The Complete Friedrich Nietzsche Philosophy Collection (Vol. 2)

*The Genealogy of Morals, Twilight of the Idols
& The Antichrist — Radical Critiques of Ethics,
Religion & Modern Values*

A Modern Translation

Adapted for the Contemporary Reader

Friedrich Nietzsche

Translated by Tim Zengerink

Table of Contents

Preface - Message to the Reader

What If You Could Help Rebuild the Greatest Library in Human History?

Thousands of years ago, the Library of Alexandria stood as the crown jewel of human achievement — a sanctuary where the collected wisdom of every known civilization was gathered, preserved, and shared freely.

And then, it was lost.

Through fire, conquest, and the slow erosion of time, humanity lost not just books — but ideas, dreams, discoveries, and stories that could have changed the world forever.

Today, the Library of Alexandria lives again — and you are invited to be a part of its restoration.

Our mission is simple yet profound:

To rebuild the greatest library the world has ever known, and to translate all timeless works into every language and dialect, so that no seeker of knowledge is ever left behind again.

By joining our movement to rebuild the modern Library of Alexandria, you become part of an unprecedented mission:

- **Unlimited Access to the Greatest Audiobooks & eBooks Ever Written:**

    Instantly explore thousands of legendary works—Plato, Shakespeare, Jane Austen, Leo Tolstoy, and countless more. All instantly available to read or listen, placing a complete literary universe at your fingertips.

- **Beautiful Paperback & Deluxe Editions at Printing Cost**

  Own any title as an elegant paperback, deluxe hardcover, or stunning collectible boxset—offered to you at true printing cost, delivered straight to your door. Build your personal Library of Alexandria, crafted for beauty, built for durability, and worthy of proud display.

- **Fresh Translations for Modern Readers—in Every Language & Dialect**

  Enjoy timeless masterpieces reimagined in clear, contemporary language—no more outdated phrases or obscure references. Alongside the original versions, we're tirelessly translating these classics into every language and dialect imaginable, ensuring accessibility and understanding across cultures and generations.

- **Join a Global Renaissance of Literature & Knowledge**

  You directly support expanding our library, publishing deluxe editions at true cost, translating works into all global languages, and bringing humanity's greatest stories to people everywhere. By joining today, you're not just preserving a legacy of masterpieces; you set in motion a powerful wave of literary accessibility.

Become a Torchbearer of Knowledge.

Join us for free now at **LibraryofAlexandria.com**

Together, we will ensure that the light of human wisdom never fades again.

With gratitude and a shared love of knowledge,
The Modern Library of Alexandria Team

Visit:

www.libraryofalexandria.com

Or scan the code below:

Introduction

Diagnosing the Soul of the West:
Nietzsche's Moral Critique in Full Force

In The Complete Friedrich Nietzsche Philosophy Collection (Vol. 2), we encounter Nietzsche at his most forceful, most polemical, and most unrelenting. This volume contains three of his sharpest and most provocative works: The Genealogy of Morals, Twilight of the Idols, and The Antichrist. Each of these texts is a direct challenge to the moral, religious, and cultural foundations of the Western world. Together, they form the philosophical apex of Nietzsche's campaign to tear down inherited systems of thought in order to clear the path for a new kind of life—healthier, freer, and more honest.

Nietzsche's style in these works is combative but not without wit. He provokes to awaken. He shocks to challenge the anesthetizing effects of conventional morality. He is not writing from an ivory tower but from a battlefield, where truth is not something passively accepted, but something forged in struggle. For Nietzsche, to think clearly is to suffer the collapse of old ideals and to find strength not in comfort but in confrontation.

These works are also deeply psychological. Nietzsche writes not only as a philosopher, but as a moral diagnostician. He asks: What are the origins of our values? What do they say about us? Are they life-affirming or life-denying? Are they the result of strength, or of weakness masquerading as virtue?

This introduction offers a close reading of each of the three major works in this volume, situating them within Nietzsche's philosophical project and highlighting their relevance to modern readers. They are challenging. But in their fire, Nietzsche offers something rare: a call not to believe, but to become.

The Genealogy of Morals:
Excavating the Foundations of Ethical Life

Published in 1887, The Genealogy of Morals is Nietzsche's most sustained and structured analysis of morality. Composed of three essays, the work explores the historical and psychological roots of our ethical values. Nietzsche is not content to ask what is good. He asks: where did the concept of "good" come from? What impulses shaped it? Who benefits from its definitions?

The first essay, "Good and Evil," traces morality to a fundamental conflict between two perspectives: master morality and slave morality. Master morality, Nietzsche claims, arises from the strong who affirm themselves—those who define good in terms of power, vitality, and excellence. Slave morality, by contrast, is a reaction—created by the weak, resentful, and oppressed. They redefine good as meekness, obedience, and suffering, while labeling strength and freedom as evil.

Nietzsche introduces the concept of ressentiment—a psychological state in which the powerless reframe their envy and hatred into moral superiority. Christianity, he argues, is the pinnacle of slave morality, teaching that the poor are blessed, the meek are exalted, and the body is a prison.

In the second essay, "Guilt, Bad Conscience, and Related Matters," Nietzsche explores the origin of guilt and punishment. He suggests that guilt originally arose not from a sense of moral transgression, but from a commercial idea: debt and repayment. With the development of conscience, this external accounting became internalized. Human beings turned their aggression inward, breeding self-loathing and guilt. The result, for Nietzsche, is the sick soul—tormented by an inherited morality that condemns its instincts.

The third essay, "What Do Ascetic Ideals Mean?" examines the religious glorification of suffering and denial. Nietzsche argues that asceticism—rejection of the body, pleasure, and power—is not a sign of holiness, but of decadence. It is the triumph of the will to nothingness over the will to life. Even science and philosophy, when used to deny or escape life, fall under this critique.

The Genealogy of Morals is both historical and therapeutic. It seeks to expose the hidden roots of our values so that we might overcome them. Nietzsche is not merely tearing down. He is diagnosing in order to liberate. His goal is to make space for a revaluation of values—one that affirms life, creativity, and strength.

Twilight of the Idols: A Hammer for False Gods

Subtitled "How to Philosophize with a Hammer," Twilight of the Idols (1888) is Nietzsche's concise and often aphoristic summation of his mature thought. The "idols" are the dominant ideas of Western culture: morality, religion, democracy, equality, and metaphysics. Nietzsche smashes these idols not with brute force, but with the subtle tapping of critique, exposing the hollow sound beneath their revered surfaces.

The book opens with "Maxims and Arrows," a series of short aphorisms that set the tone for what follows. Nietzsche's targets include the belief in free will, the elevation of reason over instinct, and the idealization of suffering. He insists that life is not to be judged by external standards, but to be lived and affirmed in all its immediacy.

In "The Problem of Socrates," Nietzsche critiques the father of Western philosophy, suggesting that Socratic rationalism is a symptom of decline. Socrates, he claims, represents a turning point where instinct was subordinated to logic, leading to the degeneration of Greek culture. Similarly, he attacks Plato for inventing a metaphysical world of "true being" that devalues the real world.

In "Morality as Anti-Nature," Nietzsche condemns moral systems that seek to suppress natural instincts. He argues that Christian morality in particular tries to destroy the passions rather than cultivate them. Virtue, for Nietzsche, is not about repression, but about channeling and affirming one's drives.

"The Four Great Errors" section debunks common fallacies—such as the belief in causality based on will, or the attribution of moral responsibility to action. These errors, Nietzsche argues, sustain the illusion of moral judgment and obstruct human flourishing.

The most famous section, "Skirmishes of an Untimely Man," offers sharp critiques of German culture, education, and philosophy. Nietzsche mocks the herd mentality, the rise of nationalism, and the decline of artistic greatness. He ends the book with "What I Owe to the Ancients," reaffirming his admiration for the tragic wisdom of pre-Socratic Greece, which embraced the fullness of life without resorting to metaphysical consolation.

Twilight of the Idols is both a philosophical bomb and a literary performance. It distills Nietzsche's worldview into sharp, memorable blows. It is accessible, witty, and lethal to complacency.

The Antichrist:
The War Against Christianity

Written in 1888, The Antichrist is Nietzsche's most direct and uncompromising attack on Christianity. It is not a critique of religion in general, but of a specific historical phenomenon: the Christian moral worldview, which he sees as a perversion of natural vitality and a glorification of weakness.

Nietzsche's title is intentionally provocative. He is not setting himself up as a satanic figure, but as the philosophical opposite of Christ as understood by the Church. He respects the historical Jesus as a moral exemplar who lived a life of non-resistance and love, but he condemns Paul and the institutional church for turning that life into a doctrine of guilt, fear, and submission.

The book is structured as a series of explosive aphorisms. Nietzsche accuses Christianity of being a slave religion, designed to protect the weak and envious by denouncing strength, beauty, and power as evil. He sees in Christian doctrine a hatred of the body, of pleasure, of this life.

Nietzsche's central argument is that Christianity has poisoned Western civilization by replacing natural instincts with moral illusions. It teaches people to hate what is noble and to venerate suffering as redemptive. He calls for a return to health—spiritual, physical, and philosophical—through the rejection of Christian values.

His vision is not nihilistic. It is life-affirming. But it affirms a life free from guilt, free from dogma, and free from the self-negating ethos of sacrifice. The Antichrist is not a call to destroy faith, but to recover it—in a higher, stronger form that serves life rather than denies it.

Fire and Clarity: Nietzsche's Final Reckoning with Morality

These three works form the core of Nietzsche's moral critique. They do not ask the reader to agree. They demand the reader to think. To question. To trace every value, every belief, to its root and ask: does this serve life, or does it deny it?

Nietzsche was not content to be a philosopher. He sought to be a cultural physician, diagnosing the sickness of Western civilization and calling for its healing through the embrace of strength, creativity, and truth. He believed that most of what we call morality is a mask—an inherited system designed to tame the human animal and to elevate weakness into virtue.

To read Nietzsche is not to passively absorb doctrine. It is to be challenged, even assaulted, by a thinker who believed that growth comes through fire. These works are not comfortable. But they are clarifying. They ask us to look in the mirror and ask not whether we are good—but whether we are honest.

Welcome to The Complete Friedrich Nietzsche Philosophy Collection (Vol. 2). May these books confront you, provoke you, and awaken in you the power to see with your own eyes, feel with your own strength, and live with your own truth.

The Genealogy of Morals

Friedrich Nietzsche

Prologue

We don't truly know ourselves—we who try to understand so much. And there's a good reason for that. We've never really looked for ourselves, so how could we possibly expect to find ourselves? It's been wisely said, "Where your treasure is, there your heart will be also." Our treasure lies in the things we strive to understand. It's like a beehive for us, filled with the knowledge we're always working to gather. As creatures of the air, born to roam, we're like bees gathering honey for our hive. Deep down, we care about one thing: bringing something valuable back home to that hive.

When it comes to the rest of life—what people call "experiences"— how many of us really care about them deeply? Who even has the time or the focus? We rarely engage seriously with those moments. To be honest, our hearts aren't truly in it, and neither are our ears. It's like someone lost in a dream, so absorbed in their thoughts that they don't even notice the loud tolling of the clock. Then, when the clock has finished striking twelve, they suddenly snap out of it and wonder, "Wait, what just happened?" That's how we often feel. We rub our ears afterward, confused, and ask ourselves in complete surprise, "What exactly have we just been through? Who are we, really?"

When we try to make sense of our experiences—those twelve striking moments of our life and being—we always miscount. We get it wrong every time. We remain strangers to ourselves, unable to truly understand who we are. For us, the saying is eternally true: "Each of us is furthest from knowing ourselves." When it comes to understanding ourselves, we are not "knowers."

The thoughts I have about the origins of our moral beliefs— because that's what this argument is all about—were first put into words in my book Human,

All- Too- Human: A Book for Free Spirits. I began writing it in Sorrento during the winter of 1876-77, a time when I could look back on the wide and challenging journey my mind had traveled up to that point. But these ideas aren't new; they're older.

The thoughts I share here are essentially the same as those I explored in that earlier book. Over the years, I hope they've become sharper, clearer, stronger, and more complete. The fact that I still hold onto them today—that they've grown and evolved together—gives me confidence. It makes me believe that these ideas didn't come about by accident or in isolation. Instead, they must have a common source, rooted in a deep and fundamental desire for knowledge. That desire has grown stronger and more focused over time, becoming clearer in its demands. For a philosopher, that's exactly how things should be.

We have no right to be disconnected. Our thoughts must not err separately, nor should we stumble upon truth by chance or in isolation. Like the fruit that a tree bears out of necessity, our thoughts, values, affirmations, denials, questions, and doubts must grow in connection with one another. They are all interrelated, bearing witness to one will, one health, one unity, one guiding light. As for whether you, the observer, find these fruits pleasing to your taste—does that matter to the tree? Should it matter to us, the philosophers?

I must reluctantly admit to a peculiar and deeply ingrained scrupulousness within myself, one that revolves around morality. This trait, evident in me from an early age, appeared so naturally, so persistently, and with such strong resistance to the influences of my environment, time, traditions, and ancestry that I might almost call it my a priori. From a young age, my curiosity and skepticism forced me to confront the question of the true origin of our ideas of "Good" and "Evil." At just thirteen years old, when most children are divided between playing games and contemplating God, I was already haunted by the problem of the origin of Evil. It was at that age that I wrote my first philosophical essay, a naïve and childlike attempt to tackle the question. My solution, as you might expect, attributed the creation of evil to God Himself— I named Him its father. Was that conclusion driven by my own a prior i? That new, immoral—or at least "amoral"—instinct, that inner imperative so far removed from Kant's ideals and yet so full of its own challenges? This imperative has since become the focus of not just my attention but something far greater.

Fortunately, I soon learned to separate theological prejudices from moral ones. I gave up the search for a supernatural origin of evil. Through a combination of historical and philological study—and an innate talent for psychological insight—I was able to shift my original question into a new and more precise form: under what conditions did humanity create these value judgments of "Good" and "Evil"? What inherent worth do they possess? Have these values up to now helped or hindered human flourishing? Are they signs of humanity's suffering, decline, and impoverishment? Or are they, instead, manifestations of life's fullness, strength, and determination—its courage, its self-assurance, its will to face the future?

To these questions, I entertained a variety of answers. I explored distinctions across different periods, cultures, and social classes. I became a specialist in my chosen problem, and each answer led to further questions, deeper investigations, new theories, and fresh possibilities. Gradually, I found myself with my own domain, my own fertile ground, a hidden world filled with growing and blooming ideas—secret gardens that no one could have suspected existed. How happy we are, we seekers of knowledge, as long as we know how to remain silent for long enough!

My initial urge to publish some of my ideas about the origins of morality came from a small, clear, well-written book— precocious even—in which a twisted and flawed kind of moral philosophy (a quintessentially English kind) was laid out plainly for the first time. This book intrigued me, pulling me in with that irresistible attraction that comes from encountering something fundamentally opposed to one's own beliefs. The book was titled The Origin of the Moral Emotions, authored by Dr. Paul Rée, and it was published in 1877.

I can almost say that I've never read anything where every argument and conclusion inspired such a strong, unequivocal rejection from me as this book did. Yet my rejection was free of irritation or intolerance. In fact, I often referred to its arguments in my own writings of that time—not to refute them (for I see no point in mere refutations), but rather to replace improbable theories with ones I found more plausible. Occasionally, of course, I might have substituted one philosophical error with another.

It was during that early phase that I began publicly expressing the theories of origin that these essays now explore, though I did so with a clumsiness I could not ignore. I lacked a specialized language for these particular topics and often found myself vacillating or falling back into old patterns.

For specific examples, one might compare what I wrote in Human, All- Too- Human, Part I, Aphorism 45, about the parallel early histories of Good and Evil—how they originated from the castes of aristocrats and slaves. Or Aphorisms 136 and following, on the birth and value of ascetic morality. Similarly, Aphorisms 96 and 99 in Volume II, and Aphorism 89, regarding the Morality of Custom—a much older and more fundamental form of morality, completely distinct from the altruistic ethics that Dr. Rée and other English moral philosophers mistake for the "essence" of ethics. Finally, see Aphorism 92.

Likewise, consider Aphorism 26 in Human, All- Too- Human, Part II, or Aphorism 112 in The Dawn of Day, where I discuss the origin of Justice as a balance of power between individuals of roughly equal strength. This equilibrium serves as the foundation for all agreements and thus for all law. Similarly, my thoughts on the origin of Punishment in Human, All- Too- Human, Part II, Aphorisms 22 and 23, challenge Dr. Rée's view. Contrary to his belief that the primary purpose of punishment is deterrence, I argue that this purpose is neither original nor essential but is instead a secondary addition that arises under specific conditions.

At that time, my focus was not so much on the theories—my own or others'—about the origins of morality. The real purpose of those theories, in my view, was to serve as a means to a greater end. My true concern was the value of morality itself. To approach this question, I had to place myself in a state of detachment, almost as though I were entirely alone with my great teacher, Schopenhauer. It was to him that my work, with all its passion and inherent contradictions (for it, too, was a polemic), turned for guidance, as if he were still alive.

The issue I grappled with was, oddly enough, the value of "unegoistic" instincts—the instincts of pity, self-denial, and self-sacrifice. Schopenhauer had persistently celebrated these instincts, portraying them in golden hues, exalting and idealizing them until they appeared to him as ultimate, intrinsic values. It was on the basis of these instincts that he pronounced his negation of both Life and himself. Yet, within me, a deep and growing mistrust arose toward these very instincts. My skepticism dug deeper and deeper, and I came to see in these instincts a profound danger to humanity. They seemed to me humanity's most sublime temptation, its greatest seduction. But seduction to what? To nothingness?

In these unegoistic instincts, I saw the seeds of humanity's decline—the beginning of its end. I saw stagnation, exhaustion, a longing to retreat, and the will turning against Life itself. These instincts appeared to me as the heralds of humanity's last illness, signaling their arrival with a delicate, sorrowful melancholy. I realized that the morality of pity, spreading ever wider and infecting even philosophers with its sickness, was the darkest symptom of modern European civilization. It was the path along which this civilization was sliding—toward what? A new Buddhism? A European Buddhism? Nihilism?

This overvaluation of pity by modern philosophers is a completely new phenomenon. Until then, philosophers were unanimous in their disdain for pity. I need only mention Plato, Spinoza, La Rochefoucauld, and Kant—four thinkers as vastly different as one could imagine, yet united on this one point: their contempt for pity.

This question about the value of pity and the morality it represents (I am deeply opposed to the modern, disgraceful softening of our emotions) might at first seem like an isolated issue—a problem standing on its own. But anyone who pauses to examine it, as I did, and learns to ask the right questions will experience what I experienced: a vast and immense new perspective unfolds before them. A sense of limitless possibilities overtakes them, almost like vertigo. Doubts, mistrust, and fears spring up everywhere. Belief in morality—indeed, in all morality—begins to waver. Finally, a new demand makes itself heard.

Let us state this demand clearly: we need a critique of moral values. The worth of these values themselves must, for the first time, be called into question. To do this, we need to understand the conditions and circumstances under which these values arose, evolved, and were distorted. Morality must be examined as both a result and a symptom, as a mask, as hypocrisy, as disease, and as misunderstanding—but also as a cause, as a remedy, as a stimulant, as a restraint, and as a drug. Such an investigation has never existed before, nor has it even been desired. Up until now, the value of these "values" has been taken as self-evident, beyond any question. No one has ever doubted or hesitated in judging the "good man" to be of higher worth than the "evil man," particularly regarding human progress, utility, and general well-being, including the future.

But what if the opposite were true? What if the "good man" turned out to be a symptom of decline—a danger, a temptation, a poison, a narcotic that allows the present to feed off the future? What if this morality is more comfortable and less risky than its opposite, but also smaller, meaner? What if morality itself is to blame for preventing humanity from reaching its highest potential for power and greatness? What if morality is, in fact, the greatest danger of all dangers?

Once this perspective opened up to me, I had every reason to search for colleagues—scholarly, bold, and diligent companions to help explore this immense, distant, and entirely uncharted territory of morality. This search continues even today. To question morality with such fresh and pressing inquiries, to see it with entirely new eyes, is practically equivalent to discovering morality for the first time. This is a morality that has actually existed, one that has been lived! And isn't discovering it for the first time like uncovering a new land?

When I thought of Dr. Paul Rée in this context, it was because I believed that his questions would eventually force him to adopt a more accurate method to arrive at his answers. Was I wrong to think so? In any case, I wanted to guide his sharp and impartial vision toward a better path. I wanted to point him toward the real history of morality and to warn him, while there was still time, against the world of English theories, which lead ultimately to the empty blue vacuum of heaven. Other colors, more grounded and powerful than blue, are far better suited for the genealogy of morals. Grey, for example, represents hard, provable facts, things that truly happened. It stands for that long, intricate script—the history of human morality—which is so difficult to decipher.

This script was unknown to Dr. Rée. What he had read was Darwin. And so, in his philosophy, the Darwinian beast and the refined, modern weakling— the polite dilettante who "bites no longer"—join hands in a way that, at least, provides an interesting lesson. The latter wears an expression of refined laziness, good-natured indifference, tinged with pessimism and exhaustion, as though it were hardly worth taking moral problems seriously.

I, on the other hand, believe there is no subject more deserving of serious attention. One of the rewards for taking these issues seriously is that, eventually, they may allow us to approach them with a light heart. This light-heartedness— or, to use my own term, this joyful wisdom—is a reward for long, courageous, and painstaking effort, a reward for digging deep. Such effort, of course, is the province of only a few. But the day will come when we can say, with full hearts, "Forward! Even our old morality is fit for comedy!" Then we will have discovered a new plot, a new possibility for the Dionysian drama of The Soul's Fate. And who better to make use of it than the ancient, eternal playwright of the grand comedy of existence?

If anyone finds this writing unclear or discordant, I do not believe the fault necessarily lies with me. My assumption is that the reader has already gone through my earlier works and has invested the effort required to grasp their essence—an effort that is far from simple. Take, for example, my Zar athustra. I do not consider anyone to truly understand that book unless every word in it has, at some point, deeply wounded them and, at another point, profoundly enchanted them. Only then can they earn the privilege of partaking reverently in the tranquil, radiant realm from which that work emerged—a realm of sunlight, vast horizons, clarity, and certainty.

In many cases, difficulty arises from the aphoristic form itself, though this is often because it is approached too superficially. A well-crafted aphorism, carefully formed and cast into its final shape, is far from being "understood" merely upon reading. On the contrary, it is only after being read that it demands interpretation and explanation— and this requires a true art of exposition. An example of what I mean by this can be found in the third essay of this book. That essay begins with an aphorism, and the essay itself serves as its commentary.

There is, however, one quality that has been largely forgotten in our time— a quality necessary to practice reading as an art. It is, in fact, why my writings will require time before they become widely readable. This quality demands, above all else, the patience of a cow— an ability completely foreign to the modern man. That quality is rumination.

Sils-Maria, Upper Engadine,
July, 1887.

Chapter 1
Good and Evil, Good and Bad

The English psychologists, who so far are the only philosophers to have made any real attempt at tracing the history of morality's origins, present us with an intriguing puzzle—not a minor one, either. To be completely honest, their personalities as living riddles are often more fascinating than their books.

They themselves are interesting! But what do these English psychologists truly aim to achieve?

We find them, consciously or unconsciously, always engaged in the same endeavor: bringing to the forefront the partie honteuse—the "shameful part"—of our inner world. They seek the driving, governing, and decisive principles of human behavior in precisely the places where intellectual pride would least want to look. They point to things like the inertia of habit, forgetfulness, blind chance, mechanical associations of ideas, or passive, reflexive, molecular, and fundamentally senseless processes. Why do these psychologists feel compelled to search in such degrading and uncomfortable corners?

Is it a dark instinct for disparagement—a sinister, vulgar, and malicious impulse, perhaps not even understood by themselves?

Or is it a residue of pessimistic jealousy, the bitterness of disillusioned idealists who have become grim and poisoned? Could it be an unspoken, subconscious grudge against Christianity (and perhaps Plato), never fully acknowledged in their minds? Or might it simply reflect a strange fascination with the grotesque, the painfully paradoxical, the mystical, and the illogical elements of life? Perhaps the answer lies in a mix of all these motives—a little vulgarity, a touch of gloominess, a sprinkle of anti-Christian sentiment, and a craving for the bizarre and provocative.

Some would say these psychologists are nothing more than cold, tiresome frogs, hopping and crawling inside people as if they were as much at home in human minds as they are in a swamp. But I reject this idea; I cannot believe it. If, in the absence of certain knowledge, one is permitted to wish, then I sincerely hope the opposite is true.

I hope that these analysts with their psychological microscopes are, at their core, brave, proud, and magnanimous beings. I wish they are individuals who know how to restrain both their hearts and their pains and have trained themselves to sacrifice what is desirable for the sake of what is true. Any truth— even the bitter, ugly, unpleasant, unchristian, and immoral truths—for such truths do exist.

All honor, then, to the noble minds who strive to surpass these historians of morality. Yet it is truly unfortunate that they lack a historical sense themselves, that they are utterly abandoned by the guiding spirits of history. Their entire mode of thinking follows the pattern of old-fashioned philosophers: thoroughly unhistorical. There can be no doubt about this. The glaring inadequacy of their genealogy of morals becomes evident the moment they try to determine the origin of the concept and judgment of "good."

Their theory declares, "Originally, humans praised and called 'good' those altruistic acts that benefited others, specifically those who received the acts' advantages. Over time, people forgot the origin of this praise, and altruistic acts came to be regarded as good in themselves, as if they contained an inherent goodness." This explanation is typical of English psychologists and contains all their signature elements: "utility," "forgetting," "habit," and finally "error." These elements combine to form a foundation for a system of values—a system upon which higher humanity has prided itself as if it were a unique and universal privilege of humankind. But this pride must be humbled; this system of values must be dismantled. Does their theory achieve that?

The first objection that comes to mind is that they have sought and located the true home of the concept of "good" in entirely the wrong place. The idea of "good" did not originate among those to whom goodness was shown. Rather, it was the good themselves—

the aristocratic, the powerful, the high-ranking, and the noble-minded—who felt that they themselves were good, along with their actions. Their "goodness" was of the first rank, standing in stark contrast to everything low, common, vulgar, and plebeian. From this sense of superiority—the pathos of distance—they claimed for themselves the right to define values, to name them, and to create a moral hierarchy that served their own nature. What concern did they have for utility?

The perspective of utility is utterly foreign and irrelevant when we consider such an explosive outpouring of supreme values— values that create and delineate their own hierarchies. This creative force stands in stark contrast to the lukewarm conditions that underpin worldly wisdom and calculations of practical expediency, conditions that are not just occasional but perpetual. The pathos of nobility and distance, as I have said—the persistent and commanding esprit de corps of a dominant higher race in contact with a subordinate or lower race—this is the true origin of the contrast between "good" and "bad."

(The masters' right to name things extends so far that language itself can be viewed as an expression of their power: they declare, "This is this," and "That is that," sealing every object and event with a sound, and in doing so, they claim possession of it.) Because of this origin, the word "good" has no necessary connection to altruistic acts, despite the superstitious assumptions of moral philosophers. On the contrary, it is only during the decline of aristocratic values that the contrast between "egoistic" and "altruistic" begins to weigh heavily on the human conscience. To use my own terminology, this contrast is an expression of the herd instinct, which eventually embeds itself in many forms of morality. Even then, it takes considerable time for this instinct to dominate so thoroughly that moral valuations become inseparable from this contrast, as we see in contemporary Europe. Today, the prejudice persists—obsessive and ingrained, like a mental affliction—that equates "moral," "altruistic," and désintéressé (selfless) as interchangeable concepts.

In addition to the historical inaccuracy of this hypothesis about the origin of "good," it suffers from a fundamental psychological

ontradiction. The theory suggests that the utility of altruistic acts led to their being praised and that this origin was subsequently forgotten. But how, exactly, could such forgetting occur? Did the utility of altruistic acts suddenly vanish at some point? Clearly not. Quite the opposite: their utility is experienced constantly, every day, and is therefore continually reinforced. This utility does not fade from memory; instead, it becomes ever more deeply imprinted on human consciousness. Far from being forgotten, it should, by all logic, grow increasingly prominent and undeniable with time.

A more coherent—though not necessarily more correct—theory is that proposed by Herbert Spencer, who equates the concept of "good" with "useful" or "purposeful." According to this perspective, judgments of "good" and "bad" are humanity's way of summarizing and formalizing its unforgettable and continually reinforced experiences of what is "useful-purposeful" and "harmful- non-purposeful." In this view, "good" is attributed to whatever has repeatedly proven to be useful and, therefore, comes to be regarded as "valuable in the highest degree," even "valuable in itself."

While I maintain that this explanation is also flawed, it at least has the merit of being internally consistent and psychologically plausible.

The key insight that set me on the right path came from asking this question: What is the true etymological meaning of the symbols for the concept of "good" across different languages? I discovered that they all traced back to the same evolution of an idea: universally, the root meaning of "good" is tied to "aristocrat" or "noble" (in the social sense). From this root developed the meanings of "good" as "possessing an aristocratic soul," "noble" as "possessing a high-caliber soul," or "having a privileged soul." This evolution consistently parallels another: the transformation of terms like "vulgar," "plebeian," or "low" into their eventual meaning of "bad."

One of the most striking examples of this is the German word schlecht. Originally, schlecht was identical in meaning to schlicht—(consider expressions like schlechtweg and schlechterdings)—which, at first, carried no negative connotation. It simply referred to someone of plebeian origin, as opposed to someone of aristocratic standing. It was only much later, around the time of the Thirty Years' War, that schlecht came to mean what it does today.

From the perspective of the Genealogy of Mor als, this discovery is significant. The delay in recognizing it can be attributed to the influence of democratic prejudice, which has long distorted questions of origin in the modern era. This bias, as I will soon demonstrate, extends even into fields like natural science and physiology, which are ostensibly the most objective of disciplines. The harm caused by this prejudice—particularly in the fields of ethics and history—is considerable once it breaks free from constraints and acts purely out of malice.

The notorious example of Buckle illustrates this point. In Buckle, the plebeianism of the modern spirit—rooted in English culture—erupted once again from its foul soil, as violent and uncontrolled as a slimy volcano. This eruption came with the same coarse, overblown, and vulgar rhetoric that has always accompanied such phenomena, mirroring the crude eloquence with which all volcanoes seem to speak.

Regarding our subject, which is undoubtedly an intimate one and appeals only to a select few, it is significant to note that in the words and roots associated with "good," we glimpse the defining traits by which aristocrats perceive themselves as beings of a higher order. Often, they name themselves based on their power and superiority, referring to themselves as "the powerful," "the lords," or "the commanders." Similarly, they might draw upon visible markers of their status, such as wealth, naming themselves "the rich" or "the possessors"—a meaning reflected in words like arya in Sanskrit, as well as parallels in Iranian and Slavic languages.

But they also name themselves according to their unique qualities, which is particularly relevant to our inquiry. For instance, they call themselves "the truthful," a designation originating with the Greek nobility, voiced through Theognis, the poet of Megara. The Greek word ἐσθλός, crafted for this purpose, etymologically means "one who is," someone real, someone true. Later, it takes on a more subjective sense as "truthful." At this stage, the concept evolves into the motto and rallying cry of the nobility, distinguishing them from the "lying," vulgar man, as Theognis describes. Over time, as the nobility decays, the term ἐσθλός comes to represent a psychological nobility, maturing into a more abstract notion of "noble."

On the other hand, words like κακ ὸς and δειλ ὸς (contrasting with ἀγαθός, the noble) emphasize cowardice. This provides a clue about the etymological origin of the ambiguous ἀγαθός, which likely developed along similar lines. The Latin word malus (possibly related to μέλας, meaning "black") reflects a similar distinction: the vulgar man was often characterized as dark-complexioned or black-haired, in contrast to the lighter- haired Aryan conquerors who subjugated them. The pre-Aryan inhabitants of Italy, marked by their darker features, became the visual antithesis of the blonde ruling class. Gaelic offers a striking parallel, with the word Fin—as in Fin- Gal—being a term of nobility that originally denoted blonde-haired individuals as opposed to dark-haired aboriginals.

The Celts, I should note, were largely a blonde-haired people. It is a mistake, as Virchow and others have suggested, to associate the dark-haired populations mapped in certain regions of Germany with Celtic ancestry. Instead, these populations are remnants of the pre-Aryan inhabitants of Europe. This phenomenon is not limited to Germany; throughout Europe, the characteristics of the older subject races—darker complexions, shorter skulls—have resurfaced, even becoming dominant. One might speculate whether modern democracy, anarchism, or the widespread socialist push for communal structures— primitive societal forms—represents a regression to this earlier state. Could it signify that the once-dominant Aryan "master race" is now in physiological decline?

As for the Latin word bonus, I propose that it originally meant "the warrior." My hypothesis derives bonus from an earlier form, duonus, as seen in the word duellum (an older form of bellum, "war"), where duonus seems embedded. Bonus, then, would signify "the man of discord," "one who divides" (duo), the warrior. This sheds light on what "the good" meant in ancient Rome: a man of battle.

Finally, consider our German word gut. Could it mean "the godlike," referring to "a man of godlike race"? Might it even share origins with the national name of the Goths, originally a noble designation? The evidence for this hypothesis lies outside the scope of this work.

Above all, there are no exceptions—though there are opportunities for exceptions—to the rule that the idea of political superiority ultimately transforms into the idea of psychological superiority. This is particularly evident when the highest caste also serves as the priestly caste, and in line with its defining traits, claims titles that specifically refer to its priestly role. In such cases, the concepts of "clean" and "unclean" emerge as markers of class distinction for the first time. Here, the notions of "good" and "bad" take on meanings that go beyond mere social distinctions.

It is important, however, not to interpret these concepts of "clean" and "unclean" too broadly, seriously, or symbolically. On the contrary, the ideas of ancient humanity must be understood in their most rudimentary and literal sense—crude, coarse, physical, and narrowly practical, without symbolic undertones. The "clean man," at the start, is simply someone who washes himself, avoids foods that might cause skin diseases, abstains from contact with lower-class women deemed "unclean," and feels a revulsion toward blood. Nothing more—at least not much more.

The nature of a priestly aristocracy itself explains why such societies are prone to dangerously intensifying opposing values at an early stage. These oppositions carve deep divisions into the social fabric, creating chasms that even the boldest free thinkers might hesitate to cross. From the beginning, there is something inherently diseased about priestly aristocracies, and this affliction permeates their way of life. Their aversion to direct action fosters a peculiar blend of introspection and intense emotional volatility. This results in a kind of introspective morbidity and nervous exhaustion—neurasthenia— that seems to cling inevitably to priests across all times and places.

As for the remedies these priestly societies devised for their own maladies, the philosopher can only observe that these so-called cures have often proven far more harmful than the original disease they sought to treat. Humanity still bears the scars of the naïve "cures" of priestly societies. Consider their dietary restrictions (such as abstaining from meat), their fasting, their insistence on sexual continence, and their withdrawal into wilderness isolation—a form of treatment reminiscent of the Weir - Mitchell rest cure, though without the system of excessive feeding and strengthening that effectively counters the hysteria of the ascetic ideal.

Reflect also on the metaphysical systems created by priests, with their war on the senses, their weakening effects, and their obsessive attention to minute details. Consider their practices of self-hypnosis, modeled on the principles of the fakir and Brahman (using metaphysical concepts like Brahman as a kind of fixation device). And finally, note the culmination of this path in an overwhelming desire for annihilation—disguised as a union with God. The longing for unio mystica with God mirrors the Buddhist's yearning for nothingness: Nirvana—and nothing else.

In priestly societies, everything operates on a more dangerous scale—not only their remedies but also their pride, vengeance, cunning, ecstasy, love, ambition, virtue, and even their morbidity. It is fair to say that on the soil of this inherently perilous form of human society, the priestly society, humanity first became an interesting animal. It was within this framework that the human soul reached new depths and developed its capacity for evil. These two traits—depth and evil—remain the fundamental markers of humanity's superiority over every other animal.

The reader will likely have already guessed how easily the priestly mode of valuation could diverge from the knightly-aristocratic mode and develop into its direct opposite. This opposition is further fueled in situations where the priestly and warrior castes confront each other with mutual jealousy, unable to agree on who should hold the highest status.

The knightly-aristocratic values are rooted in a careful cultivation of physical strength and vitality—a flourishing, rich, and exuberant health that exceeds mere survival. These values celebrate war, adventure, hunting, dancing, tournaments, and all forms of bold, free, and joyous action. In contrast, the priestly- aristocratic mode of valuation, as we have seen, rests on entirely different assumptions. For this caste, war itself is an undesirable affair! And yet, as is well known, priests are the most dangerous of enemies—why? Because they are the weakest.

Their weakness fuels a hatred that grows into something vast and sinister— subtle, cunning, and venomous. Throughout history, the greatest haters have always been priests, who are also the most intelligent haters. Compared to the ingenuity of priestly revenge, all other forms of cleverness pale into insignificance. Without the cleverness of the weak, human history would be unbearably dull. Consider the most striking example of this: all the efforts directed against the aristocrats, the powerful, the masters, and the rulers of society are insignificant compared to what the Jews—a priestly nation— achieved in their struggle.

The Jews, that priestly people, discovered that their ultimate weapon against their enemies and oppressors was a radical transvaluation of values, which was simultaneously the most ingenious act of revenge. This strategy was uniquely suited to a nation of priests, deeply steeped in the jealousy and resourcefulness of priestly vengeance. Opposing the aristocratic equation of "good = noble = beautiful = happy = loved by the gods," the Jews had the audacity to propose and fiercely uphold the opposite equation. With a terrifying logic and the deepest hatred—the hatred born of weakness—they asserted:

"The wretched are the only ones who are good. The poor, the weak, the lowly—they alone are good. The suffering, the needy, the sick, and the loathsome—they are the pious, the blessed, and only they shall be saved. But you, aristocrats, you men of power, you are evil for all eternity! You are the horrible, the greedy, the insatiable, the godless! Eternally cursed and damned shall you be!"

We know who inherited this Jewish transvaluation. In the context of the monumental and far-reaching consequences of the Jews' initiative—arguably the most fundamental declaration of war in history—I am reminded of something I wrote elsewhere (Beyond Good and Evil, Aphorism 195): that it was with the Jews that the slave revolt in morality began. This revolt, with its roots two millennia deep, has endured through history and, in our present age, has simply disappeared from view—because it has triumphed.

But you do not understand this? You cannot see the power that took two thousand years to achieve its victory? There is no surprise in that: all long processes are difficult to perceive and even harder to grasp. Yet this is what happened: from the trunk of that tree of revenge and hatred—Jewish hatred, the most profound and sublime hatred, capable of creating ideals and transforming old values into something entirely new and unparalleled on earth— there emerged a phenomenon just as incomparable: a new kind of love, the deepest and most sublime form of love ever known. And from what other trunk could such a love have grown?

But do not mistake this love as a negation of the thirst for revenge, as an opposition to Jewish hatred. Quite the opposite! This love grew out of that hatred, becoming its ultimate crown, its victorious crown. It expanded ever outward, basking in the light and fullness of the sun, while still pursuing the goals of hatred— its victory, its spoils, its cunning strategies—with the same fervor as the roots of that tree of hatred drove deeper and deeper into the dark and evil depths of existence, growing ever more stable, ever more insatiable.

Consider Jesus of Nazareth, the living embodiment of the gospel of love, this "Redeemer" who brought salvation and victory to the poor, the sick, and the sinful. Was he not, in truth, the most sinister and irresistible form of temptation? A temptation to adopt the tortuous path toward precisely those Jewish values and ideals? Did Israel not, through this "Redeemer," achieve the ultimate goal of its sublime revenge, despite his appearance as Israel's opponent and destroyer?

Could it be that this extraordinary outcome—Israel's triumph—was the result of the dark genius of a truly great policy of revenge? A revenge that was slow, far-seeing, and methodical, digging deeply into the fabric of time and history? Is it not possible that Israel had to renounce and condemn, before the eyes of the world, the very instrument of its revenge—nailing it to the cross—so that the world, all of Israel's enemies, might unsuspectingly take the bait?

Could any human mind, with all its ingenuity, have devised a bait more dangerous, more insidious? Could anything else rival the seductive, intoxicating, corrupting power of the symbol of the holy cross? This terrifying paradox of "a god on the cross," this unfathomable mystery of a god's self-crucifixion for the salvation of humanity—does it not represent the ultimate, supreme horror, a horror so profound that it defies comprehension?

It is certain, at least, that sub hoc signo—under this sign—Israel, through its revenge and its transvaluation of all values, has consistently triumphed over all other ideals, including the more aristocratic ones.

"But why speak of nobler ideals? Let us face the facts: the people have triumphed—whether you call them the slaves, the masses, the herd, or whatever other name suits you. If this triumph came through the Jews, so be it! In that case, no nation has ever had a greater mission in the history of the world. The 'masters' have been overthrown, and the morality of the common man has prevailed. This victory may be likened to a kind of blood-poisoning, as it has blended the races together—I do not deny this—but it cannot be disputed that this intoxication has succeeded. The 'redemption' of humanity (that is, its liberation from the masters) is proceeding smoothly. Everything is clearly becoming Judaised, Christianised, or vulgarised—what difference does the label make? The poisoning seems unstoppable as it spreads through the entire body politic of humanity.

However, perhaps from this point forward, its tempo can be slowed, its progress made more refined, more subtle, quieter, and more restrained—there is no rush. In this context, one might ask: does the Church still serve a necessary purpose? Does it even have a right to exist? Could humanity now do without it? Quaeritur. It seems that the Church hinders and slows this process instead of accelerating it. Perhaps that is precisely its utility.

Certainly, the Church remains a crude and clumsy institution, offensive to any mind with even a hint of delicacy or to anyone with genuinely modern tastes. Should it not, at the very least, learn to refine itself a little? Today, it repels more people than it attracts. Which of us would even bother to be a freethinker if not for the Church? It is the Church that drives us away, not its poison— because, apart from the Church, we actually like the poison."

These are the parting words of a freethinker responding to my argument— a respectable man by his own standards (as he has often demonstrated) and a democrat as well. He had listened to me patiently but could not endure my silence on this matter. As for me, there is indeed much on this subject about which I prefer to remain silent.

The revolt of the slaves in morality begins with the principle of resentment becoming creative and giving rise to values. This resentment is experienced by those who, unable to act directly, are forced to channel their frustrations into an imagined revenge. While aristocratic morality originates in a triumphant affirmation of its own existence and values, slave morality begins by saying "no"—a rejection of everything "outside itself," "different from itself," and "not itself." This "no" is its creative act.

This reversal of the valuing process—a shift from affirming the self to focusing on the external—is characteristic of resentment. Slave morality depends on an external, objective world as a condition for its very existence. To use a physiological metaphor, it requires external stimuli to activate itself; its essence is reaction, not action. It lacks the spontaneous, self-generating energy of aristocratic morality.

In the case of aristocratic values, action and growth occur naturally and independently. The aristocratic morality does not need an adversary to define itself but instead seeks an antithesis only to enhance its joyful and emphatic "yes" to itself. Its negative concepts—"low," "vulgar," "bad"—are mere afterthoughts, secondary contrasts to its primary, life-affirming essence. This essence is rich with vitality and passion, grounded in the aristocrat's self-perception: "We aristocrats, we good ones, we beautiful ones, we happy ones."

When the aristocratic morality goes astray and violates reality, this misstep is confined to the particular sphere with which it is not sufficiently familiar—a sphere that it deliberately avoids understanding and disdains to engage with. It often misjudges, in certain instances, the sphere it holds in contempt: that of the common, vulgar man and the lower classes. However, it is important to note that even if its disdain falsely represents the object of its contempt, this misrepresentation will always be far less egregious than the fabrications and grotesque distortions born of the vindictive hatred and vengefulness of the weak when they attack their enemies. Contempt inherently carries too much nonchalance, casualness, boredom, impatience, and even personal exhilaration to ever transform its object into a complete caricature or monstrosity.

Attention should be drawn to the almost benevolent nuances infused by the Greek nobility into the terms they used to distinguish the common people from themselves. Observe how, in such words, there often lingers a kind of pity, care, and consideration that softens their tone. Eventually, many of these terms evolved into expressions meaning "unhappy" or "worthy of pity." For example, words like δειλός, δείλαιος, πονηρός, and μοχθηρός, initially used to describe the vulgar man as a laborer or beast of burden, ultimately acquired connotations of misfortune. Similarly, terms for "bad," "low," and "unhappy" in Greek carried a resonance in which "unhappy" was the dominant note. This linguistic inheritance from noble morality reflects how, even in scorn, it remained consistent with its values.

The "well-born" naturally felt themselves to be the happy ones. They did not need to manufacture their happiness artificially by focusing on their enemies or delude themselves into happiness through false narratives, as is common among resentful men. Their happiness arose organically, as an outpouring of their strength and energy. To them, happiness and action were inseparable concepts; to act was to be happy. This is reflected in the etymology of the Greek phrase εὖ πράττειν ("to fare well"), which originally meant "to act well." In contrast, the happiness of the weak and oppressed is fundamentally passive—it is a sedative, a tranquilizing state of rest, peace, and quiet, akin to a Sabbath for the soul, a relaxation of the body and mind.

The aristocratic man, confident and at ease with himself, exemplified sincerity and straightforwardness. The Greek term γεννα ῖος ("noble-born") emphasizes this quality of being candid and perhaps even naïve. By contrast, the resentful man is neither sincere nor honest with himself. His soul is crooked; his mind thrives in hidden corners, on secret paths, and in backdoor dealings. For him, the concealed and indirect are his refuge, his safety, and his comfort. He is a master of silence, grudge-holding, waiting, and self-deprecation.

Over time, a race of resentful individuals necessarily becomes more prudent than any aristocratic race. For them, prudence is not a luxury or refinement, as it is for the aristocrats, but a critical necessity for survival. Among aristocratic men, prudence carries an air of indulgence and refinement. It plays a secondary role compared to the reliable functioning of their instincts and unconscious drives, or even a certain recklessness in their actions. They might charge boldly into danger or battle or exhibit bursts of passionate emotion—whether in love, reverence, or gratitude. Such displays of vitality and spirit have always been the hallmarks of noble souls.

When the aristocratic man experiences resentment, it expresses itself immediately and exhausts itself in the reaction, leaving no lingering venom. In many situations, aristocratic resentment does not even arise, where in weaker individuals it would be unavoidable. Their inability to dwell on their enemies, injuries, or misfortunes signals the fullness of their nature. Their excess of energy heals wounds and fosters forgetfulness. Mirabeau provides a modern example of this disposition; he bore no memory of the insults and petty wrongs committed against him. His inability to forgive was simply a byproduct of his tendency to forget. Such men shrug off insults like worms that would otherwise burrow into others.

In these individuals, we see the possibility—if it exists at all—of a true "love of one's enemies." An aristocratic man respects his enemies, and this respect can act as a bridge to love. He demands that his enemies be worthy adversaries—men he can admire, whose character holds much to honor and nothing to despise. He tolerates no enemy who is beneath his contempt.

In contrast, consider how the resentful man conceives of his enemy. It is here that his creativity emerges. He imagines the "evil enemy," the "wicked one," and from this fabricated figure, he derives a contrasting and corresponding idea: the "good one." This "good one" is none other than himself. Through this inversion, the resentful man defines his identity by vilifying those he opposes.

The method of the resentful man is entirely opposite to that of the aristocratic man. The aristocratic man forms the concept of "good" spontaneously and directly—arising naturally from his own being. From this starting point, he then creates the idea of "bad," which serves as a secondary concept, an afterthought. In contrast, the resentful man's concept of "evil" emerges from the cauldron of unfulfilled hatred. The aristocratic "bad" is merely a nuance, an imitation, an addition; the resentful "evil," however, is original, foundational, the central act in the creation of slave morality.

These two words—"bad" and "evil"—mark an immense difference, even though they share a common opposition in the idea of "good." But the idea of "good" itself is not the same in the two systems. Let us ask instead: Who is truly evil according to the morality of resentment? The answer, given with full seriousness, is this: precisely the good man of the aristocratic morality—the noble, the powerful, the ruler—transfigured and distorted through the venomous lens of resentment into something entirely different, into a figure of malevolence.

This much must be admitted: the man who came to know these "good" ones only as enemies also came to know them only as evil enemies. Those same aristocratic men, who among their equals were bound by strict conventions, respect, customs, and gratitude—and even more by mutual vigilance and jealousy—these same men, who within their circle displayed countless forms of courtesy, self-restraint, refinement, loyalty, pride, and friendship, behaved in entirely different ways outside their group. Toward those beyond their circle, where the foreign begins, they were little better than beasts of prey set loose.

In the wilderness, freed from the constraints of societal control, they released the pent-up tension created by their confinement in the order and peace of their own society. There, they returned to the innocence of the predator's conscience, reveling like jubilant monsters in their wild freedom. Emerging from acts of murder, arson, rape, and torture, they carried themselves with a moral ease, even a sense of playfulness, as if these horrors were nothing more than a rowdy prank from students on a spree—utterly convinced that poets would celebrate their deeds in song and story.

It is impossible to overlook the beast of prey that lies at the core of all aristocratic races. This magnificent, blonde brute, driven by a relentless hunger for plunder and victory, is a defining feature of these noble classes. This primal force demands an outlet; the beast must occasionally break free, returning to the wilderness. We see this need in the Romans, Arabs, Germans, and Japanese nobility, in the Homeric heroes, and in the Scandinavian Vikings. All these groups share this essential trait: the need to unleash their inner beast and revel in the unrestrained innocence of their savage nature.

It is the aristocratic races that have left the imprint of the word "barbarian" along every path they have traveled. Indeed, an awareness of this very barbarism, and even a pride in it, is evident even in their most advanced civilizations. For example,

Pericles, in his famous funeral oration, declares to the Athenians, "Our audacity has forced a way over every land and sea, rearing everywhere imperishable memorials of itself for good and for evil."

This audacity of aristocratic races, however reckless, absurd, and spasmodic its manifestations may seem, reflects the unpredictable and extravagant nature of their endeavors. Pericles especially highlights the ῥα θυμία of the Athenians—their nonchalance, their disregard for safety, bodily well-being, life, and comfort. He celebrates their terrifying joy and intense delight in destruction, in the ecstasies of victory, and even in cruelty. These traits— when viewed by those who have suffered at their hands—become crystallized into the image of the "barbarian," the "evil enemy," or figures like the "Goth" and the "Vandal."

The profound, icy mistrust that the German provokes as soon as he attains power—even today—is a lingering echo of the inextinguishable horror with which Europe regarded the wrath of the blonde Teutonic beast for centuries. This mistrust persists despite the fact that there is now barely any psychological, let alone physical, continuity between the ancient Germans and modern ones. I have previously pointed out Hesiod's difficulty when he attempted to describe the series of social ages in terms of gold, silver, and bronze. Hesiod faced a contradiction when trying to reconcile the Homeric world, which aristocratic families remembered as a glorious age filled with their heroic ancestors, with its simultaneously dreadful and violent reality. He resolved this by splitting one age into two: the heroic age of demigods, as it was remembered by the aristocracy, and the bronze age, as it appeared to the descendants of the oppressed, the enslaved, and the exiled. To them, it was a brutal and merciless era—a true age of bronze—hard, cold, and unfeeling, crushing everything and staining all it touched with blood.

If we accept the modern theory, now widely believed, that the very essence of civilization lies in taming humanity's beastly instincts and transforming humans into domesticated and civil animals, then it follows that the real tools of civilization must include the instincts of reaction and resentment. These are the very instincts by which aristocratic races, along with their ideals, were eventually degraded and defeated. However, this does not imply that the bearers of these tools of civilization were themselves representatives of civilization. On the contrary—this is not merely probable but evident even today.

These bearers of vindictive instincts, compelled to repress their vengeance and resentment, are the descendants of all European and non-European slaves, particularly the pre-Aryan populations. These people, I assert, represent not the advancement of humanity but its decline.

These "tools of civilization" are a disgrace to humanity and, in truth, provide more reason to question and distrust civilization than to defend it. While it is perfectly reasonable to be wary of the blonde beast that lies at the heart of all aristocratic races and to remain vigilant against it, who would not prefer to live with fear—and at the same time, admiration—than to endure the constant, revolting sight of the deformed, the dwarfed, the stunted, and the poisoned? Is that not our current condition? What drives our disgust with "man" today? For it is clear that we suffer from man—there is no denying it.

It is not fear that troubles us. Rather, it is that there is nothing left to fear from men. The worm that is "man" now crawls to the forefront, multiplying endlessly. The "tame man," the pitiful, mediocre, uninspiring creature, has come to see himself as the goal, the pinnacle, the meaning, the historic principle—the "higher man." Worse still, he may even be right to see himself this way. Compared to the overwhelming deformity, sickness, exhaustion, and decay that now pollutes Europe, he may indeed represent a kind of relative success. At least he still says yes to life.

At this point, I cannot help but express a sigh and one last hope. What is it that I find so intolerable? What chokes me, suffocates me, and makes me faint? Bad air! Bad air! The stench of something misshapen, the foul odor of the insides of a malformed soul near me—that is what I cannot endure. Beyond that, what hardship could not be borne? What privation, bad weather, illness, toil, or solitude would be insurmountable? In truth, one can endure anything, being born to dig, to battle, to survive. One always finds the light again, always experiences life's golden moment of triumph, and stands again as one was born: unbroken, tense, and ready for something more challenging, something more distant. Like a bow, stretched tauter by every strain, one prepares for the next shot.

But I beg—if there are goddesses beyond good and evil who can grant such things—grant me, from time to time, just one glimpse. Just one glimpse of something perfect, fully realized, mighty, triumphant. Grant me the sight of something that still inspires fear! Let me see a man who justifies humanity's existence. A man whose happiness, realized and embodied, redeems the idea of mankind. A man for whom one might cling to belief in humanity!

The reality, however, is bleak. The dwarfing and flattening of European man is our greatest danger. It is this trend that wears us down, for we see nothing today that strives to grow greater. The trajectory appears to move ever backward—toward something smaller, more insipid, more calculating, more comfortable, more mediocre, more indifferent, more Chinese, more Christian. There is no doubt: man is becoming "better." And it is precisely this process— this loss of fear of man—that has also robbed us of hope in man, even of the will to be man.

The sight of man now wearies us. What is modern nihilism, if not this? We are tired of man.

But let us return to the subject. The problem of a differ ent origin of "good"—as it has been imagined by the resentful man—requires an answer. It's no surprise that lambs might hold a grudge against the great birds of prey. But this doesn't mean we should blame the birds of prey for hunting the lambs. When the lambs say among themselves, "These birds of prey are evil, and anyone who is the opposite of them, who is not a bird of prey but a lamb—such a person is good," there's nothing particularly objectionable about this view. It is natural for the lambs to create such an ideal. At the same time, however, the birds of prey might mockingly say to themselves, "We don't bear any grudge against these good lambs. In fact, we like them—there's nothing tastier than a tender lamb."

To demand that strength should not show itself as strength—that it should not seek to dominate, to overcome, to rule, to thirst for challenges, opponents, and victories—is just as absurd as expecting weakness to behave like strength. A force is simply what it is: movement, will, and action—it cannot be separated from these expressions. Force is not something separate from what it does. Yet language (and the flawed reasoning built into it) misleads us. It tempts us to see every action as requiring a subject behind it, a "doer" behind the deed.

For example, people separate lightning from its flash. They think of the flash as something done by the lightning, as if lightning itself were a kind of being or subject that causes the flash to happen. In the same way, popular morality separates strength from its actions, imagining that there is some neutral, independent force behind a strong person, one that can choose whether or not to act with strength. But this is a false idea. There is no "being" behind the doing, no "doer" behind the act. The action itself is everything. The so-called "doer" is just a shadow of the action, a label we attach to it.

This is like saying the lightning "flashes," as though the flash were something separate from the lightning itself. It's a kind of doubling of the same event— making the lightning both the cause and the effect of its own flash. Scientists, too, fall into this trap when they say things like, "Force moves," or "Force causes." Even modern science, despite its cold objectivity, remains ensnared by the tricks of language. It cannot let go of the old superstition of the "subject." The atom, for instance, is one such imaginary subject, just like Kant's "Thing-in-itself."

Is it any wonder, then, that suppressed feelings of revenge and hatred seize upon this belief for their own purposes? Nothing fuels these emotions more than the idea that "the strong have the choice to be weak, and the bird of prey has the option to be a lamb." This belief gives the oppressed and downtrodden a way to hold the birds of prey accountable for being what they are. The weak and powerless, driven by their resentment, convince themselves that the strong are to blame for their strength, and that the predators are at fault for being predators.

"Let us be different from evil, let us be good! And good is anyone who does not oppress, who does not harm others, who does not attack, who does not seek revenge, who leaves vengeance to God, who keeps himself hidden as we do, who avoids evil, and who asks little from life; in short, someone like us—patient, meek, and just." Yet, when this sentiment is stripped of its pretenses and interpreted coldly and without bias, it means little more than, "The weak are weak, and it is good to avoid doing anything beyond our strength."

This grim prudence, this lowest form of survival instinct, is no different from what insects demonstrate when they feign death in the face of great danger, avoiding any action that could cost them too much. Yet this basic instinct, through the self-deception and trickery of weakness, has been dressed up in the grandeur of an ascetic, silent, and expectant virtue. It pretends, as if by choice, that the weakness of the weak—their very nature, their being, their actions, their inescapable reality—is a deliberate decision, a conscious act of will, a merit, a virtue.

Such individuals rely on the belief in a neutral, free-choosing "subject"—or, in simpler terms, the soul. This belief is essential for their self-preservation and self-assertion, where every lie about themselves can be sanctified. The notion of the subject, or soul, has perhaps been the most effective dogma ever devised because it enables the weak, the oppressed, and the frail masses to engage in the ultimate self-deception: interpreting their weakness as a form of freedom, seeing their condition—whether being one thing or another—not as necessity but as merit.

Who dares to peer into the secret of how ideals are created in this world?

Who has the courage to confront it? Come forward!

Here, a glimpse is granted into these dark and grimy workshops. But wait! Just a moment, curious and reckless soul—your eyes must first adjust to this strange, shifting light. Now, look carefully! Enough! Speak! What is happening down there, in the depths? Tell us what you see, you with the most dangerous curiosity—for now I will listen.

"I see nothing, but I hear much more. It is a careful, spiteful, soft whispering and murmuring from every corner and crevice. It seems to me they are lying; every sound is coated with a sugary sweetness. Weakness is being turned into merit—there's no question about it. It is exactly as you say."

Go on!

"And the inability to retaliate is being called 'goodness.' Cowardly baseness is being rebranded as meekness. Submission to those they hate is renamed obedience—obedience, they say, to someone who supposedly commanded this submission, whom they call God. The harmlessness of the weak, their abundance of cowardice, their standing at the door and waiting because they have no other choice—these things are given noble labels like 'patience,' which they even call a virtue. Their inability to take revenge is transformed into not wanting revenge, perhaps even forgiveness (as if they know not what they do— though we know well enough what they do). They speak of 'love for their enemies' and sweat as they say it."

Go on!

"They are wretched, without a doubt—all these whisperers and forgers in the corners, though they huddle together for warmth. And yet they tell me their misery is a special favor and distinction granted to them by God, much like one beats the dogs one loves most. They even say this misery is a preparation, a test, a form of training. Perhaps, they say, it is more than that—it might one day be repaid with immense interest, in gold or in happiness. This they call 'blessedness.'"

Go on!

"Now they are trying to convince me that not only are they better people than the mighty, than the lords of the earth—whose spittle they are forced to lick (not out of fear, of course, oh no, not out of fear! But because God commands that all authority must be honored)—but also that they have a 'better time.' If not now, then one day they will surely have a 'better time.' But enough! Enough! I can bear no more. Bad air! Bad air! These workshops where ideals are created—they reek of the rankest lies!"

Wait, hold on! You're not mentioning the masterpieces crafted by these virtuosos of black magic, these masters who can transform blackness into whiteness, guilt into innocence, and darkness into light. Have you not noticed the level of refinement they achieve in their ultimate work, their most daring, subtle, ingenious, and deceitful trick?

Be careful! These creatures of the cellar, filled with revenge and hatred—what do they make out of that revenge and hatred? Do you hear their words? Would you ever guess, if you trusted only their words, that you are among people seething with resentment and nothing else?

"I understand now—I prick up my ears (ah! ah! ah!—and hold my nose). Now, for the first time, I truly hear what they have always said: 'We are the good, we are the righteous.' What they demand is not called revenge; they call it 'the triumph of righteousness.' What they hate is not their enemies; no, they claim to hate 'unrighteousness' and 'godlessness.' What they believe in and hope for is not the joy of revenge, not the intoxicating sweetness of revenge (did not Homer call it 'sweeter than honey'?), but rather the victory of God—the righteous God— over the 'godless.' What is left for them to love in this world? Not their brothers in hate, but their 'brothers in love,' as they say: all the good and righteous people of the earth."

And what do they call that vision that comforts them through the hardships of life—their grand illusion of future blessedness?

"What? Am I hearing this correctly? They call it 'the Last Judgment,' the coming of their kingdom, 'the Kingdom of God.' But for now, they say they live 'in faith,' 'in love,' and 'in hope.'"

Enough! Enough!

Faith in what? Love for what? Hope for what? These weaklings! It is clear they also wish to be strong one day. There is no doubt about it—their kingdom must come someday. They call it "the Kingdom of God," as already mentioned. They are so meek in everything, so patient! Yet to experience that kingdom, they must live long—beyond death itself. Yes, eternal life is required to finally compensate for this earthly life of "faith," "love," and "hope."

Compensate for what? Compensate with what?

Dante, I believe, made a glaring error when, with terrifying brilliance, he inscribed over the gates of his Hell, "Me too made eternal love." Surely, the following inscription would be far more fitting over the gates of the Christian Paradise and its so-called "eternal blessedness." "Me too made eternal hate." That is, of course, assuming one is willing to put a truth above the entrance to a lie.

What is this "blessedness" of Paradise, exactly? Perhaps we could guess, but it's better to let an authority explicitly state it— someone whose expertise in such matters is beyond question: Thomas Aquinas, the great teacher and saint.

"Beati in regno celesti," says Thomas Aquinas, as softly as a lamb, "videbunt paenas damnatorum, ut beatitudo illis magis complaceat." ("The blessed in the heavenly kingdom will witness the punishment of the damned, so that their bliss will be all the greater.")

Or, if you wish to hear a stronger tone, let us take the words of a triumphant early Church Father, warning his followers against the cruel pleasures of public spectacles. Why? Because, he explains, faith offers something far greater. De Spectaculis (Chapter 29 and following) lays it out plainly: thanks to redemption, we have access to joys of an entirely different kind. Instead of athletes, we have martyrs. Do we crave blood? Then we have the blood of Christ. But what will await us on the day of His return, on the day of His triumph?

Then this enraptured visionary continues:

"But indeed, other spectacles await us—that final and eternal day of judgment, that day unexpected by the nations, that day scorned by them, when the vast age of the world and all its generations will be consumed in one fir e. What a spectacle will that be! What shall I marvel at? What shall I laugh at? Where shall I rejoice? Where shall I exult, as I watch so many mighty kings, who were once proclaimed to be taken into heaven, groaning in the deepest darkness along with Jupiter himself and their own witnesses! Then, too, the governors, those persecutors of the name of the Lord, being consumed in fir es more savage than the flames with which they tormented Christians! And what about those wise philosopher s, ashamed as they burn alongside their disciples, those same philosophers who taught that nothing pertained to God, who declared that souls either did not exist or would not return to their bodies! What of the poets, trembling not before Rhadamanthus or Minos but before the unexpected tribunal of Christ! Then, truly, the tragedies will be heard again, with voices much louder and screams far more violent in their own calamities. Then, the actors will be seen, more unrestrained in their movements through the flames. Then, the charioteer s will be on fiery wheels, their whole bodies blazing red. Then, the athletes will be thrown not in the gymnasiums, but into fire.

Unless, of course, I prefer not to see them alive even then, for I would rather direct my insatiable gaze to those who were most cruel against the Lord. 'Her e he is,' I will say, 'the carpenter 's son or the child of a prostitute' (as the following passages and especially the description of Mary in the Talmud make clear, Tertullian is here refer ring to the Jews). 'Her e he is, the break er of the Sabbath, the Samaritan possessed by a demon. Her e he is, the one whom you purchased from Judas, the one who was beaten with a reed and struck with fists, who was defiled with spit, given gall and vinegar to dr ink. Her e he is, the one whose body his disciples supposedly stole to claim he had risen—or per haps the gardener took it, to prevent visitors from trampling his lettuce!' To witness such things, to revel in such spectacles—what praetor, what consul, what priest could offer you such gifts from their generosity? And yet we already have a foretaste of these things, in a way, through faith, as the Spirit brings them to us in vivid imagination. But how much more magnificent are those things that eye has not seen, nor ear heard, nor the heart of man imagined (1 Corinthians 2 :9). I believe they will be far more pleasing than any arena or stage, whether comedic or tragic."

And so it is written: Perfidem—by faith.

Let us come to a conclusion. The two opposing value systems—"good and bad" versus "good and evil"—have waged a terrible battle across the centuries. This thousand-year struggle has shaped the world, and though the "good and evil" morality has long held the upper hand, there are still places where the outcome remains undecided. It could even be said that this conflict continues to escalate, reaching ever higher levels of complexity and intensity. It has become increasingly psychological, so much so that one might argue there is no greater mark of a higher or more psychological nature than to embody this very contradiction—to still serve as a battlefield for these opposing values.

The symbol of this struggle, etched into history in a script still worth reading, is encapsulated in the phrase: Rome against Judea, Judea against Rome. This conflict, this confrontation, this antagonism remains unparalleled in significance. There has been no greater event in history than this fight, no more profound question than the one it poses.

To Rome, the Jew represented the embodiment of the unnatural, a being utterly monstrous in its opposition to the Roman way of life. The Romans saw in the Jews a race consumed by hatred for all of humanity—and they were right, insofar as the well-being and future of humanity were tied to the unconditional dominance of aristocratic values, the values of Rome. Conversely, what did the Jews feel toward Rome? This can be gleaned from countless hints, but it is enough to turn to the Book of Revelation (the Johannine Apocalypse), which stands as perhaps the most obscene of written outbursts, a text steeped in the spirit of vengeance.

And yet, consider the profound irony—and the cunning logic—of the Christian instinct, which labeled this very book of hate with the name of the "Disciple of Love." This is the same disciple to whom the ecstatic and passionate Gospel was attributed. There is a fragment of truth in this association, even if it required considerable literary forgery to make it plausible.

The Romans were a strong and aristocratic people—perhaps the strongest and most aristocratic the world has ever known, or even imagined. Every relic of their civilization, every inscription, inspires awe, provided one can perceive the spirit behind the words. In contrast, the Jews were the quintessential priestly nation of resentment, endowed with a singular genius for shaping popular morality. To fully appreciate their exceptionalism, compare the Jews to other nations with similar tendencies, such as the Chinese or the Germans. It is only after such a comparison that one can grasp what is truly first-rate and what is merely fifth-rate.

Which of the two has been provisionally victorious, Rome or Judea? There can be no doubt. Just look at whom, even today, people bow to in Rome itself, as though before the embodiment of the highest values. And not only in Rome, but across nearly half the world—everywhere humanity has been tamed or is in the process of being tamed—people bow before three Jews and one Jewess: Jesus of Nazareth, Peter the fisherman, Paul the tent- maker, and Mary, the mother of Jesus. This fact is extraordinary. Rome has undoubtedly been defeated.

At least, that is the case for now. During the Renaissance, there was a brilliantly sinister resurgence of the classical ideal, the aristocratic valuation of all things. Rome, like a man shaking off a deep sleep, seemed to stir under the weight of the Judaised Rome that had been built over it—a Rome that had become an ecumenical synagogue and called itself the "Church." But just as quickly, Judea triumphed again, this time through that fundamentally popular (German and English) movement of revenge called the Reformation. Along with it came the inevitable restoration of the Church and, with it, the return of the graveyard peace of classical Rome.

Judea triumphed once more, and even more decisively, during the French Revolution. Here, the victory was deeper and more profound than ever. The last political aristocracy in Europe—the French aristocracy of the seventeenth and eighteenth centuries— was shattered by the instincts of a resentful populace. Never before had the world heard such jubilant celebration, such uproarious enthusiasm. And in the midst of it all, something monstrous and unexpected occurred: the ancient ideal itself was revived, parading before the conscience of humanity with unprecedented brilliance and vitality.

Against the cry of resentment—the call for equality, abasement, and the levelling of humanity, for regression into mediocrity— there resounded a counter-cry, terrible and seductive: the prer ogative of the few.

As though marking a final crossroads, there appeared Napoleon, the most singular and violent anachronism to have ever lived. In Napoleon was embodied the very problem of the aristocratic ideal itself—an ideal both magnificent and monstrous. Napoleon was a synthesis of the Monster and the Superman. Consider carefully what a profound problem he represents.

Was that the end? Was the greatest of all conflicts between ideals thereby laid to rest forever? Or was it merely postponed— postponed for a long time? Might there not come a day when the old fire reignites, more terrifying and more deliberately prepared than ever before? And further—should one not wish for such a culmination with all their strength? Should one not will it, demand it, strive for it with every fiber of their being?

For those who, like my readers, begin to reflect and think more deeply on these questions, it will not be easy to arrive quickly at a conclusion. This is reason enough for me to bring my own reflections to a close here, trusting that my meaning has by now become sufficiently clear. Surely it is evident what I mean by the dangerous motto inscribed on the body of my last book: Beyond Good and Evil. At the very least, it should be understood that this is not synonymous with "Beyond Good and Bad."

Note. I take this opportunity afforded by this treatise to express openly and formally a wish that I have, until now, shared only in casual conversations with scholars. I hope that some Faculty of Philosophy might earn the honor of advancing the study of the history of morals by initiating a series of prize essays on the subject. Perhaps this book may serve as a compelling impetus for such an endeavor.

In connection with this possibility, the following question deserves thoughtful consideration. It merits the attention not only of philologists and historians but also of professional philosophers:

"What can philology, and particularly the study of etymology, tell us about the historical evolution of moral ideas?"

At the same time, it is equally crucial to encourage physiologists and doctors to take an interest in these problems—specifically, the value of the valuations that have prevailed throughout history. In this effort, professional philosophers should act as spokesmen and intermediaries. But this requires first transforming the traditionally cold and suspicious relationship between philosophy, physiology, and medicine into one of mutual respect and productive collaboration.

Indeed, every historical and cultural "table of values"—every "thou shalt" known to history and ethnology—needs to be examined and interpreted primarily from a physiological perspective, rather than exclusively a psychological one. Additionally, all these values demand critique from the standpoint of medical science. The question, "What is the value of this or that table of values or morality?" must be examined from a variety of perspectives. For instance, the question "valuable for what?" cannot be analyzed too carefully or in too much detail.

What might have value for one purpose—such as promoting a race's capacity for endurance, its adaptability to a particular climate, or even the survival of the greatest number—might have far less value if the goal is the evolution of a stronger species. In evaluating values, the interests of the majority and those of the minority represent fundamentally opposing perspectives. It is left to the naïveté of English biologists to assume that the former perspective— the good of the majority—is inherently superior.

All the sciences must now work to prepare the ground for the philosopher's future task: to solve the problem of value. This task requires the philosopher to establish and define a hierarchy of values.

Chapter 2
Guilt, Bad Conscience, and The Like

The cultivation of an animal capable of making promises—is this not the paradoxical task that nature has set for itself in regard to humanity? Is this not the very essence of the problem of man? The fact that this problem has been largely solved is extraordinary, especially to those who recognize the immense power of forgetfulness that works against it. Forgetfulness is not simply a passive inertia, as many superficial thinkers assume. Rather, it is an active force—a positive and deliberate function. It prevents what we have lived through, experienced, and absorbed from constantly intruding upon our consciousness, just as the processes of physical digestion and assimilation operate without entering our awareness.

Forgetfulness provides a temporary closing of the doors and windows of consciousness, offering relief from the ceaseless activity of the subconscious organs working together in harmony or conflict. It allows a moment of quiet, a clean slate, so to speak—a tabula rasa— to make space for new experiences and, more importantly, for higher functions like governance, planning, and decision-making. The human organism, like an oligarchy, requires this order to function properly. Active forgetfulness, therefore, is the guardian and nurturer of mental order, peace, and proper conduct. Without it, there can be no happiness, joy, hope, pride, or even a sense of the present.

A person in whom this preventive apparatus of forgetfulness is damaged is like a dyspeptic who cannot "digest" anything, and this comparison is not merely figurative. Such a person cannot "let go" of anything. Yet this same human animal, who depends so much on forgetfulness for health and vitality, has developed within himself an opposing power: memory. Memory functions to curb forgetfulness when necessary—in situations where promises must be kept.

This memory is not a mere passive inability to forget impressions once made or words once spoken. It is an active refusal to let go. It is the persistence of the will, a deliberate desire to continue what has once been decided. It creates a bridge between the original "I will" and the ultimate execution of that will. This memory ensures that even amidst a world of new and unforeseen circumstances, distractions, and desires, the chain of intent does not break.

But what is the foundation for this remarkable ability? To regulate the future in this way, man had to learn to distinguish between what is necessary and what is accidental. He had to think causally, to envision the distant future as though it were present, to anticipate, and to determine with precision the relationship between ends and means. Above all, he had to learn to calculate and to reckon. He had to become disciplined, predictable, and reliable—even to himself. Only then could man begin to promise, to guarantee himself as a being with a future.

This is, in essence, the long history of how responsibility came into being. The task of creating an animal capable of making promises includes, as we now understand, the preliminary task of shaping man to be, in some sense, necessary, predictable, consistent with his kind, orderly, and therefore calculable. The immense undertaking I refer to as the "morality of custom" (see Dawn of Day, Aphorisms 9, 14, and 16)—the actual, painstaking work that humanity has done on itself throughout its longest and most prehistoric periods—derives its meaning and justification from this goal. Despite all its inherent harshness, despotism, rigidity, and occasional foolishness, the morality of custom made man truly calculable.

If we now consider this colossal process from its endpoint, where the tree of humanity finally bears its mature fruit—when society and its morality of custom have achieved their purpose—we find the sovereign individual. This individual is unlike anyone else, having freed himself from the constraints of the morality of custom. He is autonomous, a being who stands "beyond morality" (for autonomy and morality are mutually exclusive). He is, in short, a man of personal, enduring, and independent will—a man capable of making promises.

This individual possesses a proud awareness, felt in every fiber of his being, of what he has achieved and brought to life within himself: a genuine sense of power, freedom, and human perfection. This person, who has grown into true freedom and who is capable of binding himself with promises, is a master of his own will, a sovereign. How could he not be aware of his immense superiority over all beings incapable of committing themselves to promises or acting as their own guarantee? How could he not recognize the trust, reverence, and awe he inspires? He has earned all these. With mastery over himself, he is also granted mastery over circumstances, over nature, and over all creatures with weaker wills and less reliability.

For the free man, the man of the enduring and unbreakable will, this strength becomes his measure of value. From this vantage point, he looks outward, evaluating others. He honors and respects his equals—the strong and the reliable, those who, like him, can bind themselves with promises. Such individuals promise sparingly, carefully, and deliberately. They give their trust rarely, and when they do, it is an act of conferring honor. Their word is reliable because they know they possess the strength to uphold it, even in the face of calamity or fate.

Conversely, the sovereign man has no patience for the empty and thoughtless, for those who promise without reason or capability. He stands ready to crush the hollow fools who make promises they have no business making and to chastise the liar who breaks his word even as it leaves his lips.

The proud knowledge of this extraordinary privilege—the privilege of responsibility—and the deep awareness of this rare freedom, this power over oneself and over fate, become ingrained in him as an instinct, a ruling instinct. What does he call this instinct, this governing force within him, if he feels the need to name it? There can be no doubt: the sovereign man calls it his conscience.

His conscience? One quickly realizes that the idea of "conscience," seen here in its highest and most striking form, must have undergone a long history of development. The ability to guarantee oneself with pride, to say yes to oneself—that is a mature fruit, but also a late one. How long this fruit must have hung sour and bitter on the tree! And for an even longer period, there was no sign of it at all. No one had yet dared to promise such a thing, even though everything on the tree had been preparing and ripening for that very purpose.

"How does one create a memory in the human animal? How can an impression be so deeply fixed in this fleeting, half-thoughtless, and half- oblivious creature—this embodiment of forgetfulness— that it remains present permanently?" It is easy to imagine that this ancient problem was not solved with gentle answers or kind methods. Perhaps nothing in early human history is as dreadful and sinister as humanity's first system of mnemonics.

"Something must be burned into memory to ensure it stays there: only what continues to cause pain is remembered." This axiom comes from the oldest—and, unfortunately, the longest- lasting— psychology known to the world. One could even say that wherever we now find solemnity, seriousness, mystery, and grim colors in the lives of people and nations, we see remnants of the terror that once accompanied all promises, pledges, and obligations. The past, with all its vastness, depth, and cruelty, breathes its influence into us when we grow "serious."

When humanity deemed it necessary to forge a memory for itself, it did so through blood, torture, and sacrifice. The most horrifying sacrifices (including the sacrifice of first-born children), the most repulsive mutilations (such as castration), and the cruelest rituals of religious cults (for all religions, at their core, are systems of cruelty) all originate from this instinct that found its strongest mnemonic tool in pain.

In this sense, asceticism itself can be understood as part of this process. Certain ideas had to be rendered indelible, ever-present, and fixed in such a way that they could dominate the nervous and intellectual system. Ascetic practices and lifestyles served to eliminate competing ideas, ensuring these chosen ones became "unforgettable."

The less capable humanity was of remembering, the more horrific the signs and customs it employed. The harshness of ancient penal laws, for example, reveals how difficult it was for humans to overcome forgetfulness and hold a few basic social principles firmly in mind. These laws were directed at people ruled by every fleeting emotion and passing desire, those incapable of maintaining even the simplest agreements.

We Germans may not see ourselves as particularly cruel or hard-hearted, and certainly not as frivolous or careless. But a glance at our old penal codes reveals the tremendous effort required to evolve into a "nation of thinkers." By this, I mean the European nation that still today represents the pinnacle of reliability, seriousness, bad taste, and pragmatism—a nation that, thanks to these traits, claims the right to train Europe's intellectual elite, its mandar ins.

The Germans employed horrific means to create for themselves a memory strong enough to overcome their deeply ingrained plebeian instincts and the raw brutality of those instincts. Consider the old German punishments: stoning (as described in legend, where a millstone crushes the guilty man's head), breaking on the wheel (an original and uniquely German invention in the realm of punishment), dart-throwing, tearing or trampling by horses (the infamous "quartering"), boiling criminals in oil or wine (practiced even into the 14th and 15th centuries), the gruesomely popular flaying ("slicing into strips"), cutting flesh from the chest, and besmearing the offender with honey before exposing him to flies under the blazing sun.

It was through such vivid and horrifying images that humanity learned to retain in its memory a mere five or six "thou shalt nots," essential for societal coexistence. These were promises that man had to remember in order to enjoy the benefits of living in society. And it was, indeed, through such methods that man eventually attained r eason! But alas, reason, seriousness, control over emotions—all those somber and weighty achievements we now call reflection, all the supposed privileges and crowning glories of humanity—what a steep price they have demanded! How much blood and cruelty have laid the foundation for all the so-called "good things" in life!

But how did that other bleak phenomenon—the consciousness of sin, the pervasive sense of a "bad conscience"—enter the world? This question brings us back to our genealogists of morality. For the second time, I must say—or perhaps for the first time—that they are utterly inadequate. They possess nothing more than a few narrow spans of modern experience, lacking any deep knowledge of the past, and showing no real desire to gain such knowledge. Even less do they possess the historical instinct, that essential "second sight" needed for this kind of inquiry. Yet, despite this, they attempt to write the history of morals, and their conclusions are inevitably far removed from the truth—so far that their efforts deserve no more than a condescending glance.

Have these so-called genealogists ever entertained even a vague understanding, for example, that the fundamental moral concept of "ought" originated in the very material idea of "owe"? Or that punishment initially developed as retaliation, entirely independent of any consideration of free will or determinism? It was only when civilization reached a high level of development that humans began making more subtle distinctions such as "intentional," "negligent," "accidental," "responsible," and their opposites— distinctions which are now used in evaluating punishment.

The idea that "the wrongdoer deserves punishment because he could have acted differently," though today it seems self-evident and foundational to the notion of justice, is in fact a very late and highly refined form of human judgment. To retroactively project this idea back to the origins of human society is to commit a crude violation of the principles of early psychology.

For the vast majority of human history, punishment was never based on the offender's responsibility for their actions. It was never about punishing only the guilty. Instead, punishment functioned much like the way parents still punish their children: out of anger for a wrong suffered. This anger, often raw and instinctive, would mechanically vent itself on the source of the injury—the wrongdoer. Over time, this anger became moderated and shaped by the notion that every injury has an equivalent pr ice that could be repaid, even if the repayment took the form of pain inflicted on the perpetrator.

But from where does this deeply entrenched and seemingly indestructible idea of equivalence between harm and pain draw its strength?

I have already traced the origin of this idea to the contractual relationship between creditor and debtor, a relationship as old as the concept of legal rights itself. This points further back to the most basic forms of purchase, sale, barter, and trade.

The recognition and enforcement of these contractual relationships naturally provoke suspicion and resistance toward the primitive societies that created and upheld them. In such societies, promises were made, and mechanisms were devised to ensure the promiser would remember and honor them. These societies, as we might expect, often resorted to harshness, cruelty, and pain to achieve their goals. To instill confidence in their promise to repay, to affirm the seriousness and sanctity of that promise, and to etch the duty of repayment into their own conscience, debtors would pledge something they still owned or controlled. This might include their life, their spouse, their freedom, their body—or under certain religious frameworks, even their salvation, their soul, or their peace in the afterlife. In ancient Egypt, for example, even the corpse of a debtor could be denied rest in the grave if the debt remained unpaid—a particularly grave matter from the Egyptian perspective.

Moreover, creditors were often granted the legal right to inflict pain or torture on the debtor's body as a form of repayment. They might cut off an amount of flesh proportionate to the debt owed. This practice gave rise to elaborate, often grotesque systems of valuation for different body parts, which were meticulously detailed and legally sanctioned. Such schemes reflect the harsh precision with which early societies attempted to ensure the fulfillment of obligations.

A step forward in legal thinking—and an indicator of a freer, less pedantic, and more Roman perspective on law—can be seen in the Roman Code of the Twelve Tables. It stated that the amount creditors could cut off in such cases did not matter: "si plus minusve secuer unt, ne fr aude esto" ("if more or less is cut, it shall not be considered fraud").

Let us unpack the logic behind this entire system of equivalence. It is, indeed, a strange and revealing logic. The equivalence here does not consist of direct compensation for the injury— no payment in money, land, or goods. Instead, the creditor is compensated with a kind of emotional satisfaction. This is the satisfaction of exercising power over someone powerless, the perverse pleasure of inflicting harm simply for the sake of doing so—" de fair e le mal pour le plaisir de le fair e" ("to do harm for the pleasure of doing it"). This joy in cruelty is often most intense for creditors of lower social standing, as it allows them a fleeting sense of power and superiority. For them, it might even feel like a foretaste of a higher social position.

By punishing the debtor, the creditor momentarily participates in the privileges of the ruling class. For once, the creditor experiences the gratifying sense of being able to despise and mistreat another being as an "inferior." Even when the power to punish has already been transferred to authorities, the creditor still enjoys witnessing the debtor being despised and punished. Thus, compensation for the creditor is effectively a claim to cruelty—a right to exercise or benefit from the infliction of suffering.

It is within the realm of contractual law that we find the origins of the entire moral framework surrounding ideas such as "guilt," "conscience," "duty," and the "sacredness of duty." As with all great beginnings in human history, this moral world is steeped in blood. Should we not also acknowledge that this world has never entirely lost its connection to blood and torture—not even in the philosophy of old Kant, whose categorical imperative carries the faint yet unmistakable scent of cruelty?

In this same domain of contracts arose the dark and perhaps inseparable link between the ideas of "guilt" and "suffering." But why, again, can suffering serve as compensation for "owing"? Because the infliction of suffering brings an intense kind of satisfaction. The injured party receives, in exchange for their loss (and the frustration accompanying it), an extraordinary compensation: the pleasure of inflicting pain. This act becomes a feast for the senses—a reward that grows all the more delectable the greater the disparity in rank and social standing between creditor and debtor.

These are speculative thoughts, of course, for it is difficult, both intellectually and emotionally, to delve into such depths. The crude notion of "revenge" often introduced as a connecting concept only obscures the issue rather than clarifying it. Revenge merely redirects us to the same question: Why does inflicting suffering bring satisfaction?

It is unsettling—perhaps repellent—to the sensibilities of modern, "tame" humans (ourselves included) to fully confront how deeply cruelty once permeated human joy and pleasure. Ancient man, with a simplicity and innocence we might now find shocking, openly embraced cruelty as a natural and delightful part of life. He even institutionalized "disinterested malice" (what Spinoza calls sympathia malevolens) as a fundamental trait of human nature, something the conscience could unreservedly approve.

The more insightful observer will already have recognized this primal and enduring joy in cruelty. In Beyond Good and Evil (Aphorism 188) and earlier in The Dawn of Day (Aphorisms 18, 77, 113), I have cautiously hinted at the ongoing "spiritualization" and "deification" of cruelty that runs through the entire history of higher civilizations—indeed, that largely defines it. The time is not so distant when royal weddings or grand national celebrations were unthinkable without accompanying executions, tortures, or perhaps an auto-dafé. Similarly, aristocratic households often required the presence of a victim—someone to be baited and tormented for the amusement of the household.

Consider Don Quixote at the court of the Duchess. Today, we read Don Quixote with a bitter taste in our mouths, almost as if we are enduring a form of torture. This reaction would have been utterly foreign to Cervantes and his contemporaries, who saw the book as one of the most joyful of all comedies, a work to laugh at until they could laugh no more.

The sight of suffering soothes; the act of inflicting suffering soothes even more. This harsh principle is ancient, powerful, and fundamentally human. Perhaps even apes would agree, as they seem to demonstrate in their own inventions of bizarre cruelties— acts that prefigure and foreshadow their future humanity. Without cruelty, there can be no feast. This lesson comes from the oldest and most enduring history of mankind. Even in punishment, there has always been something of the festive.

Considering these ideas, I must clarify—let me say this in passing—that I am fundamentally opposed to providing pessimists with more fuel for their mills of dissatisfaction and despair. On the contrary, it should be emphasized that when humanity was unashamed of its cruelty, life was brighter and more vibrant than it is now, in this age of pessimism. The darkening of human existence has always paralleled the growth of man's shame in himself. The weary, pessimistic outlook, the suspicion that life itself is a problem, the icy denial born of boredom and disgust—these are not the signs of humanity's most depraved era. Rather, they bloom, like swamp flowers, only when the swamp itself comes into being— when diseased refinement and over-moralization take root, teaching "animal man" to feel ashamed of his instincts.

On the path to becoming "angelic" (to avoid using a harsher term), humanity has developed a kind of moral dyspepsia, complete with a sickly stomach and coated tongue. These have rendered not only the joy and innocence of animal existence repugnant to him but also life itself. At times, humanity stands before itself in revulsion, pinching its nose as though life stinks. Pope Innocent III's infamous list of human horrors—"unclean generation, loathsome nutrition in the womb, the vile material from which man develops, the stench of excretion, saliva, urine, and feces"— captures this attitude perfectly.

Today, suffering is trotted out as the ultimate argument against existence, the most damning indictment of life. How different this is from earlier times when people thought quite the opposite. They valued the infliction of suffering, seeing it as something magical and even a seductive lure to life itself.

Perhaps, for the more sensitive souls among us, it will be comforting to hear that pain may not have hurt as much in those days as it does now. Any physician who has treated individuals of less "refined" cultures (for instance, some African groups taken to represent prehistoric man) might confirm this. These patients, even when suffering from severe internal inflammations that would drive a modern European to the brink of despair, often endure their pain with surprising resilience. Pain simply does not have the same impact on them.

Indeed, the curve of human sensitivity to pain seems to drop dramatically, almost suddenly, once one steps beyond the narrow band of over-civilized humanity. I am personally convinced that a single painful night endured by a highly-strung, cultured woman might well outweigh the collective suffering of all the animals subjected to scientific experiments with knives.

Even now, the human craving for cruelty has likely not disappeared—it has merely been transformed. With pain now more keenly felt, this impulse has undergone a kind of sublimation and refinement. It has been redirected to the realm of imagination and the psyche, camouflaged by euphemisms so artfully contrived that even the most delicate and hypocritical consciences remain oblivious to their true nature. Terms like "tragic pity" and "the nostalgia of the cross" are among these deceptive labels, concealing the enduring appetite for cruelty beneath a veil of moral respectability.

What truly stirs indignation against suffering is not the suffering itself but its apparent senselessness. This sense of meaninglessness, however, was absent in Christianity, which framed suffering as part of a grand, mysterious system of salvation. Nor did it exist for the naive ancient peoples, who found meaning in suffering from the perspective of the spectator or the one inflicting the pain. To remove the notion of hidden, unseen suffering from the world, it became almost essential to invent gods and a hierarchy of beings—figures who could wander through secret places, peer into darkness, and never miss an intriguing or painful spectacle. Through these inventions, life managed a remarkable feat: the justification of itself, including its evils.

In our time, such justifications might require different devices (such as framing life as a riddle or a problem to be solved). But for primitive people, the logic was simple: "Every evil is justified if a god can find it edifying." And was this sentiment truly limited to primitive people? Hardly. The idea of gods as connoisseurs of cruelty extends deeply into our European civilization, even today. One might recall the perspectives of Luther or Calvin in this context. It is certain, at any rate, that even the Greeks found no greater spice for the happiness of their gods than the delights of cruelty.

What mood, one wonders, does Homer ascribe to his gods as they gaze upon the fates of mortals? What ultimate meaning lies behind the Trojan War and other such tragic horrors? There can be no doubt: these events were conceived as festival games for the gods. Moreover, since poets are of a more "godlike" breed than ordinary men, such events were also games for the poets themselves. Later, in the same spirit, Greek moral philosophers envisioned the gods' eyes fixed upon the moral struggles, heroism, and self-torture of virtuous humans. Heracles, embodying the duty-bound hero, performed on a stage and was fully conscious of his audience. For this society of actors, virtue without witnesses was utterly unthinkable.

Indeed, how could one not conclude that the bold and fateful invention of "free will"—a concept then entirely new to Europe— was created specifically to justify the notion that the gods' interest in human virtue and vice was boundless? This invention ensured that the stage of the free-will world would never lack truly fresh, novel, and exciting situations, dramatic conflicts, and catastrophic endings. In contrast, a world governed entirely by deterministic principles would be too predictable for the gods and would quickly bore them. This was reason enough for the philosophers of the time—those loyal allies of the gods—to reject the idea of a deterministic universe.

All of ancient humanity was steeped in consideration for the spectator, embodying a world where public display and theatricality were central. For them, happiness was inseparable from spectacles and festivals. And, as mentioned before, even in acts of great punishment, there was something inherently celebratory, a ritual festivity woven into the spectacle of human suffering.

The sense of "ought," of personal obligation (to return to our inquiry), originated in the oldest and most fundamental personal relationship: the relationship between buyer and seller, creditor and debtor. In this context, one individual confronted another, measuring themselves against each other. No stage of human civilization, however primitive, has been found to lack some trace of this relationship. Setting prices, assessing values, calculating equivalents, and exchanging goods—these activities dominated the earliest human thoughts so thoroughly that they essentially constituted the very act of thinking itself.

It was in this sphere that the first form of human intelligence developed, along with humanity's earliest sense of pride and superiority over other animals. Perhaps even our word "Mensch" (manas) retains a hint of this self-pride: it identified man as the creature who measures and values, the assessing animal par excellence.

Commerce—sale and purchase—along with the psychological processes they entail, predates any organized form of society or community. Instead, the awareness of exchange, trade, debt, obligation, and compensation first emerged from the most basic forms of individual interaction. This consciousness was then applied to the earliest social groups, particularly in their relations with one another. It extended the practice of comparing force against force, measuring, and calculating.

Man's focus was shaped by this perspective, and with the unyielding consistency typical of ancient thought—slow to start but relentless in its course—humanity soon arrived at a sweeping generalization: everything has a price, everything can be paid for. This concept formed the oldest and most straightforward moral code of justice and laid the foundation for ideas of fairness, goodwill, and objectivity in the world.

In this early stage, justice was essentially an agreement between individuals or groups of roughly equal power to settle disputes and restore balance through mutual understanding. As for the weaker parties, justice often involved compelling them to accept terms of settlement imposed by the stronger. This basic willingness—or enforced necessity—to come to terms marked the beginnings of what we now call fairness and equity.

When viewed through the lens of antiquity (and this kind of antiquity can arise or reemerge in any era), the relationship between the community and its members resembles that of a creditor to its debtors. Man lives within a community, enjoying its benefits—what tremendous benefits these are, though we sometimes underestimate them today. He lives protected, spared, in peace and trust, shielded from the dangers and hostilities that constantly threaten those outside the community, the "peaceless" ones. (A German might recognize this from the original meaning of the word Elend, signifying "exile" or being without a homeland.) This security is granted because the individual has pledged himself to the community, entering into obligations in exchange for this protection from harm and enmity.

But what happens when this agreement is broken? When the individual fails to uphold his obligations, the community—now the wronged creditor—will demand repayment, one way or another. In such cases, the specific harm caused by the offender becomes almost secondary. The true transgression lies in his breach of trust, his breaking of the pact with the entire community, which had granted him its protection and benefits. The criminal is not just someone who fails to repay his debt; he actively attacks his creditor. Consequently, he forfeits not only the advantages and security of communal life but also receives a forceful reminder of just how valuable those benefits were.

The wrath of the injured community strips him of his rights and casts him back into the "wild" status he had previously been protected from. The community rejects him, and in doing so, opens the door for all manner of hostility and vengeance to be unleashed upon him. At this stage of civilization, punishment serves as a grim mimicry of how one treats a despised, defeated enemy. Such an enemy is not only stripped of all rights and protection but also shown no mercy. Here we see the full enactment of vae victis— "woe to the vanquished"— in its most brutal and unrelenting form.

This perspective also explains why war itself, along with its associated sacrificial rituals, has shaped all the forms of punishment that have emerged throughout human history. The treatment of the criminal mirrors the treatment of a conquered foe, embodying the mercilessness and cruelty of a victorious celebration over the defeated.

As a community grows stronger, it begins to view individual offenses as less threatening to its overall stability. The misdeeds of individuals no longer seem as revolutionary or dangerous to the existence of the group as a whole. As a result, the wrongdoer is no longer cast out or subjected to the unrestrained wrath of the community. Instead, the community actively shields and protects the wrongdoer, particularly from the anger of those directly harmed by the offense.

With the evolution of penal law, certain patterns become increasingly evident: efforts are made to moderate the wrath of the injured party, to contain the conflict, and to prevent it from escalating or spreading. The focus shifts toward finding equivalents, settling disputes (compositio), and ultimately attempting to separate the offender from the offense itself. The more powerful and self-assured a community becomes, the more its system of justice softens. Conversely, when a community's stability is threatened or its power diminishes, the harshest and most severe forms of justice tend to resurface.

This dynamic parallels the relationship between creditors and debtors: as the creditor becomes wealthier, they grow more lenient and humane in their dealings. The true measure of their wealth becomes the degree of harm they can endure without genuinely suffering. One can even imagine a society with such immense confidence in its power that it embraces the luxury of allowing wrongdoers to go unpunished. Such a society might say, "What harm do these parasites do to me? Let them live and thrive—I am strong enough to handle it."

Justice, which began with the principle "everything can be paid off, everything must be paid off," eventually transforms into something that allows even those who cannot pay to escape punishment. Like all good things on Earth, justice ultimately undoes itself. This self-destruction of justice bears a charming name: Gr ace. And as is evident, grace remains the privilege of the strongest— their super- law.

A word of caution is necessary here regarding recent attempts to trace the origins of justice back to resentment. Allow me to offer a suggestion to psychologists who wish to study revenge up close: this particular emotion thrives most vibrantly today among anarchists and anti-Semites. Like the hidden violet, it blooms discreetly—though it carries a vastly different scent. Given that similar forces tend to create similar outcomes, it's hardly surprising that such circles often attempt to glorify revenge by rebranding it as justice. The claim seems to be that justice is nothing more than an advanced form of the consciousness of injury, which serves to validate revenge and elevate reactive emotions as a whole.

I have no fundamental objection to reevaluating these reactive emotions— indeed, from a biological perspective, their value has likely been underestimated. However, I wish to highlight that the very spirit of revenge underpins this so- called new scientific "equity." This perspective, while appearing fair at first, quickly dissolves into outright hostility and bias the moment other emotions, particularly those of higher biological value, come into play. These active emotions—like personal ambition and the drive for tangible achievement— deserve far greater scientific recognition than reactive feelings such as hate, envy, and resentment. (E. Dühring's writings, such as Value of Life and Course of Philosophy, are key examples of this bias.)

To address Dühring's claim that justice originates in the realm of reactive feelings: the truth requires us to assert the exact opposite. The final domain that justice conquers is the sphere of reactive emotions. When a truly just individual remains impartial even toward their injurer—when they go beyond being merely calm, restrained, or indifferent—this represents a rare and extraordinary achievement. True justice is an active state. To maintain an objective, clear, and balanced perspective even in the face of insult, contempt, or slander is an extraordinary form of mastery. Such an individual exhibits a profound, gentle clarity—a perfection that is almost beyond human capacity.

That said, even the most just among us is vulnerable to small provocations. A mere hint of malice, hostility, or innuendo is often enough to cloud their objectivity and inflame their emotions. Justice, for all its loftiness, is a delicate and challenging ideal to sustain.

The active man, the attacking, aggressive man, is always a hundred degrees nearer to justice than the man who merely reacts; he certainly has no need to adopt the tactics, necessary in the case of the reacting man, of making false and biased valuations of his object. It is, in point of fact, for this reason that the aggressive man has at all times enjoyed the stronger, bolder, more aristocratic, and also freer outlook, the better conscience. On the other hand, we already surmise who it really is that has on his conscience the invention of the "bad conscience,"— the resentful man! Finally, let man look at himself in history. In what sphere up to the present has the whole administration of law, the actual need of law, found its earthly home? Perchance in the sphere of the reacting man? Not for a minute: rather in that of the active, strong, spontaneous, aggressive man? I deliberately defy the abovementioned agitator (who himself makes this self-confession, "the creed of revenge has run through all my works and endeavours like the red thread of Justice"), and say, that judged historically law in the world represents the very war against the reactive feelings, the very war waged on those feelings by the powers of activity and aggression, which devote some of their strength to damming and keeping within bounds this effervescence of hysterical reactivity, and to forcing it to some compromise. Everywhere where justice is practised and justice is maintained, it is to be observed that the stronger power, when confronted with the weaker powers which are inferior to it (whether they be groups, or individuals), searches for weapons to put an end to the senseless fury of resentment, while it carries on its object, partly by taking the victim of resentment out of the clutches of revenge, partly by substituting for revenge a campaign of its own against the enemies of peace and order, partly by finding, suggesting, and occasionally enforcing settlements, partly by standardising certain equivalents for injuries, to which equivalents the element of resentment is henceforth finally referred. The most drastic measure, however, taken and effectuated by the supreme power, to combat the preponderance of the feelings of spite and vindictiveness—it takes this measure as soon as it is at all strong enough to do so—is the foundation of law, the imperative declaration of what in its eyes is to be regarded as just and lawful, and what unjust and unlawful: and while, after the foundation of law, the supreme power treats the aggressive and arbitrary acts of individuals, or of whole groups, as a violation of law, and a revolt against itself, it distracts the feelings of its subjects from the immediate injury inflicted by such a violation, and thus eventually attains the very opposite result to that always desired by revenge, which sees and recognises nothing but the standpoint of the injured party. From henceforth the eye becomes trained to a more and more impersonal valuation of the deed, even the eye of the injured party himself (though this is in the final stage of all, as has been previously remarked)—on this principle "right" and "wrong" first manifest themselves after the foundation of law (and not, as Duhring maintains, only after the act of violation). To talk of intrinsic right and intrinsic wrong is absolutely nonsensical; intrinsically, an injury, an oppression, an exploitation, an annihilation can be nothing wrong, inasmuch as life is essentially (that is, in its cardinal functions) something which functions by injuring, oppressing, exploiting, and annihilating, and is absolutely inconceivable without such a character. It is necessary to make an even more serious confession:—viewed from the most advanced biological standpoint, conditions of legality can be only exceptional conditions, in that they are partial restrictions of the real life-will, which makes for power, and in that they are subordinated to the life-will's general end as particular means, that is, as means to create larger units of strength. A legal organisation, conceived of as sovereign and universal, not as a weapon in a fight of complexes of power, but as a weapon against fighting, generally something after the style of Duhring's communistic model of treating every will as equal with every other will, would be a principle hostile to life, a destroyer and dissolver of man, an outrage on the future of man, a symptom of fatigue, a secret cut to Nothingness.

A word more on the origin and end of punishment—two problems which are or ought to be kept distinct, but which unfortunately are usually lumped into one. And what tactics have our moral genealogists employed up to the present in these cases? Their inveterate naivety. They find out some "end" in the punishment, for instance, revenge and deterrence, and then in all their innocence set this end at the beginning, as the causa fiendi of the punishment, and— they have done the trick. But the patching up of a history of the origin of law is the last use to which the "End in Law" ought to be put. Perhaps there is no more important principle for any kind of history than the following, which, difficult though it is to master, should nonetheless be mastered in every detail.

The origin of the existence of a thing and its final utility, its practical application and incorporation in a system of ends, are completely opposed to each other— everything, anything, which exists and which prevails anywhere, will always be put to new purposes by a force superior to itself, will be commandeered afresh, will be turned and transformed to new uses; all "happening" in the organic world consists of overpowering and dominating, and again all overpowering and domination is a new interpretation and adjustment, which must necessarily obscure or absolutely extinguish the existing "meaning" and "end." The most perfect comprehension of the utility of any physiological organ (or also of a legal institution, social custom, political habit, form in art or in religious worship) does not for a minute imply any simultaneous comprehension of its origin: this may seem uncomfortable and unpalatable to the older men, for it has been the immemorial belief that understanding the final cause or the utility of a thing, a form, an institution, means also understanding the reason for its origin: to give an example of this logic, the eye was made to see, the hand was made to grasp. So even punishment was conceived as invented with a view to punishing. But all ends and all utilities are only signs that a Will to Power has mastered a less powerful force, has impressed thereon out of its own self the meaning of a function; and the whole history of a "Thing," an organ, a custom, can on the same principle be regarded as a continuous "sign- chain" of perpetually new interpretations and adjustments, whose causes, so far from needing to have even a mutual connection, sometimes follow and alternate with each other absolutely haphazard. Similarly, the evolution of a "Thing," of a custom, is anything but its progress to an end, still less a logical and direct progress attained with the minimum expenditure of energy and cost: it is rather the succession of processes of subjugation, more or less profound, more or less mutually independent, which operate on the thing itself; it is, further, the resistance which in each case invariably displays this subjugation, the Protean wriggles by way of defense and reaction, and, further, the results of successful counter-efforts. The form is fluid, but the meaning is even more so—even inside every individual organism, the case is the same: with every genuine growth of the whole, the "function" of the individual organs becomes shifted—in certain cases a partial perishing of these organs, a diminution of their numbers (for instance, through annihilation of the connecting members), can be a symptom of growing strength and perfection.

What I mean is this: even partial loss of utility, decay, and degeneration, loss of function and purpose, in a word, death, are part of the conditions of genuine progress; which always appears in the form of a will and way to greater power, and is always realized at the expense of innumerable smaller powers. The magnitude of a "progress" is gauged by the greatness of the sacrifice it requires: humanity as a mass sacrificed to the prosperity of the one stronger species of Man—that would be a progress. I emphasize all the more this cardinal characteristic of the historic method, for the reason that in its essence it runs counter to predominant instincts and prevailing taste, which must prefer to put up with absolute casualness, even with the mechanical senselessness of all phenomena, than with the theory of a power-will, in exhaustive play throughout all phenomena. The democratic idiosyncrasy against everything which rules and wishes to rule, the modern misarchism (to coin a bad word for a bad thing), has gradually but so thoroughly transformed itself into the guise of intellectualism, the most abstract intellectualism, that even nowadays it penetrates and has the right to penetrate step by step into the most exact and apparently the most objective sciences: this tendency has, in fact, in my view already dominated the whole of physiology and biology, and to their detriment, as is obvious, in so far as it has spirited away a radical idea, the idea of true activity. The tyranny of this idiosyncrasy, however, results in the theory of "adaptation" being pushed forward into the van of the argument, exploited; adaptation— that means to say, a second- class activity, a mere capacity for "reacting"; in fact, life itself has been defined (by Herbert Spencer) as an increasingly effective internal adaptation to external circumstances. This definition, however, fails to realize the real essence of life, its will to power. It fails to appreciate the paramount superiority enjoyed by those plastic forces of spontaneity, aggression, and encroachment with their new interpretations and tendencies, to the operation of which adaptation is only a natural corollary: consequently, the sovereign office of the highest functionaries in the organism itself (among which the life-will appears as an active and formative principle) is repudiated. One remembers Huxley's reproach to Spencer of his "administrative Nihilism": but it is a case of something much more than "administration."

To return to our subject, which is punishment, we need to make two important distinctions: first, the relatively permanent element, the custom, the act, the "drama," a fixed sequence of steps in the process; and second, the more fluid element, the meaning, the purpose, and the expectations that come with the way the procedure works. At this point, we should assume, by analogy (following the historical method we've talked about earlier), that the procedure itself is older than its use in punishment. This use was added and interpreted into the procedure (which had been around for a long time, but with a different meaning). In short, the situation is not what our naïve moral and legal historians have thought—that the procedure was created specifically for punishment, just as the hand was once thought to have been made for grasping. Now, when we look at the second element of punishment, the more fluid one—the meaning of punishment— it's clear that in very advanced societies (for example, in contemporary Europe), punishment doesn't just have one meaning, but rather a complex mix of meanings. The general history of punishment, and how it has been used for many different purposes, eventually comes together in a kind of unity that's difficult to break down into separate parts, and this unity, it should be emphasized, can't be easily defined. (Today, it's impossible to say for sure the exact reason for punishment: all ideas that lump together a whole process in one definition tend to escape definition; only things that have no history can be clearly defined.) In earlier times, however, that collection of meanings was much less fixed and much more flexible; we can see how, in each case, the elements of the meaning shift in importance and position. Sometimes, one meaning will stand out and dominate, and in certain cases, one element (like the goal of deterring crime) might even seem to take over and eliminate all the others. To give a clearer picture of how uncertain, extra, and accidental the meaning of punishment can be, and how one procedure can be used and adapted for very different purposes, I will now provide a list based on relatively small and random examples.

- Punishment as making the criminal harmless and unable to harm others.
- Punishment as a form of compensation for the injury suffered by the victim, in any form, including sentimental compensation.
- Punishment as isolating what disrupts the balance, to stop the disturbance from spreading.
- Punishment as a way to inspire fear in those who decide and carry out the punishment.
- Punishment as a kind of compensation for the benefits the wrongdoer had enjoyed up until that point (for example, when the wrongdoer is forced into slavery in the mines).
- Punishment as removing an element of decay (sometimes even a whole part, as in Chinese laws, for the purpose of purifying the race or preserving a social type).
- Punishment as a festival, where an enemy who has been defeated is violently oppressed and humiliated.

- Punishment as a reminder, either for the person being punished (the so-called "correction") or for the witnesses of the punishment being carried out.
- Punishment as the payment of a fee, required by the power that protects the wrongdoer from the excesses of revenge.
- Punishment as a compromise with the natural act of revenge, in so far as revenge is still seen as a privilege of the stronger groups.
- Punishment as a declaration of war against those who oppose peace, law, order, and authority—those who are fought by society with the weapons of war because they are seen as a danger to the community, as someone who breaks the social contract, as a rebel, a traitor, or someone who disturbs the peace.

This list is clearly not complete; it is obvious that punishment is packed with a variety of purposes. This makes it even more reasonable to dismiss one supposed purpose, which is often considered, at least by most people, to be its most essential purpose. This idea is also the one that still provides the strongest support for the belief in punishment, a belief that is already unsteady for many reasons. Punishment is believed to have the value of awakening in the guilty person a sense of guilt; punishment is seen as the proper tool to create that psychological reaction known as a "bad conscience" or "remorse." However, this theory, even from the perspective of the present day, does not reflect reality or psychology. It is even more inaccurate when we consider the long stretch of human history, particularly the early, primitive periods.

Genuine remorse is undeniably rare among wrongdoers and those who are punished. Prisons and correctional facilities are not the environments where this "worm of remorse" tends to flourish. This is the unanimous conclusion of all honest observers, many of whom arrive at this judgment reluctantly and against their personal expectations. In general, punishment tends to harden and desensitize people. It causes individuals to become more focused and sharpens their awareness of their alienation. It strengthens their ability to resist. When punishment does succeed in breaking a person's spirit and reducing them to a pitiful state of submission and misery, the result is even less healthy than the more typical effects of punishment, which are marked by harshness and grim stubbornness.

When we consider those prehistoric times, we are led to the clear conclusion that punishment actually delayed the development of the sense of guilt—at least among those subjected to the power of punishment. Moreover, we should not underestimate the extent to which the spectacle of legal and enforcement actions prevents the wrongdoer from recognizing that their deed and its nature are inherently wrong. This is because they can plainly see similar actions being carried out in the name of justice, labeled as good, and performed with a clear conscience. These actions include espionage, deceit, bribery, entrapment, and all the cunning and covert strategies employed by law enforcement officers and informants. The system of punishment itself—a system driven not by passion but by principles—relies on acts such as stealing, oppressing, insulting, imprisoning, torturing, and even killing.

The wrongdoer sees all of this and notices that these actions are not treated as inherently blameworthy or condemnable but only as problematic in specific contexts or uses. It was not on this foundation that the "bad conscience," one of the most troubling and fascinating aspects of human nature, came into being. In fact, for a long stretch of history, the idea of dealing with a "guilty person" did not even exist in the minds of those who judged and punished. They saw themselves as dealing with someone who caused harm, an unaccountable force of fate. For the individual on whom punishment fell, it did not bring about any deeper internal suffering. Instead, it was experienced as no different from an unforeseen and unavoidable event, such as a devastating natural disaster, an avalanche that struck without warning, against which no resistance was possible.

This truth crept subtly into the mind of Spinoza, much to the frustration of his commentators (such as Kuno Fischer, for instance, who made great efforts to misunderstand him on this point). One afternoon, as Spinoza sat reflecting on who knows what memories, he began to ponder what remained for him personally of the famous morsus conscientiae—the "sting of conscience." Spinoza, who had dismissed the notions of "good and evil" as products of human imagination, passionately defended the honor of his "free" God against those who blasphemed by claiming that God acted sub r atione boni—in accordance with the concept of good. To Spinoza, such an idea subordinated God to fate, which he considered the greatest absurdity.

For Spinoza, the world had returned to the state of innocence it had known before the discovery of the bad conscience. What, then, became of the morsus conscientiae? He finally defined it for himself as "the opposite of joy—a sadness accompanied by the memory of a past event that turned out contrary to all expectation" (Ethics, Part III, Proposition 18, Scholium I and II). For thousands of years, wrongdoers faced with punishment felt much like Spinoza described regarding their "offense." They thought, "Here is something that went wrong, contrary to what I expected," rather than, "I should not have done this." They accepted punishment in the same way one endures illness, misfortune, or death—with a fatalistic and resigned stubbornness. This kind of acceptance, even today, gives people like the Russians an advantage over Westerners in dealing with the challenges of life.

In those times, if actions were judged critically, the standard was prudence. Punishment's actual effect was primarily to sharpen the sense of prudence, strengthen memory, and encourage a more cautious, secretive, and suspicious approach to life. It taught people to recognize their limitations and inspired a form of self-criticism. Punishment's broader effects on both humans and animals included increasing fear, sharpening cunning, and controlling desires. In this way, punishment tamed people but did not make them "better." In fact, one could argue the opposite: "Injury makes a man cunning," as the saying goes, and as it sharpens cunning, it often makes people worse. Thankfully, it also often makes them less intelligent.

At this point, I must offer a tentative and provisional explanation of my own hypothesis about the origin of the bad conscience. This idea is difficult to fully grasp and requires careful thought, sustained attention, and reflection. I consider the bad conscience to be the serious illness that humanity inevitably developed during its most radical transformation: when people found themselves confined within the structures of society and forced to live in peace.

Just as water-dwelling creatures faced a crisis when they had to either adapt to life on land or face extinction, so too did early humans, who were like half- animals. These creatures had thrived in a world of war, roaming, and adventure, perfectly suited to that wild life. Suddenly, their instincts became useless and "switched off." From that point on, they had to support themselves, to "carry themselves," just as water creatures had to walk on land after being carried by the water. This shift brought a crushing weight upon them. They struggled to obey even the simplest commands. Faced with a new and unfamiliar world, they could no longer rely on the instincts that had unconsciously guided them to safety in the past. Instead, they were forced to think, to reason, to calculate, and to connect causes and effects—relying on their weakest and most unreliable tool, their "consciousness."

I doubt there has ever been such a profound sense of misery in the world, such a feeling of leaden discomfort. Meanwhile, those old instincts did not disappear overnight. They continued to demand satisfaction, but it was now difficult, and often impossible, to fulfill them. Broadly speaking, these instincts were forced to find expression in new, covert ways, like a shadow of their former selves. When instincts cannot find an outlet in the external world, they turn inward. This is what I call the process of man's growing "internalization." It was through this process that what we later called the soul first began to develop.

The inner world of humanity, originally as thin and fragile as if stretched between two layers of skin, now burst open and expanded. It gained depth, breadth, and height as the external outlets for human instincts were blocked. The powerful defenses created by social organization to suppress the old instincts of freedom—especially punishment—forced these instincts to turn back against the human being himself. Feelings like hostility, cruelty, the joy of hunting, the thrill of surprise, destruction, and change—all these were now directed inward, against their possessor. This, I believe, is the origin of the "bad conscience."

Human beings, no longer facing external enemies and obstacles, found themselves trapped in the suffocating monotony and narrowness of social customs. In their frustration, they lashed out at themselves, tormenting, punishing, gnawing at, and terrifying themselves. It was like a wild animal in captivity, smashing itself against the bars of its cage. It was this being, longing desperately for the wild freedom of the past, who turned their inner life into a place of adventure, a chamber of torture, a dangerous and unpredictable desert. This homesick and despairing prisoner created the concept of the "bad conscience."

With this invention, humanity introduced a profound and sinister illness— one from which we have not yet recovered. This is the suffering of humankind caused by its own nature, a sickness born from the violent severing of humanity from its animal past. It was like a sudden, wrenching leap into a new way of life, a rejection of the instincts that had once been the source of human strength, joy, and fearsome power.

Yet, this turning of the human mind against itself produced something so new, so deep, so unprecedented, so complex, and so full of potential that it transformed the very face of the world. This was a phenomenon so dramatic, so paradoxical, so filled with possibilities that only divine observers could truly grasp its significance. The drama that began then is still unfolding, with no clear end in sight. It is too intricate, too extraordinary, too paradoxical to have happened meaninglessly or unnoticed on some random, grotesque planet.

From this moment onward, humanity must be seen as one of the most unexpected and astonishing outcomes of the game played by Heraclitus' "great child," whether you call it Zeus or Chance. Humanity now inspires interest, excitement, and hope. It even gives the impression that it is not the final goal, but a stepping stone, a bridge, an interlude—a great promise of something yet to come.

The hypothesis about the origin of the bad conscience begins with the idea that this transformation was neither gradual nor voluntary. It was not an organic adaptation to new circumstances but rather a rupture, a sudden break, a necessity imposed by fate. This change came without resistance or even a spark of resentment. Furthermore, this transformation—the shaping of a previously unrestrained and chaotic population into a rigid form—was initiated through violence and could only be maintained through violence. The earliest "state" thus emerged as a horrifying tyranny, a relentless and grinding machine that molded the raw, semi-animal masses into something pliable, structured, and disciplined.

By "state," I mean what is self-evident: a herd of blonde beasts of prey—a race of conquerors and rulers. This race, armed with all the tools of war and organization, descended with ferocious claws upon a population that, though numerically much larger, was unformed and nomadic. This is the true origin of the "state." The fanciful theory that the state began with a social contract is easily dismissed. Those who can command, who are natural masters, those whose very being is forceful and decisive—what would they have to do with contracts? These individuals are beyond calculation. They arrive like fate, without cause, without justification or warning. They are like lightning:

too powerful, too sudden, too undeniable, and too alien to even inspire personal hatred.

Such beings instinctively create and impose forms. They are the most involuntary, unconscious artists to exist. Their arrival immediately establishes a living order of sovereignty, one in which roles and functions are defined and assigned. In this order, no part exists unless it serves a meaningful role in relation to the whole. These born organizers are utterly unfamiliar with concepts like guilt, responsibility, or consideration. They embody a terrifying, artistic egoism that shines like polished metal, fully convinced of its eternal justification in its creations, just as a mother sees her child as her unquestionable right.

It was not in these individuals that the bad conscience first grew— this is a fundamental point. Yet, the bad conscience could not have developed without them. For all its repulsiveness, the bad conscience arose because their hammer blows, their violent artistry, expelled a tremendous amount of freedom from the world. This freedom was not destroyed but rendered invisible and latent.

This instinct for freedom, repressed and confined, is the key. The instinct for freedom, forced back, trampled down, imprisoned within itself, and eventually finding expression only within its own confines—this is where the bad conscience begins. It is this imprisonment, this inward turning of freedom, that marks the origin of the bad conscience.

Do not dismiss this phenomenon lightly just because of its initially painful and ugly appearance. At its core, it is the same active force at work on a grander scale in powerful artists and organizers who build states. Here, however, this force operates internally, on a smaller, more personal scale, with a tendency to turn backward on itself. It becomes a bad conscience in what Goethe calls the "labyrinth of the breast." It constructs negative ideals. This is, as I've said, the very same instinct of fr eedom (or, in my own terms, the will to power). The only difference is the material on which this force is unleashed.

In the grander, external phenomenon, the material is other people—other men. But here, it is man himself, his entire old animal self, that becomes the target.

This secret self-tyranny, this artistic cruelty, this pleasure in shaping oneself as though one were a difficult, resistant, and suffering material—this burning desire to impose a will, a critique, a contradiction, a disdain, or a rejection upon oneself— this dark and dreadful labor of love performed by a soul divided against itself, inflicting suffering upon itself for the delight of suffering, is what we call the active bad conscience. It is this same bad conscience, brimming with creative energy as the source of idealism and imagination, that has ultimately produced an extraordinary wealth of new and astounding beauty and affirmation. Indeed, it might even be said to have given birth to beauty for the first time.

What would beauty be, after all, if its opposite had not first been made conscious? If ugliness had not first declared, "I am ugly"? With this realization, the problem of tracing idealism and beauty in ideas such as selflessness, self- denial, and self-sacrifice becomes much less perplexing. It becomes clear that the original character of the pleasure felt by the selfless, the self-denying, and the self- sacrificing is rooted in cruelty.

This, then, is a preliminary explanation of the origin of "altruism" as a moral value and an outline of the soil from which this value has grown. It is the bad conscience—the will to self-punishment— that creates the conditions necessary for altruism to emerge as a value.

Undoubtedly, the bad conscience is an illness, but it is an illness in the same way that pregnancy is an illness. If we examine the conditions under which this illness reaches its most extreme and profound heights, we can begin to uncover what first brought it into the world. To do this, however, we must take a deep breath and return once more to an earlier perspective.

The relationship in civil law between debtor and creditor (which we have already discussed in detail) has been interpreted in a way that is both historically fascinating and deeply suspicious. It has been reimagined as a relationship between the current generation and its ancestors—a concept that is perhaps more incomprehensible to us today than to any other era. In the original tribal associations of primitive times, each living generation recognized a legal obligation to the generations that came before, especially to the earliest ancestors who founded the family. This obligation was far more than a sentimental one. During the longest period of human history, the mere idea of sentimental obligation was far from certain.

Instead, these early generations believed that their very existence depended on the sacrifices and efforts of their ancestors and that this debt had to be repaid through sacrifices and services. The debt was considered ongoing, growing ever larger, as the ancestors, now regarded as powerful spirits, continued to grant new privileges and advantages to the tribe. Did these benefits come for free? Certainly not, according to the harsh and "mean-souled" mindset of that era. What could be given in return? Sacrifices—at first, nourishment in its most basic form—then festivals, temples, tributes of reverence, and above all, obedience. For all customs, as works of the ancestors, were also seen as their commands and precepts. But was it ever enough to repay the ancestors? The suspicion lingered and grew over time. This suspicion occasionally demanded great acts of atonement, extravagant repayments to the creditors—such as the notorious sacrifices of the firstborn, or the spilling of blood, including human blood.

The fear of the ancestors and the sense of indebtedness to them grew stronger in direct proportion to the success of the tribe. As the tribe became more victorious, independent, respected, and feared, so too did the fear of the ancestors' power increase.

This, not the reverse, is the truth. Every step toward decay, every disaster, and every sign of degeneration or collapse diminished the fear of the ancestors' spirits and eroded the belief in their wisdom, foresight, and presence.

Imagine this crude kind of logic carried to its extreme: the ancestors of the most powerful tribes must, in proportion to the increasing fear they inspire, grow into immense, almost unimaginable figures. They become shrouded in the darkness of divine mystery and are ultimately transformed into gods. Perhaps this is the very origin of the gods: born out of fear! And for those who wish to add, "but also out of piety," it would be difficult to support that claim in relation to the earliest and longest period of human history. It is even harder to maintain with respect to the middle period—the formative era of aristocratic races. These aristocratic races repaid their founders, their ancestors (now seen as heroes or gods), with interest, attributing to them all the qualities they themselves developed over time—the qualities of the aristocrat.

Later, we will briefly examine the process of ennobling and elevating the gods (which is quite different from their sanctification). For now, however, let us follow to its conclusion this development of the consciousness of "owing."

According to historical accounts, the sense of owing a debt to the deity did not vanish with the disintegration of clan-based social structures. Just as humanity inherited the concepts of "good" and "bad" from the aristocratic nobility—along with their tendency to create social distinctions—it also inherited from the racial and tribal gods the oppressive burden of unpaid debts and the enduring desire to repay them. This inheritance was transmitted through vast populations of slaves and bondsmen, who, whether by force or through submission and imitation, adopted the religions of their masters. Through this channel, these inherited obligations spread across the world.

For centuries, the feeling of debt owed to the deity grew steadily, keeping pace with the growing prominence and exaltation of the idea of God among humanity. (The entire history of ethnic conflicts, triumphs, reconciliations, and amalgamations— everything leading to the eventual merging of social elements into grand racial syntheses—

is reflected in the chaotic genealogies of their gods, in myths of battles, victories, and reconciliations. Progress toward universal empires consistently corresponds to progress toward universal deities; despotism, by crushing the independence of the nobility, always clears the path for some form of monotheism.)

The advent of the Christian God, the most exalted deity to date, simultaneously brought with it the greatest degree of guilt consciousness. Now, if humanity has begun a reversal of this trajectory, there is reason to believe that the gradual decline in belief in the Christian God has corresponded to a significant decline in humanity's sense of moral obligation. Indeed, we can foresee the complete triumph of atheism as potentially liberating humanity from this feeling of obligation to its origin—its causa prima. Atheism might usher in a kind of second innocence, a fresh beginning free of this burden.

This, then, is a rough outline of the connection between the concepts of "ought" (owing) and "duty" with the foundations of religion. Up until now, I have deliberately avoided addressing the moralization of these concepts—their integration into the bad conscience, or more specifically, the fusion of the bad conscience with the idea of God. In the last paragraph, I even implied that such moralization did not occur and that these ideas would naturally dissipate as faith in the "creditor," in God, eroded. However, the reality is far grimmer.

The moralization of "ought" and "duty," their absorption into the bad conscience, marked the first attempt to reverse the development we have described—or at least to halt its progress. At this point, even the hope of eventual redemption is locked away in the prison of pessimism. Here, humanity's gaze recoils hopelessly from an unyielding impossibility. The concepts of "guilt" and "duty" turn backward—but against whom? There can be no doubt: they turn primarily against the debtor, the "ower," in whom the bad conscience takes root, expands, and consumes everything like a parasitic growth.

As the impossibility of repaying the debt becomes undeniable, so too arises the idea of the impossibility of atonement. This leads to the concept of inexpiable guilt—the notion of "eternal punishment."

Eventually, the bad conscience turns against the creditor as well. Whether this creditor is seen as the causa prima of humanity— the origin of the human race, its father, now cursed ("Adam," "original sin," "the bondage of the will")— or as Nature itself, the womb from which humanity emerged, and which is now held responsible for the principle of evil (the "demonization of Nature")—or as existence in general, viewed as an absurd and unbearable burden. This logic leads to nihilistic despair: the rejection of life, the desire for nothingness, or for some other form of existence, as seen in Buddhism and similar philosophies.

It is here that humanity arrives at a paradoxical and terrifying solution: the ingenious creation of Christianity. In this system, God sacrifices himself for humanity's debt. God pays himself by offering his own flesh. God, the ultimate creditor, becomes the scapegoat for his debtor—all out of love. Can you believe it? Out of love for his debtor!

The reader may already have guessed what unfolded both on the stage and behind the scenes of this drama. The will for self- torture— the turned-inward cruelty of human beings, who, once introspective and frightened by their confinement (caged within the framework of "the State" as part of their taming)—gave rise to the bad conscience as a way to hurt themselves when their natural outlet for cruelty was blocked. This man of the bad conscience seized upon the religious hypothesis to drive his self-inflicted torment to unimaginable extremes.

The idea of owing a debt to God became his tool for self- torture. In God, he imagined the ultimate antithesis to his own ineradicable animal instincts. He reinterpreted these instincts as offenses against what he "owes" to God—as hostility, rebellion, and defiance toward the "Lord," the "Father," the "Creator," the very "Beginning of the world." He trapped himself in the agonizing contradiction between "God" and "Devil." Every denial he wished to make against himself, against his nature, his naturalness, and his very reality, he twisted into an affirmation of God's existence. He transformed these negations into declarations of God's holiness, judgment, punishment, and transcendence— into eternal torment, infinite guilt, and unending hell.

This represents a madness of the will in the realm of psychological cruelty unlike anything else. Humanity's will to find itself guilty and beyond forgiveness, its will to think of itself as punished without any possibility of atonement, and its will to poison the foundations of the universe with the problem of guilt and punishment—all serve to trap humanity within this labyrinth of fixed ideas. It is a will to construct an ideal—that of the "holy God"—before which humanity can eternally prove its unworthiness.

Alas, for this despairing and deranged creature called man! What wild fantasies it conjures, what fits of perversity, hysterical irrationality, and mental savagery erupt whenever it is restrained from being the beast of action! All of this is deeply fascinating, yet it is also dark, oppressive, and draining, compelling us to resist gazing too long into these depths. Here is a sickness, undoubtedly the most horrifying disease that has ever afflicted humanity.

And if someone still has the capacity to hear—though modern man now often turns a deaf ear to such things—they may recognize that, within this night of torment and absurdity, the cry of love once echoed. It was the cry of the most intense ecstasy, the yearning for redemption through love. But anyone who truly listens to this cry recoils in unspeakable horror. For within humanity, there is so much that is monstrous. For far too long, the world has been a madhouse.

Let this be sufficient, once and for all, regarding the origin of the "holy God." The idea of gods does not inherently lead to the degradation of human imagination that we have just described. The fact that there are nobler ways to use the concept of gods—ways that do not involve the self-crucifixion and self- debasement of humanity, which has characterized the last two thousand years of Europe—remains clear. We only need to look at the Greek gods to see this. These gods were reflections of noble and grand men, mirrors in which the animal within humanity felt deified rather than destroyed by inward madness.

The Greeks used their gods in a completely different way. For them, the gods served as buffers against the "bad conscience," allowing them to preserve their inner freedom. This stands in stark contrast to Christianity's approach to its god. The Greeks, those magnificent and courageous people, embraced this principle wholeheartedly. Even the Homeric Zeus himself occasionally reminded them not to take life too lightly. Take, for instance, his commentary on the case of Aegisthus, a truly egregious example:

"Wonderful how they grumble, the mortals against the immortals.

They claim all evil comes from us, yet in their folly, They fashion their own doom, against all fate."

Yet note how this Olympian observer and judge is neither angry with mortals nor condemns them. Instead, he views their misdeeds with a certain amused detachment. "How foolish they are," he seems to think. For the Greeks, even in their strongest and most valiant era, the causes of evil and disaster were not rooted in sin but in folly, in imprudence, in a kind of temporary disturbance of the mind. Folly, not sin—do you see the distinction?

Even this "brain disturbance," however, presented a puzzle to the Greeks. "How could this happen?" they wondered. "How could such foolishness find its way into the minds of men like us— men of noble ancestry, men of wealth, men with fine natural gifts, men of the best upbringing, men of virtue?" For centuries, the Greek aristocracy asked this question whenever one of their peers committed some incomprehensible outrage or act of sacrilege. Eventually, they settled on an answer: "It must be that a god has deceived him," they concluded, nodding their heads.

This solution is quintessentially Greek. In their worldview, the gods did not punish humanity for its failings; instead, they took upon themselves the responsibility for human guilt. This approach justified human actions to a certain extent, even when those actions were evil. In those days, the gods were not seen as dispensers of punishment but as bearers of guilt—a role far nobler than that of executioner.

I conclude with three questions, as you will notice. "Is an ideal being established here, or is one being torn down?" you may ask. But have you truly considered the cost of creating every ideal in the history of the world? How much truth has had to be distorted and misunderstood, how many lies have been sanctified, how much conscience disturbed, and how many sacrifices of "God" have been made each time? To build a sanctuary, another must be destroyed—this is an unyielding law. Show me a single instance where it has not held true!

We modern men have inherited an ancient tradition of vivisecting our consciences and inflicting cruelty on our natural, animal selves. This is where we have undergone our most rigorous training, where we have perhaps honed our artistic talents—or, at the very least, indulged our dilettantism and perverted tastes. For far too long, humanity has regarded its natural instincts with suspicion, branding them as evil. Over time, these instincts have become intertwined with the bad conscience.

Wouldn't it be possible to attempt the opposite? Couldn't we attach this bad conscience to all our unnatural inclinations—our transcendental aspirations that oppose sense, instinct, nature, and our very humanity? Couldn't we apply it to all the ideals, past and present, that reject life and defame the world? But who today would be strong enough to undertake such a reversal? To whom could one turn with such aspirations?

It is precisely the "good" people who would rise against us if we tried. Alongside them would be the indolent, the conformists, the vain, the hysterical, and the weary. Nothing is more alienating or offensive than hinting at the stern rigor with which we treat ourselves. And yet, how readily the world embraces us when we simply "let ourselves go" and do as it does. For such a transformation, we would need spirits of an entirely different caliber than those of this feeble and introspective age—spirits strengthened by wars and victories, who crave conquest, adventure, danger, and even suffering.

Such spirits would need to be accustomed to rarefied air, to the sharpness of winter wanderings, to both literal and metaphorical ice and mountains. They would need a sublime malice, a supreme and conscious audacity born of great health. In summary, they would require nothing less than this great health.

Is this even conceivable today? Perhaps not. But someday, in an age stronger than this decaying and inward-looking present, such a redeemer must come. This redeemer, a spirit of great love and great scorn, will create anew. Driven by his own power, he will rebound from every transcendental ideal, not to escape reality but to penetrate it. Diving deep into existence, he will return to the surface with the means to redeem it—redeeming reality from the curse imposed upon it by the old ideal.

This man of the future will free us from the old ideal and its inevitable companions: great nausea, the will to nothingness, and nihilism. He will be the herald of a new dawn, restoring freedom to the will, purpose to the world, and hope to humanity. He will be the Antichrist and the Antinihilist, the conqueror of God and Nothingness. He must come.

But what am I saying? Enough. Enough! At this moment, the only course left to me is silence—otherwise, I overstep into a realm that belongs to someone younger, stronger, more "future" than I. This realm belongs to Zarathustra, Zarathustra the godless.

Chapter 3

What Is the Meaning of Ascetic Ideals?

What is the meaning of ascetic ideals? For artists, they mean either nothing or far too much. For philosophers and scholars, they reflect a kind of instinct or "flair" for the conditions that best support advanced thinking and intellectual pursuits. For women, at best, they add an extra layer of charm, a faint touch of delicacy on a beautiful body, the angelic quality of a plump, attractive creature. For those who are physically weak or chronic complainers (the majority of humanity), they serve as a way to appear "too good" for the world, a holy excuse for indulgence. Ascetic ideals become their main weapon in dealing with lingering pain and boredom. For priests, they represent true priestly belief, their greatest tool of power, and the ultimate justification for that power. For saints, ascetic ideals offer a reason for retreat, a longing for the ultimate glory of nothingness—"God"—and serve as a form of madness.

Yet, the fact that ascetic ideals have meant so much to humanity reveals something fundamental about the human will: its horror of emptiness. Humans need a goal, and they would rather will nothingness than have no will at all. Do you understand me? Have I made myself clear? No? "Certainly not, sir?" Well, let's start over from the beginning.

What is the meaning of ascetic ideals? Or, to take a specific example I've often been asked about: why would an artist like Richard Wagner embrace chastity in his later years? True, he had always done so in a certain way, but only near the end of his life did he do so in a fully ascetic sense. What explains this change, this complete reversal in his attitude? Wagner turned into the opposite of what he had been. What does it mean when an artist transforms into their own opposite? Let's pause to consider this question.

Think back to the boldest, happiest, and most creative period of Wagner's life. This was when he was deeply involved with the idea of

Luther's Wedding. Who knows what twist of fate led us to have The Master singer s instead of this wedding music? And how much of the latter might still echo the former? There is no doubt, however, that Luther 's Wedding would have celebrated chastity. Yet, it would also have celebrated sensuality, and it would have been entirely fitting— entirely Wagnerian. There is no inherent contradiction between chastity and sensuality. Every true marriage, every genuine and heartfelt love, transcends this division.

I believe Wagner could have shown his fellow Germans this beautiful reality through a daring and elegant "Luther Comedy." It would have reminded them that chastity and sensuality can coexist, even complement each other. Among the Germans, there have always been many critics of sensuality, but perhaps Luther's greatest achievement was his courage to embrace it. He called it, quite charmingly, "evangelical freedom." Even in situations where the conflict between chastity and sensuality does arise, there is no reason for it to be tragic. At least, this should be true for those who are healthy in both mind and body, who do not see the balance between "animal" and "angel" as a fundamental challenge to life itself. The most brilliant spirits, such as Goethe and Hafiz, even found this balance to be one of life's greatest charms. These so-called "conflicts" can actually make life more alluring.

On the other hand, it is painfully clear that when broken, miserable people worship chastity, they do so because it represents the opposite of what they are. They see chastity as the antithesis of their own ruined nature. And when such people worship chastity, the result is tragic. You can imagine the desperate grunting and pathetic eagerness with which they embrace it. They celebrate this painful, unnecessary conflict, the very conflict Wagner seemed to want to set to music and display on stage in his later years. But why? What purpose could it possibly serve? What did these broken souls mean to him? What do they mean to us?

At this point, it's impossible to avoid asking what Wagner really intended with that rustic, unmanly character, that naïve and unfortunate soul, Parsifal, whom he ultimately turned into a Catholic through such dubious means. Was Parsifal meant to be taken seriously? One might hope not—one might even suspect the opposite. Perhaps Wagner intended Parsifal to be a lighthearted farewell, akin to the final act of a trilogy or asatyric drama. Perhaps he, the great tragedian, wanted to bid farewell to us, to himself, and above all to tragedy itself, in a manner fitting his stature: by parodying the very idea of the tragic, mocking the grim seriousness and earthly sorrows of the past. This parody would also mock the most grotesque and unnatural aspects of the ascetic ideal, a phase that he had finally overcome.

Such an interpretation would indeed be worthy of a great tragedian. Every true artist reaches the height of their greatness only when they can look down on themselves and their work, when they can laugh at their own creations. Could Parsifal be Wagner's secret laugh at himself? The triumph of ultimate artistic freedom and transcendence? We might wish it so. For what else could Parsifal amount to if taken seriously? Are we to see in it, as some have suggested, a work driven by an insane hatred of knowledge, reason, and the body? A curse against flesh and spirit uttered in one breath of bitter contempt?

Could Parsifal be Wagner's retreat into the sickly ideals of Christianity, his return to a decayed and obscurantist morality? Was it a self-negation, a complete reversal by an artist who had previously poured all his will into the highest artistic expressions of both soul and body? And not just in his art, but in his life as well? Recall the enthusiasm with which Wagner once followed Feuerbach's teachings. Feuerbach's motto of "healthy sensuality" was, during the 1830s and 1840s, like a word of salvation to Wagner and many other Germans, especially the so-called "Young Germans."

Did Wagner later change his mind about this? It certainly seems that he wanted to change his message on the subject. This shift isn't only apparent in the Parsifal trumpets resounding onstage; it echoes in the somber, constrained, and troubled writings of his later years. In countless passages, Wagner reveals a hidden desire, a hesitant and unspoken will to preach retreat, to advocate for conversion, Christianity, medievalism. It's as if he wanted to say to his followers, "All is vanity! Seek salvation elsewhere!" At one point, he even invokes the "blood of the Redeemer."

What, then, are we to make of all this? Could Wagner's Parsifal truly represent the turning point where he gave up his earlier ideals and turned toward something entirely opposed to what he once stood for? Or is it something else altogether?

This list is certainly not complete; it is obvious that punishment is overloaded with utilities of all kinds. This makes it all the more permissible to eliminate one supposed utility, which passes, at any rate in the popular mind, for its most essential utility, and which is just what even now provides the strongest support for that faith in punishment which is nowadays for many reasons tottering. Punishment is supposed to have the value of exciting in the guilty the consciousness of guilt; in punishment is sought the proper instrumentum of that psychic reaction which becomes known as a "bad conscience," "remorse." But this theory is even, from the point of view of the present, a violation of reality and psychology: and how much more so is the case when we have to deal with the longest period of man's history, his primitive history! Genuine remorse is certainly extremely rare among wrongdoers and the victims of punishment; prisons and houses of correction are not the soil on which this worm of remorse pullulates for choice— this is the unanimous opinion of all conscientious observers, who in many cases arrive at such a judgment with enough reluctance and against their own personal wishes. Speaking generally, punishment hardens and numbs, it produces concentration, it sharpens the consciousness of alienation, it strengthens the power of resistance. When it happens that it breaks the man's energy and brings about a piteous prostration and abjectness, such a result is certainly even less salutary than the average effect of punishment, which is characterised by a harsh and sinister doggedness. The thought of those prehistoric millennia brings us to the unhesitating conclusion, that it was simply through punishment that the evolution of the consciousness of guilt was most forcibly retarded—at any rate in the victims of the punishing power. In particular, let us not underestimate the extent to which, by the very sight of the judicial and executive procedure, the wrong-doer is himself prevented from feeling that his deed, the character of his act, is intrinsically reprehensible: for he sees clearly the same kind of acts practised in the service of justice, and then called good, and practised with a good conscience; acts such as espionage, trickery, bribery, trapping, the whole intriguing and insidious art of the policeman and the informer—the whole system, in fact, manifested in the different kinds of punishment (a system not excused by passion, but based on principle), of robbing, oppressing, insulting, imprisoning, racking, murdering.—All this he sees treated by his judges, not as acts meriting censure and condemnation in themselves, but only in a particular context and application. It was not on this soil that grew the "bad conscience," that most sinister and interesting plant of our earthly vegetation—in point of fact, throughout a most lengthy period, no suggestion of having to do with a "guilty man" manifested itself in the consciousness of the man who judged and punished. One had merely to deal with an author of an injury, an irresponsible piece of fate. And the man himself, on whom the punishment subsequently fell like a piece of fate, was occasioned no more of an "inner pain" than would be occasioned by the sudden approach of some uncalculated event, some terrible natural catastrophe, a rushing, crushing avalanche against which there is no resistance.

What, then, is the meaning of ascetic ideals? In the case of an artist, we are starting to understand their meaning: Nothing at all... or so much that it is almost nothing. So, what is the point of them? For a long time now, artists have not taken an independent enough stance, either in the world or against it, to make their views and the changes in these views worth paying attention to. They have always been the servants of some morality, philosophy, or religion. And, unfortunately, they have often been excessively obedient courtiers to their clients and patrons, and overly curious sycophants to the existing powers, or even to new powers that are rising. To put it simply, they always need a shield, a support, some established authority: artists never stand on their own. Standing alone goes against their deepest instincts. So, for example, when the time came, Richard Wagner took the philosopher Schopenhauer as his shield, his support. Who would even think it possible that he would have had the courage for an ascetic ideal without the backing of Schopenhauer's philosophy, without the authority of Schopenhauer, which ruled Europe in the 1870s? (This is without considering whether an artist could have even existed without the support of an orthodoxy.) This leads us to a deeper question: What does it mean for a real philosopher to embrace the ascetic ideal, a truly independent intellect like Schopenhauer's, a man with the courage to be himself, who knows how to stand alone without waiting for others to protect him, and without needing approval from his superiors? Now, let us think about Schopenhauer's remarkable attitude toward art, an attitude that even fascinates certain types of people. This is clearly the reason why Richard

Wagner suddenly turned to Schopenhauer (as we know, influenced by the poet Herwegh), turning so completely that it caused a major shift in his views, creating a sharp contradiction between his earlier and later aesthetic beliefs. His earlier ideas are expressed in his work *Opera and Drama*, while his later writings, starting in 1870, show his change of heart. In particular, from that time on (and this is the change that most alienates us), Wagner had no hesitation in changing his opinion on the value and role of music itself. What did he care if, until that point, he had seen music as a tool, a medium, a "woman" that needed an end, a "man"—that is, drama—in order to thrive? He suddenly realized that much more could be achieved by applying Schopenhauer's theory to music, in *majorem musicae gloriam*—meaning, through the idea of music's sovereignty, as Schopenhauer understood it. Music was now seen as separate from and opposed to all other arts, as the independent art in itself—not like other arts, which reflect the world of appearances, but as the voice of the will itself, speaking directly from the "abyss" as the most personal, original, and direct expression. This huge increase in the value of music (which seemed to grow from Schopenhauer's philosophy) was accompanied by an unprecedented rise in the status of the musician. He became an oracle, a priest—no, more than a priest, a kind of spokesperson for the "intrinsic essence of things," a messenger from another world. From then on, he spoke not just of music, this ventriloquist of God, but also of metaphysics. So, is it any surprise that, eventually, he spoke of ascetic ideals?

Schopenhauer made use of the Kantian approach to the aesthetic problem—but he certainly did not see it in the same way as Kant. Kant thought that he honored art by emphasizing those qualities of beauty that also contribute to the dignity of knowledge: impersonality and universality. This is not the place to discuss whether this was a complete mistake; all I want to highlight is that Kant, like many other philosophers, did not approach the aesthetic problem from the perspective of the artist (the creator). Instead, he only considered art and beauty from the perspective of the spectator, and in doing so, he unknowingly brought the spectator into the very idea of the "beautiful"! But if only the philosophers of beauty had a better understanding of this "spectator"!—an understanding of him as a great personality, as a rich experience, as a wealth of powerful and most individual events, desires, surprises, and raptures within the realm of beauty! But, as I feared, the opposite was always the case. And so, from the very beginning, we get definitions from philosophers that are burdened with a coarse mistake, like Kant's famous definition of beauty. "That is beautiful," says Kant, "which pleases without interest." Without interest! Now, compare this definition with another, made by a true "spectator" and "artist"—by Stendhal, who once called beauty *une promesse de bonheur*

(a promise of happiness). Here, at the very least, the one point Kant makes in his aesthetic theory—disinterest—is rejected and eliminated. Who is right, Kant or Stendhal? When, after all, our aesthetes never tire of pointing to the fact that under the magic of beauty, men can look at even naked statues of women "without interest," we can certainly laugh a little at their expense. In this respect, the experiences of artists are much more "interesting," and, at any rate, Pygmalion was not necessarily an "unaesthetic man." Let us think all the better of the innocence of our aesthetes, reflected in such arguments. Let us, for example, count as a point in Kant's favor the country-parson naivety of his doctrine on the peculiar character of the sense of touch! And here we return to

Schopenhauer, who was much closer to the arts than Kant was, yet still never fully escaped the Kantian definition. How can this be? The situation is remarkable: he interprets Kant's phrase "without interest" in the most personal way, drawing on an experience that must have been a part of his regular routine. Few topics are discussed with such certainty by Schopenhauer as the workings of aesthetic contemplation: he claims that it simply counteracts sexual interest, like hops and camphor. He never tires of glorifying this escape from the "will to live" as the great advantage and utility of the aesthetic state. In fact, one might be tempted to ask whether his fundamental idea of Will and Idea—the thought that freedom from the "will" can only be achieved through the "idea"—didn't stem from a generalization of this sexual experience. (And, by the way, in all discussions of Schopenhauer's philosophy, one should never forget that it reflects the thinking of a young man of twenty- six, so it carries not only the peculiarities of Schopenhauer's life but also the characteristics of that particular stage in his life.) Let us now listen to one of the most striking passages he wrote in praise of the aesthetic state (from *World as Will and Idea*), and pay attention to the tone, the suffering, the happiness, and the gratitude with which these words are spoken: "This is the painless state that Epicurus praised as the highest good and the state of the gods; during this moment, we are freed from the vile pressure of the will. We celebrate the Sabbath of the will's hard labor, and the wheel of Ixion stands still." What power in the language! What images of agony and long-lasting revulsion!

How extreme is the contrast between "that moment" and everything else— the "wheel of Ixion," "the hard labor of the will," and "the vile pressure of the will." But even if Schopenhauer was absolutely right for himself, how does that help us understand what the beautiful really is? Schopenhauer describes one effect of beauty— the calming of the will—but is this effect something that usually happens? As mentioned before, Stendhal, who had a more balanced and happier nature than Schopenhauer, highlights a different effect of beauty. "The beautiful promises happiness." To him, the excitement that beauty creates in us, the "interest," is what matters most. And doesn't Schopenhauer leave himself open to criticism here, by claiming he understands Kant's view on beauty when he really doesn't? Kant defined beauty as something that pleases without making us feel any personal interest in it. But Schopenhauer actually found beauty interesting—perhaps even through the most personal kind of interest of all, the feeling of relief from suffering, like a tortured person escaping their pain. So, if we return to our original question—"What does it mean for a philosopher to admire ascetic ideals?"—we get our first clue: he wants to escape from suffering.

Let's be careful not to overly focus on the word "torture"—there is definitely room for some criticism and even some humor here. We shouldn't ignore the fact that Schopenhauer, who treated sexuality as an enemy (and even woman, whom he saw as "the instrument of the devil"), needed enemies to keep himself in a good mood. He loved using dark, bitter, and harsh words. He often raged just for the sake of raging, out of sheer passion. Without his enemies—without Hegel, without women, without sensual pleasures, and without the "will to live"—Schopenhauer would have become ill. He would have become a pessimist (although he wasn't really one, despite wanting to be). Without his enemies, he wouldn't have been able to continue at all. He would have given up. But his enemies kept him going. They always dragged him back into life, and his anger, just like that of the ancient

Cynics, was his source of strength, his way of coping, his way of finding relief and happiness.

So much for what is most personal in Schopenhauer's case; on the other hand, there is still a lot that is typical of him— and now we return to our main question. It is an accepted and undeniable fact, as long as there are philosophers in the world, and wherever philosophers have existed (from India to England, for example, at opposite ends of the spectrum of philosophical ability), that philosophers often feel irritated or even angry at sensuality. Schopenhauer is just the most passionate, and if you can listen closely, the most captivating and enchanting example of this. There is also a real philosophical bias and love for the entire ascetic ideal; there should be no illusions about this. Both of these feelings, as I have mentioned, are common in the type of philosopher we are talking about. If a philosopher lacks both of them, you can be sure that he is, at best, only a "pseudo- philosopher."

What does this mean? This situation must first be understood: in itself, it stands there, pointless and unchanging, like any "Thing- in-itself." Every living creature, including the "philosophical beast," naturally strives for the best conditions where it can fully express its power, and experiences the most satisfaction in doing so. Similarly, and with a keen sense that is even sharper than reason, every animal, including humans, instinctively fears any kind of disturbance or obstacle that could block or prevent its ability to reach these optimal conditions (I am not talking about happiness here, but about the way to power, action, and the most powerful actions, which often lead to unhappiness). Likewise, the philosopher deeply fears marriage, along with anything that could lead to it—marriage is seen as a deadly obstacle to reaching the ideal conditions for intellectual freedom.

So far, how many great philosophers have been married? Heraclitus, Plato, Descartes, Spinoza, Leibniz, Kant, Schopenhauer— they were not married, and one can't even imagine them being married. A married philosopher is something of a joke—that is my rule. As for the exception of Socrates—he married out of a kind of ironic humor, seemingly just to prove this very rule. Every philosopher would say, just as Buddha said when he heard that he had a son: "Rahoula has been born to me, a fetter has been forged for me" (Rahoula here means "little demon"); every "free spirit" must have his moment of reflection, just like Buddha did at one point: "Life is too narrow in a house; it is a place of impurity; true freedom is found by leaving the house." Because Buddha thought this way, he left his house.

There are so many ways to seek independence shown in the ascetic ideal, that philosophers can't help but feel joy and excitement when they hear the stories of those who, with great resolve, said no to all forms of servitude and chose to live in the desert— though they may have been, in reality, just strong donkeys, far from strong minds. So, what does the ascetic ideal mean for a philosopher? This is my answer—it probably won't surprise you: when a philosopher sees this ideal, he smiles because he sees it as a perfect condition for the highest and boldest intellectual freedom. By embracing this ideal, he doesn't reject "existence" as a whole; on the contrary, he affirms only his own existence, and perhaps even to the point where he is not far from wishing in a blasphemous way, "let the world perish, but let philosophy, let the philosopher, let me, exist!"

These philosophers, you see, are by no means untainted witnesses or judges of the value of the ascetic ideal. What do they think of themselves—what does the "saint" mean to them? They think of what is most essential to them personally; of freedom from force, disturbance, and noise; freedom from work, responsibilities, and worries; of a clear head; of the flow and freedom of thoughts, like a dance or spring or flight; of good air—fresh, clear, free, dry air, like the air at high altitudes, where every living creature becomes more intellectual and gains wings; they think of peace in every room; of all the hounds neatly chained, with no barking of anger or rough hatred; no regrets from wounded pride; quiet and obedient internal organs, busy like mills, but unnoticed; a heart that is distant, transcendent, future, even posthumous— to sum it up, they mean by the ascetic ideal the joyful asceticism of a deified and newly born animal, one that sweeps through life instead of resting. We know the three main ideas of the ascetic ideal: poverty, humility, chastity; and if you closely examine the lives of all the great, creative, and inventive minds, you will repeatedly find these three qualities, to a certain extent. Not for a moment, of course, as if these were their virtues—what does this type of person have to do with virtues?—but as the most essential and natural conditions of their best existence, their greatest productivity.

In this regard, it is possible that their strong intellectualism had to first control a proud or easily irritated nature, or an excessive sensualism, or that it had to work hard to keep its desire for the "desert" against a temptation for luxury, indulgence, or even a generous and excessive nature. But their intellect did all this because it was the dominant instinct that carried out orders over all the other instincts. It still does: if it stopped, it would simply no longer be dominant. But there is not the slightest trace of "virtue" in all of this. Moreover, the "desert" I just mentioned, where strong, independent, and well-prepared minds retreat to their hermitages—oh, how different it is from the dream of a desert that the cultured classes have! In some cases, the cultured classes themselves are the desert. It is certain that none of the intellectual giants could tolerate this desert for even a minute. It is not romantic enough, not enough like the mystical, Syrian deserts they dream of! Yes, there are still many donkeys here, but the resemblance stops there. But what a desert means today is something more like this—it might be a deliberate obscurity; a way of getting away from one's own self; a fear of noise, fame, papers, influence; a small office, a daily task, something that hides rather than reveals; sometimes associating with harmless, cheerful animals or birds, the sight of which refreshes; a mountain for company, but not a dead one, one that has life (that is, with lakes); and sometimes, even a room in a busy hotel where one can count on not being recognized, and be able to speak freely to everyone—this is the desert—oh, it is lonely enough, believe me! I admit that when

Heraclitus retreated to the courts and halls of the massive temple of Artemis, that "wilderness" was worthier; why do we lack such temples? (Perhaps we do not lack them: I just think of my wonderful study in Piazza di San Marco, in spring, of course, and in the morning, between ten and twelve.)

But what Heraclitus avoided is still what we try to avoid today: the noise and endless chatter of the Ephesians, their politics, their news from the "empire" (which I mean, of course, Persia), their market-trade in "the things of today"— for there is one thing from which we philosophers especially need rest—from the things of "today." We honor the quiet, the cold, the noble, the distant, the past—everything that, in fact, does not force the soul to tense up and defend itself— something we can connect with without needing to speak out loud. Just listen to the way a spirit speaks; each spirit has its own tone and loves its own tone. That one over there, for example, must be an agitator, a hollow mind, an empty vessel: whatever goes into him, everything comes back from him dull and thick, heavy with the echo of an empty space. That spirit over there almost always speaks hoarsely: has he, perhaps, thought himself hoarse? Maybe so—ask the physiologists—but he who thinks in words, thinks as a speaker, not as a thinker (this shows that he does not think about objects or think objectively, but only about his relationship with objects—that, in fact, he only thinks of himself and his audience). This third one speaks aggressively, coming too close to us, his breath touching us—we involuntarily shut our mouths, even though he is speaking to us through a book: his tone of style explains why—he has no time, he has little faith in himself, and he thinks this is his one chance to express himself. But a spirit who is sure of himself speaks softly; he seeks privacy, he lets himself be awaited. A philosopher is recognized by the fact that he avoids three bright and noisy things—fame, princes, and women—which is not to say that they do not come to him. He avoids any glaring light: that is why he avoids his time and its "daylight." In this way, he is like a shadow; the lower the sun sinks, the longer and darker the shadow becomes. As for his humility, he accepts, just as he accepts darkness, a certain dependence and obscurity: also, he fears the shock of lightning, he shudders at the danger of a tree that is too isolated and too exposed, where every storm blows with full force. His "maternal" instinct, his secret love for that which grows within him, leads him into states where he is relieved from the need to take care of himself, much like the "mother" instinct in women has always kept women in a dependent position. After all, philosophers demand very little; their favorite motto is, "He who possesses is possessed." All of this is not, as I must say again and again, due to a virtue, or a worthy desire for moderation and simplicity: but because their highest master demands it of them, demands it wisely and relentlessly; their master who cares for only one thing, and for which he gathers and hoards everything—time, strength, love, attention. This type of man does not like to be disturbed by enemies, nor by friends; he is a person who forgets or despises easily. He finds it bad form to play the martyr, "to suffer for the truth"—he leaves all of that to the ambitious, to the stage-heroes of the intellect, and to everyone, in fact, who has enough time for such luxuries (the philosophers themselves have real work to do for truth). They use big words sparingly; they are said to dislike the word "truth" itself: it sounds too pompous. Finally, when it comes to the chastity of philosophers, the creativity of this type of mind clearly lies in a different area than that of having children; perhaps in some other area as well, they achieve a kind of immortality, a small, lasting legacy (philosophers in ancient India would be even bolder in expressing this: "What use is posterity to someone whose soul is the world?"). In this mindset, there is no trace of chastity because of any ascetic belief or hatred of the body, just as an athlete or jockey's abstaining from women is not really chastity. It is simply the will of the dominant instinct, at least during their period of deep philosophical reflection. Every artist understands how sexual activity can harm the mind during times of intense focus and preparation; for the greatest artists and those with the most refined instincts, this is not necessarily learned through hard experience—it is just their "maternal" instinct, which, in order to nurture the growing work, carelessly uses up (beyond all its usual resources) the strength of their physical life; the stronger power then takes over the weaker. Let's now apply this idea to Schopenhauer, a case we have already discussed: for him, the sight of beauty acted like a kind of irritant that triggered the main power of his nature (the power of deep thought and intense focus); so this strength erupted and suddenly took control of his consciousness. But this doesn't rule out the possibility that the special sweetness and fullness of the aesthetic state, which is linked to sensuality (just like the "idealism" seen in young girls at puberty), could also come from this same source. Therefore, it may be that sensuality isn't removed when the aesthetic state arises, as Schopenhauer thought, but instead, it transforms and no longer enters the mind as sexual desire. (I will come back to this point later, when discussing the more detailed aspects of the physiology of the aesthetic experience, a topic that has been largely unexplored and not well explained up until now.)

A certain asceticism, a serious yet joyful renunciation, is, as we have seen, one of the most favorable conditions for the highest intellectualism. And, as a result, it will not surprise us that philosophers, in particular, always have a certain affection for the ascetic ideal. A serious historical investigation shows that the bond between the ascetic ideal and philosophy is even tighter and stronger than we might expect. It could be said that it was only in the leading strings of this ideal that philosophy really learned to take its first steps and baby paces—oh, how clumsily, oh, how crossly, oh, how ready to tumble down and lie flat was this shy little creature with its bandy legs! The early history of philosophy is like that of all good things; for a long time, they lacked the courage to be themselves. They kept always looking around to see if anyone would come to their help; moreover, they were afraid of everyone who looked at them. Just enumerate in order the particular tendencies and virtues of the philosopher— his tendency to doubt, his tendency to deny, his tendency to wait (to be "ephectic"), his tendency to analyze, search, explore, dare, his tendency to compare and to equalize, his will to be neutral and objective, his will for everything to be "without anger and prejudice."

Has it yet been realized that for quite a long time, these tendencies were opposed to the first demands of morality and conscience? (Let us not even speak of reason, which even Luther called "Frau Klüglin," the sly whore.) Has it yet been recognized that a philosopher, upon arriving at self-consciousness, must indeed feel himself an incarnate "we strive for the forbidden," and thus guard himself against "his own sensations," against self-consciousness? It is, I repeat, the same with all good things, on which we now pride ourselves; even judged by the standard of the ancient Greeks, our whole modern life, as far as it is not weakness but strength and the awareness of strength, appears as pure "Hybris" and godlessness. The things that are the complete opposite of those we honor today have long had conscience on their side and God as their guardian. "Hybris" is our entire attitude toward nature nowadays, our violation of nature with the help of machinery, and all the unscrupulous inventiveness of our scientists and engineers. "Hybris" is our attitude toward God, that is, toward some alleged teleological and moral spider behind the webs of the great trap of cause and effect. Like Charles the Bold in his war with Louis the Eleventh, we could say, "I fight the universal spider"; "Hybris" is our attitude toward ourselves—for we experiment on ourselves in a way we would not allow with any animal, and with curiosity, we open our souls in our living bodies: what does the "salvation" of the soul matter to us now? We heal ourselves later: being ill is instructive, we do not doubt it, even more instructive than being well—inoculators of disease seem to us today even more necessary than any medicine-men or "saviors." There is no doubt that we do violence to ourselves today, we crackers of the soul's kernel, we incarnate riddles, who are forever asking riddles, as though life were nothing more than cracking a nut; and even through this, we must inevitably become more and more worthy of being asked questions and worthy of asking them, and in this way, we perhaps also become more worthy to—live?

All good things were once bad things; from every original sin, an original virtue has grown. For example, marriage was once seen as a violation of the rights of the community. A man used to pay a fine for the audacity of claiming one woman for himself (this idea connects to things like the jus primae noctis, the right of the priest to be the first to sleep with a bride, which is still a custom in Cambodia today, as a part of the "old traditions").

The soft, kind, yielding, and sympathetic feelings we now value so highly were once looked down upon by those who had them. Gentleness was once a source of shame, just as hardness is seen as a fault now (see Beyond Good and Evil, Aph. 260). The submission to law: how difficult it was for the noble people around the world to give up their personal vendettas and accept the law's power over them! Law was once considered forbidden, a blasphemy, an unwelcome change; it was forced upon people like a power they reluctantly accepted with personal shame.

Every small step forward in the world used to come at the cost of great mental and physical suffering. Today, the idea that not just progress, but any step forward, any movement or change, required countless martyrs sounds strange to us. I mentioned this in Dawn of Day, Aphorism 18. "Nothing is bought more dearly," says the same book a little later, "than the small amount of human reason and freedom that we now take pride in. But that pride is why it's almost impossible for us to sympathize with those vast periods in history, the 'Morality of Custom,' that shaped the early stages of the 'world's history,' and set the course for human nature. I repeat, during those times, suffering was seen as a virtue, cruelty as a virtue, deceit as a virtue, revenge as a virtue, and rejecting reason as a virtue. Meanwhile, well-being was seen as a danger, the desire for knowledge as a danger, pity as a danger, peace as a danger, being pitied as a shame, work as a shame, madness as divinity, and change as immorality and corruption!"

In the same book, Aphorism 12, there is an explanation of the burden of unpopularity under which the earliest group of contemplative men had to live— despised almost as widely as they were first feared! Contemplation first appeared on earth in a disguised shape, in an ambiguous form, with an evil heart and often with an uneasy head: there is no doubt about it. The inactive, brooding, unwarlike element in the instincts of contemplative men long invested them with a cloud of suspicion: the only way to combat this was to excite a definite fear. And the old Brahmans, for example, knew to a nicety how to do this! The oldest philosophers were well versed in giving their very existence and appearance meaning, firmness, background, by reason whereof men learned to fear them; considered more precisely, they did this from an even more fundamental need, the need of inspiring in themselves fear and self-reverence. For they found even in their own souls all the valuations turned against themselves; they had to fight down every kind of suspicion and antagonism against "the philosophic element in themselves." Being men of a terrible age, they did this with terrible means: cruelty to themselves, ingenious self- mortification—this was the chief method of these ambitious hermits and intellectual revolutionaries, who were obliged to force down the gods and the traditions of their own soul, so as to enable themselves to believe in their own revolution. I remember the famous story of the King Vicvamitra, who, as the result of a thousand years of self-martyrdom, reached such a consciousness of power and such a confidence in himself that he undertook to build a new heaven: the sinister symbol of the oldest and newest history of philosophy in the whole world. Every one who has ever built anywhere a "new heaven" first found the power thereto in his own hell… Let us compress the facts into a short formula. The philosophic spirit had, in order to be possible to any extent at all, to masquerade and disguise itself as one of the previously fixed types of the contemplative man, to disguise itself as priest, wizard, soothsayer, as a religious man generally: the ascetic ideal has for a long time served the philosopher as a superficial form, as a condition which enabled him to exist… To be able to be a philosopher he had to exemplify the ideal; to exemplify it, he was bound to believe in it. The peculiarly etherealized abstraction of philosophers, with their negation of the world, their enmity to life, their disbelief in the senses, which has been maintained up to the most recent time, and has almost thereby come to be accepted as the ideal philosophic attitude—this abstraction is the result of those enforced conditions under which philosophy came into existence, and continued to exist; inasmuch as for quite a very long time philosophy would have been absolutely impossible in the world without an ascetic cloak and dress, without an ascetic self-misunderstanding. Expressed plainly and palpably, the ascetic priest has taken the repulsive and sinister form of the caterpillar, beneath which and behind which alone philosophy could live and slink about… Has all that really changed? Has that flamboyant and dangerous winged creature, that "spirit" which that caterpillar concealed within itself, has it, I say, thanks to a sunnier, warmer, lighter world, really and finally flung off its hood and escaped into the light? Can we today point to enough pride, enough daring, enough courage, enough self-confidence, enough mental will, enough will for responsibility, enough freedom of the will, to enable the philosopher to be now in the world really— possible?

And now, after we've seen the ascetic priest, let's address our main question. What does the ascetic ideal really mean? This is when it becomes very serious— critically serious. We are now facing the real representatives of seriousness. "What is the meaning of all seriousness?" This even deeper question might already be on our minds: it's a question more for scientists, but we will skip it for now. In this ideal, the ascetic priest finds not only his beliefs, but also his will, his strength, and his interest. His right to exist depends on this ideal. No wonder we run into a fierce opponent (assuming, of course, that we are the ones opposing this ideal), someone fighting for his very survival against those who reject this ideal! On the other hand, it's already unlikely that such a biased attitude towards our problem will help him much; the ascetic priest will hardly be the best champion of his own ideal (just like a woman often fails when she tries to defend "woman")—let alone being the most objective critic or judge of this debate. So, it's clear that we will more likely have to help him defend himself properly against us, rather than worry about him defeating us too easily. The idea we're debating is the value of life from the perspective of the ascetic priests: this life (and everything it's part of—"Nature," "the world," everything that is always changing) is seen by them in relation to a different kind of existence, which it pushes away unless life denies itself: in the case of the ascetic life, life is seen as a way to get to another existence. The ascetic views life as a puzzle, where one must move backwards to find where it began; or he sees it as a mistake that must be corrected by action: he demands that others follow him; he enforces his view of existence wherever he can. What does this mean? Such a strange view is not a rare case, or a curiosity in history: it's one of the most common and enduring facts we have. If we looked at the big picture of human life from the perspective of a distant star, we might think that Earth is especially ascetic, a place full of unhappy, proud, and ugly creatures, who never stop hating themselves, the world, and all of life, and who hurt themselves out of the pleasure of causing pain—probably their only pleasure. Let's think about how regularly, how universally, the ascetic priest appears: he doesn't belong to any one group; he thrives everywhere; he comes from all walks of life. It's not that he inherited this view and passed it down—quite the opposite. There must be a deep, powerful need that makes this kind of person, so hostile to life, appear again and again.— Life itself must have a reason for letting this type of self- contradiction continue. For the ascetic life is a self-contradiction: it is based on deep resentment, the resentment of a never-satisfied desire and ambition, wanting to control not just one part of life, but life itself, with all its deepest, strongest, and most basic forces. The ascetic tries to use power to block the sources of power. The green-eyed jealousy even targets physical well-being, especially things like beauty, happiness, or pleasure, while the ascetic finds satisfaction in suffering, decay, pain, misfortune, ugliness, and even in punishing and sacrificing themselves. This is all deeply paradoxical: we're faced with a split that chooses to be a split, that enjoys the suffering, and only becomes more confident and victorious as its own basis—its physical life—diminishes. "Triumph in the greatest agony": this is the symbol under which the ascetic ideal has fought throughout history; in this mix of temptation, pleasure, and torture, it found its brightest light, its salvation, and its final victory. Crux, nux, lux—all three in one.

If a will so driven by contradiction and unnaturalness is compelled to philosophize, where will it direct its peculiar obsession? It will aim its skepticism at those things most firmly believed to be true and real. It will seek out error precisely where the instinct for life has most confidently established truth. Following the example of the ascetics of Vedanta philosophy, it might declare matter to be an illusion, dismiss pain and multiplicity as errors, and even reject the logical distinction between "subject" and "object" as falsehoods. To abandon belief in one's own self, to deny one's own "reality"—what a victory!

This is a higher kind of triumph, not just over the senses or the physical, but an act of violence and cruelty against reason itself. This ecstasy reaches its peak in ascetic self-contempt, where reason, despised and scorned, is forced to decree: there exists a realm of truth and life, but reason is excluded from it. Even Kant's idea of the "intelligible character of things" retains traces of this schism so beloved by ascetics—the tendency to turn reason against itself. In Kant's view, the "intelligible character" of things refers to a quality that reason can only understand as being beyond comprehension.

Despite this, as seekers of knowledge, we should not be entirely ungrateful for such radical reversals of perspectives and values. The mind's relentless rebellion against itself, even when it seems futile, has value. The very act of seeing the world from a different angle, the very desire to do so, serves as a form of training for the intellect, preparing it for true objectivity. Here, objectivity is not understood as "disinterested contemplation"—a concept that is impossible and absurd—but as the ability to command both sides of an argument and to shift perspectives at will, using the contrast between viewpoints and emotional interpretations to advance understanding.

However, let us, as philosophers, be cautious of the dangerous mythology surrounding ancient ideas that have enthroned concepts like a "pure, will-less, painless, timeless subject of knowledge." Let us be wary of such contradictory notions as "pure reason," "absolute spirituality," or "knowledge-in-itself." These ideas demand something absurd: they require an eye that does not see, an eye without direction, stripped of the active and interpretive functions that make perception possible. In these theories, seeing is divorced from context, and vision itself is reduced to nonsense.

There is no seeing without perspective, no knowing without a viewpoint. The more emotions we engage with, the more perspectives we apply, the more different "eyes" we turn toward an object, the fuller and more complete our understanding of it becomes—this is true objectivity. But to eliminate all will, to silence every emotion—if such a thing were even possible—what would we call that? Surely it would amount to nothing less than intellectual castration.

But let us return to the topic. The apparent contradiction seen in ascetics— "life turned against life"—is, from a physiological standpoint (and not merely a psychological one), complete nonsense. It can only seem to be a contradiction. It must be a temporary explanation, a formula, a misunderstanding—a psychological attempt to explain something deeper, something that could not be fully understood or articulated for a long time. It is merely a term placed over an old gap in human knowledge.

Let me state the facts more plainly: the ascetic ideal arises from the instincts of self-preservation and self-defense found in a decaying form of life. It is a strategy employed by a life form struggling to hold its ground and fight for its survival. This ideal signals a state of partial physiological exhaustion and decline, against which the strongest and most intact life instincts continually battle, creating new tools and strategies. The ascetic ideal is one such tool. Its purpose is precisely the opposite of what its worshippers imagine—life fights within and through this ideal against death. The ascetic ideal is a strategy for sustaining life.

History provides an important clue to this. The dominance of the ascetic ideal, particularly in times and places where human civilization and taming were most developed, reveals something significant: the diseased condition of humanity up to now. Specifically, the condition of tamed humanity shows a physiological struggle against death—or more accurately, against the weariness of life, exhaustion, and the longing for an end. The ascetic priest embodies the desire for another kind of existence, one on a different plane. He represents the highest point of this yearning, its official ecstasy and passion. Yet it is this very strength of the desire that binds him to earthly life. It makes him a tool for creating better conditions for human existence on this plane. Paradoxically, this power is what allows the ascetic priest to keep the entire herd of failures, distortions, outcasts, and self- tormentors tethered to life, even as he himself leads them forward, instinctively acting as their shepherd.

Do you see it now? This ascetic priest, this supposed enemy of life, this denier of life—he is, in fact, one of life's greatest conservative and affirmative forces.

What, then, is the cause of this diseased condition? For it is certain that man is sicker, more uncertain, more changeable, and more unstable than any other animal. He is the sick animal—there is no question about it. But why? Certainly, man has also dared, innovated, and risked more than all other creatures combined. He is the great experimenter with himself, the restless and insatiable being who challenges beasts, nature, and even gods. He is ever striving for mastery, driven relentlessly forward by the future pressing upon the present. How could such a bold and resourceful creature not also be the most endangered, the one with the longest and deepest sickness of all the sick animals?

Man grows weary of himself. Entire epidemics of this weariness have swept through humanity, as during the Dance of Death in 1348. But even this exhaustion, this disgust with himself, is transformed into something powerful. Man discharges his nausea and fatigue with such force that it becomes a new chain that binds him to life. His "no" to life somehow conjures countless graceful "yeses." Even in wounding himself, this master of destruction and self- destruction is forced by the wound itself to continue living.

The more common this sickness in humanity becomes—and we cannot deny its prevalence—the more we should honor those rare individuals who possess both mental and physical strength, the true gifts of humanity. These exceptional individuals should be protected even more carefully from the worst kind of environment—the atmosphere of the sickroom. But is that being done? The sick pose the greatest threat to the healthy. It is not the strong who harm the strong, but the weak. Do we recognize this?

On a larger scale, it is not fear of humanity that we should wish to diminish. Fear forces the strong to remain strong, even to be fearsome at times, preserving the vitality of humanity's healthiest type. What is truly dangerous is not the fear of humanity but the nausea with humanity—and just as much, the excessive pity for humanity. If these two emotions were ever to merge, they would unleash the greatest monstrosity imaginable: the ultimate will of humanity, the will to nothingness—Nihilism. The path toward this is already well-paved. Anyone who uses their senses—who not only smells but also sees and hears—can detect the faint yet pervasive odor of madness and sickness wherever they go. I am speaking, of course, of the so-called cultured regions of humanity, of every "Europe" that exists in the world today.

It is the sick who are the greatest danger to humanity, not the evil or even the "beasts of prey." Those who are flawed from the start, crushed, broken— these are the weakest among us, and they undermine the ground beneath humanity's feet. They inject the most dangerous poison into our trust in life, in humanity, and in ourselves. How can we escape it? How can we avoid the covert glance of the malformed and miserable, a glance that leaves us deeply saddened? That glance, turned away from life, reveals their inner monologue: "I wish I were something else, but there is no hope. I am what I am. How could I escape myself? And truthfully—I am sick of myself!"

From such soil—this swampy ground of self-contempt—springs a weed, a poisonous growth. It is small, hidden, ignoble, and sickeningly sweet. Here, the worms of revenge and resentment crawl. The air reeks of secrecy and unmentionable things. In this foul environment, a malicious web is spun—a conspiracy of the suffering against the healthy and the victorious. Here, the sight of success and strength is met with hatred. And yet, what efforts they make to conceal this hatred! What grand words and virtuous postures they adopt! What skillful lies they tell to disguise their bitterness!

These wretched beings—what a noble tone their complaints take on! How their eyes ooze sugary humility and submission! But what do they really want? Above all, they want to appear righteous, loving, wise, and superior. This is the ambition of the "lowest" and the sick. How clever this ambition makes them! You cannot help but marvel at the skill with which they counterfeit virtue, even forging the golden seal of righteousness. They have taken virtue for themselves, beyond all doubt. "We alone are the good and the righteous," they declare. "We alone are the homines bonae voluntatis—the people of good will." They move among us as living accusations, as warnings, as if health, strength, pride, and the joy of power were sins for which we must one day atone. How they long, in their hearts, to make us atone! How they thirst to become our executioners!

Among them are countless vengeful individuals masquerading as judges, constantly invoking the word "righteousness" as if it were a venom they are ready to spit. Their mouths are always pursed, prepared to attack anything that does not wear a mask of discontent, anything that dares to move through life with cheerfulness and ease. Among them, too, is the most repulsive type of the vain and deceitful—those twisted creations who present themselves as "pure souls," peddling their warped sensuality disguised as "purity of heart," wrapped in poetic verses and other such coverings. They are the self-comforters, the ones who indulge in their own illusions, masturbators of their own souls.

The sick have a relentless will to project some form of superiority, to seek out devious paths that lead to power over the healthy. Where can this will to dominate—the will to power of the weakest— not be found? Especially in the sick woman: no one surpasses her in inventiveness when it comes to ruling, oppressing, and tyrannizing. The sick woman spares nothing—neither the living nor the dead. She digs up even the most buried and forgotten things. (As the Bogos say, "Woman is a hyena.") Look into the private lives of families, communities, and institutions: everywhere you will see this ongoing, silent battle of the sick against the healthy. It is often fought with subtle poisons, pinpricks, and spiteful grimaces disguised as patience. Yet sometimes, it escalates into a diseased kind of self-righteousness, a pure pantomime of "moral indignation."

This battle even reaches into the sacred spaces of knowledge, where the yelping of these sick hounds can be heard. Their lying and frenzied moralism infect even the noblest pursuits. Think, for instance, of that Berlin preacher of revenge, Eugen Dühring, who shamelessly exploits the most vile moral refuse in modern Germany. He stands out even among the Anti-Semites as the loudest and most repugnant moral hypocrite of the age.

These individuals are consumed by resentment. They are physiological distortions, worm-eaten remnants of humanity, a kingdom of festering revenge. They are tireless, insatiable in their attacks on the happy and equally ingenious in finding ways to disguise and justify their revenge. When will they reach their ultimate triumph? Likely when they succeed in planting their misery—and all misery— into the minds of the happy. At that point, the happy might begin to feel ashamed of their happiness and say to one another, "It is wrong to be happy when there is so much suffering."

But there could be no greater or more disastrous misunderstanding than for the healthy, the strong, and the joyful to doubt their right to happiness. Away with this "perverse world"! Away with this sickly sentimentality! Preventing the sick from infecting the healthy—this must be our highest goal. To achieve this, it is essential that the healthy remain separate from the sick, guarding themselves even from their gaze, avoiding any association with them. Is it their mission to play nurse or doctor to the sick? Certainly not. To do so would be the grossest denial of their true purpose. The higher must never degrade itself into becoming a tool for the lower. The pathos of distance must always maintain this separation.

The right of the happy to exist, the right of full-toned bells to ring above the discordant cracked bells, is infinitely greater. The happy, the healthy, and the strong are the true guarantees of humanity's future. They alone are bound to its destiny. What they can and must do, the sick cannot and should not attempt. But for the healthy to fulfill their unique role, they cannot waste themselves as the doctors, comforters, or "saviors" of the sick.

…And so, good air! Good air! Let us move away, at all costs, from the madhouses and hospitals of civilization. Let us seek good company—our own company—or, if need be, solitude. But at any rate, let us escape the foul stench of inner decay and the rotting corruption of the sick. This, my friends, is how we must defend ourselves, if only for a little longer, against the two worst afflictions that could ever befall us: the great nausea with man and the great pity for man.

If you have truly grasped—deeply and profoundly—the reasons why it is impossible for the healthy to act as nurses for the sick, to take on the task of healing them, then you must also understand another necessity: the need for doctors and nurses who are themselves sick. And now, with both hands, we hold the essence of the ascetic priest. The ascetic priest must be understood as the predestined savior, shepherd, and defender of the sick herd. It is only through this lens that we can comprehend his terrifying historical role. His domain is the rule over sufferers; this is his kingdom, his instinct, his unique art, his craft, and even his form of happiness.

To fulfill this role, he must be sick himself, a kin to the sick and the deformed, so that he can understand them and communicate with them. Yet, at the same time, he must also be strong—stronger than both himself and others. He must possess an unshakable will to power to win the trust and reverence of the weak. He becomes their anchor, their bulwark, their guide, their overseer, their tyrant, even their god. His duty is to protect the herd—but against whom? Against the healthy, of course, and against the envy the herd feels toward the healthy.

The priest naturally opposes every form of untamed, wild, predatory strength and power. He is the first embodiment of a more refined creature, one that scorns more easily than it hates. He will inevitably find himself in conflict with the beasts of prey, but his weapons are not brute force; they are cunning and spirit. He may even need to summon from within himself, or at least project, a new form of predator—a hybrid monstrosity, part polar bear, part stealthy panther, and part fox. This combination is as mesmerizing as it is terrifying.

When necessary, the priest appears with the gravity of a bear—serious, wise, cold, and full of deceitful superiority. He presents himself as the voice of mysterious powers, even venturing into the realm of other predators. His goal is to sow suffering, discord, and self-doubt among them, and he is certain of his skill to remain the master of sufferers at all times.

The priest arrives with salves and balms, but before healing, he first wounds. And as he soothes the pain of the wound, he poisons it further. He excels at this, this wizard and beast-tamer, who turns everything healthy sick and makes the sick docile. He guards his herd well—this strange shepherd—protecting them even from themselves. He shields them from the sparks of malice, deceit, and wickedness that smolder within the herd, for these are the ailments of the sick.

He fights tirelessly, using cunning, harshness, and secrecy, to stave off anarchy and the ever-present danger of the herd's collapse. For within the herd, resentment—the most dangerous and volatile of all explosives—constantly accumulates. It is the priest's task to manage this brewing storm, to keep the herd together and obedient, even as he strengthens his own rule.

Diverting this volatile resentment in a way that prevents it from destroying both the herd and the herdsman—this is the true achievement of the ascetic priest. It is his most significant function. If one were to summarize the value of the priestly life in the briefest formula, it would be this: the priest is the diverter of resentment. Every sufferer instinctively seeks a cause for their suffering. More specifically, they seek a doer—an agent they can hold responsible. Even more precisely, they long for a sentient, accountable being upon whom they can place the blame. In short, they need something alive, something tangible, upon which to direct their emotions. Whether this target is real or symbolic, it serves the same purpose: it provides an outlet for the sufferer's pent-up emotions.

For the sufferer, venting emotions becomes their most desperate attempt at relief—a kind of self-induced numbness, a narcotic they turn to in their struggle to deaden any kind of pain. This phenomenon, in my judgment, reveals the true physiological root of resentment, revenge, and related emotions. These are not merely defensive reflexes, as they are often misunderstood. They are not the protective reactions that help one avoid further harm, like the way a decapitated frog might reflexively react to corrosive acid. No, the purpose here is different. It is not about avoiding harm but about numbing a deep, persistent, almost unbearable pain by replacing it with a more violent emotion—any violent emotion will do.

For this purpose, an excuse is needed to provoke such emotion. The more intense the emotion, the more effective it is in temporarily driving the pain out of consciousness. This is why sufferers instinctively conclude, "It must be someone's fault that I feel this way." This reasoning is universal among those in pain, but it becomes more pronounced the less they understand the true physiological cause of their suffering. The source of their pain could be anything—an imbalance in the nervous system, an excess of bile, a deficiency in vital minerals like potassium, intestinal pressure disrupting blood flow, ovarian degeneration, and so forth. Yet, instead of addressing these actual causes, sufferers turn to imaginative and emotional explanations.

Sufferers possess an almost inexhaustible creativity in finding excuses to amplify their painful emotions. They revel in jealousy, wallow in dark suspicions, and relive supposed injustices. They dig through the depths of their past and present, searching for hidden grievances that allow them to indulge in torturous doubt and drink deeply from the poison of their own malice. They reopen old wounds, make scars bleed once more, and transform loved ones— friends, spouses, children—into perceived enemies. Their inner voice constantly repeats, "I suffer; it must be someone's fault."

This is where the ascetic priest steps in. He speaks to the suffering sheep and says, "Yes, my sheep, it is someone's fault—but that someone is you. You are the one to blame. It is your fault, and it is your fault alone." Bold, even false, as this declaration may be, it achieves one critical outcome: it redirects the resentment inward.

Now you see the purpose of the ascetic priest's role, the remedy that life's instinct has attempted through him. To achieve this, the priest employed a temporary tyranny of paradoxical and extreme ideas such as "guilt," "sin," "sinfulness," "corruption," and "damnation." The goal was not to heal the sick in any real physiological sense. Instead, it was to make them harmless, to a certain extent, by turning their destructive tendencies inward. The incurable were, in effect, destroyed by their own self-accusations. The milder cases were redirected toward self-discipline, self- surveillance, and self-mastery. Their resentment became a tool for controlling and policing themselves.

It is evident that this emotional "medication" never aimed to truly heal the sick. Healing, in the physiological sense, was never the goal of this instinct of life. Instead, two outcomes were achieved. First, there was a kind of consolidation and organization of the sick—a systematized management of suffering, which we often call the "Church." Second, a provisional safeguarding of the comparatively healthy was achieved. A deliberate separation was created between the healthy and the sick—a rift that kept the two groups distinct.

For a long time, this was all that could be achieved, and yet it was significant. It was a great deal—more than could have been imagined in such a state of widespread suffering and decline. It was an accomplishment of enormous importance.

As you can see, I am proceeding in this essay from a hypothesis that, for the kind of readers I address, does not need proof: the idea that "sinfulness" in humanity is not an actual fact but rather an interpretation of a fact—a physiological discomfort viewed through a moral and religious lens that no longer holds authority over us. Therefore, the feeling of being "guilty" or "sinful" is not evidence that one is justified in feeling so, any more than feeling healthy is proof of actual health. Consider, for example, the infamous witch trials. Even the most intelligent and humane judges of the time firmly believed they were dealing with guilt. The so-called witches themselves believed it. And yet, guilt was absent.

Let me expand on this hypothesis. I do not accept the concept of "pain in the soul" as a fact. Rather, I see it as an explanation—a temporary one—for phenomena that could not previously be clearly defined. In this sense, it is still unsubstantiated and scientifically unsupported, a convenient term that takes the place of a question mark. When someone cannot escape their "pain in the soul," the cause lies not in the "soul" itself but far more likely in the body—in the stomach, for instance. (I speak crudely, though I do not mean to encourage a crude interpretation of my words.)

A strong and well-balanced individual processes their experiences—both their deeds and misdeeds—just as they digest their food, even when some morsels are tough to swallow. If they fail to "digest" an experience, this indigestion is physiological as much as it is psychological. In fact, the two forms of indigestion are often interlinked, with one contributing to the other. You could embrace this perspective and still remain, in principle, an opponent of materialism.

But is the ascetic priest truly a physician? We already have reasons to hesitate before calling him one, no matter how much he enjoys portraying himself as a "savior" and being worshipped as such. His efforts are focused entirely on addressing the sufferer's discomfort, not the root cause of the suffering or the underlying illness itself. This is the most fundamental objection to priestly "medicine."

However, if you adopt the priest's perspective, it is difficult not to marvel at what he has seen, sought, and achieved from this vantage point. His genius lies in mitigating suffering, in providing consolation. Consider the inventiveness with which he has interpreted his role as a consoler and the boldness with which he has selected the tools for his task. Christianity, for instance, could be considered a vast treasure trove of ingenious consolations. It has amassed a remarkable storehouse of remedies—refreshing, soothing, even numbing drugs. Christianity has ventured some of the most daring and dangerous psychological strategies. With unparalleled refinement, often with a distinctly Oriental subtlety, it has identified emotional stimulants capable of countering the profound depression, crushing fatigue, and black melancholy of those who are physiologically unwell.

Indeed, all religions share this common goal: combating a kind of weariness that weighs down life. It is likely, even inevitable, that in certain times and places large portions of the population would experience waves of physiological depression. Without the scientific understanding of bodily health that we possess today, such depression would not have been recognized as physiological. Instead, its causes and cures were sought within the realm of moral and psychological explanations. This, I propose, is the most general framework for what is often called "religion."

Religions, then, can be seen as grand systems of consolation, designed to manage the fatigue of life that spreads among societies. By addressing this fatigue, they provide temporary relief and create narratives that help individuals endure the burdens they cannot fully understand or escape. This is the ascetic priest's domain: offering solace for suffering while leaving its true sources untouched.

Such feelings of depression can arise from a wide variety of causes, each shaped by unique circumstances and influences. For example, depression may result from the intermingling of races or classes that are too different from each other. Genealogical and racial distinctions often manifest in class structures, and the European "Weltschmerz" or the pessimism of the nineteenth century can be traced back to absurd and abrupt class mixing. Similarly, depression may be triggered by ill-fated migrations, such as when a race moves into a climate it cannot adequately adapt to, as in the case of the Indians in India.

Other causes might include the natural decline brought on by old age and fatigue, such as the Parisian pessimism that emerged after 1850, or poor dietary habits like the rampant alcoholism of the Middle Ages or the peculiar nonsense of vegetarianism, even though vegetarianism has been endorsed humorously by figures such as Sir Christopher in Shakespeare. Further contributors include deteriorating blood health or diseases like malaria and syphilis, which devastated Germany after the Thirty Years' War and left behind a population marked by submissiveness and timidity.

When such widespread depression arises, humanity instinctively wages war against it on a grand scale. This battle unfolds in various practices and stages. For brevity, I leave aside the philosophical struggles against depression, which often accompany these efforts. These philosophical battles, though intellectually engaging, are largely ineffective and impractical. They are riddled with abstract theorizing, such as the notion that pain is merely a mistake to be corrected—an assumption that, when tested, invariably fails to make the pain disappear.

The dominant approach to combating depression is through methods that reduce life's intensity to its absolute minimum. The strategy seeks to suppress the consciousness of life itself, lowering it as much as possible. This often involves eliminating desires and avoiding anything that provokes emotion or "stirs the blood." Practitioners of such methods might abstain from salt (as in the hygiene of fakirs), avoid love and hate, embrace equanimity, renounce revenge, wealth, and labor, and sometimes even resort to begging. They shun the company of women or limit their interactions with women to the barest minimum. Intellectually, this strategy aligns with Pascal's principle, "il faut s'abêtir"—the need to dull one's mind.

In ethical and psychological terms, these practices are labeled as "self- annihilation" or "sanctification." Physiologically, they resemble a form of "hypnotism," an effort to simulate the human equivalent of hibernation in animals or aestivation in tropical plants. The goal is to achieve a minimal level of metabolism and assimilation, allowing life to persist without fully entering consciousness. An extraordinary amount of human energy has been invested in achieving this state— possibly to no avail.

Still, it is undeniable that such "saintly athletes," who have appeared throughout history in nearly every culture, often find genuine relief from the physiological depression they battle. Through rigorous training and their system of hypnotism, they have managed to escape the deepest forms of depression in countless cases. This success places their methods among the most universal practices documented in ethnology.

It is incorrect to dismiss such strategies, aimed at starving the physical desires and instincts, as mere madness. While some blunt, roast-beef-eating "freethinkers" and Sir Christophers may be eager to label these practices as insanity, their view is overly simplistic. That said, there is no doubt that such methods frequently lead to mental disturbances. These may include experiences of "inner light," auditory or visual hallucinations, ecstatic raptures, or heightened sensualism, as exemplified in the cases of the Hesychasts of Mount Athos or St. Theresa.

The victims of these phenomena often provide explanations filled with fanatical falsehoods. Yet, even in their explanations, one detects a profound tone of gratitude—a sense that their suffering has granted them a higher understanding. They interpret their final state of salvation, the ultimate goal of their hypnotic practices, as a profound mystery beyond words. To them, it is a return to the essence of existence, a liberation from illusions, desires, and all forms of action. It is seen as a state beyond Good and Evil, transcending every boundary and dichotomy.

As the Buddhists say, "Good and Evil are both chains. The perfect man is the master of both."

"The done and the undone," says the disciple of the Vedanta, "do him no harm; the good and the evil he shakes off, for he is wise. His kingdom remains unaffected by actions; he transcends both good and evil." This is a thoroughly Indian conception, shared by both Brahmanism and Buddhism. In neither Indian nor Christian doctrines is "redemption" achieved through virtue or moral improvement, no matter how much they might value the hypnotic power of virtue. This is a key point to understand—and it aligns entirely with reality. The fact that these traditions stayed true to this principle may be one of the best examples of realism within the otherwise morality-saturated framework of the three great religions.

"For those who know, there is no duty." Redemption, according to these teachings, is not something attained by accumulating virtues. Redemption means unity with Brahman, who cannot gain perfection because he is already perfect. Similarly, it is not about shedding faults, for Brahman, with whom unity constitutes redemption, is eternally pure. These ideas are well-articulated in the commentaries of Cankara, as cited by Paul Deussen, one of the first true European experts on Indian philosophy and a personal friend.

We must, therefore, give due respect to the concept of "redemption" in these great religions, but it is hard to remain entirely serious when faced with how these exhausted pessimists—too weary even to dream—praise deep sleep. To them, deep sleep is seen as a merging into Brahman, the ultimate unification with God, the unio mystica.

The oldest and most revered scriptures express it this way: "When he has completely gone to sleep and reached perfect rest, so that he sees no more visions, then, oh dear one, he is united with Being. He has entered his true self—enclosed by the Self with its absolute knowledge. He has no more consciousness of anything within or without. Day and night do not cross these bridges, nor do age, death, suffering, good deeds, or evil deeds." Similarly, the adherents of this deepest of the three great religions claim, "In deep sleep, the soul rises out of this body, enters the supreme light, and takes its true form: it becomes the supreme spirit itself. There, it moves about freely, rests, plays, and enjoys itself—whether with women, chariots, or friends. Its thoughts no longer return to the burdens of the body, to which the vital breath ('prana') is yoked like an animal to a cart."

Yet, as with the concept of "redemption," we must note that this elaborate and extravagant Oriental imagery ultimately conveys the same critique of life as did the Greek philosopher Epicurus. His approach, while clear and cold in its simplicity, expressed the same underlying sentiment. The hypnotic sensation of nothingness, the peace of deep sleep, and the numbness of complete anesthesia— this is what the suffering and utterly dejected regard as their highest good, their ultimate value.

For them, this state of absolute negation becomes something positive, the essence of what they consider the highest achievement. By this same emotional logic, all pessimistic religions declare that nothingness is God. In their eyes, to embrace the void is to find peace, and the absence of everything is exalted as the ultimate liberation.

This hypnotic dulling of sensitivity and resistance to pain—requiring rare qualities like courage, disregard for public opinion, and intellectual stoicism—is far less common than another, simpler method often employed to combat depression: mechanical activity. Undeniably, the burden of a painful existence can be significantly lightened through such activity. Today, this phenomenon is often referred to, somewhat crassly, as the "blessing of work."

The relief it provides comes from its ability to divert the sufferer's attention entirely away from their pain. By monopolizing the consciousness with constant action, little room is left for suffering to take hold. After all, human consciousness is a narrow space, easily filled. Mechanical activity, combined with its byproducts—absolute regularity, rigid and unthinking obedience, the monotony of routine, the total occupation of time, and even a certain freedom found in impersonality—becomes a powerful tool. This "training in impersonality" or incuria sui (carelessness about the self), has been utilized with great skill by the ascetic priest in his ongoing war against pain.

When addressing the lower classes—slaves, prisoners, or women (who, in many cases, exist as a blend of laborer and captive)— the priest requires little effort beyond linguistic manipulation. By renaming and reinterpreting their circumstances, he can make them view their hated conditions as blessings. It is important to note that dissatisfaction with one's lot as a slave was not a creation of the priests, but the priests were adept at redirecting that discontent.

A complementary and equally popular method for combating depression is the prescription of small joys, particularly joys that are easy to attain and can be integrated into daily routines. This remedy often works alongside the discipline of mechanical activity. Among the most common forms of this "medication" is fostering joy through producing joy—acts such as doing good, giving gifts, helping others, offering comfort, praising someone, or extending kindness. These acts of generosity are often linked with the moral commandment to "love your neighbor."

The ascetic priest, however cautiously, also prescribes a controlled stimulation of one of the strongest and most vital instincts: the Will to Power. Even the smallest feeling of superiority, which naturally accompanies acts of helping, comforting, or praising others, becomes a profound source of consolation for the afflicted. Physiological distortions and those suffering from depression wisely use this instinct to their advantage, finding happiness in the smallest affirmations of power. Where this instinct is not harnessed constructively, the same drive often leads to harmful actions, as people injure one another in their pursuit of even the most minor dominations.

An exploration of Christianity's origins in the Roman world reveals that cooperative organizations for addressing poverty, illness, and burial emerged among the lowest social strata. These groups deliberately fostered the antidote of shared, mutual benefits as a way to combat depression. At the time, this approach may have been a novel discovery—a true innovation. By promoting cooperation, family structures, community life, and gatherings in shared spaces (Caenacula), these groups stimulated the Will to Power on a communal level, albeit in modest doses. This collective drive for mutual aid blossomed into a more potent and expansive manifestation of that instinct.

The development of these herd organizations marked a genuine advancement in the battle against depression. As communities grew, individuals often found a new focus of interest that drew them away from their personal despair or self-loathing—what Geulincx termed despectus sui (contempt for oneself). Through communal bonds and shared purposes, individuals could escape the narrower confines of their own dissatisfaction, finding solace and meaning in collective life. This was, in many ways, a triumph—not only for the community but for the individuals within it, who discovered a form of redemption through their integration into something greater than themselves.

All sick and suffering individuals instinctively strive for herd organization, driven by a deep desire to alleviate their overwhelming discomfort and sense of weakness. The ascetic priest recognizes and nurtures this instinct, fostering the formation of herds. Wherever herds arise, they are the product of the instinct of the weak, who crave union, and the cunning of priests, who structure and lead them. This dynamic reflects a natural divide: the strong, by necessity, strive for isolation as much as the weak seek union.

When the strong join together, it is not out of love for community but rather a reluctant alliance aimed at achieving aggressive collective action and fulfilling their shared Will to Power. Such cooperation is often against their individual inclinations, each strong individual wrestling internally against this compromise. Conversely, the weak unite with genuine delight in the organization, feeling their instincts gratified. For them, the herd is a source of solace and strength, whereas for the "born master"— the solitary predator type of man— any form of organization is a wound to their very nature, an affront to their instincts.

History teaches us an inescapable lesson: lurking within every oligarchy is the seed of tyranny. Oligarchies are perpetually tense, as each individual member must constantly suppress their own tyrannical desires. (The Greeks exemplify this dynamic; Plato, with his deep understanding of his contemporaries—and himself—revealed it time and again in his writings.)

The ascetic priest's methods, which we have already examined— suppressing vitality, enforcing mechanical labor, offering small joys, and promoting "love your neighbor"—are all tools for herd organization. By awakening a shared sense of communal power, the priest enables individuals to find joy in the success of the group, thus overshadowing their disgust with themselves. These strategies, according to contemporary standards, are considered "innocent" methods in combating depression.

Let us now turn to the "guilty" methods, which are far more intriguing. These methods center on the deliberate creation of emotional excess, a strategy used to provide temporary relief from the chronic pain of depression. Emotional excess acts as a powerful anesthetic, dulling the sufferer's awareness of their agony. This need for intense emotion has driven priestly ingenuity to extraordinary lengths, leading to the invention of countless techniques to provoke overwhelming feelings.

This may sound harsh. One might prefer a gentler phrasing: "The ascetic priest has always harnessed the enthusiasm inherent in strong emotions." But why should we sugarcoat this for the delicate sensibilities of modern listeners? To do so would only cater to the verbal Pecksniffianism of our age. For a psychologist, to indulge in such euphemisms would not only be hypocritical but nauseating. Good taste—or perhaps what some might call integrity—demands that we challenge the sickly moralized language that infects modern discourse about humanity and the world.

Do not be deceived: the defining trait of modern souls and modern literature is not outright dishonesty but the innocence that accompanies their intellectual dishonesty. This innocence is what makes modern psychology such a distasteful and dangerous enterprise. It is a path that leads directly to the "great nausea"—a revolt against the sugary moralism and falsity saturating contemporary culture.

I am well aware of the role modern works, and modernity as a whole, will serve for future generations (should they endure and should a healthier, stricter generation eventually arise): modernity will function as an emetic. It will purge the moral and intellectual systems of those future people, ridding them of the cloying sweetness, the ingrained softness and false idealism that masquerades as high-mindedness today.

Our contemporary "cultured" men and "good" men do not lie—this much is true. Yet this is hardly to their credit. Their unwillingness to lie is not a sign of virtue but a reflection of the same ingrained dishonesty that defines them. It is not a conscious choice but a symptom of their weakness, their inability to confront or express uncomfortable truths. Such is the state of modern idealism, cloaked in moral sugar and falsehood, steeped in the sentimental idealism they mistake for greatness. And such is the legacy that modernity will leave behind: a purgative for a future stronger, healthier humanity.

The real lie—the deliberate, intentional, and "honest" lie, the kind Plato speaks of so highly—is far too bold and difficult for most people to handle. Asking them to embrace it would require them to do something they are fundamentally unwilling to do: look inward, confront their own truths, and learn to differentiate between what is true and what is false within themselves. Instead, the dishonest lie is what suits them best—a lie that fools even the "good" man. Such people are entirely incapable of being anything other than dishonorable liars, absolute liars, yet they remain innocent liars, virtuous liars, and naïve, well-meaning liars.

These "good men" are completely steeped in morality, so much so that their sense of honor has been irreparably corrupted. They are morally tainted, disgraced for all eternity. Which of them could withstand hearing more truths about humanity—or, more specifically, about themselves? Who among them could bear the weight of an honest biography? A few examples will suffice. Lord Byron once wrote a deeply personal autobiography, but Thomas Moore, being "too good" for such raw honesty, burned his friend's papers. Similarly, Schopenhauer's executor, Dr. Gwinner, is said to have destroyed many of Schopenhauer's self-reflective writings, including some that may have even been critical of himself (εἰς ἑαυὸν). And consider the virtuous American Thayer, who, while writing Beethoven's biography, abandoned the project partway through. At a certain point, even he could no longer continue exposing the truths of Beethoven's otherwise noble and simple life.

The moral here is clear: who among us, in this age, would dare to write an honest word about themselves? To do so would require one to belong to an order of holy fools, a rare breed indeed. An autobiography from Richard Wagner is promised, but does anyone doubt that it will be anything less than a carefully constructed narrative? Consider the outrage caused by the Catholic priest Janssen in Germany with his overly simplistic and harmless depictions of the Reformation. Now imagine the chaos that would erupt if a true psychologist were to present us with an authentic account of Luther—not with the timid modesty of a Protestant historian or the moralizing simplicity of a parish priest, but with the fearless precision of someone like Taine, whose boldness comes not from deference to power but from genuine inner strength. (The Germans, by the way, already have a classic example of such deference in Leopold Ranke, the quintessential advocate of every causa fortior, a master of opportunism disguised as objectivity.)

But you can see my point. To put it simply, there are plenty of reasons why we psychologists must approach even ourselves with a degree of mistrust. It is quite likely that we too are still "too good" for the work we attempt to do. Despite whatever contempt we may feel for the modern obsession with morality, we are not immune to its influence. We are, perhaps, still its slaves and victims. This moral infection seeps into even our own judgments. What else could that diplomat have meant when he warned his colleagues, "Distrust your first impulses, gentlemen! They are almost always good"? This should be the mantra of every psychologist when speaking to their peers.

And so, we return to our problem, which demands a certain level of rigor and mistrust, especially of first impulses. The ascetic ideal as a tool for inducing emotional excess—those who recall my earlier thoughts will already understand part of what I mean. This ideal seeks to unsettle the human soul completely, throwing it into states of terror, ecstasy, rapture, and despair, as though through a sudden lightning strike. This method aims to jolt the individual out of their unhappiness, depression, and discomfort. But which paths lead to such a result? And which of them are the safest?

In truth, all strong emotions hold the potential to achieve this, provided they find a sudden and dramatic outlet. Rage, fear, lust, revenge, hope, triumph, despair, and cruelty—any of these can provide a release. The ascetic priest has never hesitated to employ the entire arsenal of human emotions, unleashing them selectively to awaken people from prolonged melancholy. He chases away their dull pain and misery, if only temporarily, always under the guise of religious meaning and justification.

Of course, this emotional excess comes at a cost. It must be repaid—it inevitably worsens the condition of the sick. For this reason, such remedies are deemed "guilty" by modern standards. Still, the priest's methods are undeniably effective, even if the price is steep and the long-term consequences dire.

Fairness requires us to acknowledge that this remedy was applied by the ascetic priest with a good conscience. He prescribed it with a profound belief in its necessity and effectiveness, even though he often struggled with the very pain he created in others. The priest, as a healer of sorts, genuinely believed this was the best path forward. Even the severe physiological consequences of these methods— sometimes leading to mental disturbances— were not entirely inconsistent with the purpose of the remedy. After all, the priest was not attempting to cure diseases in a conventional sense but to combat the misery of depression and its accompanying unhappiness. The goal was to alleviate and numb the pain of existence, and in that sense, the remedy succeeded.

The central tool that the ascetic priest used to pluck every agonizing and ecstatic chord in the human soul was the feeling of guilt. As I have previously explained, the origins of guilt lie in animal psychology—it began as a primal feeling tied to the instincts of creatures struggling with survival. In its raw, unshaped form, guilt was a simple mechanism of conscience. Yet, in the hands of the priest, this crude feeling was transformed into something far more elaborate and dangerous—a masterwork of emotional manipulation.

The priest gave this new version of guilt a name: "sin." Sin became the religious reinterpretation of the animal's bad conscience, a reversal of cruelty turned inward. Up to now, "sin" has been the most monumental event in the history of the human soul afflicted by disease. It is, without question, the most perilous and fatal creation of religious interpretation.

Imagine a man already suffering, burdened by his existence, trapped in a cage of his own making, and without understanding why. He searches desperately for reasons—anything to explain his suffering—and for remedies, perhaps even narcotics, to dull the pain. When he turns to the ascetic priest, the priest provides him with his first "answer": the cause of his suffering lies within himself, in his guilt, in a piece of his past. His suffering, the priest explains, is a punishment—a direct consequence of his own actions.

The man hears and understands. But now he is trapped, like a hen that has had a line drawn around it, unable to step outside the circle. The sick man becomes the sinner. And for thousands of years, humanity has been haunted by the image of this new invalid, the sinner. Can we ever escape it?

Everywhere we look, we see the hypnotic gaze of the sinner, always fixated on guilt as the sole cause of suffering. Everywhere is the evil conscience—what Luther called the "ghastly beast"—obsessed with the past, distorting actions through the lens of guilt and fear of punishment. The sinner's suffering is endlessly misunderstood, transformed into feelings of blame and a terror of divine retribution. The consequences are everywhere: the scourge, the hair shirt, the starving body, acts of contrition. We see the sinner breaking themselves on the wheel of a restless, insatiable conscience. We see silent pain, overwhelming fear, hearts tormented by their own guilt, and cries for redemption.

And yet, this system achieved its intended purpose. The old depression, dullness, and lethargy were completely vanquished. Life, once heavy and meaningless, became deeply interesting again—so much so that it burned with an almost unbearable intensity. The sinner became a figure of endless energy, awake and sleepless, consumed by his inner fire. Exhausted but never allowed to rest, humanity, as the sinner, was thrust into a state of perpetual tension and spiritual urgency.

The ascetic priest, the master manipulator, had triumphed. His kingdom had arrived. No longer did people complain about pain; instead, they began to crave it. "More pain! More pain!" became the cry of his followers, his initiates, echoing through the centuries. What had begun as a fight against depression and despair was transformed into an insatiable hunger for suffering—a perverse new vitality born from the ashes of misery.

Every form of emotional excess that inflicted pain—everything that shattered, overwhelmed, crushed, exalted, or transported the soul—became a tool for the ascetic priest. The horrors of torture chambers, the twisted ingenuity of hell itself, and every imaginable torment were uncovered, imagined, and exploited to serve the triumph of his ideal: the ascetic ideal. "My kingdom is not of this world," he proclaimed, both at the beginning and the end of his work. But did he truly still have the right to say so? Goethe once claimed there are only thirty-six tragic situations. If we didn't know better, we might assume Goethe was no ascetic priest—because the priest surely knows more.

Regarding this "guilty" form of priestly medicine—the emotional excess prescribed by the ascetic priest to his ailing followers—criticism is almost unnecessary. The idea that such methods have genuinely helped any sick person seems laughable. Who could seriously argue that emotional extremes, wrapped in sacred language and applied under the guise of divine purpose, have ever truly cured anyone? If by "be of use" one means that these methods have reformed individuals, I won't dispute it. But let's clarify: "reformed," to my understanding, means something closer to "tamed," "weakened," "discouraged," "refined," "delicate," or "emasculated"—all of which amount to a form of harm.

When dealing primarily with the sick, depressed, and downtrodden, such treatments might indeed make them seem "better," but they also make them far worse. Ask any physician who treats mental illness: what is the outcome of systematically applying penance- tortures, acts of contrition, and ecstatic salvation experiences? The result is clear—a nervous system further shattered, piled atop whatever existing malady the sufferer endured. History corroborates this. Everywhere the ascetic priest implemented this "cure," disease spread rapidly, infecting not only individuals but entire populations.

What were the results of these methods? Time and again, they left communities and nations riddled with broken nerves and deep psychological scars. Consider the epidemic of epileptic fits in the Middle Ages, such as the St. Vitus and St. John dances—mass outbreaks of uncontrollable convulsions, born out of penance and redemption training. Another result was the emergence of chronic depression and twisted emotional states that reshaped entire cities or nations, like Geneva or Basel, transforming their temperaments into something permanently somber and repressed.

This training was also directly responsible for the witch-hysteria—epidemics of mass delusion akin to somnambulism. Between 1564 and 1605 alone, there were eight significant outbreaks of this phenomenon. Similarly, we find entire populations gripped by suicidal fervor, like the mass death-cravings of certain periods in Europe, where crowds would shout the horrifying cry, "Evviva la morte!" (Long live death!). These episodes often swung unpredictably between orgiastic ecstasy and a destructive frenzy, a pattern seen wherever the doctrine of sin and asceticism found success. Religious neuroses are unmistakably tied to these symptoms—what else could they be? (Quaeritur— we must ask).

The ascetic ideal, along with its lofty moral cult, stands as one of humanity's most ingenious, reckless, and dangerous systems of emotional excess. It has left a terrifying and indelible mark on the history of mankind, a scar that is both unforgettable and undeniable. Worse still, this history is not confined to the past. Its influence continues to manifest in the present, haunting us with its legacy of suffering and manipulation.

I can scarcely think of any force that has harmed the health and vitality of European people more than the ascetic ideal. It can rightly be called the true catastrophe in the history of European health. At most, it can be compared to the uniquely German influence: the widespread poisoning of Europe with alcohol. This plague, running parallel with the rise of German political and racial dominance, left its mark wherever their influence extended—not only their blood but also their vice was spread. Third in this grim sequence is syphilis, though the gap between these calamities is significant (magno sed proximo intervallo).

Wherever the ascetic priest has gained control, he has corrupted the health of the soul. And, inevitably, where he has corrupted the soul, he has also corrupted taste in the arts and literature—he continues to do so even now. "Inevitably," I say. I trust I will be granted this conclusion without the need to prove it exhaustively here. Allow me to offer one striking example: consider the chief book of Christian literature, their ultimate standard, their "book above all books." This book was born in the midst of the Graeco- Roman splendor—a golden age for books, when the ancient world still brimmed with literary treasures that had not yet been lost to decay and ruin.

Imagine a time when people could still read works that we, today, would trade half our modern literature to possess. Yet, in this era of greatness, Christian agitators—those we now call the "Fathers of the

Church"—had the audacity to declare: "We too have our classical literature; we have no need of the Greeks." They held up their books of legends, their apostles' letters, and their apologetic pamphlets with pride. The comparison is almost absurd, akin to how the English Salvation Army today pits its tracts against Shakespeare and other "heathens" with similar misplaced self- importance.

Let me say it plainly: I do not like the New Testament. In fact, it nearly unsettles me to admit how isolated I feel in my disdain for this highly esteemed and excessively praised scripture. Two thousand years of admiration and reverence weigh against me— but so be it! "Here I stand; I cannot do otherwise." I have the courage of what some might call my bad taste.

The Old Testament, on the other hand—that is something entirely different. It commands respect! Within its pages, I find great men, a landscape full of heroic grandeur, and one of the rarest phenomena in history: the raw, unpretentious naivety of a strong heart. In the Old Testament, I see a people, a true collective identity. But in the New Testament? It is nothing more than a crowded hostel for petty sects, a spiritual rococo with its ornate twists, exaggerated flourishes, and overly sentimental embellishments. The air of small religious gatherings permeates it, a stifling atmosphere with hints of provincial sweetness that belong more to the Hellenistic world of the Roman provinces than to anything truly Jewish.

Here, meekness and bravado stand awkwardly side by side. The New Testament is filled with noisy, emotional chatter that nearly drowns out all else. There is hysteria in abundance, but no true passion; theatrical gestures, but no substance. These "pious little people" lack all dignity. How can they make such a spectacle of their minor failings, parading them with such earnestness? Who cares about their petty sins—let alone God?

And then, they have the audacity to demand the crown of eternal life. For what? On what grounds? The arrogance of it all is almost unbearable. An immortal Peter? Who could endure such a figure?

These small, self-important provincials seem convinced that their trivial troubles and mundane lives are matters of cosmic significance, as though the universe itself were obligated to revolve around their personal struggles. They never tire of dragging God Himself into the midst of their insignificant grievances, entangling the divine in their narrow, self-absorbed misery.

This is the New Testament: a book born of small minds and small ambitions, written by and for people who elevate their everyday struggles into the grand stage of universal importance. It is impossible not to see the absurdity—and, in some cases, the insufferable insolence—of it all.

And what about the dreadful form of this constant, intrusive familiarity with God? This Jewish—and not solely Jewish— endless pleading and clawing at the divine, this desperate, shameless insistence? There are small, so-called "heathen" tribes in East Africa from whom the first Christians could have learned much, especially a bit of tact in worship. These tribes do not even speak their god's name aloud—a delicacy so refined it far surpasses anything the early Christians could have mustered. It is certainly too refined, not just for primitive Christians, but also for the loud and irreverent worshippers that came later. For contrast, just think of Martin Luther—the most "eloquent" and audacious peasant Germany has ever known. Recall the tone of Luther in his personal exchanges with God, where he felt most at home: blunt, brash, and utterly without restraint.

Luther's rebellion against the medieval saints and the Church— especially his animosity toward "that devil's hog, the Pope"— was, at its core, the revolt of a crude man offended by the etiquette of worship. That code of priestly conduct maintained the sacred distance between the divine and the profane, admitting only the initiated and reverent to the holy of holies while shutting out the unrefined masses. Luther, the peasant, could not abide this. It was not "German" enough for him. He wanted to speak directly, personally, and without ceremony to his God—straightforward and plain. And he succeeded.

Yet, as you might guess, the ascetic ideal has never been a school for good taste, much less for refined manners. At its best, it has taught a particular form of priestly decorum—a manner fundamentally opposed to all genuine civility. Its essence is one of excess, a relentless defiance of balance and moderation, a refusal to adhere to any proper limits. It is the ultimate "non plus ultra" of poor taste and unchecked fanaticism.

But the damage caused by the ascetic ideal extends far beyond health and taste. It corrupts in countless ways—third, fourth, fifth, and sixth dimensions of ruin. Listing all its effects would be endless, and exhausting the catalogue would serve little purpose. Instead, my aim is not to enumerate its outcomes but to uncover what it means, to reveal the foundation it rests on, the forces lurking beneath it, and the hidden motives it expresses—often in vague, distorted, and misleading ways.

This is why I have not spared my readers a look at its disastrous consequences: to prepare them for the ultimate and most terrifying question—what is the true meaning of the ascetic ideal? What is the source of its immense, monstrous power? Why does it wield such dominance? Why is it given so much space to flourish, and why is there no stronger resistance to it? The ascetic ideal embodies a single will. But where is the opposing will—the counter-ideal that resists and stands against it?

The ascetic ideal has one clear aim: to make every other interest in human life seem small and unimportant by comparison. It interprets entire eras, nations, and people solely in relation to this goal. It rejects and accepts, denies and affirms, only within the confines of its own interpretation. Is there any other system of meaning that has been so thoroughly worked out? The ascetic ideal refuses to submit to any other power. Instead, it claims precedence over all forces, asserting that nothing powerful in the world can exist without first being assigned meaning, value, and legitimacy by the ideal itself.

Everything is treated as a tool for its purpose, a means to its singular end.

So, where is the counterpart to this vast, all-encompassing system of will and interpretation? Why is such a counterpart absent? Where is the alternative "one aim"?

I am told that this counterpart is not absent—that it has long fought against the ascetic ideal, successfully challenging it, and has even gained dominance over it in some respects. Look, they say, to modern science—the purest form of real- world philosophy. Science, they argue, has achieved what the ascetic ideal never could: the courage to believe in itself, the will to exist on its own terms, unburdened by God, another world, or the ascetic virtues of denial and negation. Science, they say, is the true conqueror of the ascetic ideal.

All their loud, clumsy agitation leaves me unmoved; these self-proclaimed heralds of reality are poor performers, incapable of producing a sound deep enough to resonate with true understanding. They are not the voice of science's vast and profound abyss—for modern science is an abyss. In their mouths, the word "science" is reduced to a vulgarity, an abuse, an insult to its true meaning. The reality is quite the opposite of what the ascetic ideal's defenders claim. Science today has no faith in itself, much less in any ideal greater than itself. And wherever science still possesses passion, love, dedication, or even suffering, it is not an adversary of the ascetic ideal—it is its finest and most advanced form.

Does this sound strange? Perhaps, but consider this: even now, there are plenty of diligent and honorable workers among the learned, people who are genuinely pleased with their small spheres of activity. Because they enjoy their work, they sometimes become embarrassingly loud in demanding that everyone else should be content as well, especially with science. After all, they say, "There is so much useful work to do in science!"

I do not deny this; indeed, I would be the last to interfere with the joy these honest laborers find in their tasks. Their enthusiasm for their craft brings me some delight as well. But the fact that science requires hard work, or that it has contented workers, is no evidence that science as a whole possesses a unified purpose, a shared will, a single ideal, or a deep passion rooted in faith. On the contrary, the truth is precisely the opposite.

When science is not functioning as the newest incarnation of the ascetic ideal—a rare occurrence, reserved only for the most exceptional and refined cases—it often serves instead as a refuge for all kinds of cowardice, doubt, guilt, and self-loathing. It becomes a sanctuary for those plagued by a lack of ideals, those suffering from the absence of a great passion, and those tormented by their enforced restraint and moderation. Oh, how much does science obscure today? How much, at the very least, does it try to obscure?

The tireless diligence of our most accomplished scholars, their obsessive industriousness, their endless sacrifices at the altar of intellectual labor—how often is the true purpose of all this effort simply to avoid seeing a particular truth? Science, in such cases, acts as a form of self-anesthesia. Have you noticed this?

Anyone who spends time with scholars knows the experience: a single harmless word, unintentionally spoken, can wound them deeply. What you might think is a compliment can provoke an extreme bitterness, not because you intended offense, but because you failed to recognize the nature of the people you were dealing with. These scholars are sufferers—though they might not admit it even to themselves. They are dazed, unaware of their own condition, gripped by one overriding fear: the fear of becoming fully conscious.

Now, turn your attention to the other side—to those rare figures I previously mentioned, the supreme idealists among philosophers and scholars today. Could it be that we have found in them the true opponents of the ascetic ideal—its genuine anti-idealists? These "unbelievers" (for they all claim that title) believe so; they cling to this belief as their last vestige of faith. They are so earnest, so fiery in their declarations and gestures, so insistent that they stand in opposition to the ascetic ideal. But does their belief make it true?

We, who claim to "know," have become deeply suspicious of all believers, no matter their creed. Over time, this suspicion has led us to draw the opposite conclusions from those drawn by others. Where belief is strongest, we suspect the greatest difficulty in proving it; the strength of a belief often signals its actual improbability. We do not deny that faith brings comfort or even salvation; in fact, it is precisely because of this that we doubt faith proves anything at all. Strong faith, capable of creating happiness, raises suspicions about its object rather than validating its truth. Instead, it points to the likelihood of illusion.

What, then, is the situation with these figures—these solitary spirits, these self-proclaimed deniers, these champions of intellectual purity, these heroic seekers of truth? They are the pride of our age: pale atheists, anti-Christians, immoralists, Nihilists, sceptics, and "ephectics" (those who suspend judgment) as well as "hectics" (those burning with intellectual fever). These are the highest idealists of knowledge, the sole bearers of the intellectual conscience in our time. They believe themselves to be as distant as possible from the ascetic ideal, thinking of themselves as "free spirits."

And yet, if I may speak the truth they cannot see—for they are too close to themselves—this ideal is their ideal. They are, in fact, its most spiritualized embodiment. They are its most refined scouts, its sharpest weapon, and its most subtle and persuasive expression. If I am at all adept at unraveling riddles, then let me propose this: for some time, there have been no truly free spirits. Why? Because they still believe in truth.

Consider the Christian Crusaders in the East who encountered the infamous Order of Assassins—a group that epitomized free spirits, disciplined far beyond anything the strictest monastic orders could achieve. Among their highest initiates was shared a secret motto: "Nothing is true; everything is permitted." This was the ultimate expression of freedom in thought—freedom that rejected even the belief in truth. Have any Europeans, any self-proclaimed freethinkers, ever truly confronted this idea? Have they grappled with its consequences or ventured into the labyrinth it creates? I doubt it. No, I know otherwise.

The so-called "free spirits" of today are, in fact, bound tighter than ever. Their belief in truth has an absolutism that is unmatched, even fanatical. I speak from experience, having encountered it firsthand. This belief binds them to a form of dignified intellectual asceticism— a stoicism of the mind that prohibits negation as firmly as it does affirmation. They remain paralyzed before the brute fact, the factum brutum, as though standing still is their ultimate virtue.

This small-minded fatalism, this "petit faitalism" (as I term it), is especially evident in the French scientific mindset, which tries to claim moral superiority over the German approach. But this renunciation of interpretation—this refusal to modify, challenge, or creatively engage with facts—this so-called objectivity is nothing more than a modern variation of ascetic virtue. It is, in essence, another form of the same repudiation of the senses, merely disguised under a new guise. At its core, it is still the ascetic ideal in operation, perpetuating itself through intellectual austerity.

The force that drives science into its relentless pursuit of truth is none other than faith in the ascetic ideal itself, even when this faith operates as an unconscious imperative. Do not be mistaken—this is still faith, faith in the metaphysical value and intrinsic worth of truth, a belief that is legitimized and sustained only within the framework of the ascetic ideal. This ideal upholds and guarantees the worth of truth; if the ideal falls, so does the belief in the inherent value of truth.

Strictly speaking, there is no science without its guiding "hypotheses." The very concept of a science that stands independent of assumptions is illogical, even inconceivable. Before science can take form, there must first be a philosophy, a faith, something that provides it with direction, meaning, boundaries, methods, and ultimately, the right to exist. Anyone who imagines otherwise—who claims, for instance, to establish philosophy on a "purely scientific basis"—must first overturn not only philosophy itself but also truth as we understand it. This would be the gravest affront to both, an unforgivable insult to the foundations of thought.

Make no mistake: the unwavering pursuit of truth, conducted with such daring and extremity as demanded by the faith in science, inherently asserts the existence of a world distinct from life, nature, and history. By affirming such a world, does it not simultaneously reject its counterpart—this world, our world? This paradox was already noted in my earlier work, The Joyful W isdom (Book V, Aphorism 344): "The one who pursues truth in this radical, uncompromising way presupposes the existence of another world. And in so doing, must they not reject this one— the very world in which we live?"

Even now, we so-called knowers, we godless opponents of metaphysics, remain bound to a legacy born of ancient belief. Our zeal for truth, the very fire that drives us, is drawn from a thousand-year-old blaze ignited by faith—a Christian faith, a Platonic faith. This faith declared that God is truth and that truth is divine. But what happens when this belief crumbles? What if nothing proves to be divine except error, blindness, and lies? What if God Himself turns out to be the oldest and most tenacious lie?

At this point, we must pause to consider the consequences carefully. Science, which has long appeared as self-justifying, now finds itself in need of justification. This is not to say such justification necessarily exists; rather, it highlights a fundamental problem that has been ignored by nearly all philosophers, ancient and modern alike. Why this blind spot? Because all philosophy to date has been shaped by the ascetic ideal, where truth was enshrined as absolute—whether as Being, God, or the ultimate arbiter of reality.

Truth was sanctified, removed from scrutiny, and treated as unquestionable. Do you grasp the significance of this "unquestionable"?

Once belief in the God of the ascetic ideal is rejected, a new and pressing question arises: what is the value of truth itself? This becomes a problem for the first time—a question that the ascetic ideal never allowed to surface. The Will to Truth, which has driven humanity for centuries, now demands a critique. This is the task we must take upon ourselves: to examine, even challenge, the value of truth itself.

If this seems overly concise, I encourage readers to revisit The Joyful Wisdom, particularly the aphorism titled "How Far We Too Are Still Pious" (Aphorism 344) and the entirety of its fifth book. For further reflection, the preface to The Dawn of Day also offers valuable insights into this ongoing inquiry. Through these works, one might better understand the profound questions we must now face in our reevaluation of truth, its worth, and the faith that has sustained it for so long.

No, you cannot deceive me with science when I seek the natural opposition to the ascetic ideal or when I ask: "Where is the counter-will, the opposing ideal that expresses itself against it?" Science is far too dependent to fulfill this role. In every field, science relies on an ideal, a value-creating force that gives it direction, a purpose in which it can believe. Science does not create values on its own. Its relationship to the ascetic ideal is not inherently antagonistic. On the contrary, it often acts as a driving force in the inner evolution of that ideal.

If we examine more closely, science does not attack the core of the ascetic ideal but merely its outward manifestations—its rigid forms, surface expressions, and dogmas. Science liberates the inner life of the ideal by stripping away its superficialities, but it does not overthrow the ideal itself. In fact, both science and the ascetic ideal rest on the same foundation: an overvaluation of truth, or more precisely, a shared belief in the impossibility of questioning or valuing truth itself. This shared foundation makes them allies. If one is to critique the ascetic ideal, one must also critique science. Recognize this connection; it is crucial.

Art, in contrast, holds a far more genuine opposition to the ascetic ideal. Art, where deception is sanctified, and the will to create illusions is celebrated, stands fundamentally opposed to the ascetic ideal. Plato understood this deeply; he was the greatest adversary of art that Europe has ever known. His opposition to Homer reflects the full antagonism: on one side, Plato represents the life- denying transcendentalist, the great critic of existence. On the other side, Homer stands as life's unconscious celebrant, its golden admirer. For art to serve the ascetic ideal is the deepest corruption of its essence— a sad but frequent reality, as artists are often susceptible to such compromise.

Physiologically speaking, both science and the ascetic ideal stem from similar conditions: a certain decline in vitality, a frugality of life. Both reflect a cooling of emotions, a slowing of life's tempo, and the replacement of instinct with analysis and reason. Seriousness becomes their shared hallmark—a clear sign of life's struggle, a strenuous effort to maintain balance. Consider the eras in which scholars and intellectuals gain prominence; they often coincide with periods of cultural fatigue, societal decline, and the fading of confidence in life and the future.

The ascendancy of intellectuals, like the rise of democracy, arbitration instead of war, equal rights for women, or religions based on pity, are all symptoms of life's weakening vitality. They signify moments when a society has shifted from the vitality of creation to the slower rhythms of maintenance and decline. Science, when considered as a problem, raises questions about its very meaning and purpose. For a deeper exploration of this, one might refer to the preface of The Birth of Tragedy.

Modern science, despite its celebrated independence, often acts as the unwitting ally of the ascetic ideal. This partnership is subtle and unconscious, but it is undeniable. Science and the ascetic ideal have long reinforced one another. Their apparent opposition is misleading; they serve the same underlying purpose. Even the so-called victories of science often strengthen the ideal, not weaken it. When science dismantles a theological framework, it does not destroy the ideal itself. Instead, it refines it, making it more elusive, abstract, and insidious.

For instance, did the collapse of theological astronomy herald the end of the ascetic ideal? Hardly. If anything, the need for transcendental solutions to life's mysteries has only grown stronger. Since Copernicus, humanity has seen a continuous process of self-diminishment. The idea that we are mere accidents in a random and indifferent universe has not freed us from the ascetic ideal but has intensified our longing for meaning. This relentless will to belittle ourselves, to make existence seem smaller and more inconsequential, reveals the enduring grip of the ascetic ideal.

Science, with all its achievements, has yet to confront this core issue. It has not provided an alternative to the ascetic ideal but has instead evolved alongside it, refining and reinforcing its foundations. The need for critique remains. Only by addressing the shared underpinnings of science and the ascetic ideal can we begin to question the deeper values that continue to shape humanity.

Alas, humanity's belief in its own dignity, uniqueness, and indispensable role in the grand scheme of existence has eroded. Once, man regarded himself as almost divine—"a child of God," or even a "demi-God." But now, that sense of sacredness is gone, and he sees himself as nothing more than an animal—plain, literal, unremarkable, and unqualified. Since Copernicus, it feels as though mankind has been slipping down a steep incline, rolling faster and faster away from the perceived center of existence. But to where? Into the void? Into the "thrilling sensation of his own nothingness"?

Perhaps this descent is merely a direct path back to the old ideal. Consider how all branches of science—whether astronomy or even philosophy, including the harsh self-examination of reason itself—have labored to dismantle man's lofty opinion of himself. Kant, for instance, confessed to feeling diminished by the discoveries of astronomy, admitting it "annihilates my own importance." Science seems to take a strange pride in this project, finding its satisfaction in maintaining the very state of self- contempt it worked so hard to cultivate in humanity. For science, this disdain for man becomes his final and most profound claim to self-worth—a bitter, stoic form of pride. After all, only one who understands value can truly despise something, even himself.

But does this mean science has effectively countered the ascetic ideal? Hardly. If anything, it reinforces it. Take Kant's so-called "victory" over theological dogmas concerning God, the soul, freedom, and immortality. Many theologians believed this victory marked a blow to the ascetic ideal, but has it really? In truth, transcendentalists have thrived since Kant. Freed from direct ties to theologians, they've found a new respectability under the guise of science. Kant taught them the tools and methods to pursue their deepest aspirations without theological oversight, cloaked in scientific respectability.

Consider the agnostics, who revere the unknown and the absolute mystery. These modern worshippers elevate their very questioning into a form of divinity. They have turned their reverence for what they cannot comprehend into a new kind of faith. Xaver Doudan remarked on this phenomenon, noting how the habit of admiring the unintelligible has led to confusion, displacing a simpler stance of merely accepting the unknown. Ancient peoples, he speculated, may have been spared such ravages.

Suppose that everything humanity has ever come to know contradicts or horrifies its desires. In such a situation, how convenient it is to shift the blame— not onto the desires themselves but onto the act of knowing! "There is no knowledge; therefore, there is a God."

What an elegant syllogism! What a masterstroke for the ascetic ideal! It manages to transform humanity's dissatisfaction with the world into a divine affirmation of its own worldview. In doing so, the ideal emerges not weakened but stronger, perpetuating its hold over humanity.

Or, does modern history seem to reflect a greater confidence in life or its ideals? Quite the opposite—it prides itself on being merely a mirror, rejecting any teleological purpose or claims of proving anything. It disdains judgment, deeming such roles beneath it, which it might call an act of "good taste." Instead, it avoids both assertions and denials, merely fixing its gaze and "describing." This approach, while seemingly detached, is highly ascetic and, even more so, deeply nihilistic. Make no mistake about that.

Consider the historian's gaze: it is stern, somber, and determined, much like that of a solitary explorer in the Arctic, peering outward as if to avoid looking within or back. What does he see? A barren wasteland. Life lies silent beneath the snow, and the only echoes are bleak murmurs: "Whither?" "Vanity," "Nothingness." This desolate landscape yields nothing—no growth, no vitality— except perhaps the hollow intellectualism of "meta-politics" in St. Petersburg or Tolstoy's overwrought pity.

And then there is that other, perhaps even more modern, school of historians—a group enamored with life and the ascetic ideal alike. They romanticize and fetishize the contemplative life, praising it as though it were an art form, and establishing for themselves a smug little corner of pseudo- intellectual worship. These "sweet intellectuals," with their pretentious adoration of winter landscapes and ascetic ideals, inspire in me a deep and furious longing—for action, for vitality, even for the icy mists of historical nihilism. Yes, I'd prefer the company of those historical nihilists trudging through grey, cold fog over these effete, self- satisfied contemplators.

But worse still are the "objective" historians—those detached scholars perched on their worm-eaten chairs, feigning neutrality while oozing hypocrisy.

They are neither fully priests nor wholly men of passion; instead, they are grotesque hybrids, half-priest and half-satyr, their entire existence marked by a false refinement. Renan, for instance, reeks of perfume but lacks substance, a perfect example of this type. Such figures make me bristle with irritation. They sap my patience, and their very presence enrages me more than the supposed "play" of history itself. How could one not feel disdain? These eunuchs of thought, these weak-kneed admirers of ascetic ideals, deserve nothing but contempt.

Nature, in its wisdom, granted horns to the bull and teeth to the lion. For what purpose did it give me feet, if not to kick? Yes, kick—to trample down these cowardly intellectuals, these groveling contemplators who flinch at vitality and flirt shamelessly with ascetic ideals. They are hypocrites, eunuchs, and frauds, wrapping themselves in the guise of wisdom or objectivity, but inside, they are hollow. They are tragic clowns posing as priests, agitators masquerading as heroes, and opportunists exploiting idealism for personal gain.

Take, for example, the modern Anti-Semites, who cloak themselves in the supposed virtue of "Christian-Aryan honour." They roll their eyes and posture with cheap moralistic tricks, aiming to manipulate the most gullible elements of society. Their success reveals the sad state of modern intellectual life, particularly in Germany, where the mind has been dulled by an unhealthy diet of newspapers, politics, beer, and Wagnerian bombast. Combine this with the isolationist arrogance of "Germany above all," and you have the perfect storm of intellectual stagnation, a kind of mental paralysis that grips the nation and prevents any genuine progress or vitality.

All reverence to the ascetic ideal, but only insofar as it is honest and believes in itself. When it plays no games or flirts with pretensions, it retains a certain dignity. But the insipid bugs who cling to it, feeding on its infinite aspirations, until even the infinite stinks of their corruption—I cannot abide them. Nor can I stomach the empty facades of life these hypocrites parade, the exhausted souls wrapped in hollow wisdom, or the theatrical agitators hiding their triviality behind grand ideals. They represent everything that stifles life, everything that dulls the spark of vitality and replaces it with the rotting specter of pretense and decay.

Europe today seems consumed by its craving for stimulation. It overflows with ingenious means of excitement, as if it knows no greater need than for stimulants, whether intellectual or alcoholic. This has led to a widespread counterfeit of ideals—a flood of artificial inspirations and theatrical displays of passion. The atmosphere is thick with a pseudo-alcoholic stench of pretense, suffocating and false.

I can only imagine how many shipments of fake idealism, heroic posturing, and melodramatic moralism would need to be exported from Europe to cleanse its air. How many barrels of saccharine pity labeled as "the religion of suffering"? How many props for limp-minded intellects—crutches of righteous indignation? How many actors parading as champions of the Christian moral ideal? There's clearly a new business opportunity here: a trade in small, mass-produced idols of idealism and compliant "idealists." The market is wide open! With boldness—or perhaps just a free, uninhibited hand—one might imagine rebranding the entire world under these ready-made ideals.

But enough! Let's set aside these absurdities and grotesque spectacles of the modern spirit. They elicit as much ridicule as revulsion, and our present problem—the meaning of the ascetic ideal—does not depend on them. I will address these matters in more depth elsewhere, under the title "A Contribution to the History of European Nihilism." This will appear in a larger work I am preparing, The Will to Power: An Attempt at a Transvaluation of All Values. My only reason for mentioning them here is to note a peculiar irony: the ascetic ideal's most dangerous adversaries are not its critics, but its comedians. These performers of the ideal inspire distrust, undermining its seriousness.

In all other domains where intellectual work is done earnestly and authentically, without counterfeit, the ideal is often dispensed with entirely. This abstention is popularly labeled "Atheism," but even this so-called rejection is deceptive. The will to truth, which persists even in atheism, is in fact the most distilled and severe formulation of the ascetic ideal. Stripped of its adornments and external structures, this will to truth represents the ideal's core, not its remnant.

Consider this carefully: unadulterated, honest atheism—breathed in by the most intellectually rigorous minds of our time—does not oppose the ascetic ideal as it might seem. Rather, it is one of its final, logical expressions. It is a culmination, an awe-inspiring catastrophe born from two millennia of training in the pursuit of truth. This discipline has finally forbidden itself from indulging in the "lie" of belief in God.

This trajectory is not unique to Europe. A strikingly similar development occurred in India, providing independent and therefore illustrative evidence of the pattern. The same ideal drove to the same conclusion centuries earlier, culminating with Buddha around 500 years before the European era. This evolution began in the Sāmkhya philosophy and was later popularized by Buddha, transforming it into a religion.

The parallel is fascinating: two cultures, separated by vast distances, reaching the same endpoint through the relentless logic of their ideals. Europe, following its path of rigorous devotion to truth, finds itself arriving at a stark, godless reality—not an opposition to the ascetic ideal, but its ultimate refinement. The story of this ideal is not yet finished, and its ramifications continue to unfold in ways both profound and disquieting.

What, I ask in all seriousness, has truly triumphed over the Christian God? The answer is stated in my Joyful Wisdom, Aphorism 357: "Christian morality itself has triumphed—the idea of truth, taken with increasing seriousness, the intricate subtlety of the Christian conscience transformed and elevated into the scientific conscience, into an intellectual rigor at any cost." Viewing nature as proof of God's benevolence, interpreting history as evidence of divine reason and a moral order, seeing personal experiences as though every event were orchestrated for the salvation of the soul—such ideas are now entirely overturned. The sharper conscience rejects these interpretations, deeming them dishonorable, cowardly, and false. This severity, this demand for intellectual integrity, makes us, indeed, good Europeans, inheritors of the most rigorous self- discipline Europe has ever known.

All great things, however, crumble by their own weight, by acts of self- destruction; this is the law of life, the rule of inevitable "self-mastery" intrinsic to existence itself. Even the lawgiver must eventually face the verdict of his own law: pater e legem quam ipse tulisti—"submit to the law you have made." Christianity as a dogma fell through the consequences of its own morality, and now Christianity as a morality is unraveling in the same way. We are on the verge of this event. Christian truthfulness has led, step by step, to conclusions that ultimately turn against itself. It culminates in the question: "What is the meaning of all will for truth?"

Here lies our challenge, my unknown friends (for I know of no friends yet): what is the sense of our existence if not that the will for truth has become self- aware in us as a problem? With this self-awareness, morality as we know it collapses. This is the grand drama of the next two centuries in Europe—the most terrifying, enigmatic, yet potentially hopeful of all dramas.

Without the ascetic ideal, man—the human animal—lacked meaning. His existence had no purpose, no justification. The question "What is man for?" was met with silence. There was no will for man or the world; a vast emptiness surrounded human existence. Behind every great life echoed an even greater refrain of "Vanity!" The ascetic ideal answered this vacuum. It signified that something was missing—

that man needed justification, explanation, affirmation. He suffered not just physically but from the problem of his own meaning.

Man's issue was not suffering itself, but rather the lack of an answer to the searing question: "Why do we suffer?" The bravest and most resilient of creatures, man does not inherently reject suffering; he embraces it when it has meaning. He seeks suffering if it serves a purpose. What humanity could not bear was the meaninglessness of suffering, and the ascetic ideal gave it meaning. For the first time, suffering was explained. The immense void was filled. The door to suicidal nihilism was shut.

Granted, the explanation brought new and more agonizing suffering— more corrosive, more brutal—but it gave suffering purpose. It recast suffering through the lens of guilt. Despite this, humanity was saved. Man now had meaning and could "will" something—anything. The content of the will mattered less than the act of willing itself. The will was preserved, and with it, humanity was saved from nihilism.

This ascetic ideal, however, expressed profound contempt for life. It represented a hatred of the human, a disdain for the animal, and an aversion to the material. It loathed the senses, feared reason, rejected happiness, and recoiled from beauty. It yearned to escape illusion, change, growth, decay, desire—even life itself. At its core, the ascetic ideal revealed a will for Nothingness—a will fundamentally opposed to life. Yet it remains a will.

And as I said at the start: humanity would rather will Nothingness than not will at all.

Peoples and Countries

The Europeans today see themselves as the highest examples of humanity on Earth.

A common trait of Europeans is the inconsistency between their words and actions, unlike the people of the East, who stay true to themselves in daily life. The way Europeans established colonies can be explained by their nature, which resembles that of a predator.

This inconsistency stems from Christianity having abandoned the class it originally came from.

This marks a significant difference between us and the Greeks: their morals were shaped by the ruling classes. The morality we see in Thucydides is the same as the one that erupted in Plato's time. Honesty, for example, saw an effort during the Renaissance, often to benefit the arts. Michelangelo's view of God as the "Tyrant of the World" reflected an honest perspective.

I hold Michelangelo in higher regard than Raphael because Michelangelo, through all the Christian limitations of his era, glimpsed a nobler cultural ideal than the one embodied by Christian-Raphaelite art. Raphael merely and respectfully celebrated the values handed down to him without striving for something beyond. Michelangelo, in contrast, grappled with the immense challenge of creating new values. He sought to embody the conqueror perfected, the one who must first overcome his inner hero, a figure standing at the highest pedestal, mastering even his pity, and ruthlessly destroying anything that does not reflect his vision. Michelangelo at times surpassed his age and Christian Europe. However, he often yielded to the softer, eternal feminine elements of Christianity. In the end, it seems he abandoned the bold ideal of his greatest moments—a vision too immense for anyone but a man in his prime to carry. As he aged, he could no longer bear it. To fulfill his ideal, he would have had to destroy Christianity itself, but he lacked the philosophical depth to do so.

Perhaps only Leonardo da Vinci among the artists achieved a truly post- Christian perspective. Leonardo seemed to carry within him an understanding of the East—the "land of dawn"— both internally and externally. There is something transcendent and silent about him, a trait shared by all who have seen too much of both the good and the bad in the world.

How much we have learned in just fifty years! The Romantic School and its belief in "the people" have been entirely discredited. Homeric poetry is not "popular" poetry. The powers of nature are no longer deified. Relationships between languages no longer imply relationships between races. There is no mystical contemplation of the supernatural, no hidden truth in religion.

The question of truthfulness has become a completely new challenge. I am amazed. From this perspective, figures like Bismarck seem guilty due to carelessness, and Richard Wagner seems culpable for his lack of humility. Even Plato's noble falsehoods (pia fraus) and Kant's derivation of the Categorical Imperative now appear flawed, as these ideas were not truly their own beliefs.

In the end, even doubt turns upon itself, leading to doubt about doubt. The question of the value of truthfulness and how far it should go lies before us.

What I appreciate in the German character is its Mephistophelian quality. However, to truly understand this, one must have a greater concept of Mephistopheles than Goethe had. Goethe reduced Mephistopheles to make his "inner Faust" appear larger. The true German Mephistopheles is far more dangerous, daring, wicked, and cunning—yet also more open and honest. Consider the character of Frederick the Great or, even more so, Frederick II of Hohenstaufen.

The true German Mephistopheles crosses the Alps and claims everything he sees as his own. Then, like Winckelmann or Mozart, he collects himself. He views Faust and Hamlet as exaggerated figures made for ridicule, and he even looks at Luther the same way. Goethe, during his better German moments, likely laughed quietly at such things. But even Goethe could not avoid slipping back into his more somber moods.

Perhaps the Germans simply grew up in the wrong environment! There is something within them that could have been Hellenic— something that stirs when they come into contact with the South, as seen in Winckelmann, Goethe, and Mozart. However, we must remember that as a culture, the Germans are still young. Luther remains their last significant historical figure, and their most recent defining book is still the Bible. The Germans have never truly "moralized" in a philosophical sense. Even their diet has been a curse, contributing to a certain Philistinism.

The Germans are a dangerous people, experts at inventing intoxicants of all kinds. Gothic art, rococo (as Semper described), their sense of history and exoticism, Hegel, Richard Wagner— even Leibniz, who still exerts influence today—all are evidence of this. They even turned the servile spirit into an ideal, celebrating it as the virtue of scholars, soldiers, and the humble-minded. Germans may well be the most complex and mixed people on Earth.

They are "the people of the middle," inventors of porcelain and a peculiar type of bureaucratic Privy Councillor, resembling something out of Chinese tradition.

The smallness and pettiness of the German soul were not caused by their history of small states. History shows that people from even smaller states could still be proud and independent. Nor does a large state automatically foster freer, stronger souls. A man whose spirit bows to the command, "Thou shalt and must kneel!"—a man whose very body instinctively submits to titles, medals, and favors from above—will bow even lower under a greater ruler than under a lesser one. There is no doubt about this.

In contrast, in the lower classes of Italy, there is still a sense of aristocratic self-assurance. The discipline and self-respect that come from a long history of greatness are still visible. A poor Venetian gondolier cuts a more impressive figure than a Privy Councillor from Berlin and is, in many ways, the better man. Ask the women—they know this.

Most artists, even the greatest among them, have historically come from the serving classes. Whether they served nobility, princes, women, or the masses, they remained tied to their patrons, not to mention their dependence on the Church and moral conventions.

Rubens, for example, painted the nobility of his time, but he adhered to their vague notions of taste rather than his own sense of beauty. He worked against his personal standards.

Van Dyck, however, was nobler in this regard. He elevated those he painted, infusing them with qualities he admired most. He did not lower himself to match them; instead, he brought them up to his level through his art.

The artist's submissive humility to his audience, which Sebastian Bach revealed in bold and shocking terms in the dedication of his High Mass, may be harder to detect in music, but it is deeply ingrained. If I were to explain my views on this subject, I might not even find a willing audience.

Chopin, like Van Dyck, carried himself with distinction. Beethoven had the proud spirit of a peasant, while Haydn carried the pride of a servant. Mendelssohn, too, had a natural elegance, much like Goethe.

German scholars with wit have always been few—countable on one hand— while the rest possess understanding, and some, fortunately, that famous "childlike quality" that enables them to intuitively sense things. This ability has led German science to uncover phenomena that we can scarcely imagine—and which, perhaps, do not exist. Yet, this quality of "divination" is not shared by the Jews among the Germans.

Just as French scholars reflect the wit and courtesy of French society, Germans mirror the deep, contemplative seriousness of their mystics and musicians, along with a certain naive childishness. Italians, on the other hand, exude a sense of republican refinement and artistry; they can appear noble and proud without slipping into vanity.

It is my hope that more of Germany's talented individuals will eventually gain enough self-control to abandon their poor taste for affectation and sentimental gloom. Such men will, I trust, turn against the influences of Richard Wagner and Schopenhauer. These two figures, dangerous as they are, flatter Germany's most perilous traits and lead the nation toward decline. Instead, a stronger and more promising future lies with the legacy of Goethe, Beethoven, and Bismarck, not with such deviations from the path. After all, Germany has yet to produce true philosophers.

The peasant represents the most common form of nobility because he relies primarily on himself. Peasant blood remains the strongest in Germany, as seen in figures like Luther, Niebuhr, and Bismarck. Regarding Bismarck, one cannot ignore his Slavic ancestry. German faces often reveal this mixture—those with vigorous, masculine blood left Germany for foreign lands, while the remaining population, largely docile and subservient, saw improvement through an infusion of Slavonic elements. Today, the Brandenburg and broader Prussian nobility, as well as the peasants from specific northern regions, embody the most masculine natures in Germany. It is natural for such men to rule; indeed, the future of German culture rests with the sons of Prussian officers.

Germany has always suffered from a lack of wit. Even average minds achieve high honors there simply because they are uncommon. Qualities like diligence, persistence, and a dispassionate, critical perspective are what Germany values most. These traits have allowed German scholarship and the German military system to dominate Europe.

Parliaments can be of use to a strong and capable statesman; they provide something stable to rely on, something that can bear responsibility. However, Germany should not adopt the counting obsession and faith in majorities seen in Latin nations. There is still an opportunity to innovate in politics, and universal suffrage, which is relatively new and could easily be uprooted, should not be allowed to take deeper root. It was introduced only as a temporary solution to pressing problems.

Can anyone genuinely care about the German Empire as it stands? Where is its new and innovative thinking? If it is merely a new combination of power, that's even worse—especially if it lacks a clear vision. Peace and laisser - aller are not the kind of politics I respect. What interests me in Germany is the potential to rule effectively and to champion the most elevated ideas.

The greatest threat in the world today is England's narrow-mindedness. Remarkably, I observe more ambition for greatness among Russian Nihilists than among English Utilitarians. To achieve true mastery, Germany must forge a union with the Slavic races and incorporate the skills of the Jews, who are the most capable financiers.

To achieve this, several elements are necessary: (a) A firm grasp of reality. (b) Abandoning the English principle of popular representation and replacing it with representation of major interests. (c) An unconditional alliance with Russia and a joint strategy to ensure that English schemes have no influence in Russia. The future must not be Americanized. (d) Nationalistic politics are unsustainable, and the entanglement of Christian ideals is a major hindrance. In Europe, all rational minds are skeptics, even if they do not openly admit it.

I see beyond these national conflicts, new empires, and whatever else appears on the surface. My true concern is with what I perceive slowly taking shape—the vision of a United Europe. This has been the only meaningful labor, the singular impulse in the souls of all the broad-minded and forward-thinking individuals of this century. Their aim has been to prepare a new synthesis, an effort to anticipate and shape the future of "the European." Only in moments of weakness or as they grew older did they revert to the narrow nationalism of "Fatherland" sentiments—then they once again became "patriots." Figures such as Napoleon, Heinrich Heine, Goethe, Beethoven, Stendhal, and Schopenhauer come to mind. Perhaps even Richard Wagner, with his peculiar brand of German obscurity, belongs among them, though his inclusion warrants some hesitation.

Supporting the minds that seek this unity is a significant and clarifying economic reality: the small states of Europe—our current kingdoms and empires—will soon become economically unsustainable. The frenzied, unregulated competition for control of local and international trade is pushing Europe toward amalgamation into a single power. Money is driving this necessity. For Europe to effectively engage in the looming struggle for global dominance (and it is easy to imagine against whom this struggle will be fought), an agreement with England will likely become unavoidable. England's colonies will be essential in this endeavor, just as modern Germany, in its emerging role as broker and middleman, will find itself reliant on the colonial assets of Holland.

It is clear that no one believes England can maintain its current global role alone for another fifty years. The impossibility of preventing homines novi from entering government will undermine her stability, while the constant rotation of political parties will obstruct any efforts requiring long-term planning. Today, a man must first be a soldier to secure his reputation as a merchant later. Suffice it to say, the next century will likely follow the path laid by Napoleon—the foremost figure of his era and the most innovative and visionary of modern times. For the challenges of the coming century, the methods of popular representation and parliamentary governance seem woefully inadequate.

Europe's condition in the next century will once again demand the cultivation of manly virtues, as life will be defined by constant danger. Universal military service already serves as a curious counterbalance to the softness introduced by democratic ideals, born as it was out of the nations' struggles. And what is a nation?

A group of people who speak the same language and consume the same news. These groups call themselves "nations" and are all too eager to trace their ancestry and history to a single, unbroken source. Yet, even with the help of the most outrageous falsehoods about the past, they have never fully succeeded in doing so.

What confusion and falsehood must exist for questions of "race" to even be raised in the chaotic mixture that is modern Europe! (Assuming, of course, that the origins of these writers are not in some far-off place like Horneo or Borneo.) A simple principle: avoid associating with anyone who participates in the deceitful "race" charade.

With the freedom of travel available today, people of like minds and shared heritage can gather and create communities with shared customs and practices. This is how nations can be overcome. To make Europe a true center of culture, we must rise above the foolishness of national divisions. At higher levels, there is already an interconnectedness that we cannot ignore. Think of France and German philosophy, Richard Wagner and Paris during the 1830s to 1850s, or Goethe and Greece. There is a natural momentum toward unifying Europe's past in the minds of its greatest thinkers.

Humanity still has much ahead of it—how could anyone believe the ideal lies in the past? Perhaps the past can only offer meaning when seen in contrast to our present, which might well be a lower phase of development.

This persistent uncertainty haunts us, keeping us awake, raising questions that no one wants to acknowledge. It's our riddle, our Sphinx, standing near more than one precipice. We suspect that today's Europeans are deeply mistaken about what they value most, and some indifferent, childlike force—a pitiless demon— seems to toy with our passions and ideals, just as it has perhaps toyed with all that has lived and loved before us.

I suspect that much of what we Europeans admire today—values like "humanity," "sympathy," and "pity"—might have some worth only because they weaken and tame certain powerful, primal drives. Over time, however, these virtues seem to shrink the potential of the human type, reducing us to mediocrity. If I may use a desperate phrase for a desperate situation: all of this leads to the belittling of man. For an epicurean god watching this human comedy unfold, it must be amusing to see Europeans believe, with all their moral earnestness and self-satisfaction, that they are advancing. The truth, however, is that they are sinking—lower and lower. By cultivating herd-friendly virtues and suppressing the contrary qualities that could create a new, stronger, and more masterful race, we are merely refining the herd-animal within man. And yet, man remains the animal that has not yet stabilized itself.

Genius and the times in which it arises are intricately connected. Heroism, for example, is not a form of selfishness—it often leads to ruin. The strength of an individual often finds its direction shaped by the era into which they are born, giving rise to the misconception that such a person is a product of their time. In reality, this strength could manifest in many different ways. There is always a disconnect between the individual and their time. Public opinion tends to celebrate the herd instinct—the instinct of the weak—while the strong individual fights for ideals that defy this collective mindset.

The looming fate of Europe is clear: her strongest individuals emerge rarely, and even then, often too late in life. In their youth, they are already burdened by sorrow, disillusionment, and a darkness of mind. This happens because, with the intensity of their strength, they confront the full weight of their era's despair— the despair of knowledge and disillusionment—and drain it completely. Yet, this is the ultimate test of their power: they must rise above the sickness of their age to find their own health. Their distinction is marked by their late blooming—late joy, late folly, and a late but exuberant springtime of spirit.

But here lies the danger of our time: everything we cherished in our youth has betrayed us. Even our last love—the one we placed in Truth herself— threatens to betray us if we are not careful. Let us guard this final love with vigilance, for it represents our deepest acknowledgment and our most profound hope.

The End

Twilight of the Idols

Friedrich Nietzsche

Prologue

To stay cheerful while dealing with a grim and extremely serious task is no small artistic skill. Yet, what could be more essential than cheerfulness? Nothing is ever truly successful unless vibrant energy has helped create it. Only extra strength proves real power. A rethinking of all values—a question so dark and massive that it even casts a shadow over the one who raises it—is a task so heavy with consequence that anyone who takes it on must occasionally step into the sunlight to shake off a seriousness that becomes overwhelming, unbearably so. This goal justifies any method, and every event along the way becomes an unexpected benefit. Above all, war. War has always been the ultimate strategy for those who have delved too deeply into their own thoughts or grown too profound; a wound provokes the strength to heal.

For many years, I've lived by a saying, though I'll keep its origin a secret from curious scholars: "The spirit grows, virtue flourishes through a wound."

At other times, another way to recover, one I prefer even more, is to question idols. There are more idols than truths in the world, and this is why I have such a "sharp eye" for this world. It is also why I have such a "sharp ear." To ask questions of these idols with a hammer, and maybe hear that familiar hollow sound that comes from something empty—what joy this brings to someone who listens carefully, even with a mind attuned to what isn't spoken. For an old psychologist and Pied Piper like me, even the things that wish to remain silent cannot help but reveal themselves.

This book, as its title suggests, is mainly a kind of relaxation, a flash of light, a playful escape for a psychologist in his free time. But could it also be a new kind of battle? Are we once again questioning new idols? This small work is a bold declaration of war. As for questioning idols, this time, it isn't just the idols of the present day but the eternal ones that are struck with a hammer, as though they were tuning forks. These idols are certainly the oldest, the most self-assured, and the most puffed-up. None are more hollow. Yet this doesn't change the fact that they are believed in more than any others. They are never even called idols—at least, not the most revered ones among them.

Chapter 1
Maxims – And Missiles

Idleness is the root of all psychology. What? Does that mean psychology is a kind of vice? Even the bravest among us rarely has the courage to face what they truly know. Aristotle said that to live alone, a person must be either an animal or a god. But there's a third option missing: one must be both—a philosopher.

"All truth is simple."—Isn't that a double lie? Sometimes, I choose to remain blind to certain things. Wisdom places limits even on knowledge. A person recovers best from their extraordinary nature—from their intellect—by letting their instincts take over for a while.

So which is it? Is humanity just a mistake made by God? Or is God simply a mistake made by humanity?

From life's school of war: That which doesn't kill me makes me stronger.

Help yourself, and others will help you too. This is the true meaning of loving your neighbor.

A person should never be ashamed of their actions. Once a deed is done, they shouldn't disown it. Feelings of guilt are indecent.

Can a donkey be tragic? To be crushed under a burden it can neither carry nor throw off—isn't this the fate of a philosopher?

If someone knows why they exist, they can figure out how to live. Happiness isn't the goal of life; only the English make that their aim.

Man created woman—out of what? Out of a rib taken from his god, from his "ideal."

What are you searching for? Do you wish to multiply yourself tenfold, a hundredfold? Are you seeking followers? Look for zeros, not people!

Those of us who belong to the future, like myself, are harder to understand than those who mirror their time, but we're treated with more respect. Simply put: we are never fully understood— that's why we have authority.

On women: "Truth? Oh, you don't understand truth! Isn't it an insult to all our sense of modesty?"

There is an artist after my own heart, humble in his needs. He only desires two things: his bread and his art—panem et Circem.

Those who cannot impose their will onto the world at least give it some meaning. They believe there's already a will within it. (This is the essence of faith.)

What? You chose virtue and a heart full of passion, yet you still glance enviously at the rewards of the shameless? But by choosing virtue, you've renounced all "advantages"... (this belongs nailed to the door of an anti-Semite).

The perfect woman writes literature as if it were a minor vice, a passing experiment, all the while looking around to see if anyone is noticing—and hoping that someone does.

One should only choose situations where fake virtues are unnecessary, where, like a tightrope walker on their rope, one must either fall, stand firm, or find a way out.

"Evil men have no songs."—How, then, do the Russians have songs?

"German intellect"—for eighteen years this phrase has been a contradiction in terms.

When a man tries to find the origins of everything, he becomes like a crab. The historian always looks backward; eventually, he even starts believing backward.

Feeling content keeps a person from catching a cold. Has a woman who knew she was well-dressed ever gotten sick?—No, not even if she was barely covered by rags.

I distrust anyone who builds elaborate systems and avoid them. The desire to create a system shows a lack of honesty.

Man thinks women are profound—why? Because he can never fully understand them. Women are not even shallow.

When a woman has masculine virtues, she can make you want to run away.

When she doesn't have any masculine virtues, she runs away herself.

"How often conscience used to sting in the past! It must have had strong teeth back then! But today, what's gone wrong?"—A question for the dentist.

Mistakes made in haste rarely come alone. The first time, a person always overdoes things. Because of that, they make a second mistake, where they end up doing too little.

When a worm is stepped on, it curls up. This shows its caution—it lowers the chances of being stepped on again. In moral terms, this is called humility.

There is a kind of hatred for lies and deceit that comes from a sharp sense of humor. There is also the same hatred, but born from cowardice—the fear of lying because it's forbidden by divine law. Too cowardly to lie...

What tiny things bring happiness! The sound of bagpipes. Life without music would be a mistake. The German even imagines God as a singer.

"One can only think and write while sitting" (G. Flaubert). Now I've got you, you nihilist! Living a sedentary life is the true sin against the Holy Spirit. Only the thoughts that come to you while walking have any real worth.

Sometimes, we psychologists are like restless horses, growing uneasy as we see our own shadow rise and fall before us. A psychologist must look away from himself if he wants to see anything clearly.

Do we immoralists harm virtue in any way? No more than anarchists harm royalty. In fact, only after being shot at have princes returned to their thrones with greater strength. The moral of the story: morality must be tested by attack.

Are you rushing ahead?—Are you doing so as a leader or as an exception? Or perhaps you're just running away?... This is the first question of conscience.

Are you authentic, or are you just acting? Are you the real thing or merely a representative of it? Or, worse, are you just a copy of an actor?... This is the second question of conscience.

The disappointed man says: "I searched for great men, but all I found were imitators of their ideals."

Are you someone who observes from the sidelines, or someone who lends a hand? Or are you someone who looks away or even turns their back? This is the third question of conscience.

Do you want to follow, lead, or walk your own path alone? A person must know what they desire—and that they truly desire something. This is the fourth question of conscience.

They were merely rungs on my ladder, steps I used to climb higher. For that purpose, I had to move past them. But they thought I wanted to stop and rest on them.

Does it matter whether others agree that I'm right? I am far too right. And the one who laughs best today will also laugh last.

The formula for my happiness: a Yes, a No, a straight path, and a goal.

Chapter 2
The Problem of Socrates

Throughout history, the wisest minds have always agreed on one thing: life is not good. No matter the time or place, their words have been the same— filled with doubt, sadness, weariness, and even hostility toward life. Even Socrates, in his final moments, said: "To live is to be sick for a long time. I owe a cock to the god Æsculapius." Even Socrates had had enough of life. But what does that mean? What does it suggest? In the past, people would have said—and it was said loudly, especially by the Pessimists—"Surely there must be some truth in this! The agreement of the wisest proves it." Should we say the same thing today? Can we?

Instead, we now respond: "Surely there must be some sickness here." These so-called great thinkers of every age need to be examined more closely! Could it be that they all shared something physically or mentally fragile, something decadent? Is it possible that wisdom comes to earth like a crow drawn to the faint smell of decay?

This bold and disrespectful thought—that these great thinkers were actually signs of decline—first came to me in connection with a case where both scholarly and common opinions stood firmly against my own view. I came to see Socrates and Plato as symptoms of a culture in collapse, as tools of the disintegration of Greece, as fake Greeks, even anti-Greek (this was my argument in The Birth of Tragedy, 1872). The agreement of these sages— the consensus sapientium, as I increasingly realized—was not evidence that they were right about life. Instead, it suggested that they all shared some underlying physical or mental weakness that made them take the same negative stance toward life. Their judgments about life, whether positive or negative, are not true in themselves. Their value lies only in what they reveal about their creators. Such judgments are symptoms, and nothing more. In themselves, these opinions about life are meaningless.

You must grasp this critical idea: the value of life cannot be measured. A living person cannot judge it because they are too involved—they are part of the conflict, not a neutral observer. A dead person cannot judge it either, for obvious reasons. For a philosopher to see life's value as a problem suggests something is flawed in their perspective. It raises a question about their wisdom—or even their lack of wisdom.

Could it be that all these so-called great thinkers were not only signs of decline but also not wise at all? Let us now return to the case of Socrates.

Judging by his origins, Socrates came from the lowest social class—Socrates was part of the common mob. You know, and can still observe in the descriptions of him, how remarkably ugly he was. In Greek society, where beauty was highly valued, ugliness was not only an objection but often taken as evidence of deeper flaws. Was Socrates truly Greek? Ugliness often reflects a thwarted or disrupted development, or perhaps one stunted by mixed influences. In other cases, it signals a degenerative decline. Anthropologists who study criminals say that the typical criminal is often ugly: monstrum in fronte, monstrum in animo—a monster in appearance, a monster in spirit. Does that mean the criminal is a degenerate? Was Socrates, then, a typical criminal?

This idea wouldn't conflict with the infamous judgment made about Socrates by a physiognomist, which deeply upset his friends. While passing through Athens, a foreigner skilled in reading faces told Socrates directly that he was a monster and that his body harbored every kind of vice and passion. Socrates simply replied: "You know me, sir!"

Not only do Socrates' wild and chaotic instincts point to degeneracy, but so do his extreme reliance on logic and the peculiar malice that seemed tied to his disfigured features. We must also not forget his auditory hallucinations, which he religiously interpreted as "the demon of Socrates." Everything about him was excessive, exaggerated, almost comical—a caricature. His nature was also secretive, filled with hidden motives and underlying currents. I attempt to understand the strange personality behind the Socratic equation: Reason = Virtue = Happiness. This is perhaps the strangest formula ever devised, and it fundamentally contradicted the instincts of the earlier Greeks.

With Socrates, Greek taste shifted toward dialectics. What happened as a result? First, the refined and noble taste of earlier Greek culture was overthrown. Dialectics allowed the common crowd to rise to prominence. Before Socrates, the art of argument was avoided in polite society; it was considered improper and even disgraceful. Young men were warned against indulging in it. Arguing and constantly explaining oneself were seen as suspicious behaviors. Honest people, like honest things, don't need to constantly justify themselves. It was considered poor form to put everything on display. Anything that required proof was seen as having little inherent value.

In societies where authority was respected, where people gave commands rather than explanations, the dialectician was viewed as a kind of jester. People laughed at him and didn't take him seriously. Yet Socrates, a master of dialectics, managed to make people take him seriously. How did this happen? What was going on?

A person resorts to dialectics only when they have no other options available. People know that using it creates suspicion and that it's not particularly persuasive. Nothing is more easily overturned than the effect of a dialectical argument—this is clear from the experience of any debate or discussion. Dialectics can only be a last resort, the weapon of someone who has no other tools left. One must be desperate to demand their rights this way; otherwise, they wouldn't need to rely on it. This is why the Jews became skilled in dialectics.

Reynard the Fox was a dialectician. But what about Socrates—was he one too?

Is Socratic irony a form of rebellion, a weapon of resentment from the common people? Did Socrates, oppressed and suffering, enjoy his inherent cruelty by inflicting sharp attacks through his arguments? Was he taking revenge on the noblemen he managed to charm? As a dialectician, a person wields a ruthless weapon; they can dominate and even humiliate their opponents. By defeating someone in debate, the dialectician undermines them; their victory is always a compromise. The dialectician forces their opponent to prove they're not a fool, which often provokes anger and renders them defenseless. A dialectician paralyzes their opponent's thinking. Could dialectics, for Socrates, have been a form of revenge?

I have explained why Socrates could repel people; now it's just as important to understand why he was so captivating. One reason is that he invented a new kind of Agon, a competitive struggle, becoming the first master of verbal combat in Athens' elite circles. He charmed others by appealing to the Greek love of competition—he transformed intellectual debate into a new kind of contest between men and youths. Socrates also had an intense and magnetic personality, one deeply rooted in eroticism.

But Socrates saw even further. He understood his noble Athenian peers better than they understood themselves. He recognized that his situation—his unusual inner conflict—was not unique. The same kind of decline was quietly spreading everywhere: ancient Athens was dying. Socrates realized that the entire world needed him—his method, his remedy, and his unique technique for self-discipline and survival. Everywhere, instincts were in chaos; everywhere, people were teetering on the edge of excess. The monstrum in animo—the monster within—had become a widespread threat. "Instincts must be tamed," he thought. "We need to find a counterforce, a ruler stronger than they are."

When the physiognomist unmasked Socrates, calling him a volcano of evil desires, Socrates, the great Master of Irony, uttered a few revealing words that explain his nature. "That is true," he admitted, "but I overcame them all."

How did Socrates manage to master himself? His case was, at its core, simply the most extreme and visible example of a widespread crisis. It was a time when no one could control themselves, and instincts constantly clashed with one another. As the clearest example of this disorder, Socrates fascinated people. His shocking ugliness made him impossible to ignore, and his ability to present himself as a solution—a cure for this state— made him even more compelling.

When a man feels compelled, as Socrates did, to turn reason into a tyrant, it is a clear sign that something else is attempting to seize control. In Socrates' case, reason was seen as a savior. Neither Socrates nor his followers had the freedom to choose whether to be rational—they had no choice. At that time, being rational was mandatory, a last resort. The intensity with which all of Greek thought embraced reason reveals the severity of their situation: humanity was at a critical crossroads. The options were stark— either perish or cling desperately to excessive rationality.

The moral focus of Greek philosophy from Plato onward, and its reverence for dialectics, stemmed from a pathological state. The equation Reason =

Virtue = Happiness essentially meant: we must follow Socrates' example and constantly confront our dark passions with the light of reason. We must prioritize cleverness, precision, and clarity above all else. To yield to instinct or the unconscious was seen as a descent into chaos.

I have now explained why Socrates was so captivating: he appeared as a healer, a savior. But should we examine the flaws in his faith in "reason at any cost"? It was an illusion, a self- deception among philosophers and moralists, to believe they could free themselves from decline simply by fighting against it. This approach cannot lead to liberation. The tools they used, the path they chose as a solution, were themselves symptoms of the very degeneration they sought to overcome. They only altered the form of the problem—they did not eliminate it. Socrates was a misunderstanding. The entire morality of "improvement," including that of Christianity, was also a misunderstanding.

The brightest light of reason—this insistence on clarity, coldness, caution, and conscious control—opposed to instinct and detached from it, was itself a disease, simply a different kind of sickness. It was not a path back to "virtue," "health," or "happiness." To be forced to fight against one's instincts is the very definition of degeneration. As long as life is ascending, happiness is synonymous with instinct.

Did Socrates, the most intelligent of self-deceivers, understand this? Did he admit it to himself at the end, in his brave acceptance of death? Socrates wanted to die. It wasn't Athens that gave him the hemlock—it was his own hand. He pushed Athens to hand him the poisoned cup. "Socrates is not a doctor," he may have whispered to himself. "Only death can heal this. Socrates himself has simply been sick for a very long time."

Chapter 3

"Reason" In Philosophy

You ask me what defines the peculiarities of philosophers? For example, their lack of a sense of history, their disdain for the idea of change, and their obsession with preserving things like the ancient Egyptians did. They believe they honor something by removing it from its history, placing it "under the aspect of eternity"—essentially turning it into a mummy. For thousands of years, philosophers have dealt with mummified ideas; nothing alive has ever emerged from their work. These worshippers of concepts kill and preserve things when they idolize them—they endanger the life of everything they claim to revere. To them, death, change, aging, and even growth and creation are flaws, even arguments against life itself. What is, they claim, cannot change; and what changes, they insist, is not real.

All philosophers believe—desperately—in the idea of Being. But because they cannot grasp it, they search for reasons why this understanding is denied to them. "There must be some illusion, some trick, preventing us from knowing the true nature of Being," they say. "Where is this deceiver?" Then, triumphantly, they declare: "We've found it—it's sensuality!" The senses, they argue, are immoral in other ways and deceive us about the true world. The moral they draw is this: we must rid ourselves of the illusion brought by the senses, of change, of history, of lies. For them, history is nothing but belief in the senses, belief in falsehood. Their conclusion: we must reject everything the senses tell us. We must reject humanity and everything connected to it. Let us become philosophers—mummies, believers in monotony, grave-diggers! Above all, they cry, let us cast aside the body, this miserable obsession of the senses. The body, they claim, is infected with every flaw of logic and is neither real nor possible, even though it has the audacity to pretend otherwise.

With great respect, I make an exception for Heraclitus. While other philosophers dismissed the senses because they revealed variety and change, Heraclitus dismissed them because they seemed to show permanence and unity. Yet even Heraclitus was unfair to the senses. The senses do not lie, as the Eleatics thought, nor as Heraclitus believed. They don't lie at all. It is our interpretation of what the senses reveal that introduces falsehood—the lies of unity, matter, substance, and permanence. Reason is the source of these distortions. As long as the senses show us a world of change and impermanence, they are truthful. Heraclitus was entirely correct, however, in saying that the idea of Being is an empty illusion. The "apparent" world is the only world that exists; the so-called "true world" is nothing but a false add-on to it.

What delicate instruments our senses are! Take the human nose, for example—no philosopher has ever spoken of it with the reverence and gratitude it deserves. Yet, for now, it is the most finely tuned instrument we have. It can detect even the tiniest changes in motion, subtleties that even a spectroscope cannot measure. Our scientific achievements today reach as far as we have trusted our senses, sharpened them, enhanced them, and followed their evidence to its limits. What lies beyond that is incomplete and not yet science—it is metaphysics, theology, psychology, epistemology, or abstract systems like logic and mathematics. In all of these fields, reality is not even considered, not even as a problem, just as the broader value of these symbolic conventions like logic is not questioned.

Another strange trait of philosophers is just as dangerous. They confuse the last things with the first. They take what appears last— unfortunately, as it often shouldn't appear at all—"the highest concept," the most general, emptiest, and vaguest shadow of reality, and place it at the beginning, treating it as the origin. This, too, reflects their habit of reverence: the highest thing must not have arisen from anything lower, it must not have grown or developed at all. Their moral: anything of the highest rank must be causa sui—its own cause. If something derives from something else, it loses value and becomes suspect.

All the so-called higher values—like Being, the Absolute, Goodness, Truth, and Perfection—are assumed to be of the highest rank. They cannot have evolved; they must be self- caused. Moreover, these concepts must be alike, never in conflict with one another. And so they arrive at their grand concept of "God," the final, most diluted, and emptiest thing, which they declare to be the first cause, the ens r ealissimum, the ultimate reality. Imagine humanity taking the mental cobwebs spun by these diseased minds seriously! And yet, humanity has paid a high price for doing so.

Let us contrast this with how we approach the problem of error and deception in things (and notice, I politely say "we"). In the past, people saw change and evolution as proof that the world was deceptive, that something was leading us astray. Today, however, we understand that the real source of error lies in our rational thinking. Whenever we insist on unity, identity, permanence, substance, cause, materiality, or Being, we are driven into error— despite knowing from careful study that the error lies here.

This is similar to how people once believed their eyes deceived them about the sun's motion. In this case, it isn't our eyes but our language that keeps reinforcing these mistaken concepts. Language was developed in a time when human psychology was still very primitive. If we look at the origins of language metaphysics—that is, reasoning itself—we find it rooted in a kind of fetishism. Language imposes the idea of a doer behind every deed; it assumes that willpower is a cause and that the self, the "ego," is a kind of Being or substance. This faith in the ego as a substance is then projected onto the world, creating the concept of "things." From the ego alone comes the idea of Being.

At the root of all this is a grave mistake: the belief that the will is something active, a force. Now we know it's just a word. Much later, in a far more enlightened world, philosophers marveled at how certain and reliable these categories of reason seemed. They concluded that these concepts could not have come from experience since experience actually contradicts them. Where, then, do they come from? In both India and Greece, people made the same mistake: "We must have lived in a higher world once," they thought, "because we possess reason!" But the truth is, we came from a much simpler and less developed state.

Nothing has been more convincing than the error of Being, as first proposed by the Eleatics. Their concept of Being is supported by every word and sentence we speak! Even those who opposed the Eleatics fell into the trap of their idea, such as Democritus with his theory of the atom. "Reason" in language—what an old and cunning deceiver it is! I suspect we will never rid ourselves of the idea of God as long as we believe in grammar.

To make this important and novel perspective clear, I will summarize it in four points to simplify understanding and encourage discussion.

Proposition One. The arguments claiming this world is only "apparent" actually support its reality. No other kind of reality can be proven.

Proposition Two. The qualities people attribute to the "true Being" of things are actually qualities of nonexistence. The "true world" was constructed by denying the real world, and it is indeed an illusion—a moral and optical trick.

Proposition Three. Imagining another world makes no sense unless there is a deep, instinctual urge to slander, diminish, and distrust this life. In that case, this imaginary "better" world is just an act of revenge against the life we live.

Proposition Four. Dividing the world into a "true" and "apparent" world, whether in Christianity or Kant's philosophy (which is essentially Christianity in disguise), is a sign of decline and a symptom of decaying life. The fact that an artist values appearances more than reality does not contradict this. For the artist, "appearance" is reality, but in a refined, intensified, and improved form. The tragic artist is not a pessimist—they affirm even the most troubling and terrifying aspects of life. They are Dionysian.

Chapter 4
How The "True World"
Ultimately Became a Fable the History of An
Error

The true world is reachable by the wise, the virtuous, and the devout. They live in it—they are it.

(This earliest version of the idea was relatively simple, clever, and convincing. It was essentially a rewording of "I, Plato, am the truth.")

The true world, though unattainable for now, is promised to the wise, the virtuous, and the devout—especially to the sinner who repents.

(The idea evolves: it becomes subtler, more deceptive, more elusive. It takes on a new form—it becomes feminine, it becomes Christian.)

The true world is beyond reach. It cannot be proven or promised, but merely thinking about it provides comfort, obligation, and direction.

(This is essentially the same old sun, but seen through a haze of doubt and skepticism. The idea becomes lofty, pale, northern—Königsbergian.)

The true world—is it unattainable? In any case, it is unattained. And because it is unattained, it is also unknown. As something unknown, it can no longer comfort, save, or command. How could the unknown demand anything of us?

(The first light of dawn. Reason begins to stir and stretch. The cockcrow of positivism.)

The "true world"—an idea that no longer has any use, that no longer demands anything—a pointless, unnecessary idea, now discarded: let us get rid of it!

(The brightness of morning; breakfast; the return of common sense and joy.

Plato blushes in shame, and all free spirits celebrate wildly.)

We have abolished the true world. What remains? The apparent world, perhaps? Certainly not! By getting rid of the true world, we have also done away with the world of appearances!

(Noon; the time of the shortest shadows; the end of the longest mistake; the height of humanity. Thus Spoke Zarathustra begins.)

Chapter 5
Morality as The Enemy of Nature

There is a time when all passions are destructive, dragging people down with their reckless force. But there comes a much later time when passions merge with the spirit and refine themselves—they become "spiritualized." In the past, because of the inherent foolishness of passion, people waged war against it. They committed themselves to eradicating it. All ancient moralists agreed on this point: "Il faut tuer les passions"—passions must be killed. The most famous version of this idea is found in the New Testament, in the Sermon on the Mount, where, let's be clear, things are hardly viewed from an elevated perspective. It says there, for example, about sexuality: "If your eye offends you, pluck it out." Thankfully, no Christian truly follows this advice.

Destroying passions and desires simply because of their foolishness or to avoid the unpleasant outcomes of their excess now seems to us like an even greater form of foolishness. We no longer admire dentists who pull teeth just so they won't ache again. On the other hand, it's fair to say that the soil from which Christianity grew could never have allowed for the idea of "spiritualizing passion" to take root. Everyone knows the early Church waged war on intelligence in favor of the "poor in spirit." Under those conditions, how could passions have been fought intelligently? The Church combats passion through methods of removal and suppression. Its solution, its "remedy," is castration. It never asks, "How can desire be refined, elevated, or even sanctified?"

Throughout history, the Church's discipline has always focused on eradicating passions entirely—on destroying sensuality, pride, the thirst for power, the desire for wealth, and even the urge for revenge.

But attacking passions at their roots is the same as attacking life at its source. The Church's approach is fundamentally hostile to life itself.

The same methods—castration and eradication—are instinctively chosen to battle passions by those who are too weak-willed or degenerate to impose some form of moderation. These are the kinds of people who, metaphorically (or even literally), need La Trappe or some extreme declaration of war against their desires, a vast gulf separating them from temptation. Only degenerates need such drastic methods. A weak will—or, more precisely, an inability to resist reacting to stimuli—is itself a form of degeneration.

A radical and absolute hatred of sensuality is always a suspicious sign. It gives good reason to doubt the overall health of the person who takes such an extreme stance. Moreover, this hatred reaches its peak only when such people no longer have the strength of character to commit to the ultimate remedy—to renounce their inner "Satan."

Consider the history of priests, philosophers, and even artists. The most venomous attacks on the senses have not come from those who are impotent or naturally ascetic, but from those who found it necessary to become ascetics. These were people whose inner struggles forced them into extreme positions, and their attacks on sensuality reflect their personal battles more than any genuine wisdom.

The spiritualization of sensuality is called love: this represents a great victory over Christianity. Another triumph is the spiritualization of hostility. This means we are beginning to deeply understand the value of having enemies. In short, we now act and think in the exact opposite way from how we once did. Throughout history, the Church sought to destroy its enemies. But we, the immoralists and Antichrists, see an advantage in the Church's survival. Even in politics, hostility has become more refined—more cautious, thoughtful, and restrained. Nearly every political party now sees its self-interest in ensuring its opposition doesn't collapse. The same is true in global politics.

A new creation—such as the new Empire—needs enemies more than friends. It only becomes necessary as a contrast to what opposes it; it defines itself through opposition. We approach our inner conflicts in much the same way. Here too, we have spiritualized enmity and come to understand its value. A person is productive only when they are rich in opposing instincts; they stay youthful only so long as their soul resists comfort and rejects the yearning for peace.

The "peace of the soul," which Christianity holds as its highest goal, has become entirely foreign to us. Nothing could make us less envious than the moral complacency and contentment of a clean conscience—the happiness of a "moral cow." A man who renounces conflict also renounces a life of grandeur.

Of course, in many cases, what people call "peace of the soul" is really something else, disguised and unable to name itself honestly. Let me, without hesitation or bias, suggest a few examples.

"Peace of the soul" could be the radiant glow of abundant animal energy within the realm of morality or religion. Or it might be the first sign of fatigue, the shadow cast by the evening, as all evenings cast shadows. Or it could be a signal of humid air and southern winds on the horizon. Perhaps it is an unconscious gratitude for good digestion, sometimes mistaken for "brotherly love." It could also be the calmness of someone recovering from illness, savoring every flavor of life anew and waiting patiently. Or it might follow the satisfaction of a powerful passion, the comfort of an unfamiliar fullness.

"Peace of the soul" might be the weariness of our will, desires, and vices as they grow old. Or it could be laziness, dressed up by vanity in the clothes of morality. Sometimes, it's the relief that follows the end of long periods of uncertainty, even if that end is marked by terrible certainty. It might also be the expression of mastery during a creative effort, the deep, steady breathing of someone who has achieved true freedom of will.

Who knows? Perhaps even The Twilight of the Idols is nothing more than a form of "peace of the soul."

Let me lay down a principle: all natural morality—that is, every healthy morality—is guided by the instinct for life. It fulfills one of life's fundamental laws by creating definite rules like "you shall" or "you shall not," and in doing so, it clears obstacles from the path of life. In contrast, morality that opposes nature—which describes almost every morality that has been taught, praised, and preached so far—is aimed directly against life's instincts. It secretly or openly condemns these very instincts. When it says, "God sees into the heart of man," it denies the deepest and most vital desires of life, turning God into life's enemy. The saint, whom God supposedly favors, is nothing more than an ideal eunuch. Life ends where the "Kingdom of God" begins.

If you understand the wickedness of this rebellion against life, which Christian morality has made almost sacred, you also see its emptiness, its falseness, and its absurdity. For any condemnation of life by a living being is merely a symptom of a specific kind of life. The question of whether such a condemnation is right or wrong doesn't even arise. To even approach the question of life's value, one would need to be outside life itself and yet know it as completely as everyone who has ever lived. This makes the question entirely inaccessible to us.

When we speak of values, we do so under the influence and perspective of life itself. Life urges us to create values; life evaluates through us. This means that even morality that opposes life—one that sees God as the rejection and condemnation of life—is still an evaluation of life. But what kind of life does it reflect? I have already answered: it is the perspective of declining, weakened, exhausted, and doomed life. Morality, as it has been understood up to now—as Schopenhauer put it in his idea of

"The Denial of the Will to Life"—is the instinct of degeneration turned into a command. It says, "Perish!" It is the death sentence pronounced by those already marked for death.

Now, consider how absurdly simple it is for someone to say, "Man should be like this or that!" Reality shows us a wondrous abundance of types, an endless variety of forms and transformations. Yet the first petty moralist who comes along declares, "No! Man should be different!" This self-righteous fool even imagines he knows what man should be like. He draws his own face on the wall and proclaims: "Behold the man!"

Even when the moralist addresses an individual and says, "You should be this way or that way!" he still makes a fool of himself. The individual, with their past and future, is part of fate—a law, a necessity added to the universe. To say to someone, "Change yourself," is the same as demanding that the entire world change, even retroactively. These moralists have been consistent in their madness—they wanted man to be different, to be virtuous, to reflect their own image. In doing so, they denied the world itself. This is no small form of insanity! Nor is it a humble kind of arrogance!

Morality, when it condemns for the sake of condemnation itself—without any regard for life's goals, needs, or motives—is a specific kind of error. It is a degenerative quirk that has caused immeasurable harm, and no one should feel pity for it. We, the immoralists, on the other hand, have opened our hearts to understanding, acceptance, and affirmation. We do not reject life lightly; instead, we take pride in saying "yes" to things.

Our vision has widened to include the economy of life—a system that knows how to use even what priests and moralists reject. It finds value even in what the sanctimonious or the sickly-minded condemn. It turns the so-called repulsive elements—priests, bigots, and the "virtuous"—to its own advantage. What is that advantage? We, the immoralists, are the living answer to that question.

Chapter 6
The Four Great Errors

The error of confusing cause and effect—there is no more dangerous mistake than mistaking the effect for the cause.

I call this mistake the fundamental perversion of reason. Yet, this error has been one of humanity's oldest habits, and one that persists even today. In some parts of the world, it has even been elevated to sacred status, taking the form of "religion" and "morality." Every principle put forth by religion and morality is built upon this very error. Priests and moral lawgivers have been the most enthusiastic promoters of this distortion of reason.

Take, for example, the famous book by Cornaro, in which he promotes a strict, modest diet as the key to a long, happy, and virtuous life. This book, widely read and still reprinted in large numbers, has likely caused more harm and shortened more lives than almost any other well-intentioned work—except, of course, the Bible. Why? Because it confuses cause and effect. Cornaro believed his longevity was caused by his restricted diet. However, the truth is that his unique physiology, marked by an unusually slow rate of molecular change and low energy expenditure, was the actual cause of his meager diet. His constitution didn't allow him to eat much—if he had eaten more, he would have fallen ill.

For most people, especially those with a different metabolism, such a diet would be disastrous. A modern scholar, for example, whose nervous energy is rapidly consumed, would waste away on Cornaro's diet. Crede exper to— trust someone who knows from experience.

The same confusion of cause and effect lies at the heart of every religion and morality. Their central message is always: "Do this and avoid that, and you will be happy. Otherwise—" This "otherwise" is an unspoken threat. Every moral or religious imperative repeats this same formula. I call this the original sin of reason—immortal unreason.

But in my hands, this principle is turned on its head. This is the first example of my "transvaluation of all values." A well-constituted person, one who is a masterpiece of nature, instinctively performs certain actions and avoids others. Such a person embodies the natural order and harmony their body expresses. Their virtue is not a cause but an effect of their excellent constitution. Their longevity and ability to have many children are not rewards for their virtue; rather, these qualities result from their robust and healthy nature. This is the true basis of what I call Cornarism.

In contrast, the Church and traditional morality assert, "A race or a people perishes because of vice and luxury." My reinstated reason says the opposite: when a people are already in decline, when they are physically degenerating, vice and luxury naturally emerge. These are not the causes of their downfall but symptoms of their exhaustion. Their declining energy leads them to crave stronger and more frequent stimuli, which is typical of all weakened natures.

Consider a young man who becomes pale and sickly. His friends may blame an illness, but I say the illness itself is merely a symptom of his already weakened state, the result of hereditary exhaustion. Similarly, when a political party makes a fatal mistake, the common view is that the mistake leads to its demise. But my superior understanding of politics says: a party capable of making such errors is already in its death throes. It has lost its instinctual certainty.

Every error, in any context, is the consequence of a degeneration of instincts and a disintegration of the will. This is the essence of what we call "evil." Everything truly valuable arises from instinct and is therefore effortless, necessary, and free. Strain and effort are objections to value. The divine is characterized not by struggle but by lightness—the god has light feet, unlike the hero who battles against obstacles.

The error of false causality also runs deep. Throughout history, humans have believed they understood causality. But where did this belief come from? What gave us such confidence in causality? It came from what we call the "inner facts of consciousness." Yet not one of these so-called facts has ever been proven.

We assumed we were the causes of our own actions, that our will was an undeniable proof of causality. We believed that all the motives for our actions could be found in our consciousness, as if they were sitting there waiting to be uncovered. Without these motives, we thought, we wouldn't be free or responsible. Finally, we believed that thoughts themselves were caused by the ego, the "self."

But now, we have come to our senses. Today, we know none of this is true. The "inner world" is a collection of illusions. The will doesn't cause anything; it doesn't explain anything. It merely accompanies processes and sometimes isn't even present. What we call "motive" is another falsehood, a surface ripple that often conceals the deeper causes of action rather than revealing them. As for the ego, it is now nothing more than a myth, a fiction, an empty word.

What's the result of all this? There are no such things as spiritual causes. The entire foundation of popular experience—our belief that the world is built on causes and effects, wills and spirits—has collapsed. Humanity blissfully projected its own inner illusions onto the world, turning it into a vast system of agents and actions. Man imagined his ego as the root of all things and built the concept of "Being" upon this illusion.

Even the concept of the atom, cherished by physicists, still carries remnants of this old psychological error. And the metaphysicians' notion of the "thing-in- itself" is the ultimate example of this confusion—a disgraceful relic of primitive thinking.

The greatest error of all has been to regard the spirit as a cause, to mistake it for reality, and to use it as a measure of the real. This error was even elevated to the status of a deity—it was called God.

The Error of Imaginary Causes

Starting in the realm of dreams, we often ascribe causes to sensations after the fact. Take, for instance, the sound of a distant cannon shot in a dream. We frequently weave a story around such sensations, turning them into little dramas where we ourselves are the central figures. The sensation lingers, echoing and intensifying, until our instinct for causality demands an explanation. But instead of recognizing the sensation as random, we interpret it as something meaningful—a direct result of a fabricated cause. In dreams, this often leads to a reversal of the natural order of events: the sensation, which should be the starting point, is made the result of the imagined cause. The cannon shot is explained as though it were caused by events that supposedly happened earlier in the dream.

What occurs here? Ideas associated with a particular sensory state are misinterpreted as the cause of that state. This same process happens when we are awake. Many of our general sensations— like tension, pressure, obstacles, or explosions in the interplay of our bodily systems, particularly in the sympathetic nervous system— trigger the instinct to search for a cause. We need an explanation for why we feel good or bad, ill or well. It is not enough for us to simply recognize that we feel a certain way. We only become fully conscious of the feeling when we have assigned it a cause.

Memory plays a key role in this process, unconsciously recalling past states that were similar, along with the causal interpretations we previously attached to them. However, memory rarely retrieves the actual causes. Instead, it presents familiar interpretations. The belief that our thoughts or conscious processes are the causes of these sensations stems from the way memory works. This mechanism leads us to accept a fixed interpretation of causes, one that often hinders or entirely blocks us from investigating the real causes of our sensations.

The Psychological Explanation

Why do we trace the unfamiliar back to the familiar? Because doing so brings relief, comfort, and a sense of control. The unfamiliar provokes fear, anxiety, and unease. Our most basic instinct is to eliminate these uncomfortable feelings. Thus, our first principle becomes: any explanation is better than none at all. Since our goal is simply to free ourselves from troubling ideas, we are not overly picky about the explanations we adopt. The first explanation that makes the unfamiliar seem familiar gives us such comfort that we readily accept it as true.

This process relies on the "proof" of happiness or relief to determine truth. In this way, the instinct for causality is closely tied to feelings of fear and the need to alleviate it. Whenever possible, the question "why?" doesn't just seek any cause but rather a particular kind of cause—one that comforts, liberates, and reassures us.

The easiest way to achieve this is by attributing causes to something we already know, something familiar and stored in memory. The new, unfamiliar factor is excluded from consideration as a possible cause. We prefer explanations that remove the sensation of strangeness, novelty, or unpredictability. Over time, a particular way of explaining causes becomes dominant, solidifies into a system, and eventually crowds out alternative explanations.

For example, a banker instinctively attributes everything to business, a Christian sees sin behind every event, and a young woman interprets everything through the lens of her love life.

The Domain of Morality and Religion as Imaginary Causes

The entire realm of morality and religion can be categorized under the heading of "imaginary causes." Consider how unpleasant sensations are explained in these frameworks. Such sensations are often attributed to malevolent external forces, like evil spirits. For example, the hysteria of women in the past was frequently interpreted as possession by witches. Similarly, feelings of guilt or sinfulness are seen as evidence of moral failings, yet they are often just symptoms of physiological imbalances. People have always found reasons to be dissatisfied with themselves, projecting these feelings onto moral or religious explanations.

Religions often go further, interpreting unpleasant sensations as punishment for wrongdoing, as if suffering proves guilt or sinfulness. Schopenhauer took this idea to its extreme, claiming that all great suffering reveals what we deserve, as it could not happen without a reason rooted in guilt. In this way, morality and religion turn life's natural challenges into accusations and condemnations.

Even physiological conditions like exhaustion or illness are interpreted through this lens. The passions and bodily senses are blamed as causes, and their effects are deemed deserved punishments for indulging in sinful behavior. This moralization of suffering twists natural occurrences into a system of guilt and penalty.

Similarly, pleasant sensations are explained through imaginary causes. They are attributed to faith, good deeds, or divine favor. A "good conscience," for instance, may simply be the result of good digestion, yet it is often interpreted as a reward for moral virtue. Even successful outcomes of endeavors are misattributed; a hypochondriac or someone like Pascal, for example, would not feel general happiness simply because of a fortunate result.

Religious virtues like faith, love, and hope are also misinterpretations. The feelings of strength and abundance that underpin these states are mistaken for their causes. A person trusts in God because they feel strong and peaceful, not the other way around.

Morality and Religion as Psychology of Error

At their core, morality and religion belong to the psychology of error. They consistently confuse cause and effect. They mistake feelings of pleasure or pain for their supposed causes and interpret them through a lens of moral or religious belief. They turn subjective states of consciousness into explanations, obscuring the true causes behind these sensations.

In every case, morality and religion invert the relationship between cause and effect, making them systems of misinterpretation. Truth is conflated with the effects of what is believed to be true, and the underlying processes that produce sensations are hidden behind a false dialect of moral and religious explanations. These systems are not rooted in reality but are deeply embedded in the errors of human psychology.

The Error of Free Will

Today, we have no patience for the concept of "free will." We know too well what it really is: the most audacious theological trick ever devised to make humanity "responsible" in a theological sense—that is, to make humanity dependent on theologians. Let me explain the psychology behind how this sense of responsibility is instilled.

Whenever people assign responsibility to someone, it is driven by the instinct for punishment and judgment. The innocence of Becoming—the natural unfolding of events—is destroyed the moment any state of affairs is attributed to a will, intentions, or deliberate actions. The doctrine of the will was invented primarily as a tool for punishment, specifically to assign guilt.

The entire foundation of ancient psychology, or the psychology of the will, arose because its creators—the priests who ruled early societies—sought to justify their power to punish. They wanted to grant themselves, or their gods, the right to judge and condemn. To make this possible, humanity had to be considered "free," so that individuals could be judged and held guilty. Consequently, every action was framed as voluntary, and the origin of every action was imagined to lie in conscious choice. This fraud became the foundation of psychology: the deliberate falsification of human nature to serve the interests of power and control.

Now, we are moving in the opposite direction. We immoralists are working tirelessly to eliminate the concepts of guilt and punishment from the world. We aim to cleanse psychology, history, nature, and all social customs and institutions of these poisonous ideas. Our most determined adversaries in this effort are the theologians, who still cling to the notion of a "moral order of things." They continue to pollute the innocence of Becoming with the concepts of punishment and guilt. Christianity, in this regard, is nothing more than the metaphysics of the executioner.

What, then, can our teaching be? It is this: No one gives a person their qualities—not God, not society, not parents, not ancestors, and certainly not the person themselves. This nonsensical notion, which has been perpetuated for centuries, was called "intelligible freedom" by Kant and perhaps even earlier by Plato. But it is utterly refuted here.

No one is responsible for their existence, for being the way they are, or for the circumstances in which they find themselves. A person's existence is inextricably linked to the entire chain of events that has been and will be. It is not the product of an intention, a will, or an aim. There is no striving for some "ideal man," "ideal happiness," or "ideal morality." To think otherwise is absurd.

The concept of "purpose" is something we invented—it does not exist in reality. There is no purpose driving existence. Each individual is a necessary part of the whole, a fragment of fate, inseparably bound to the totality of existence. No one can judge, measure, or condemn an individual's existence because to do so would mean judging, measuring, and condemning the entirety of existence. But there is nothing outside the whole to serve as a basis for such judgment.

The liberation we offer is this: no one can be made responsible. Existence cannot be traced to a causa prima—a first cause. The world is not an entity driven by a central consciousness, a divine spirit, or a purpose. This realization restores the innocence of Becoming. It frees the world from the burden of guilt and condemnation.

The concept of "God" has been the greatest obstacle to accepting existence as it is. For centuries, God has been used to justify the idea of ultimate responsibility, judgment, and guilt. But we deny God. We deny responsibility in God. Only by doing so can we truly save the world. This denial restores the innocence of existence and frees us from the chains of metaphysical guilt. This is the great liberation.

Chapter 7
The "Improvers" Of Mankind

You are familiar with my demand upon philosophers: that they rise above the notions of Good and Evil, leaving behind the illusion of moral judgment. This demand arises from a perspective I was the first to articulate—that there are no moral facts. Moral judgment, like religious judgment, believes in unrealities, in things that do not exist. Morality is merely an interpretation of certain phenomena—or, more accurately, a misinterpretation.

Moral judgment belongs to a stage of ignorance, a time when the very idea of reality, the distinction between what is real and imagined, had not yet emerged. At this stage, "truth" was applied to a multitude of things we now consider imaginary. For this reason, moral judgment should never be taken literally. On its own, it is nonsense. However, as a system of signs, it is invaluable to those who understand it. It offers insight into the cultural and psychological conditions of societies that lacked the knowledge to understand themselves. Morality, in essence, is a kind of language, a symptomatology. To make use of it, one must already grasp what it signifies.

Let me offer a preliminary example. Throughout history, certain individuals have sought to "improve" humanity—a goal that has always been closely tied to morality. But beneath this single word, vastly different tendencies are concealed. The "improvement" of humanity has sometimes meant the taming of the wild animal in man, while at other times it has meant the cultivation of a specific type of human being. These two approaches are fundamentally distinct, though both are described as moral.

Take the taming of an animal as an example. To call this process an "improvement" seems almost laughable to modern ears. Anyone who has observed a menagerie knows that animals are not improved there—they are weakened. Their natural power and danger are subdued through fear, pain, and deprivation, transforming them into sick, broken creatures. The same holds true for humanity under the influence of the priestly "improvers."

Consider the Middle Ages, when the Church acted as a menagerie for humanity. The Church hunted down the most vital and noble individuals—the "blond beasts," such as the Germans—and set about "improving" them. But what did this "improved" person look like after the process? He became a shadow of himself, a distorted caricature of humanity. Lured into monasteries, stripped of his instincts, and imprisoned behind oppressive concepts of sin and guilt, he was rendered sick and wretched, filled with self- hatred and suspicion of all that is strong and joyful in life. In short, he became a Christian.

From a physiological standpoint, this "improvement" was no different than what one does to an animal: weakening it by making it sick. The Church understood this strategy well. It ruined man, drained his strength, and then claimed to have made him better.

Now, let us consider a very different example of morality: the deliberate cultivation of a particular type of humanity. The most striking example of this is found in Indian morality as laid out in the Law of Manu. This text describes the structured breeding of four distinct castes: priests, warriors, merchants and farmers, and finally servants (the Sudras). Here, we are no longer dealing with the taming of wild animals. To conceive of such a system presupposes a level of mildness and rationality far beyond that of the lion-tamer.

Emerging from the Christian atmosphere of prisons and hospitals, one can breathe more freely in the world of Manu. Here, the goal is not to break humanity but to cultivate it. The vision is vast, orderly, and noble. By comparison, the New Testament reeks of pettiness and decay. Yet even this grand system had to confront challenges, particularly from those who did not fit into its carefully crafted structure—the "non-caste" people, the Chandala.

For the Chandala, the morality of Manu was as harsh as the Church's morality was to the strong. Unable to assimilate these "mixed" people into the system, Indian morality sought to render them weak and harmless by making them sick. This was a struggle against the sheer numbers of the Chandala, whose very existence threatened the structure of the caste system.

Some of the measures taken against the Chandala are repugnant to modern sensibilities. For instance, the Avadana- Sastra decrees that their diet should consist solely of garlic and onions; they were forbidden access to grains, clean water, or fire. Their drinking water had to be drawn from ditches and animal tracks, and they were prohibited from washing themselves or their clothing. Chandala women were barred from assisting one another during childbirth, and Sudra women were forbidden from helping them as well.

Such sanitary regulations had predictable results: deadly epidemics and venereal diseases ravaged the Chandala population. In response, the Law of the Knife—circumcision for males and genital mutilation for females—was introduced. Manu himself described the Chandala as the offspring of adultery, incest, and crime. Their clothing was to be made from rags taken from corpses, their utensils from broken pottery, and their jewelry from old iron. They were to worship malevolent spirits, wander endlessly, and were even forbidden to write using their right hand or in the direction reserved for virtuous people.

This is the logical outcome of a morality focused on breeding: the deliberate dehumanization of those who threaten the system. The Chandala were treated as the living embodiment of chaos, their suffering justified as the necessary cost of order.

The stark contrast between these two examples—the Christian taming of man and the Indian cultivation of castes—reveals the true diversity hidden within the concept of morality. While both systems aimed to "improve" humanity, their methods and goals were fundamentally different. The Christian moralist sought to weaken and break the strong, while the Indian lawgiver aimed to build a structured and lasting society. Yet both relied on the same principle: to make the undesirable elements weak and subservient, even at the cost of their health and humanity.

These regulations are profoundly revealing: they offer a glimpse into the primal and unfiltered humanity of the Aryans. From them, we see that the concept of "pure blood" is far from innocent—it carries with it a profound and often ruthless seriousness. At the same time, these regulations help us identify the people in whom a deep-seated hatred of this Aryan humanity—the Chandala hatred—has been immortalized. Among these people, this hatred was transformed into both religion and genius.

From this perspective, the gospels are invaluable historical documents, and the Book of Enoch is even more significant. Christianity, having sprung from Jewish roots and comprehensible only in the context of this heritage, represents the exact opposite of the morality of breeding, race, and privilege. Christianity is, at its core, an anti-Aryan religion. It is the transvaluation of all Aryan values— a complete reversal. It is the triumph of Chandala values, the gospel of the poor, the lowly, and the oppressed.

Christianity embodies the general uprising of the downtrodden— the miserable, the failed, and the broken—against the concept of "race." It is the eternal revenge of the Chandala, disguised as the "religion of love."

When comparing the morality of breeding to the morality of taming, we see that the methods employed by each are equally ruthless. Both rely on a deep commitment to immorality in order to enforce their respective visions of morality. One could even propose a principle: to create morality, one must possess an absolute will to immorality.

This paradoxical principle forms the basis of a profound and perplexing problem that I have studied for years: the psychology of those who claim to "improve" humanity. This problem first presented itself to me in the form of a seemingly trivial yet deeply significant phenomenon known as the pia fraus— the "pious fraud." This concept, the shared legacy of all philosophers and priests who have sought to improve mankind, opened the door to my exploration of this issue.

Figures like Manu, Plato, Confucius, and the teachers of Judaism and Christianity have all relied on the pia fraus. None of them ever doubted their right to deceive. Moreover, they never questioned their right to many other tools of manipulation and control.

To summarize this idea in a formula: every method ever used to make humanity "moral" has been, at its core, thoroughly immoral.

Chapter 8
Things the Germans Lack

Among Germans today, it is not enough to simply possess intellect; one must actively claim it, assert it, even lay hold of it.

Perhaps I know the Germans well enough to tell them a few uncomfortable truths. Modern Germany possesses a vast reserve of inherited and cultivated abilities, so vast that it could afford to spend this accumulated wealth liberally for some time. However, what has emerged in modern Germany is not a superior culture, nor refined taste, nor noble instincts for beauty. Instead, it is a set of virtues— admirable, yes, but also heavily pragmatic—more robust and "manly" than those of other European nations.

Germany still demonstrates a remarkable level of good spirits and self- respect, along with strength in human relationships and a reliable sense of mutual obligations. There is an abundance of industriousness and perseverance, paired with an inherited sobriety that seems to require stimulation rather than restraint. It is worth noting that Germans still know how to obey without feeling that obedience diminishes them, and they maintain respect for their opponents rather than despising them.

You can see that I wish to be fair to the Germans; it is my intention not to betray my commitment to balance, even when critiquing them. But fairness requires me to voice my objections as well. Achieving a position of power comes at a cost, for power inevitably stultifies.

Once upon a time, the Germans were known as a nation of thinkers. But do they truly think anymore? Today, Germans seem bored by intellect, mistrustful of it. Politics has consumed the seriousness once reserved for intellectual pursuits. The rallying cry, "Ger many, Ger many above all," seems to have delivered a fatal blow to German philosophy. Abroad, people ask me, "Are there still German philosophers? Are there still German poets? Are there any good German books?" I feel ashamed, though I muster the courage to answer, even in my moments of despair, "Yes, Bismarck!"

But could I dare to reveal what books are actually being read in Germany today? The curse of mediocrity dominates.

What could German intellect have become? Who has not lamented this question! For nearly a thousand years, this nation has deliberately dulled its own edge. Nowhere else have Europe's two great narcotics—alcohol and Christianity—been so excessively and destructively consumed as in Germany. To these, a third opiate has been added, one that could alone have sufficed to extinguish the spark of intellectual daring: music. German music—ponderous, bloated, and stifling—has completed the paralysis of German thought. How much sluggishness, heaviness, dampness, lethargy, and beer-fueled languor are entangled in German intellect!

How can it be that young men who dedicate their lives to intellectual pursuits lack the most basic instinct for intellectual self-preservation and drink beer? The alcoholism of academic youth doesn't prevent them from becoming scholars—after all, one can be a great scholar without being truly intelligent. But in every other respect, this is a disaster. What kind of intellectual softness, what kind of dull degeneration, comes from beer?

I once pointed out an infamous example of this kind of intellectual degeneration: the decline of David Strauss, once a leading German free spirit, who devolved into the author of a pedestrian gospel and a "New Faith." His intellect succumbed not just to mediocrity but to the very spirit he himself had celebrated—"the dear old brown liquor," to which he remained faithful to the end.

This kind of degeneration—soft, indulgent, and self-defeating— offers a troubling reflection of the broader intellectual culture in Germany, one that undermines the potential for brilliance with a relentless embrace of comfort, conformity, and the narcotics of religion, alcohol, and art.

I have spoken about the state of German intellect, noting that it has become coarser and shallower. But is that enough? In truth, what concerns me far more is the steady and alarming decline of German seriousness, depth, and passion in intellectual matters. It is not just intellect that has diminished; even the emotional force— what we might call the pathos—behind intellectual pursuits has been transformed.

When I occasionally encounter German universities, I am struck by the atmosphere that prevails there. What barrenness! What smug, tepid intellectuality! These institutions have grown content with mediocrity, and the once-earnest German intellectual spirit now feels lukewarm, drained of vitality.

Some might point to German science as a counterargument to my observations. Such a claim would only prove they have misunderstood me and failed to grasp even a single page of my writings. For seventeen years, I have devoted myself to exposing the dehumanizing and de-intellectualizing effects of modern scientific pursuits. The rigid, mechanical labor demanded by the vast scope of modern sciences has left individuals shackled, unable to cultivate the fuller, richer, and deeper natures that once thrived in intellectual endeavors.

Our age suffers from an overabundance of shallow dilettantes and fragmented personalities—half-formed individuals who flit aimlessly through life. The universities, though unintentionally, have become factories for producing this kind of intellectual decay, training people whose instincts for genuine intellectuality have withered. And this problem is not confined to Germany. All of Europe is beginning to recognize this trend. Large-scale politics, the realm in which Germany has invested so much, fools no one. Germany is becoming, ever more clearly, the flatland of Europe, a place devoid of the peaks of culture and thought.

I am still searching for a German with whom I could engage in the kind of seriousness that defines my way of thinking. And even more elusive is a German with whom I could share genuine cheerfulness. The Twilight of the Idols— what man today could grasp the kind of seriousness from which a philosopher recovers in such a work? Of all things, our cheerfulness is the most misunderstood.

Now let us shift our focus slightly. It is not just that German culture is visibly in decline; there are also clear reasons behind this fall. No one, whether an individual or a nation, can expend more energy than they possess. If your resources of reason, seriousness, will, and self-discipline are poured entirely into pursuits such as political power, economics, large-scale commerce, parliamentary systems, or military ambitions, then you cannot also spend them on culture.

Culture and the state are fundamentally opposed to one another. Let no one be misled: the idea of a "culture-state" is a modern illusion. One thrives at the expense of the other. Throughout history, every great period of culture coincided with political decline. That which is culturally great is always unpolitical, even anti-political.

Consider Goethe. His heart swelled with hope at the rise of Napoleon, a figure of cultural vitality, but it closed at the thought of the "Wars of Liberation," which signaled Germany's move toward becoming a political power. Similarly, when Germany emerged as a dominant force in global politics, France rose anew as a cultural powerhouse. Even now, much of Europe's intellectual seriousness and passion have migrated to Paris. Questions of pessimism, the works of Wagner, and other psychological and artistic debates are approached in France with a level of subtlety and depth that Germany seems incapable of matching.

In matters that truly define culture—those that demand intellectual and artistic earnestness—the Germans are no longer relevant. This shift marks a profound displacement of Europe's intellectual center of gravity. In the history of European culture, the rise of the German Empire signifies not progress but a retreat from cultural significance.

I challenge you to name a single German thinker today who can stand alongside the great figures of Europe's intellectual past. Where is the modern equivalent of Goethe, Hegel, Heinrich Heine, or Schopenhauer? The absence of any contemporary German philosopher worthy of comparison with such minds is an ever-growing marvel—and a deeply troubling one.

The entire higher educational system in Germany has lost sight of everything that truly matters—both the ultimate goals and the means to achieve them. People seem to have forgotten that education itself is the goal, the process of cultivation an end in itself—not "the Empire" or any other external objective. They forget that education demands true educators, not merely public- school teachers or university scholars. What is needed are educators who are themselves cultivated, superior, and noble minds—individuals who can demonstrate their worth at every moment of their lives through their words and their actions. These are individuals who are ripe and refined products of culture.

Instead, Germany is plagued by an abundance of learned louts—"superior wet-nurses"—foisted upon its youth by public schools and universities. These are not educators in the true sense, but mere functionaries. What Germany lacks, with few exceptions, is the very foundation of education: genuine educators. And without educators, there can be no culture. This deficit has led to the decline of German culture.

One of those rare exceptions, and a man I deeply respect, is my friend Jacob Burckhardt of Bâle. It is to him, above all, that Bâle owes its position as a center of true human culture. He stands as a shining example of what an educator should be.

What, then, do Germany's higher schools actually achieve? They ruthlessly and rapidly train vast numbers of young men to become useful and exploitable servants of the state. This process prioritizes utility over cultivation, treating education as a means to an end rather than an end in itself. The very concept of "higher education" contradicts the idea of catering to the masses. True higher education can only concern the exceptional few; it is a privilege reserved for those capable of appreciating and embodying it.

Great and beautiful things cannot belong to the masses. As the Latin phrase goes, pulchrum est paucorum hominum—the beautiful is for the few. This democratization of education— this attempt to make cultivation "general" and common—is one of the root causes of Germany's cultural decline. When higher education is treated as a universal right rather than a privilege, it inevitably deteriorates in quality.

Another factor undermining German education is the influence of the military profession. The privileges associated with military careers drive far too many people into the higher schools, flooding the system and degrading its standards. In modern Germany, no parent has the freedom to provide their children with a noble education. The teachers, curricula, and goals of the higher schools are all built on a fundamentally mediocre foundation.

Everywhere one looks, haste reigns supreme. It is as if something vital would be lost if a young man were not "finished" by the age of twenty-three, or if he were unable to answer the all-important question: "What career should I choose?" But the superior individual, the one truly capable of higher culture, does not think in terms of "careers." Such a person feels called to something higher and cannot simply conform to the idea of a "calling" imposed by society.

The superior individual takes their time—they must take their time. For such a person, the idea of being "finished" is absurd. In the realm of higher culture, a man of thirty is still a beginner, still a child.

Meanwhile, our overcrowded public schools and the mass production of mediocre teachers are nothing short of a scandal. While some may present serious motives for defending this state of affairs— like the professors at Heidelberg recently did—there can be no legitimate reasons to support it. The rush to "complete" education and the focus on quantity over quality are destroying the very foundation of culture.

Germany's educational system is not cultivating exceptional individuals; it is churning out uniform, functional tools for the state. This is a betrayal of what education should be and a clear indication of the decline of German intellectual and cultural life.

To remain true to my affirmative nature—a nature that deals with contradictions and criticism only reluctantly and as a secondary matter—I will begin by stating the three essential goals for which we require educators. People must learn to see, they must learn to think, and they must learn to speak and write. These three abilities are the foundation of a noble culture.

To learn to see means to train the eye in calmness, patience, and the ability to let things present themselves. It involves postponing judgment and approaching every individual case from all possible angles. This is the first and most essential preparation for intellectual development. One must not react immediately to stimuli; one must cultivate the instincts of restraint and isolation. To learn to see, as I understand it, is closely related to what is popularly referred to as "strength of will." Its core is the ability not to want to see immediately, to defer decisions, and to resist impulses.

All lack of intellectuality and all vulgarity stem from the inability to resist stimuli. Such people feel compelled to respond to every impulse and indulge every reaction. In many cases, this immediate response is a sign of decline, a symptom of exhaustion or morbidity. Most of what common language calls "vices" is simply the physiological inability to refrain from reacting.

To illustrate what it means to have learned to see, consider a person who has undergone this training. As a learner, this individual will likely become cautious, slow, and resistant. With a calm and almost hostile skepticism, they will allow strange and unfamiliar things to approach them but will refrain from immediately engaging or forming judgments. They will withdraw their hand, metaphorically speaking, as the new comes near, watching and observing instead.

In contrast, to be perpetually open, to have the "doors of one's soul" flung wide for every trivial fact, to constantly lie in submission before the flood of external impressions—this is what modern people call "objectivity." But such objectivity is in poor taste; it is vulgar and cheap. It is the intellectual equivalent of being at the mercy of every passing whim, ready to leap into others' souls and experiences without discernment or control.

As for learning to think—our schools have long since abandoned any understanding of this process. Even at the universities, among scholars of philosophy, the discipline of logic is withering away, both as a theory and as a practical skill. Look into any German book, and you will find no trace of the understanding that thinking has a technique, a structure, and a discipline. There is no recognition that thinking must be learned, much like dancing must be learned. Thinking, like dancing, demands practice and a will to mastery.

Who among the Germans today knows, from experience, the subtle joy— the delicate shudder—that comes when intellectual movements are as graceful as light footfalls? Instead, intellectual clumsiness abounds. Awkward postures of the mind and a heavy-handed approach to grasping ideas are so distinctly German that outside of Germany, they are mistakenly equated with the German spirit itself. The German mind has no "fingers" for fine nuances.

The Germans' tolerance for their philosophers, particularly for Kant—the most malformed and crippled figure in the realm of ideas—speaks volumes about their lack of elegance. Kant is a testament to their coarse intellectual habits and their inability to recognize intellectual grace.

In truth, no noble education can exclude dancing in all its forms. This includes dancing with one's feet, but also with ideas, with words, and, above all, with the pen. Writing is, in its highest form, a kind of intellectual dance, requiring rhythm, precision, and lightness. Yet at this point, I must acknowledge that these thoughts will likely remain utterly incomprehensible to most German readers.

Chapter 9

Skirmishes in A War with The Age

My Impossible People.—Seneca, the showman of virtue, performing like a bullfighter in the ring of morals. Rousseau, the preacher of returning to nature, lost in his own unpolished, raw state. Schiller, the trumpet of morality, blasting his tunes from Säckingen with little depth behind the noise. Dante, the scavenger who writes poetry over the graves he haunts. Kant, whose moral preaching is nothing more than a cleverly disguised form of empty rhetoric. Victor Hugo, a beacon on the vast sea of nonsense, shining brightly but without direction. Liszt, master of chasing not only after musical greatness but also after women. George Sand, overflowing with creativity, like a cow with an endless supply of beautiful milk. Michelet, all fire and passion, but dressed casually in the everyday garb of enthusiasm. Carlyle, the voice of pessimism, but one born of a poorly digested meal rather than deep reflection. John Stuart Mill, whose clarity is so sharp it feels almost offensive. The brothers Goncourt, two literary warriors battling Homer with their pens, their drama set to Offenbach's music.

Zola, who finds inspiration in the repulsive and thrives in the stench of decay.

Renan. Theology personified, corrupted by the original sin of Christianity. His thoughts are tainted with the contradictions of faith. Even when Renan dares to take a stance, to say "yes" or "no" on a major issue, he almost always misses the point entirely. He tries to combine science with nobility, seemingly unaware that science is inherently democratic and cannot be aligned with his aristocratic ideals. He dreams of an intellectual aristocracy, yet at the same time, he bows down to the gospel of humility and grovels before it. What good is his modern free-spiritedness, his wit, his irony, and his intellectual acrobatics, if deep inside he remains tied to the faith of a Christian, a Catholic, and even a priest?

Renan's strength, much like that of a Jesuit or a confessor, lies in his ability to seduce. His intellect has the same unctuous, self- satisfied tone as a parson. Like all priests, he becomes dangerous when he loves, because his love distorts the truth. He has a rare talent for worshipping dangerous ideas in such a way that they appear benign. But his intellect, rather than invigorating, weakens and softens. For France, already suffering from a broken will and diminishing strength, Renan is one more calamity—a soothing voice at a time when sharp clarity and decisiveness are needed.

Sainte-Beuve. There is nothing manly about him. He is filled with petty malice toward all strong and noble spirits. He drifts aimlessly, subtle yet spiteful, always restless and curious. He listens at keyholes, gathering whispers, but never facing things head-on. At heart, he is more like a woman, full of revenge and sensuality. As a psychologist, he is a genius of slander, endlessly creative in his ability to add a touch of poison even to his praise. His instincts are plebeian, closely aligned with the resentful spirit of Rousseau. This makes him a Romanticist, for beneath all Romanticism lies Rousseau's vengeful nature, grumbling and restless.

Sainte-Beuve is a restrained revolutionary, his actions kept in check by fear. He flinches before strength, whether it comes in the form of public opinion, the Academy, the court, or even the cloistered thinkers of Port Royal. He is filled with bitterness toward all that is great, toward everything that has confidence in itself. He is enough of a poet, enough of a sensualist, to recognize power when he sees it, but he writhes under its weight like a worm being trodden upon.

As a critic, Sainte-Beuve lacks a foundation—no standard of judgment, no clear principles, no backbone. While he speaks with the versatility of a worldly libertine, chattering endlessly about countless subjects, he lacks the courage to own his own libertinism. As a historian, he has no philosophical depth, no ability to see history as a coherent whole. This lack of vision leads him to avoid making judgments, opting instead for a mask of "objectivity" in matters of importance.

Yet when it comes to things that demand subtlety and refined taste, Sainte- Beuve finds his footing. Here, he dares to embrace his true nature, enjoying his own personality and even achieving mastery. In this sense, he is a precursor to Baudelaire, though without Baudelaire's courage to push boundaries.

"The Imitation of Christ." This is a book I cannot even touch without feeling physically repulsed. It reeks of the "eternally feminine," a cloying sweetness that can only appeal to French sensibilities or to Wagnerites. Its saintly musings on love are delivered in a tone so saccharine that even the most worldly Parisian women might find themselves intrigued.

I have been told that Auguste Comte, the clever Jesuit disguised as a man of science, took inspiration from this book in his attempt to lead his countrymen back to Rome by way of science. I can believe it. This is the essence of the "religion of the heart"—a sentimental, deceptive path back to the old faith, cloaked in modern rhetoric. It is as much a symbol of decline as it is of misplaced devotion.

G. Eliot.—They have let go of the Christian God, yet they cling even harder to Christian morality. This is a very English way of thinking, and while it might seem strange, one can hardly blame moral women like George Eliot for following it. In England, even the smallest step away from theology must be balanced by an extreme embrace of morality. It's their way of making amends, their form of penance. Anyone who begins to stray from religious belief feels compelled to prove their virtue by becoming a moral fanatic.

We, however, are different. When we abandon Christian faith, we also give up any claim to Christian morality. This connection might not be obvious to everyone, but it must be emphasized repeatedly, especially to counter the shallow thinkers so common in England. Christianity is not a loose collection of values; it is a complete system, a worldview where every part supports the whole. If you remove its central pillar—the belief in God—the entire structure collapses. What remains is empty, lifeless, and without meaning.

Christianity assumes that humans cannot know what is good or bad for themselves. It teaches that only God knows these things. Christian morality, therefore, is not a product of human reasoning but a divine command. It is immune to criticism because it rests entirely on the belief that God is the ultimate truth. Without God, Christian morality loses its foundation and cannot stand on its own.

The English, however, seem to believe otherwise. They think they can intuitively know what is good or evil without needing Christianity to guide them. But this belief only shows how deeply Christian values still shape their thinking. Their moral standards remain rooted in Christian teachings, even when they deny the religion itself. This is not evidence of independence; it is proof of how strong Christianity's influence remains. The English no longer recognize the origins of their morality, nor do they realize how fragile it is without its theological base. For them, morality is not a question to be examined—it is simply assumed, a problem they have yet to confront.

George Sand.—I recently read the first Lettres d'un Voyageur, and like everything influenced by Rousseau, it felt artificial, exaggerated, and insincere. The style reminded me of cheap wallpaper—bright, decorative, but ultimately shallow. The writing seems overly concerned with appearing noble and generous, yet lacks any genuine depth. What struck me most was Sand's affected masculinity, which came across as forced and unconvincing, like the awkward swagger of a poorly mannered schoolboy.

And how cold she must have been beneath this performance! She seemed like a machine, wound up and ready to produce her work, writing not out of passion but out of routine. This coldness is not unique to her; it is the hallmark of Romanticists like Hugo and Balzac, whose writing often feels detached from true feeling. Sand's self-satisfaction is evident in her prolific output, as if she took pride in her ability to churn out words endlessly. There was something undeniably German in her style—not in the good sense, but in the clumsy, heavy-handed way that marks the decline of true French taste. And yet Renan adores her!

A Moral for Psychologists.—Never engage in psychology just for the sake of observing. Observing for its own sake leads to a distorted view of things, to exaggeration, and to a forced perspective. Experiencing something intentionally, with the purpose of analyzing it, is not helpful. When in the middle of an experience, a person should not turn their attention inward to observe themselves. In such moments, even the clearest vision becomes clouded—it turns into the "evil eye." A true psychologist avoids observing for the sake of observation. The same is true for a true artist. A born painter, for instance, does not work directly "from nature." Instead, they rely on their instinct, their internal lens, to filter and shape their perception of reality. For them, only the general idea, the final impression, reaches conscious thought. They do not bother with the painstaking process of building conclusions from small, particular details.

But what happens when someone approaches this differently? Take, for example, the Parisian novelists who practice "note- book psychology," recording every detail, large or small, that catches their attention. Such people are constantly spying on life, collecting observations like trinkets to carry home at the end of each day. The result? A chaotic mess, at best resembling a mosaic of unrelated fragments. Their work is restless and garish, more like a patchwork quilt than a coherent picture. The Goncourts are the worst offenders in this regard. They cannot write three sentences without causing pain to anyone with an eye for psychology or aesthetics.

From an artistic perspective, nature is no model to imitate. Nature exaggerates, distorts, and leaves gaps—it is full of accidents. To study "from nature" is, in my view, a bad sign. It shows submission, weakness, and a kind of fatalism. This slavish worship of trivial facts is beneath a true artist. The ability to see "what is" belongs to a different kind of intellect altogether—one that is practical and matter-of-fact, not artistic. An artist must know who they are and what their purpose is, rather than bowing before the randomness of nature.

To make art possible—that is, to create an aesthetic way of acting and seeing—a certain physiological state must come first: ecstasy. Without this heightened state of being, art simply cannot exist. Ecstasy heightens the sensitivity of the whole body and mind, making them more receptive and powerful. Many kinds of ecstasy can lead to art, no matter how they arise. Sexual excitement, for example, is the oldest and most fundamental form of ecstasy. Similarly, ecstasy can come from powerful desires, intense passions, the energy of celebration, the thrill of a battle, the bravery of a daring act, the joy of victory, or the rush of destruction. Even seasonal changes, such as the vibrancy of spring, or the use of drugs can trigger this state. Another form of ecstasy arises from a strong surge of willpower, when one feels driven and overflowing with determination.

At its core, ecstasy creates a feeling of increased strength and abundance. In this state, a person projects their inner wealth onto the world around them. They impose their energy onto things, forcing them to reflect their own richness and power. This act of projecting oneself onto the world is called idealizing. Contrary to popular belief, idealizing does not mean removing details or simplifying things. Instead, it emphasizes the main characteristics so powerfully that lesser details fade away.

In this state of abundance, a person enriches everything they encounter. Whatever they see or desire appears to them as larger, stronger, and more alive. They transform objects and ideas until these reflect their own strength and perfection. This drive to transform things into something beautiful is what we call art. Through art, a person celebrates themselves as a reflection of perfection, even in things they are not.

It is also possible to imagine the opposite of this artistic state—an anti- artistic condition. In such a state, a person drains energy from everything around them. Instead of enriching and enhancing, they weaken and impoverish. These individuals lack vitality and draw from others to sustain themselves. History is full of such anti-artists—individuals like Pascal, whose Christian faith exemplifies this draining tendency. A true Christian, by nature, cannot also be an artist. Even suggesting otherwise by pointing to figures like Raphael misses the point entirely. Raphael affirmed life, celebrated beauty, and said "yes" to the world, which means he was not a Christian in the true sense.

The terms Apollonian and Dionysian, which I introduced to aesthetics, represent two opposing forms of ecstasy. Apollonian ecstasy sharpens vision, giving the eye a heightened ability to see and understand. This type of ecstasy inspires painters, sculptors, and epic poets, who are fundamentally visionaries. On the other hand, Dionysian ecstasy awakens the entire system of passions, intensifying them and causing them to pour out in a flood of expression. This state drives transformation and imitation, releasing all forms of mimicry and artistic display at once. The Dionysian artist is incredibly sensitive to every emotion and suggestion. They instinctively grasp and communicate emotions, transforming themselves into whatever role or passion they encounter. Music, as we understand it today, is a surviving fragment of this broader Dionysian expression—a remnant of a once richer form of emotional discharge. For music to become its own art form, many other senses, such as the sense of touch and movement, had to be partially suppressed. Rhythm, however, still appeals to our physical senses to some extent, linking music to its Dionysian roots.

Actors, mimes, dancers, musicians, and lyricists all share a common foundation in their instincts. Over time, however, they have specialized, developing their own distinct fields of art, even to the point of becoming opposites. Among these, lyricists remained closely connected to musicians for the longest period, while actors were similarly linked to dancers. Architects, however, represent something different. Their art is born not from

Dionysian or Apollonian ecstasy but from the overwhelming will to create. Architecture expresses human pride, triumph over nature, and the will to power in physical form. Great men have always inspired architects, who in turn translate this power into structures that symbolize strength and security. Architecture becomes a language of power, speaking through form. It can persuade, command, or simply exist with quiet confidence. True grandeur in architecture reflects power that is self-assured, needing no validation, unconcerned with opposition, and relying only on itself.

Recently, I read about Thomas Carlyle's life, a mix of unintended comedy and moral posturing. Carlyle was a man of dramatic words and gestures, forever in search of a strong faith that he could not find. This unfulfilled longing makes him a quintessential Romantic. The desire for strong faith, however, is not a sign of having it but rather the opposite. A person with true faith can afford the luxury of doubt and skepticism because their foundation is firm. Carlyle's loud proclamations of reverence for those with strong faith, combined with his anger at those who lacked it, reveal his inner turmoil. He needed noise—both literal and figurative—to distract himself from his doubts.

Carlyle's defining trait was his persistent dishonesty with himself. This quality makes him fascinating, though it also explains why he was so admired in England. Honesty, as the English understand it, often overlaps with hypocrisy, and Carlyle fits this mold perfectly. At heart, he was an atheist who stubbornly refused to admit it, making his struggle with faith all the more dramatic and emblematic of the English spirit.

Emerson is far more enlightened, versatile, and refined than Carlyle, and most importantly, he is happier. He lives instinctively, enjoying the best parts of life while discarding what he finds unpleasant. Compared to Carlyle, Emerson has better taste and a lighter, more joyous intellectuality. Carlyle, who admired him greatly, complained that Emerson "does not give us enough to chew." While this criticism may be true, it hardly counts as a flaw—it is simply a reflection of Emerson's different approach. Emerson's cheerfulness shields him from the heaviness of life. He does not burden himself with excessive seriousness, and he approaches existence with a kind of perpetual youthfulness, blissfully unaware of his age or the weight of time. He might have described himself, in Lope de Vega's words, as someone who constantly succeeds himself, always renewing and reimagining his life. His mind naturally seeks reasons to be content, even grateful, and he often approaches a carefree joyfulness akin to the bourgeois simplicity of a man returning from a romantic escapade, satisfied with life's fleeting pleasures.

The "struggle for existence," a centerpiece of Darwinian thought, strikes me as more of an assumption than an established fact. It does happen, but it is the exception, not the rule. Life's general state is not one of scarcity and competition but one of abundance, extravagance, and even absurd excess. Where struggle does occur, it is more often a struggle for power than for mere survival. The idea of nature as fundamentally Malthusian is misleading. Even if the struggle for existence does take place, its outcomes are often the opposite of what Darwin and his followers might hope. Instead of favoring the strong, the exceptional, and the privileged, it often benefits the weak, simply because they are the majority and frequently more cunning. Darwin overlooked the role of intellect—an oversight that seems distinctly English. The weak are often more intelligent, driven by necessity to develop cleverness and adaptability. By contrast, the strong, having less need for such traits, may grow complacent and neglect their intellect, letting it atrophy. Intellect, after all, demands caution, patience, and subtlety—qualities the powerful may disdain in favor of brute strength.

Those who study humanity deeply often have ulterior motives. A politician, for instance, uses his understanding of people to gain power or advantage. But what of the so-called disinterested observer, the one who claims to seek no personal benefit? A closer look often reveals a darker purpose: the desire to feel superior, to distance oneself from humanity, to no longer belong. This kind of person despises mankind, even if they claim objectivity and fairness. By contrast, the more "self-serving" politician may actually be more humane, for at least he sees himself as part of the same world as those he studies.

The German approach to intellect and psychology leaves much to be desired, as evidenced by certain cultural missteps. Consider, for example, the pairing of names like Goethe and Schiller, or worse, Schiller and Goethe, as if they were equals. Has no one yet recognized the vast gulf between them? And then there are other egregious pairings, such as Schopenhauer and Hartmann. Such thoughtless associations reflect a lack of discernment and an inability to appreciate true intellectual refinement.

The most intelligent and courageous individuals often endure the greatest tragedies because they confront life's most daunting challenges. Yet, paradoxically, these struggles lead them to honor life all the more, for it forces them to grapple with its fiercest adversaries. In this way, their suffering becomes a testament to their strength and their profound engagement with existence.

In today's world, genuine hypocrisy has become increasingly rare. Hypocrisy requires a strong belief, a faith so deeply held that one is willing to outwardly adopt another, contradictory stance while maintaining one's inner conviction. Such duality thrives only in an era of fervent faith, where abandoning one's belief is unthinkable. Modern culture, however, allows for a multiplicity of beliefs, making hypocrisy almost obsolete. People no longer feel the need to maintain a façade; instead, they adopt multiple convictions and live comfortably with them, ensuring these beliefs never truly conflict or demand consistency.

This tolerance for contradictions is both a sign of our age and a symptom of its weaknesses. Modern individuals avoid compromising themselves by avoiding consistency. They cultivate convenience rather than conviction, preferring a life free of challenges or demands on their integrity. Even vices, once expressions of strong will, have degenerated into virtues in this climate of comfort and ease. The few hypocrites I've encountered are mere imitations of the real thing, like actors playing a role. They lack the depth and complexity of true hypocrisy, reduced instead to shallow performances in a world that no longer requires or even understands the profound struggles of belief and deceit.

Beautiful and Ugly:—Our sense of the beautiful is deeply relative, tightly bound to the limitations of human perception and context. To try and separate beauty from the joy humans derive from their surroundings, especially other humans, would be to sever it from its grounding altogether. "Beauty in itself" is nothing more than an abstract phrase, a hollow idea without true substance or universal agreement. In perceiving beauty, humans essentially declare themselves as the measure of perfection. At times, in exceptional circumstances, they even idolize themselves as that ultimate standard. This impulse stems from the most basic instinct of survival and self-preservation. Even the loftiest ideas of beauty are, at their core, expressions of humanity's need to affirm and expand itself.

Man views the world as brimming with beauty, failing to recognize that he is the source of this projection. The beauty he perceives is merely a reflection of himself, a human imprint upon the world. Alas, it is not a universal beauty, but rather one that is all-too-human. In truth, man mirrors himself in everything he beholds, deeming things beautiful because they resonate with his own image.

The judgment of beauty is thus the vanity of the human species, an echo of its own self-love. A skeptic might wonder, "Is the world genuinely beautiful because man finds it so?" Perhaps not. Perhaps all man has done is to humanize the world, to imprint it with his desires and perceptions. Yet, there is no definitive proof that man is the ultimate standard of beauty. What if, in the eyes of a more refined judge of taste, mankind appeared peculiar, comical, or arbitrary? Imagine Dionysus teasing Ariadne about her ears during a philosophical conversation, playfully suggesting, "Why are they not a little longer?" The joke may contain a deeper truth.

From this perspective, nothing in itself is beautiful; it is man alone who declares beauty. Aesthetic sensibility begins with this innocent assumption, the first axiom of aesthetics. Alongside it stands a second principle: nothing is truly ugly except the degenerate man. Together, these principles define the bounds of aesthetic judgment. From a physiological standpoint, ugliness weakens and demoralizes. It reminds humanity of fragility, decay, and the loss of vitality. In the presence of ugliness, man's strength diminishes, as if the sight itself drains him of energy. This reaction, measurable even by a dynamometer, reveals a deep instinctual response: ugliness signals something threatening, something that disrupts the will to power.

When a man feels a sudden drop in confidence or courage, it often stems from encountering something that he perceives as ugly. This reaction emerges from deep within his instincts, stored with countless associations between appearances and their inferred meanings. Ugliness is perceived as a symptom of decline and degeneration. Anything that even faintly suggests a deterioration of the human type—be it physical exhaustion, aging, stiffness, or the crudeness of decomposition—is judged as ugly. Colors, smells, and forms associated with decay, even when abstracted into mere symbols, provoke the same visceral rejection.

This response is not simply distaste; it is hatred, a primal and profound aversion. What is it that man hates in ugliness? He hates the signs of decline in his own kind. This hatred is rooted in the deepest instincts of survival, resonating with the need to preserve the strength and vitality of his type. It is a hatred tinged with horror and caution, expressing a far-sighted instinct for the preservation of life. This reaction is not shallow; it is the most profound hatred man possesses, one that is etched into the very fabric of his being.

It is this hatred of decline, this refusal to accept degeneration, that gives art its depth. Art draws from the profound tension between man's yearning for beauty and his rejection of what threatens his sense of vitality and perfection. In this way, art is more than an expression of the beautiful; it is an affirmation of life, shaped by man's most primal fears and desires.

Schopenhauer, the last German thinker of significance, stands alongside figures like Goethe, Hegel, and Heinrich Heine as a European, not merely a national, event. For a psychologist, he is a fascinating case of the highest order. His work represents a cunning and skillful effort to turn the most life-affirming aspects of human existence—such as art, heroism, genius, beauty, deep compassion, the pursuit of truth, and even the grandeur of tragedy—into arguments for a nihilistic rejection of life. In this, Schopenhauer engages in what could be called one of history's greatest intellectual forgeries, rivaled only by Christianity. He reinterpreted all the noble affirmations of life as if they were but expressions of the denial of the "will to live" or as steps leading inevitably toward that denial.

When scrutinized more closely, Schopenhauer appears as an inheritor of the Christian worldview, repackaged for a secular age. Unlike Christianity, which outright rejects many aspects of human culture, Schopenhauer found a way to nihilistically "approve" of them. To him, these elements of culture—art, beauty, and even human striving—were not ends in themselves but tools to draw the soul toward "salvation," mere appetizers to stimulate a hunger for deliverance from life itself.

Take, for example, his view of beauty. Schopenhauer speaks of beauty with a sorrowful intensity, valuing it as a bridge to something beyond, a fleeting liberation from the burdens of the "will to live." He sees beauty as a temporary escape, particularly from the "burning core" of the will—sexuality. To him, beauty negates the reproductive instinct, offering a glimpse of salvation. Singular saint, indeed! But someone challenges this notion— Nature herself. Why does Nature create beauty in sound, color, fragrance, and rhythm if not to affirm life and reproduction? Why does beauty compel and captivate? Schopenhauer's own idol, Plato, offers a striking contradiction to his thesis.

Plato, whom Schopenhauer venerates as a divine authority, takes an entirely different view. For Plato, beauty is not a denial of life; it is an irresistible lure toward creation and procreation. Beauty inspires both the lowest sensual desires and the highest intellectual pursuits. With a Greek innocence utterly foreign to the Christian mindset, Plato claims that without the beauty of young men in Athens, there would have been no Platonic philosophy. It was their radiance that stirred the philosopher's soul, igniting a passion that refused to rest until it had planted the seeds of great ideas in such captivating soil. Plato himself, then, was a singular saint of a different kind—one for whom the aesthetic and the erotic were deeply intertwined.

This reveals a starkly different approach to philosophy in Athens, where it was pursued openly, even playfully. Unlike the cloistered, abstract cogitations of later thinkers such as Spinoza with his intellectual love of God, Platonic philosophy was an extension of the Greek tradition of competitive games, agon, infused with an erotic dimension. Plato's philosophy was, in many ways, an elevated and spiritualized form of the Greek gymnastic competitions, with dialectics becoming a new art form born of this philosophic eroticism.

In defense of Plato and against Schopenhauer's austere view, it is worth noting that much of the higher culture and literature of classical France also flourished on the fertile ground of sexual interests. Whether in gallantry, the passions, sexual rivalry, or the role of women, these themes pervade French culture and cannot be overlooked. The sensual and the intellectual intertwined seamlessly, revealing that higher culture, far from denying life, often springs from its most vibrant and primal energies.

The idea of l'ar t pour l'ar t—art for art's sake—has often been interpreted as a rebellion against the notion that art must serve a moral purpose or improve humanity. This phrase essentially declares, "Let morality go to hell!" Yet, even in this rejection, we see how deeply entrenched the moral bias remains. The act of opposing morality in art still acknowledges its overwhelming influence. If art is stripped of its role as a preacher of morals or a tool for human betterment, this does not mean it is left entirely without purpose or meaning. To say that art has no purpose, no point, no sense—this is what l'art pour l'art suggests. It is like a snake biting its own tail: a pure passion insisting, "No purpose at all is better than a moral purpose."

But a psychologist must question this: What does art actually do? Does it not praise? Does it not elevate certain ideas while diminishing others? Does it not highlight and amplify? In doing so, art reinforces or diminishes certain values. Can this be dismissed as an incidental outcome or a mere accident, independent of the artist's intentions? Or is it, rather, a fundamental instinct of the artist to shape and serve life through art? Is the artist's true drive concerned with art itself, or does it instead lie in the aim of art—to enrich and enhance life, to advocate for a specific way of living? Art is a tremendous stimulus to life; how, then, can it be seen as pointless or purposeless? It is not simply l'art pour l'art.

And what of the dark and unsettling aspects that art sometimes reveals? When art exposes what is ugly, harsh, or deeply troubling, does it not risk making life unbearable? Some philosophers have thought so. For example, Schopenhauer argued that the purpose of art, especially tragedy, was to free us from the relentless desires of the will and to lead us toward resignation. Tragedy, for him, was valuable because it made us more willing to renounce life. But this view reflects a pessimistic perspective—a deeply negative outlook. To understand art, we must consult the artist, not the pessimist. What does the tragic artist convey to us? Surely it is not resignation but rather a fearless embrace of life's terrors and uncertainties. The artist shows us how to face profound suffering with courage and strength. This attitude is a triumph in itself, and those who have experienced it know it is something to be revered. The artist must share this perspective. A true artist and a genius in communication cannot help but share it.

The tragic artist exalts a heroic spirit, one that confronts overwhelming challenges, sublime catastrophes, and terrifying mysteries with dignity and resolve. This spirit celebrates itself in tragedy, finding joy even in suffering. The tragic artist extends this "cup of sweetest cruelty" to those who are attuned to hardship, who seek it out and embrace it as a defining aspect of life. Tragedy is not about giving up; it is about finding meaning and affirmation in struggle.

A related notion is the idea of hospitality in one's soul. To welcome anyone and everyone into one's inner world may seem generous, but it lacks discernment. A truly noble heart holds its finest chambers in reserve, waiting for worthy guests—guests who are not merely anybody but rather individuals of real substance. Such hearts are rich in depth, with shutters closed and windows veiled, not out of fear or selfishness, but in anticipation of those who merit their best.

Too often, we undervalue ourselves when we attempt to articulate the deepest contents of our souls. Our most profound experiences are not verbose; they are beyond words and would resist even the most earnest attempts at expression. The very act of finding words for something suggests that it has already been overcome or rendered less significant. Speech itself diminishes, for in speaking, we simplify and vulgarize. Words are the currency of the average, the mundane, the communicable. To speak is to betray the depth of what one truly feels, revealing instead only a shadow of the truth. This recognition might well serve as a moral guide for philosophers and others who value the unspoken.

And what of those who strive for objectivity, who pride themselves on their detached and impartial perspectives? Their wisdom, patience, and tolerance may seem impressive, even virtuous, but it often comes at the cost of passion and genuine self-control. Such individuals, drenched in their indulgence and sympathy, should occasionally permit themselves a dose of raw emotion, even a small emotional vice. It may feel uncomfortable, even ridiculous, to them, but it serves as a form of self-discipline—a kind of asceticism for those who have mastered detachment but risk losing touch with their own humanity.

In becoming personal, the so-called "objective" individuals reveal their own virtues, for objectivity often masks a deeper desire: the need to feel above the fray, detached from the common lot. Yet true nobility lies not in keeping oneself apart but in knowing when and how to connect with others authentically. The virtues of objectivity are limited without the courage to embrace and engage with life's messy, subjective truths.

Excerpt from a doctor's exam paper: "What is the ultimate goal of all advanced education?" To transform a human being into a machine. "What methods are employed to achieve this?" Teaching the individual how to endure boredom. "And how is this boredom instilled?" Through the concept of duty. "What model of duty is presented to the student?" The philologist, who embodies the art of relentless, uninspired diligence. "Who, then, is the ideal human being?" The government official. "And which philosophy provides the definitive framework for this ideal?" Kant's philosophy: envisioning the government official as the ultimate abstraction—the thing- in-itself— presiding over his worldly role as mere appearance.

The Right to Stupidity: Picture the exhausted worker, his breath measured, his demeanor mild, his actions guided by inertia rather than intent. This archetype, a product of our era of relentless labor (and "Empire"), now inhabits every class. This weary figure seeks escape and leisure, claiming even Art for himself—books,

newspapers, and, most notably, beautiful landscapes like Italy. This man of the evening, with his "wild instincts lulled," as Faust might say, requires his summer holidays, his coastal retreats, his alpine glaciers, and his pilgrimage to Bayreuth. In times like these, Art gains the right to be utterly frivolous—a playful retreat for wit, spirit, and emotion. Wagner, of course, understood this well. Pure silliness becomes a form of refreshment, a tonic for the fatigued.

A Further Question of Discipline: Consider the methods Julius Caesar used to safeguard himself against illness and headaches: grueling marches, a life stripped to its simplest essentials, constant exposure to the elements, and enduring hardships without respite. These strategies represent the necessary defenses and survival tactics for those intricate, high-performing organisms called geniuses. Such lives, always teetering at the edge of their capacity, demand such rigorous measures to maintain their vitality.

The Immoralist Speaks: Nothing is more repugnant to true philosophers than observing man in the act of wishing. When they see man purely in his actions—this most fearless, cunning, and resilient of animals, navigating life's calamities with remarkable ingenuity—he earns their admiration. They may even encourage him.

Yet the moment man begins to wish or pursue "ideals," he becomes contemptible in their eyes. They reject not only the man of desires but also the very concept of "desirability" and all the ideals and aspirations that humans project upon the world.

Were a true philosopher inclined to nihilism, it would not be because of the absence of meaning but because every human ideal reveals not grandeur but something base: futility, absurdity, frailty, cowardice, fatigue, and the residue left over from life's excesses. Why is it that man, so admirable in his tangible existence, becomes unworthy of respect the moment he begins to desire? Is it some kind of cosmic balancing act? Must the heights of his reality be counterbalanced by the lowliness of his imagination and aspirations? Humanity's history of desires has always been its most shameful chapter; one would be wise not to delve too deeply into it.

What redeems mankind is not its dreams or ideals but its tangible reality. This reality justifies humanity—now and forever. A real man, living and acting in the world, is infinitely more valuable than the mere shadow of a man shaped by desires, fantasies, and delusions. Any ideal man, no matter how elevated he may seem, pales in comparison to the flesh-and-blood individual who embodies the truth of existence. And it is precisely the "ideal man"—the product of abstractions, longings, and lies—that a philosopher finds most insufferable.

The Natural Value of Egoism: The worth of selfishness depends entirely on the inherent value of the individual who practices it. This value may be immense, or it may be insignificant and even contemptible. Every person can be evaluated based on whether they represent the ascending or descending trajectory of life. Once this determination is made, it becomes possible to measure the value of their egoism. If a person embodies the upward movement of life—its growth, strength, and vitality—then their worth is extraordinary. For the collective progress of humanity, which advances through such individuals, it is essential to focus on ensuring their well-being and creating the optimal conditions for them to thrive. These individuals are not isolated entities, mere atoms, or passive inheritors of history; instead, they represent the entire trajectory of humanity culminating in their existence.

Conversely, if an individual represents decline, degeneration, or chronic decay, their value diminishes significantly. Sickness, for instance, is often the result, rather than the cause, of such decline. In such cases, it would be most equitable if these individuals took as little as possible from those who are nature's fortunate creations. These declining individuals become parasitic, drawing from the vitality of others without contributing to life's upward momentum.

The Christian and the Anarchist: When the anarchist, as the voice of the decaying elements in society, cries out for "rights," "justice," or "equality," it is not an enlightened demand but a symptom of their deeper ignorance. They do not understand the true source of their suffering: a poverty not of material possessions but of life itself. An instinct for finding blame is at work here; someone must bear responsibility for their discomfort and unease. Their anger, their dramatic indignation, serves as a fleeting relief—a kind of temporary intoxication that offers them a sense of power, however small. To complain, to bewail one's condition, even to hurl accusations, is a twisted consolation. It allows them to endure their existence by adding a layer of satisfaction to their misery.

There is always an element of revenge in lamentation. In every complaint lies the unspoken accusation: "Because I suffer, you ought to suffer too." This logic, though bitter, is the foundation of revolutions. To grumble about one's plight, however, is always degrading. It stems from weakness, whether one blames others or oneself for one's suffering. The socialist blames society; the Christian, by contrast, blames themselves. But both share a common flaw—the need to identify a scapegoat for their pain. This shared instinct, ignoble in both cases, is driven by the desire to alleviate suffering with the sweet, temporary balm of revenge.

The targets of this vengeful instinct are often incidental, chosen simply because they offer a convenient outlet. The Christian turns their blame inward, condemning their own sinfulness, while the anarchist directs their anger outward, railing against society and its perceived injustices. Yet, both are products of decline, symptoms of decadence. Even the Christian, in their acts of condemnation, slander, and defamation, mirrors the same instinct that drives the socialist worker to vilify society. The ultimate Christian fantasy— the Last Judgment—is nothing more than a dramatic extension of this need for vengeance, a cosmic reckoning that satisfies their desire to see wrongs avenged on the grandest scale.

In this way, the Christian's idea of the "Beyond" serves as nothing more than a tool to defame the "Here." It is not born out of a genuine belief in transcendence but from the need to disparage and denigrate this world. Similarly, the anarchist's dream of revolution is merely a more immediate expression of the same instinct—a wish for upheaval to punish those they blame for their suffering. Whether through the promise of an apocalyptic reckoning or the hope for societal collapse, both use these fantasies to lash out at life, unable to embrace its reality or its challenges.

An "altruistic" morality, one that causes selfishness to weaken and fade away, is always a troubling sign. This holds true not only for individuals but especially for nations. When selfishness starts to diminish, it signals the absence of the best and strongest qualities. To instinctively choose what harms oneself or to be drawn to so-called "selfless" motives is nearly a definition of decadence. The idea of "not prioritizing one's own interests" is nothing more than a moral disguise for a deeper problem, a physiological one: the person no longer knows what truly benefits them. This is the collapse of instincts, the breakdown of life's natural guidance system. A person who becomes overly altruistic is on a dangerous path. Instead of admitting honestly, "I am no longer any good," the lie that decadents tell themselves through morality is, "Nothing is any good— life itself is worthless."

This kind of judgment is deeply harmful, as it can spread like a poison, infecting others. On the polluted soil of society, such ideas grow wildly and take root, appearing now as religion, like Christianity, or as philosophy, like Schopenhauer's worldview. In some cases, even the faintest trace of such toxic ideas, sprouting as they do from the decay of life itself, can harm humanity for thousands of years.

The sick man, in this context, becomes a parasite to society. There are times when continuing to live becomes indecent. When life's meaning and one's right to live have been lost, clinging to existence through doctors and treatments should be viewed with disdain. Doctors themselves should be the ones to instill this sense of contempt; instead of prolonging such lives with prescriptions, they should daily serve their patients a dose of disgust. A new duty should fall upon the doctor—to mercilessly prevent and eliminate degenerate life in cases where the higher interests of life demand it. This would include defending the right to be born, the right to live, and even the right to procreate. One should embrace death proudly when living proudly is no longer possible. Death should be a conscious choice, welcomed at the right time, with clarity and joy, and shared with loved ones in a way that allows a proper farewell. A person should remain fully themselves, able to reflect on their achievements and measure the value of life itself before departing.

This vision is the complete opposite of the grotesque drama that Christianity has turned the moment of death into. Christianity has abused the vulnerability of dying people, violating their conscience and exploiting their final moments as a way of judging them and their lives. For this, Christianity deserves no forgiveness. It is our duty to restore the dignity of death, reclaiming it as a natural, physiological process, even though "natural death" is often nothing more than a euphemism for suicide. No one perishes because of someone else; one dies only because of their own nature. Yet the kind of death that happens by chance, at the wrong time, or under cowardly circumstances, is the most disgraceful. Out of love for life itself, one should strive for a death that is deliberate and free, neither accidental nor unexpected.

Let me offer some advice to the pessimists and other decadents among us. We cannot undo the fact of our birth—that mistake, if it was one—but we can choose to correct it if we wish. The act of taking one's own life can be the most honorable deed. In fact, the person who ends their life almost earns the right to live for having had the strength to do so. Such an act benefits society—and life itself—far more than a life wasted in weakness, self-denial, or other so-called virtues. At the very least, the one who takes their own life spares others the burden of their existence and removes one more objection to the value of life.

Pure pessimism can only truly be proven by the actions of pessimists themselves. They must go further in their logic. To merely deny life in theory, as Schopenhauer did in The World as Will and Idea, is not enough; the next step is to deny Schopenhauer himself. Incidentally, pessimism, no matter how contagious it might appear, does not actually increase the decay of an era or a species. It merely reflects the decay that already exists. Like cholera, it only afflicts those who are already susceptible. Pessimism does not add a single person to the ranks of the world's degenerates. Let me remind you of an important fact: during years when cholera rages, the overall number of deaths does not exceed those of other years.

Have we really become more moral? Many insist that we have, yet I find this belief itself to be grounds for skepticism. In Germany, for instance, the entire force of moral indignation—the kind that passes for morality—was directed against my idea of "Beyond Good and Evil." People argued passionately that modern moral sentiment demonstrates our progress, claiming that compared to us, a figure like Cæsar Borgia could not be seen as a "higher man" or the kind of "superman" I described him to be. One editor even congratulated me for my boldness while accusing me of aiming to abolish all decency.

A curious compliment indeed! But I pose this question in return: Have we truly become more moral?

We modern people like to imagine our heightened sensitivity and mutual consideration as evidence of moral advancement. This collective sense of care and support, this avoidance of harm or offense, seems to us a significant step forward—proof that we surpass the brutal and daring men of the Renaissance. Yet every era believes itself superior in such ways; it is inevitable.

One thing is certain: we could not survive the raw reality of the Renaissance, nor could we imagine enduring its conditions. Our nerves and constitutions are simply too frail. But this does not signify progress. It only reflects the weakened, more delicate nature of our current state, a kind of physiological aging that has given rise to a morality of tenderness and caution.

If we strip away this frailty and delicateness, our so-called morality of "humanization" loses all meaning. In such a context, it might even appear contemptible. Let us also consider how our humanitarian virtues would have seemed to Renaissance men— those accustomed to a richer, bolder, and more overflowing vitality. They would have laughed themselves to death at our modern notions of virtue. Unwittingly, we have become laughable. Our supposed "progress" in reducing suspicion and hostility is simply a byproduct of our dwindling vitality. Living in such dependency and fragility requires endless caution and cooperation. In this environment, we become a society of mutual invalids and caregivers, calling this arrangement "virtue."

To men of a fuller, more daring era, our lifestyle might be seen as cowardice, weakness, or the morality of the old and infirm. What I call our softening of morals is not progress but evidence of decline. By contrast, a harder, fiercer moral code often arises in times of surplus vitality. When life overflows with energy, people take risks, embrace challenges, and even waste their strength freely. What once added zest to life might now poison us. Even indifference—a form of strength—is beyond our reach because we are too sensitive, too frail. Our morality of pity, which I was the first to criticize, reflects the hyper- irritability that marks all decadence. Attempts to give this morality a scientific foundation, as Schopenhauer's morality of pity sought to do, are fundamentally decadent and closely aligned with Christian ethics.

Strong ages and noble cultures regarded pity, neighborly love, and self- denial as contemptible traits. They measured their worth by their positive forces, their creative tension, and their ability to stand apart. By this measure, the Renaissance stands as the last great age, while we moderns—obsessed with self- preservation, neighborly love, and cautious virtues like industry and equity— represent a weak one. Our virtues arise from our frailty. The modern idea of "equality" and the process of leveling everyone to the same standard are hallmarks of a declining culture. Strong ages celebrated the differences between people, the "pathos of distance," the instinct to distinguish oneself, and the courage to embrace hierarchy. These qualities are eroding. The gap between extremes is closing, and society is flattening into sameness.

All our political theories, including the structure of "The German Empire," reflect this decline. Even the ideals of modern science are unconsciously shaped by the forces of decadence. My critique of English and French sociology remains the same: it takes the symptoms of societal decline—its frailty and leveling instincts— and mistakes them for universal norms. Sociology today idealizes descending life, the decay of all organizing power, and the erosion of rank and distinction. This is what our socialists champion as progress. But it is not only socialists who are guilty of this error. Herbert Spencer, with his vision of altruism's triumph, was equally a decadent. To him, and to many others, this collapse of vitality appeared as an ideal to be pursued.

My Concept of Freedom.—The value of something is not always found in what it helps us achieve but often in what it demands from us—the price we must pay. Liberal institutions, for example, lose their essence of freedom the moment they become securely established. Once they are no longer contested, they turn into oppressive forces that stifle true freedom. These institutions undermine the Will to Power, promoting mediocrity as a virtue. They encourage conformity, making people timid, complacent, and fixated on comfort. Under them, the herd instinct triumphs, and humanity is reduced to a collective of obedient cattle. Liberalism, stripped of its idealism, becomes nothing more than the domestication of mankind.

However, the same liberal institutions, when fought for and not yet fully realized, can inspire the very opposite. Struggle for their creation and survival fosters freedom because it involves conflict. And it is war—war for freedom— that preserves the untamed, illiberal instincts essential for liberty. War trains individuals to be free. So, what is freedom? Freedom is the will to take responsibility for oneself. It is the capacity to maintain the distance that distinguishes you from others, to embrace hardship, endure privation, and remain indifferent even to life itself when necessary. It is the willingness to sacrifice, not only others but also yourself, for a cause you believe in. Freedom is the triumph of warrior instincts—those that revel in challenge and victory— over the instincts that crave mere comfort and happiness.

The truly free man despises the shallow comfort idolized by merchants, Christians, cattle, women, Englishmen, and democrats. For him, comfort is contemptible. The free man is a warrior. The measure of freedom, whether in individuals or nations, is determined by the resistance they have to overcome and the effort it takes to stay above it all. True freedom is greatest where the challenge is fiercest— just steps away from tyranny, on the threshold of being overpowered. Psychologically, tyranny represents the inner, powerful instincts that demand the utmost discipline to subdue. Julius Caesar is the finest example of such a free spirit, a man who mastered his instincts with an iron will. Politically, the same holds true: history shows that nations worth admiring were never formed under liberal institutions. It was great danger that shaped them into something worthy of reverence. Danger reveals our hidden strengths, awakens our virtues, and compels us to innovate and defend ourselves. It forces us to become resourceful and discover our inner genius.

The first principle of freedom is this: strength is born of necessity. Without the need to be strong, no one becomes strong. The greatest incubators of strength, the strongest individuals and societies to ever exist, emerged from aristocratic communities like Rome and Venice. These societies understood freedom as I do—not as a given, but as something that must be seized, something you either have or do not have, something you will for yourself and take by force.

A Criticism of Modernity.—We all agree on one thing: our institutions are failing. Yet the fault does not lie with these institutions themselves but with us. We no longer possess the instincts that once gave rise to institutions and sustained them. Without those instincts, the institutions themselves are crumbling and disappearing because we are no longer capable of upholding them. Democracy has always marked the decline of organizational power. I pointed this out as early as "Human,

All Too Human," where I described modern democracy, along with its half-measures like the "German Empire," as forms of a decaying State.

For institutions to exist and thrive, a particular kind of will is necessary—a will that is instinctive, commanding, and even harshly anti-liberal. This will demands allegiance to tradition, authority, and a responsibility that spans generations, stretching infinitely backward and forward in time. When such a will is present, empires with lasting power emerge, like the imperium Romanum or, in our era, Russia. Russia is the only nation today that demonstrates the endurance, strength, and patience required for genuine stability, a nation that can afford to wait, that can still promise a future. Russia stands as the antithesis of the petty- statism, fragility, and nervous exhaustion that plague Europe, particularly brought to the forefront by the foundation of the German Empire.

The modern Western world no longer harbors the instincts that produce institutions or the future. These instincts are fundamentally at odds with what is called the "modern spirit." People live recklessly in the moment, at breakneck speed, with little thought for long-term responsibility. And yet, this is celebrated and called "freedom." But all the qualities that make institutions enduring and meaningful are now despised, ridiculed, and rejected. Even the faintest whisper of authority sends people into a panic about a potential new slavery. In our politics and political parties, the instinct to value and preserve what is solid has decayed so deeply that people instinctively prefer what dissolves, what speeds up the collapse of everything.

Take modern marriage as an example. Its original rationality has vanished completely, but this is not a criticism of marriage itself— it is a criticism of modernity. Marriage once had a clear, rational foundation. It rested on the exclusive legal responsibility of the husband, which acted as a stabilizing force within the union. This stability gave marriage a weight and seriousness that countered the fleeting impulses of sentiment, passion, or momentary desires. Marriage also relied on the absolute indissolubility of the bond, which instilled it with permanence, regardless of the accidents of emotion. Additionally, the responsibility of choosing marriage partners fell to the family, which ensured a certain strategic and long-term coherence in these unions.

The increasing preference for love marriages, however, has undermined the very foundation of matrimony. No institution can ever be built upon a fleeting idiosyncrasy such as "love." Love is too transitory, too unstable to bear the weight of a lasting structure. Marriage can be based on more enduring forces: sexual desire, the instinct of property (with the wife and children seen as possessions), or the instinct of dominion. The latter is particularly vital, as it drives the creation of the smallest yet enduring unit of governance—the family. The family requires children and heirs to carry forward its acquired power, wealth, and influence, ensuring a continuity of purpose and solidarity in instincts from one generation to the next.

Marriage, as an institution, assumes a commitment to the greatest and most enduring forms of organization. It presupposes that society as a whole is willing to secure its own continuity into the distant future. Without this shared commitment, marriage loses its meaning. And this is exactly what has happened to modern marriage: it has lost its meaning, and as a result, it is gradually being abolished.

The question of the working man arises from a combination of foolishness and the underlying degenerate instincts that fuel the intellectual confusion of modern times. There are matters so basic and essential to the order of things that they should never even be questioned. This principle, rooted in instinct, serves as the foundation for survival and continuity. Yet here we are, asking what we should do about the European working class, having transformed their existence into a "question." What is expected now? These workers have been made too aware of their position, their situation framed as an issue, and their sense of entitlement has grown. They question more and more, with increasing boldness, and why wouldn't they? They know they have the numbers on their side.

There's no chance now of cultivating a humble, contented worker like the kind found in China—a course that would have been both reasonable and necessary. Instead, thoughtless and shortsighted decisions have destroyed the very instincts required for the existence of a functional and stable working class. By declaring the working man fit for military service, granting him the right to unionize, and giving him a vote, society has made his discontent inevitable. What did people expect? These concessions have led him to see his position not as a fact of life but as a moral outrage, as an injustice. And yet I ask again, what is the goal here? If people desire a certain outcome, they must also desire the means to achieve it. If society wants workers, it is madness to educate them into believing they are masters.

The kind of freedom being clamored for today is not the kind I mean when I speak of freedom. In our era, leaving individuals to their instincts only leads to chaos. These instincts often contradict and destroy one another, tearing individuals apart from within. Modern life itself can be described as a state of physiological self-contradiction. A rational system of education would seek to suppress some instincts with rigorous discipline, allowing others to grow strong and dominant. This pruning would make individuals coherent and capable. Instead, what we see today is the opposite. The loudest calls for independence, for unchecked development, and for "letting go" come from those who most desperately need restraint. This phenomenon extends to politics and even art. It is a sign of decline, another proof of our instincts faltering. The modern understanding of "freedom" is not a triumph; it is evidence of our degeneration.

When faith becomes necessary, honesty among moralists and saints becomes exceedingly rare. They may claim to value honesty; they may even believe they practice it. But when belief is more effective, more convincing, and ultimately more useful than deliberate hypocrisy, instinct makes that hypocrisy innocent. This principle is key to understanding the behavior of great saints. The same can be said for philosophers, who are their own kind of saint. Their role requires them to uphold certain truths, truths that bolster their craft and grant it public approval. To borrow from Kant, these are the truths of "practical reason." Philosophers know what they must prove. This is their pragmatism, their trade secret. They recognize one another by their shared adherence to these "essential truths." The commandment "Thou shalt not lie" is, for the philosopher, merely a warning: Do not dare, dear philosopher, to speak the entire truth.

A quiet reminder to conservatives: What we have learned—or should have learned—is that regression is impossible. Reverting to a previous state, whether biologically, culturally, or morally, is a fantasy. As physiologists, we know this for a fact. Yet priests and moralists have always believed otherwise. They have tried to bend and force humanity back into older molds of virtue, imposing the rigid standards of morality as if humanity could fit back into them. Even modern politicians mimic these moralists. Today, some political movements aim to force the world into a backward march, longing for an imagined past where everything supposedly worked. But not everyone is suited to move backward like a crab.

The truth is, humanity must move forward, even if this means deeper descent into decadence. This is how I define modern "progress": each step forward is another step further into decay. We cannot halt this trajectory entirely. At best, we might delay it, creating bottlenecks of degeneration that will only result in more violent and catastrophic outbursts later on. But we cannot turn back the tide. Progress, as we conceive of it today, is no more than the managed advance of decline.

My concept of genius begins with the idea that great men and great eras are like explosive forces, holding within them a tremendous amount of stored energy. Their very existence depends on both historical and physiological conditions. They arise only when energy has been conserved, hoarded, and preserved over long periods without any premature release. Once the tension has built to an extreme, even the slightest trigger can ignite the force, giving rise to genius, extraordinary deeds, and monumental changes in the world.

What, then, is the significance of external factors like environment, historical periods, or the so-called "spirit of the age"? Consider Napoleon as an example. Revolutionary France, and even more so the years preceding the Revolution, cultivated values and produced types of people entirely contrary to what Napoleon represented. Yet Napoleon emerged not as a product of that age, but as a legacy of a stronger, older, and more enduring civilization—a civilization whose vitality France was busy dismantling. Precisely because he was different, because he drew from a deeper reservoir of power and tradition, Napoleon became the uncontested master of his time. His strength surpassed that of his contemporaries, allowing him to dominate them.

Great individuals are essential, yet the era in which they appear is largely a matter of chance. Their near-inevitable mastery of their time stems from their greater strength, maturity, and the longer duration for which power has been stored within them. The relationship between genius and its era is like that between strength and weakness, or maturity and immaturity. A genius always towers above his age, which is comparatively youthful, feeble, indecisive, and naive.

Today, however, many people hold a different view, especially in France, where the idea that the "environment" or "zeitgeist" shapes genius has gained almost scientific credibility, even among physiologists. This belief—a sort of nervous disorder disguised as intellectual insight—is a troubling and disheartening sign. England, too, subscribes to this view, but this is hardly surprising. The English tend to interpret genius in only two ways: either through a democratic lens, as exemplified by Buckle, or through a religious perspective, as Carlyle does.

Great individuals and great ages bring with them immense danger. They exhaust what came before and often leave sterility in their wake. A great man signifies an ending, just as a great age—take the Renaissance, for instance— marks the conclusion of a long buildup of energy. Genius, in both action and creation, is inherently extravagant. Its greatness lies in its uncontainable outpouring of energy. The instinct for self-preservation is overridden in such figures; their overwhelming energy compels them to give and expend themselves completely, without restraint. This process is not calculated or deliberate—it is as inevitable as a river bursting through its dams.

People often misinterpret this self-expenditure, labeling it "self-sacrifice" or admiring it as "heroism." They speak of the genius's disregard for personal well- being, their unwavering dedication to an idea, a cause, or a nation. But these are misconceptions. A genius does not act out of deliberate self-sacrifice; they overflow naturally, consuming themselves in the process. They cannot help but give everything—they are compelled by their very nature to do so, just as a river must flow.

Humanity, having reaped countless benefits from such explosive forces, has responded with a peculiar kind of gratitude. It has attributed to these figures a higher morality, seeing in them ideals of selflessness and devotion. Yet this, too, is a misunderstanding. It is not morality that drives the genius; it is the sheer necessity of their nature. Humanity thanks its benefactors in the only way it knows— by misinterpreting them.

The criminal and those like him represent the strong man placed in conditions that do not suit him—a strong nature forced into sickness. He is a man who thrives in wild and untamed environments, where freedom and danger shape life, where the instincts of strength—his shield and sword—find their rightful place. But within society, these very virtues are outlawed. His natural instincts are immediately entangled with emotions like fear, suspicion, and shame. Such a conflict is nearly a formula for physical and psychological decline. When a person must carry out what he is best at—what he most loves—not openly but in secrecy, with constant caution, restraint, and craftiness, it saps his vitality. The repeated necessity of paying for his instincts through danger, persecution, or punishment causes him to turn against those very instincts. He comes to see them as his curse.

This process unfolds most severely in our society, which is tame, average, and emasculated. A natural man, one unshaped by civilization, coming from the mountains or the open seas, is almost certain to decay into a criminal in such an environment. Yet, not always: there are cases where the natural man is stronger than society itself. Napoleon, the Corsican, stands as the most famous example of this triumph.

To explore this further, we can turn to Dostoevsky, a witness of singular importance on this issue. Dostoevsky—incidentally the only psychologist from whom I have learned anything—was among the great discoveries of my life, even more rewarding than Stendhal. This deeply insightful man, who had every reason to hold the shallow Germans in contempt, found among the Siberian convicts he lived with for years—those utterly hopeless criminals with no chance of returning to society—a type of humanity very different from what he had anticipated. These convicts were made of the hardest and most valuable material to be found in Russian society, carved from a superior stock.

Now let us generalize the case of the criminal. Let us think of all individuals who, for whatever reason, fail to gain society's approval. These are people who know they are not seen as beneficial or respectable. They exist with the feelings of outcasts, akin to the Chandala, aware that they are not treated as equals but as untouchables, proscribed, or polluted. Their thoughts and actions are shaped by this awareness, marked by a certain shadowy, subterranean quality. Their inner world becomes dimmed compared to those who live in the sunlight of public favor.

Interestingly, many of the figures we now admire and respect once lived under such conditions. The scientist, the artist, the genius, the independent thinker, the actor, the entrepreneur, and the great adventurer—all of these lived lives that were once disdained. As long as the priest stood as the highest type of man, all others of value were diminished, seen as less worthy. However, the time is coming—this I assert with certainty—when the priest will be regarded as the lowest type of man, as our Chandala, the most dishonest and disreputable among us.

Even now, under the most lenient and humane customs ever known in Europe, any life that stands apart, that is prolonged in obscurity or strangeness, begins to resemble the criminal type. All pioneers of the spirit bear for a time the grim and fateful mark of the Chandala. It is not because they are directly seen as such by others, but because they themselves feel the enormous gulf that separates them from what is accepted and honored in tradition. Nearly every genius experiences this phase of the "Catilinarian life"—a stage filled with hatred, revenge, and rebellion against everything stagnant and established. Catiline—the early form of every future Caesar.

Here the outlook is free. When a philosopher chooses silence, it can signify the greatness of his soul; when he contradicts himself, it might stem from love; and when he lies, it may well be the courtesy of a knight of knowledge. As someone aptly remarked, "It is unworthy of great hearts to spread the turmoil they feel." Yet, it is equally true that there can be greatness in not avoiding what seems undignified. A woman in love may sacrifice her honor, a knight of knowledge who "loves" may sacrifice his humanity, and a god who loved became a Jew.

Beauty is no accident. Even the beauty of a race or family, the grace and perfection of all its movements, does not come easily. Like genius, it is the culmination of generations of effort. Great sacrifices have always been made on the altar of good taste, and much has been deliberately left undone. The 17th century in France serves as a prime example of this, a time when both action and restraint worked hand in hand to elevate aesthetics. A principle of selection was applied to everything—company, environment, clothing, and even the expression of sexual desire. Beauty was prioritized over profit, habit, public opinion, and laziness. The first rule was simple: no one should "let themselves go," not even in private.

Good things are exceedingly expensive. This is true not only in monetary terms but in the discipline required to acquire them.

Whoever possesses beauty or refinement is different from someone still striving for it. Everything good is an inheritance, something passed down and refined over time. What isn't inherited is incomplete; it is only a beginning. In ancient Athens, during Cicero's time, men and boys were more beautiful than women. But this was the result of centuries of rigorous effort and self-discipline devoted to male beauty. Let us not be deceived: refining feelings and thoughts alone is insufficient. This is the great failing of German culture, which emphasizes abstract ideals but neglects the body.

The body must be persuaded first. Maintaining a refined and tasteful demeanor, associating only with others who do the same, shapes one's entire being over a few generations. The destiny of a people or humanity is determined by where they begin their cultural efforts. The starting point must be the body, behavior, diet, and physiology—not the "soul," as priests and moralists insist. The Greeks understood this foundational truth and acted upon it, which is why they remain the first true creators of culture. Christianity, with its disdain for the body, has been the greatest misfortune to ever befall humanity.

Progress, as I see it, is not about returning to a primal state but ascending into a more profound and untamed naturalness. It is about reaching a height where one can grapple with grand challenges, even play with them. Take Napoleon as an example of what I mean by a "return to nature." In his tactics and strategy, he exemplified this ascent. But Rousseau? Where did he wish to return? Rousseau, that first modern man, was both an idealist and a scoundrel. Needing moral dignity to endure his own reflection, he was a creature of vanity and self-loathing. He camped on the threshold of modernity, calling for a "return to nature." But what kind of nature did he envision? I detest Rousseau even in the Revolution. The Revolution's bloody spectacle does not disturb me as much as its Rousseau-inspired morality. It was the morality of mediocrity masquerading as justice.

The doctrine of equality is the deadliest poison of all, for it pretends to speak in the name of justice while veiling true justice. Justice would say, "To equals, equality; to unequals, inequality." Never should unequal things be made equal. The horrors and bloodshed associated with this doctrine have granted it an undeserved aura of sanctity. The Revolution, as a drama, has deceived even noble minds. Only Goethe, as far as I can see, viewed it as it should be seen— with utter disdain.

Goethe was not merely a German figure but a European one. He was a bold attempt to overcome the 18th century by reclaiming the naturalness of the Renaissance. In Goethe, the instincts of his century—its sentimentality, its idolization of nature, and its anti-historical spirit—were transformed. He was a realist who embraced life rather than shrinking from it. Goethe sought wholeness, uniting reason, feeling, sensuality, and will, in opposition to the fragmented doctrines of Kant. He disciplined himself into a harmonious whole and became a master of himself.

Goethe dreamed of a complete human being: cultured, physically skilled, self-respecting, and capable of indulging in life's richness without being destroyed by it. He was tolerant not from weakness but from strength, turning adversity to his advantage.

He embodied a cheerful fatalism, embracing the universe with confidence. Such faith, the highest of all, is what I have called Dionysian—a celebration of life that affirms all existence.

In some ways, the 19th century aspired to Goethe's ideals: broad understanding, bold realism, and reverence for life's facts. Yet, the result was chaos, fatigue, and a retreat into the sentimental mediocrity of the 18th century—romanticism, socialism, and altruism. This century, especially in its later years, became an intensified version of its predecessor: a period of decline. Goethe, despite his greatness, was merely an episode—a magnificent but futile effort.

Great men should not be judged by their immediate utility. Humanity often misunderstands its benefactors, attributing to them motives they never had. Goethe is the last German I respect. He understood the cross, as I understand it, and shared my disdain for what it symbolizes. People often ask why I write in German when I am so little read in Germany. My aim is not immediate recognition but to create works that time itself cannot erode. Both in form and content, I strive for a degree of immortality. The aphorism and the concise sentence, forms in which I am a master, are eternal. My ambition is to say in ten sentences what others cannot say in a whole book.

With Thus Spoke Zarathustra, I have given humanity its deepest book.

Soon, I will give it its most independent one.

Chapter 10

Things I owe to The Ancients

In conclusion, I want to say a few words about that world to which I have sought new ways of access and for which I may have discovered a new passage—the ancient world. My taste, which is perhaps the opposite of tolerant, does not wholeheartedly embrace even this world. In general, I am not eager to say Yes to things. I would rather say No, or, better yet, say nothing at all. This is true of entire cultures; it is true of books; and it is true of places and landscapes.

To be honest, there are very few ancient books that hold a special place in my life, and the most famous ones are not included among them.

My sense of style, particularly for the epigram as a form of expression, seemed to awaken almost instantly when I first encountered Sallust. I still recall the astonishment of my respected teacher Corssen when he was compelled to give his worst Latin student the highest marks. Suddenly, and all at once, I understood everything there was to learn. The condensed and austere language, packed with meaning and with an almost mischievous indifference to "beautiful words" and "beautiful feelings"—in these I found my own inclination. In my writings leading up to Thus Spoke Zarathustra, you will notice a serious effort to achieve a Roman style—a style that aspires to the permanence of "more enduring than bronze."

The same thing occurred when I first read Horace. No poet, even to this day, has given me the same intense artistic pleasure as an ode by Horace did from the very beginning. In some languages, it would be ridiculous to even attempt what Horace achieves. His writing is like a mosaic where every word radiates its influence both to the left and the right. Its placement, sound, and meaning all work together to create an extraordinary effect. This economy of words—where the least amount of signs produces the maximum energy—is distinctly Roman. And, if you trust my judgment, it is the very definition of noble excellence. Compared to this, all other poetry seems almost crude, like meaningless, sentimental rambling.

I cannot say that I owe the Greeks anything resembling the profound impressions I have received from the Romans. To be frank, the Greeks can never hold the same significance for us as the Romans do. The Greeks are not teachers in the same way. Their style is too peculiar, too fluid, to impose itself as a model or to attain the weight of a true classic. Who has ever truly learned how to write from a Greek? It is impossible to imagine anyone mastering writing without the Romans. They are our true instructors. And do not suggest Plato to me—I remain fundamentally skeptical of him. I have never been able to align myself with the tradition among scholars of admiring Plato as an artist.

Even in antiquity, the most refined critics of taste were not taken by Plato as we are led to believe. To my mind, Plato jumbles all the forms of style into a chaotic mix. In this sense, he is one of the earliest examples of stylistic decadence. He shares this fault with the Cynics, who created the satura Menippea. The Platonic dialogue—a smug, almost juvenile form of dialectics—could only charm someone who has never read good French writers, such as Fontenelle. Plato, I must confess, bores me. At heart, my distrust of him is fundamental. I see him as profoundly removed from the essential instincts of the Hellenes, steeped in moral prejudices, and, in some respects, as a precursor to Christianity. For Plato, the idea of "good" is already the supreme value—a concept that foreshadows the Christian morality to come. If I had to give Plato's philosophy a blunt name, I might call it "lofty nonsense," or, if preferred, "idealism."

Humanity has paid a high price for this Athenian's education among the Egyptians—or perhaps among the Jews in Egypt? Plato, with his double-edged charm—the so-called "ideal"— became the bridge by which the nobler spirits of antiquity were led to misunderstand themselves and cross into the ideology that culminated in the Christian cross. And even now, how much Plato remains entrenched in the concepts of the "church," in its architecture, its system, and its practices!

For me, the cure, the antidote, and the reprieve from all this Platonism has always been Thucydides. His work represents my ideal of clarity and realism.

Perhaps Machiavelli's The Prince is his closest relative in spirit. Both refuse to delude themselves. They seek reason in reality, not in abstract rationality or morality. Thucydides is the antithesis of the sugary, romanticised vision of the Greeks that modern "classical education" instills in young minds. His writings should be read with great care, each line scrutinised, and his unspoken ideas considered just as seriously as his explicit words. Few thinkers possess so much depth in what they leave unsaid.

Thucydides is the consummate expression of the Sophist tradition, that movement grounded in realism which resisted the idealistic pretensions and moral posturing of Socratic thought as it spread in all directions. For me, Greek philosophy represents the decline of Greek instincts, whereas Thucydides encapsulates the unflinching, rigorous realism of the ancient Hellene.

The distinction between Thucydides and Plato is ultimately one of courage versus fear. Thucydides confronts reality with bravery and clarity, while Plato shrinks from it, retreating into the comforting arms of ideals. Thucydides is a master of his own mind and therefore a master of life. Plato, on the other hand, flees from life into the shadows of abstract ideals. This makes Thucydides not just a historian, but a thinker of unyielding power and strength, unmatched in his affirmation of reality.

To unearth examples of "beautiful souls," "golden means," or other supposed perfections among the Greeks, to admire their serene grandeur, their so-called ideal attitudes, or their exalted simplicity—this "exalted simplicity," which in truth is nothing more than a piece of German naivety, was something from which my inner psychologist always saved me. What I saw instead was their most powerful instinct: the relentless Will to Power. I saw them driven by the fierce and untamed force of this will, trembling with its violence. I recognized that their institutions were not built on harmony but on strategies of containment, created to protect every individual from the volatile, explosive energy simmering within their neighbor.

This immense internal tension found its outlet in violent and ruthless aggression directed outward, toward other states. Their cities tore at one another in brutal conflict, each striving to maintain peace within by externalizing the chaos. Strength became an absolute necessity in this environment, for danger was constant and ever-present, lurking at every corner. The extraordinary grace and flexibility of their bodies, the bold realism, and even the characteristic amorality of the Hellenes—these were not innate attributes but rather survival mechanisms. These traits were forged under the pressures of their circumstances, not gifts they were born with.

Even their festivals and artistic achievements were not mere expressions of joy or creativity but instruments of self-assertion and self-glorification. These were deliberate efforts to heighten their sense of superiority, to project it outward, and sometimes to inspire terror in those who observed them. Imagine judging the Greeks through a lens shaped by German interpretations—seeing them through the narrow focus of their philosophers. Worse yet, imagine using the staid, suburban respectability of the Socratic schools as the key to understanding the essence of what is truly Hellenic!

The truth is that the philosophers were the decadent offshoots of Hellas, a counter-movement that ran against the grain of their original and noble values. They opposed the agonal instinct, the competitive drive that defined the Hellenic spirit; they rejected the spirit of the polis, the pride in racial excellence, and the authority of deep-rooted traditions. Socratic virtues were only preached to the Greeks because the Greeks had already begun to lose their virtue. Irritable, cowardly, unsteady, and increasingly prone to theatricality, they were a people in decline, desperate for the moral sermons directed at them.

But these moral prescriptions did not save them. They could not. Instead, these grand gestures and lofty words were little more than adornments for a society in decay. Decadents are always drawn to such displays, for they cling to the illusion of greatness even as it slips further from their grasp. Morality, as the Greeks came to know it through their philosophers, was not a cure but a symptom—a symptom of a people who had already lost their way.

I was the first to take the phenomenon of Dionysus seriously in order to understand the ancient, vibrant, and abundantly rich Hellenic instinct. This phenomenon, remarkable in its essence, can only be interpreted as an expression of overflowing energy. Whoever has studied the Greeks as profoundly as Jakob Burckhardt of Basel, one of the finest connoisseurs of their culture, would immediately recognize that this interpretation opened a new path of understanding. In his Cultur der Griechen, Burckhardt even dedicated a special chapter to this subject, acknowledging its significance. On the other hand, consider the almost laughable deficiency of instinct displayed by German philologists when they approach the question of Dionysus. The famous Lobeck, for example, burrowed into this mysterious realm with the assuredness of a dried-up bookworm, convinced he was being scientific when, in truth, his approach was painfully superficial and immature.

With all the pomp of erudition, Lobeck reduced the mysteries to trivialities, suggesting that the orgies merely taught participants banal facts like how wine stirs desire or that plants bloom and fade with the seasons. He explained away the immense wealth of rites, symbols, and myths rooted in these rituals—which permeate the entirety of antiquity—with the dismissive notion that the Greeks merely invented festivals and myths as idle diversions. His conclusion, that celebratory behaviors like laughing, weeping, and dancing formed the basis of elaborate traditions, is nothing short of absurd. This reductionist nonsense, presented as scholarship, deserves no serious consideration.

Contrast this with the more profound vision of the Greeks as seen by figures like Winckelmann and Goethe. Yet even they misunderstood something essential. Their idealized image of the Greeks—one of calm grandeur, rational simplicity, and harmonious beauty—could not accommodate the Dionysian essence. Goethe, for instance, likely dismissed the ecstatic fervor of Dionysian rites, failing to recognize that these mysteries revealed the core of the Greek soul. This core was their "will to life," expressed most powerfully in the Dionysian state. Through these mysteries, the Greeks secured for themselves a profound connection to life eternal, embracing its cyclical nature and celebrating the continuity of existence through procreation and renewal.

To the Greeks, the mysteries of sexuality symbolized the sacred foundation of life itself. Every aspect of birth, creation, and renewal was steeped in reverence and seen as divine. Even pain, particularly the pain of childbirth, was sanctified, as it was inseparable from creation and growth. This sanctification of pain carried a deeper message: to ensure the endless joy of creation, the "pains of childbirth" must be eternal. Such is the symbolism of Dionysus, the affirmation of life in all its fullness, including its suffering, its ecstasy, and its inexhaustible capacity for renewal.

Christianity later distorted this profound connection, branding sexuality as impure and casting filth upon the very foundation of existence. In doing so, it severed humanity from the instinctual reverence for life that the Greeks held sacred. Yet it was the psychology of orgiasm—this experience of overwhelming vitality, where even pain becomes a stimulant—that gave me the key to understanding the concept of tragic feeling. Aristotle and the pessimists misunderstood tragedy entirely. Far from being an expression of Greek pessimism, as Schopenhauer claimed, tragedy represents the ultimate rejection of such a worldview. It is a triumphant affirmation of life, embracing even its most perplexing and terrifying aspects.

The essence of tragedy lies in its exultation of life's inexhaustible energy, even in the sacrifice of its highest forms. This is the Dionysian spirit, the bridge to the psychology of the tragic poet. It does not aim to escape terror and pity or to purge dangerous passions through catharsis, as Aristotle supposed. Instead, it transcends terror and pity, rejoicing in the eternal cycle of creation and destruction, the endless becoming that is life itself. This lust for life, which includes a love for destruction as part of creation, is at the heart of the Dionysian worldview.

With this understanding, I return to the foundation of my philosophy, to the starting point of my intellectual journey. The Birth of Tragedy was my first attempt to reevaluate all values, and here, once again, I stand upon the same ground from which my will and power originate. I am the last disciple of the philosopher Dionysus, the prophet of eternal recurrence.

The End

The Antichrist

Friedrich Nietzsche

Prologue

This book is meant for the rarest kind of people. Perhaps none of them are alive today. Maybe they are among those who will one day understand my Zarathustra. How could I mistake myself for those who are just now beginning to listen? My time is not now; it will come the day after tomorrow. Some men are born only to be understood after their death.

I know all too well what it takes to understand me, and why one must. To endure the weight of my seriousness and my passion, a person must have intellectual integrity, a strength so sharp it borders on hardness. He must be used to living at great heights, looking down on the petty chatter of politics and nationalism as something far beneath him. He must be indifferent, never questioning whether the truth benefits him or brings him misfortune. He must have a strength that draws him toward questions no one else dares to ask—the courage to confront what is forbidden and a destiny tied to navigating life's labyrinth. He must know the solitude of seven lifetimes. He must have new ears to hear unheard music, new eyes to see what lies furthest away, and a conscience open to truths no one has dared to discover before. He must also possess the ability to conserve his energy with great discipline, to channel his passion and strength wisely. Above all, he must have a deep reverence for himself, a love for himself, and absolute freedom over himself.

Such are my readers—my real readers, my destined readers. What value do the rest have? The rest are simply humanity. To understand me, one must rise above humanity in power, in greatness of soul—and in scorn.

The Antichrist

Let us look at each other directly. We are Hyperboreans—we know just how far removed we are from the rest. "Neither by land nor by water can you reach the Hyperboreans," said Pindar long ago. We live beyond the North, beyond the ice, even beyond death—our life, our happiness lies there. We have found that happiness; we know the way to it. It came from thousands of years wandering in the labyrinth. Who else has found it? The modern man? "I don't know the way in or out; I am whatever doesn't know either the way in or out," says the modern man with a sigh.

This modern age made us sick—sick with its lazy peace, its cowardly compromises, and the self-righteous dirtiness of its constant "Yes" and "No." This tolerance, this wide-open heart that "forgives" because it "understands," feels like a hot, stifling wind to us. We would rather live in the cold ice than among these modern virtues and soft southern breezes. We were brave; we spared neither ourselves nor others, but it took us a long time to figure out where to direct that courage. We became somber, and they called us fatalists. Our fate was one of fullness, tension, and stored-up strength. We longed for lightning and great deeds, not for the weakling's happiness or resignation. The air around us was heavy with thunder, and as we embodied nature, even the skies seemed dark—because we had not yet found our path. Our formula for happiness: a Yes, a No, a straight line, a goal.

What is good? Whatever increases the feeling of strength, the will to power, and power itself in a person.

What is evil? Whatever comes from weakness.

What is happiness? The feeling that strength grows, that resistance is overcome.

Not satisfaction, but more power. Not peace at any cost, but struggle. Not virtue in the moral sense, but effectiveness—virtue in the Renaissance sense, free from moral constraints.

The weak and the flawed should perish: this is the first principle of our kindness. And one should even help them perish.

What is more damaging than any vice? Active compassion for the weak and flawed—Christianity.

The problem I am setting here is not what will replace mankind in the chain of life—man is an end—but what kind of man should be created, should be desired, as the most valuable, the one most worthy of life, the one who can secure the future.

This higher type of man has appeared many times in history, but always as a rare accident, an exception, never something deliberately created. Often, this type has been the most feared; in fact, it has been seen as the ultimate terror. Out of this fear, the opposite type has been nurtured and achieved: the tame animal, the herd animal, the sickly human—the Christian.

Humanity does not represent progress toward something better, stronger, or higher as people think today. This idea of progress is modern—and false. The European today is far beneath the European of the Renaissance in terms of worth. Evolution does not automatically mean improvement, growth, or strength.

True, in isolated cases and different parts of the world, a higher type of person can and does emerge. Compared to the masses, this person may appear as a kind of superhuman. These rare, fortunate occurrences have always been possible and will likely remain so. Entire races, tribes, or nations may occasionally represent such strokes of luck.

We must not dress up or beautify Christianity: it has waged a relentless war against the higher type of man. It has suppressed the deepest instincts of this type, turning these instincts into the very definition of evil. Christianity created its concept of "the Evil One" from the traits of the strong man, labeling him as the ultimate outcast. It has sided with the weak, the lowly, and the flawed, elevating opposition to life's natural instincts of self- preservation into an ideal.

Even the brightest minds have been corrupted by it, as Christianity painted the highest intellectual values as sinful, misleading, and full of temptation. The most tragic example of this is Pascal, who believed his brilliant mind had been ruined by original sin, when in truth, it was Christianity that destroyed it.

What a tragic and painful picture I see: I have pulled back the curtain to reveal humanity's decay. When I use the word "decay," it carries no moral judgment—it is free from that suspicion. I emphasize this again: I mean decay in the sense of decline, of décadence. Strangely, I find this decay most evident in those who have aimed highest at "virtue" and "godliness." What I argue is that the values humanity holds in the highest regard today are décadence values.

I call an animal, a species, or an individual corrupt when it loses its instincts—when it chooses what harms it. A history of humanity's "higher feelings" and "ideals" (a task I may yet undertake) would likely explain why man has degenerated. To me, life is an instinct for growth, survival, accumulating strength, and achieving power. When the will to power is absent, disaster follows. My claim is that the highest values of humanity have been emptied of this will, and that the values of décadence and nihilism now dominate under the guise of sacred names.

Christianity calls itself the religion of pity. Pity, however, opposes all the invigorating passions that enhance the energy of life; it weakens and drains power. When a man pities, he loses strength. Pity amplifies the suffering that already exists, spreading it like a contagion. In extreme cases, pity can demand total sacrifice, an enormous cost for an often trivial cause—as in the death of the Nazarene. That's one way to see it. But there's a deeper issue: the reactions pity provokes reveal its true danger to life. Pity goes against the very law of evolution, the principle of natural selection. It preserves what is ready to perish; it sides with the weak, the disinherited, and the condemned. By supporting the flawed and the suffering, pity makes life appear bleak and uncertain.

Humanity dared to call pity a virtue. In fact, in some moral systems, pity was hailed as the ultimate virtue, the foundation of all others. But this view came from a nihilistic philosophy, one that essentially denied life. Schopenhauer recognized this: pity denies life and makes it seem unworthy of living. Pity is the tool of nihilism. Let me stress this again: this weakening, contagious instinct undermines all the instincts that sustain and enhance life. Pity, as a protector of the miserable, becomes an agent of décadence. It encourages extinction—not openly, of course, but under the guise of "the other world," "God," "true life,"

Nirvana, salvation, or blessedness. This seemingly innocent language from religious and ethical teachings hides its true aim: the destruction of life.

Schopenhauer hated life, which is why pity seemed virtuous to him. Aristotle, on the other hand, recognized pity as a sick and dangerous state of mind. His remedy was tragedy, a kind of purging. The instinct for life demands that we find ways to puncture and release the dangerous build-up of pity, like the one we see in Schopenhauer's work or in modern culture, from Tolstoy to Wagner. This accumulation of pity must be burst, its poison discharged.

Nothing in our modern age is more harmful than Christian pity. To heal this sickness, we must be unmerciful, wield the knife without hesitation. This is our task, our responsibility as philosophers. This is what it means to be Hyperboreans.

We need to be clear about who we see as our opponents: theologians and anyone with theological influence in their blood—that sums up our entire philosophy. To truly understand the danger they pose, one must have confronted it up close, or better yet, experienced it personally and almost succumbed to it. Only then can one realize it's no small matter. The so-called free- thinking of many naturalists and scientists strikes me as a joke— they lack real passion about these issues; they haven't suffered. This poison spreads much further than most people imagine. I see the arrogant attitude of theologians in all who call themselves "idealists." These are people who claim a higher perspective, allowing them to look down on reality with suspicion.

The idealist, like the priest, holds onto lofty concepts and uses them with a kind of benevolent disdain against reason, the senses, honor, enjoyment, and science. To them, these things are inferior, corrupting forces. They imagine the soul as a pure thing that rises above it all. As if humility, chastity, poverty—in short, so-called holiness—haven't caused far more harm to life than any imaginable vice or horror. The idea of the "pure soul" is a complete lie. As long as priests—these professional deniers, slanderers, and poisoners of life—are seen as a higher kind of human being, there can be no answer to the question, "What is truth?" The truth has already been turned upside down when the advocate of emptiness is mistaken for its representative.

I wage war against this theological instinct because I see its traces everywhere. Anyone with theological blood in their veins is dishonest and untrustworthy in everything. The pitiful product of this condition is called faith. Faith means closing one's eyes to oneself forever, to avoid seeing the lies that cannot be undone. On this false foundation, people build their ideas of morality, virtue, and holiness. They make their flawed perspective sacred by calling it "God," "salvation," or "eternity." They declare that no other way of seeing the world has value.

I uncover this theological instinct wherever I look—it is the most widespread and deeply rooted falsehood on earth. Whatever a theologian declares as true is almost certainly false. This can serve as a reliable guide to truth. Their instinct for self-preservation is so strong that they resist truth in every form, ensuring it can never be honored or even spoken. Wherever theologians hold influence, they reverse values, forcing the meanings of "true" and "false" to switch places. Whatever harms life is called "true," while whatever uplifts, strengthens, and celebrates life is labeled "false."

When theologians, through the "conscience" of rulers or the masses, seize power, there is no doubt about their ultimate goal: they aim to bring everything to an end. Their nihilistic will to destruction is always at the heart of their actions.

Among Germans, I am immediately understood when I say that theological blood is the downfall of philosophy. The Protestant pastor is the grandfather of German philosophy, and Protestantism itself is its original sin. Protestantism can be defined as a half-paralyzed form of both Christianity and reason. Simply mentioning the "Tübingen School" makes it clear what German philosophy essentially is—a refined form of theology. The Suabians are known as the most skilled liars in Germany; they lie without malice, almost innocently.

Why was there such celebration among German scholars— most of whom are the sons of pastors and teachers—when Kant appeared? Why does the echo of their conviction that Kant marked a new beginning still resonate? The theological instinct in German academia immediately recognized what Kant's work made possible once again. A secret path back to the old ideals was reopened. The concept of the "true world" and morality as the foundation of existence—the two most harmful errors ever conceived—were, thanks to Kant's crafty skepticism, made less vulnerable. They might not have been proven, but they were no longer easily refuted. Reason no longer claimed the right to demolish these ideas. Reality was reduced to mere "appearance," while an entirely false notion of existence was elevated as reality. Kant's success was a theological success, not a philosophical one. Like Luther and Leibniz before him, Kant became another obstacle to German integrity, which was already fragile.

Now, a word against Kant as a moralist. True virtue must be something we create for ourselves; it must emerge from our personal needs and as a defense of our life. In every other case, it is a threat. Virtue that does not belong to one's own life endangers it. A virtue rooted in mere reverence for the abstract idea of "virtue," as Kant proposed, is destructive. Ideas such as "virtue," "duty," or "the good for its own sake"—virtues grounded in impersonality or universal validity—are mere illusions. They reflect the decay and ultimate breakdown of life, embodying the stagnant spirit of Königsberg.

In contrast, the deepest laws of survival and growth demand that each individual discover their own virtue, their own unique imperative. A nation collapses when it confuses its specific duty with some general, abstract concept of duty. Nothing leads to a more complete disaster than impersonal duties or sacrifices made to serve lifeless abstractions. Yet, no one seems to have recognized Kant's categorical imperative as a danger to life. It was only protected because of the theological instinct. A life- driven action proves itself right through the joy it brings. And yet, that nihilist, Kant, with his deeply Christian instincts, treated joy as an objection.

What destroys a person faster than working, thinking, and feeling without inner necessity, without personal desire, and without pleasure? To act as a mere machine of duty is a recipe for decline and even for madness. Kant himself became a victim of this—a true descent into idiocy. And this man lived in the same era as Goethe! This spinner of lifeless abstractions was celebrated as the German philosopher and is still held in high regard today.

I hesitate to even speak about what I think of the Germans. Didn't Kant see the French Revolution as a transformation of the state from something inorganic to something organic? Didn't he ask if there was any event that could be explained without assuming some moral faculty within humanity? And, according to Kant, this faculty demonstrated "mankind's tendency toward the good," once and for all. His answer to this was "revolution." Instinct gone wrong in every possible way, instinct rebelling against nature— that is German decay transformed into philosophy. That is Kant!

I exclude a few skeptics, those rare examples of decency in the history of philosophy; the rest lack even the slightest idea of intellectual honesty. These so- called great minds and prodigies behave like women—they consider "beautiful feelings" as valid arguments, believe that an emotional outburst is proof of divine inspiration, and treat conviction as the mark of truth. In the end, Kant— with his "German" innocence—tried to give this kind of intellectual corruption a scientific spin by naming it "practical reason." He intentionally created a version of reasoning meant for moments when actual reasoning was inconvenient, especially when the moral command "thou shalt" needed to take center stage.

If we recall that philosophers originally evolved from the priestly type, then this inherited self-deception ceases to surprise. When a man feels he has a divine mission—perhaps to uplift, save, or free humanity—when he senses a divine spark within and believes himself a voice for supernatural commands, it's only natural that he considers himself above mere logical standards of judgment. He feels sanctified by his mission, a figure of a higher order. What does such a priest have to do with philosophy? He sees himself as far above it. And throughout history, the priest has held authority, defining what is "true" and "false."

We shouldn't underestimate the importance of this: we free spirits are already a "revaluation of all values." We stand as a visible rebellion and triumph over the old concepts of "truth" and "untruth." The most valuable insights are the last to be achieved, and the greatest of these insights are about the methods we use. For thousands of years, the methods and principles of the scientific spirit—so commonplace today—were despised. Anyone who leaned toward them was cast out from "decent" society, labeled an "enemy of God," a mocker of truth, or even "possessed." A man of science was treated as untouchable, like a member of an outcast class.

For centuries, we faced humanity's overwhelming foolishness and their shallow ideas of what truth should be. Their expectations of what serving the truth meant, along with all their moral commands, were hurled at us. Our goals, methods, and careful, skeptical approaches were viewed as shameful and contemptible. Looking back, we might even wonder if people's blindness wasn't tied to an aesthetic preference. They demanded truth to be dramatic, something that thrilled their senses. From scholars, they expected spectacle and strong emotional appeal. It was likely our modesty, our quiet approach, that clashed with their tastes.

How accurately they sensed it—these self-important defenders of God!

We have forgotten certain ideas and grown more humble in every way. We no longer see humans as descended from the "spirit" or the "divine"; instead, we place them back among the animals. Humans are the strongest of animals because they are the cleverest, and their intelligence is a result of this. However, we are cautious not to let this lead to arrogance, such as thinking humans are the pinnacle of evolution. In truth, humans are far from being the crown of creation; many animals exist at similar levels of development. Even saying this might be overstating it, for humans are, relatively speaking, the most flawed and unhealthy of all animals. They have strayed the farthest from their instincts, yet they remain the most fascinating.

As for the lower animals, Descartes had the daring to describe them as machines. Modern physiology supports this view. However, Descartes' mistake was setting humans apart. Today, we know humans only to the extent that we see them as machines too. Previously, humans were said to possess "free will" as a gift from higher beings, but now this idea no longer makes sense. What we once called "will" is now understood as a result of various conflicting and harmonious stimuli—a reaction, not an independent force. The will does not "act" or "move" as we once thought.

In the past, people believed that human consciousness, or "spirit," was proof of divine origin. To perfect themselves, people were told to withdraw from earthly experiences and shed their physical selves, leaving only the "pure spirit." We now see consciousness as a sign of imperfection—a trial, an experiment, or even a misunderstanding. It consumes energy needlessly and cannot achieve anything perfectly.

The idea of a "pure spirit" is sheer foolishness; remove the body, the senses, and the nervous system, and all that remains is error.

Christianity disconnects morality and religion from reality entirely. It offers imaginary causes like "God," "soul," "spirit," and "free will" (or "unfree will"), and imaginary effects like "sin," "salvation," "grace," and "forgiveness." Its stories involve imaginary beings—God, spirits, and souls—and its version of natural history is centered on humans while denying natural causes. Its psychology misinterprets feelings and bodily states, labeling them with terms like "repentance," "temptation," or "the presence of God." Its teleology imagines destinations like "the kingdom of God" or "eternal life." Unlike dreams, which reflect reality in some way, this fictional world distorts, cheapens, and denies it.

When "nature" was set against "God," the natural became synonymous with the "bad." This entire fabricated world stems from a hatred of nature, or reality, and reveals a deep discomfort with the real. Who feels compelled to escape reality? Those who suffer in it. To suffer from reality is to be a flawed reality. The imbalance of pain over pleasure drives this false morality and religion. That imbalance, in turn, is the very definition of decay.

A closer look at the Christian concept of God inevitably leads to one conclusion—a criticism that must be faced. A nation that still has confidence in itself clings to its own god as a representation of its strength and identity. Through this god, the people honor the values and conditions that ensure their survival and celebrate their virtues. The god becomes a projection of their pride and their sense of power, a figure to whom they can give thanks. A wealthy people will naturally offer from their abundance; a proud people will need a god to whom they can make sacrifices as an expression of their vitality. Religion, in this sense, becomes a form of gratitude—a way to acknowledge the miracle of their own existence, for which they feel compelled to create a god to thank.

Such a god must have the capacity to do both good and harm, to be a friend or a foe, and to inspire awe through acts of both kindness and wrath. To strip a god of these dual traits, reducing him to a god of pure goodness, would go against human nature itself. People need a god who reflects their full range of experiences and emotions— good and evil alike. A god who cannot express anger, revenge, envy, scorn, cunning, or the exhilaration of victory and destruction is a god no one could understand, let alone revere. Why would anyone desire a god so one-dimensional?

However, when a nation begins to lose its belief in its own future—when hope for freedom fades, and submission seems like the only path to survival— its concept of god also begins to change. This god, once a representation of collective strength and the thirst for power, transforms into a figure of meekness, humility, and peace. He preaches "peace of soul," forbids hatred, and promotes universal love, extending even to one's enemies. Such a god becomes moralistic, personal, and all-encompassing. No longer the god of a strong people, he turns into the god of private lives and cosmopolitan ideals.

Once, this god embodied the might of a nation, the strength and ambition that fueled its people. But now, this god is no longer aggressive or commanding. Instead, he is reshaped to align with weakness, embodying the virtues of those who lack power. When gods are stripped of strength, passion, and masculine virtues, they become the gods of those in physical or moral decline. These people do not see themselves as weak; they call themselves "the good."

The dualistic idea of a good god versus an evil god emerges from this decline. Those who feel oppressed reimagine their god as pure goodness, while stripping the gods of their oppressors of any redeeming qualities, turning them into devils. This transformation of gods into either purely good or purely evil figures is a byproduct of societal and moral decay. Both the overly good god and the concept of the devil are the products of decadence.

How, then, can anyone seriously regard the evolution of the Christian god—from the god of Israel, a national deity, to the Christian god, a universal embodiment of goodness—as progress?

Even intellectuals like Renan fall into this naïve interpretation. Yet the opposite is true. When everything essential to life's ascension—strength, courage, pride, and mastery—is removed from the concept of god, he becomes nothing more than a crutch for the weak, a comfort for sinners, and a refuge for the sick. He is reduced to a savior, a redeemer, the last vestige of divinity's purpose.

This transformation represents the decline of the godhead itself. Once the god of a chosen people, rooted in a specific nation and its power, he becomes a wanderer, like the people who created him. No longer tied to one place or people, he spreads across the world, becoming a universal god. As his following grows, so does his detachment from his original identity. He becomes the god of the masses, of the weak, and his once-proud attributes are lost.

This universal god does not grow into a majestic figure like the gods of proud, ancient peoples. Instead, he remains a shadow of his former self—still marked by his origins in a small, oppressed nation. His earthly kingdom is not one of grandeur but of the underworld, hidden in the shadows and ghettos of the world. He is pale, weak, and a reflection of human frailty.

Even the intellectuals—those pale thinkers who analyze reality through abstraction—have taken over this god. They spun their webs of metaphysics around him until he was subdued and transformed into one of them. He began spinning his own abstract theories, embodying the ideals of philosophers like Spinoza. Over time, he grew thinner and more abstract, becoming the "pure spirit," the "absolute," the "thing-in-itself." This final stage marks the collapse of a once-great god, reduced to an idea, a shadow of his former strength.

The Christian concept of God—a god who is the champion of the weak, a spinner of metaphysical webs, a being reduced to pure spirit—stands as one of the most corrupted and degenerate ideas of divinity ever conceived. It marks a dramatic low point in the evolution of what gods have historically represented. This god, rather than celebrating life, vitality, and existence, becomes a direct contradiction to these very forces. Instead of affirming life and glorifying its essence with a resounding "Yes!" he becomes the eternal "No!"—a declaration of war against life, nature, and the will to live. This god transforms into a symbol for rejecting the here and now, denying the world as it is, and replacing it with fabrications of an imagined "beyond." In him, emptiness itself is worshipped, and the will to embrace nothingness is sanctified.

The failure of the robust northern European races to discard this frail, lifeless god reflects poorly on their spiritual insight and their capacity to distinguish true vitality in religion. These people, whose physical and cultural strength could have driven them to dismiss such a decayed and worn-out relic of human weakness, instead absorbed this god into their instincts. In doing so, they allowed disease, resignation, and contradiction to infiltrate the core of their values. The consequences of this failure still reverberate through their culture, evident in the inability to create new gods or fresh expressions of divine power. Two millennia have passed, and yet no new gods have emerged. Instead, the world continues to cling to this pitiful deity of Christian monotony—a bland, uncreative projection of human decay. This god is a grotesque hybrid of emptiness and contradiction, a hollow image conjured from the collective weariness of the soul. He embodies the instincts of decadence, giving legitimacy to cowardice, resignation, and spiritual exhaustion.

In condemning Christianity, I do not wish to neglect its distant relative, Buddhism, a faith with an even larger number of followers. Both religions fall into the category of nihilistic systems, born from similar physiological and psychological conditions. However, there is a profound difference between them. For this insight, critics of Christianity owe a debt to Indian scholars who have illuminated the nuances of Buddhism. Unlike Christianity, Buddhism is grounded in realism—a hundredfold more so. It reflects a tradition of profound philosophical inquiry and retains an ability to confront reality objectively and without illusion. By the time Buddhism emerged, it had already discarded the concept of "god."

In fact, Buddhism is perhaps the only historical religion that can be described as genuinely positive, even in its approach to knowledge and truth. Its epistemology aligns with strict phenomenalism, focusing solely on observable phenomena and experiences. Buddhism does not frame life as a struggle against "sin"; rather, it addresses the reality of human suffering directly. This acknowledgment of suffering replaces the moral self- deceptions that Christianity clings to, transcending simplistic notions of good and evil. In this way, Buddhism situates itself, in my terms, "beyond good and evil."

The foundation of Buddhism lies in two significant physiological realities: first, an extreme sensitivity to sensory experience, which manifests as an acute susceptibility to pain; and second, an extraordinary intellectualism, characterized by prolonged engagement with concepts and logical processes. These traits lead to a state where the sense of individuality is overtaken by an ideal of the "impersonal." For those who have lived as objectivists or possess a heightened capacity for detached observation, these conditions are all too familiar.

These physiological and intellectual traits often culminate in a state of depression, which Buddha sought to alleviate with specific, pragmatic solutions. His teachings prescribed living outdoors and embracing a life of travel to maintain balance. Moderation in eating and careful dietary choices were emphasized, as well as caution in the use of intoxicants. Similarly, Buddha warned against stirring up passions, as they can disrupt emotional equilibrium and intensify physical agitation. Above all, he advised against excessive worry— whether about oneself or others.

Buddha's approach was methodical and focused on fostering a state of quiet contentment and cheerful tranquility. He encouraged the cultivation of thoughts that support well-being while discouraging those that lead to distress. For him, "goodness" was synonymous with health and vitality—a condition where the body and mind flourish in harmony. His vision of goodness and health stands in stark contrast to Christianity's idealization of suffering and self- denial, making Buddhism a practical, life-affirming system rather than a nihilistic rejection of existence.

Prayer is absent in Buddhism, as is asceticism. There is no rigid system of categorical imperatives or disciplinary practices, even within the walls of monasteries—leaving is always an option.

These methods would only serve to amplify the already heightened sensitivity that Buddhism aims to address. For the same reason, Buddha does not advocate for conflict with unbelievers. His teachings oppose revenge, hostility, and resentment, with their refrain echoing through Buddhist texts: "Enmity never ends enmity." He understood that these emotions are unhealthy for those striving to follow his path. Buddha observed mental exhaustion as a result of excessive "objectivity"—a condition where individuals lose focus on themselves and their inner balance, leading to a weakening of self-interest or egoism. To counteract this, his teachings emphasize returning all spiritual interests to the self. In Buddhism, taking care of oneself is a moral responsibility. The central question, "How can one escape suffering?" becomes the axis around which the entire spiritual practice revolves. It's worth noting the parallel to Socrates, who similarly waged war against empty intellectualism and elevated self-interest to the status of morality.

Buddhism thrives in conditions marked by mild climates, societies of gentleness and openness, and the absence of militarism. It takes root among well- educated and culturally refined individuals. Cheerfulness, calm, and freedom from desire are its principal goals—and they are fully attainable. Unlike other faiths, Buddhism does not merely aspire to perfection; it achieves it as the norm.

Christianity, on the other hand, reflects the instincts of the downtrodden and oppressed. It is a faith embraced by those at the bottom, seeking salvation from their suffering. Its central practices revolve around examining sin, engaging in self-criticism, and constantly interrogating one's conscience. Emotional connection to a perceived power—called "God"—is heightened through prayer, while salvation is portrayed as a gift, an unattainable ideal, something granted by "grace." Christianity operates in secrecy and shadow; it despises openness. Hygiene and care for the body are scorned, labeled as indulgent or sensual, and the church has historically opposed cleanliness—such as when Christian rulers in medieval Spain closed Cordova's 270 public baths after driving out the Moors.

Cruelty is another hallmark of Christianity, both toward oneself and others. Hatred of unbelievers, a willingness to persecute, and an embrace of somber, troubling thoughts are central to its ethos. Christianity values epileptoid mental states—emotional extremes glorified as religious experience. Its dietary practices encourage poor health and overstimulate the nerves. It promotes disdain for earthly rulers and the aristocratic class while fostering a secret competition with them. Christians surrender their physical selves to rulers but claim their souls as their own. This attitude reflects Christianity's fundamental hatred for intellect, pride, courage, and freedom. It opposes the joy of the senses and resents joy in general.

When Christianity expanded beyond its original roots among the impoverished and marginalized of the ancient world, it faced a new challenge: gaining power among barbarian peoples. These were not weary or defeated individuals, but raw, untamed men, strong yet maladjusted. Their dissatisfaction with themselves and the world stemmed not from over- sensitivity, as in Buddhism, but from an intense drive to inflict harm and achieve satisfaction through acts of hostility. To conquer these barbaric societies, Christianity absorbed their concepts and values, adopting practices such as the sacrifice of firstborn children, the drinking of blood as a sacrament, and a general contempt for intellect and culture. It embraced physical and psychological torture, as well as the ostentatious rituals of a dramatic cult.

Buddhism, by contrast, is suited for societies that have advanced in their moral and cultural development—those that have grown gentle, refined, and overly spiritualized. Its call is one of return: to peace, to balance, to cheerfulness, and to temperance in both spirit and body. Europe, in its current state, is not ready for Buddhism. Christianity, however, appears at a much earlier stage of societal evolution, where it seeks to tame beasts of prey by making them ill. Weakness is Christianity's strategy for taming and "civilizing" its followers.

Buddhism offers guidance for civilizations nearing their peak, weary from centuries of progress. Christianity, by contrast, arises in uncivilized conditions, sometimes serving as the very foundation upon which societies begin to build. Its purpose is not to elevate or refine but to subdue, to weaken, and to control.

Buddhism and Christianity are not just different; they are complete opposites in many ways. Buddhism does not rely on prayer or ascetic practices. It avoids imposing strict disciplines or rules that would heighten sensitivity and stress. Monastic life, while organized, is flexible—leaving is always an option. Buddha's teaching discourages conflict and enmity, rejecting revenge, hostility, or resentment. The Buddhist refrain, "Enmity never ends enmity," captures its essence. These passions, harmful to health and peace, stand opposed to the purpose of his teachings.

Buddha observed that mental fatigue often arose from over-objectivity, where individuals lost connection with themselves and their personal interests. This imbalance weakened the instinct of self-preservation. His solution was to direct spiritual focus back toward the self. In Buddhism, self-care is not just encouraged—it is a moral imperative. The core question of his philosophy, "How can one escape suffering?" shapes every practice and teaching. This emphasis on personal well-being recalls Socrates' focus on self-knowledge and morality rooted in individual needs.

For Buddhism to flourish, specific conditions are necessary: a mild climate, a culture of gentleness, and a lack of militarism. Its teachings appeal to educated and spiritually advanced societies. It seeks calm, cheerfulness, and the absence of harmful desires— not as unreachable ideals but as realities. In Buddhism, perfection is not something to strive for; it is something achievable here and now.

Christianity, in stark contrast, is the religion of the downtrodden, rooted in the instincts of the oppressed. It appeals to those who suffer and struggle with their own existence. At its core, Christianity revolves around sin, self-criticism, and guilt. It glorifies suffering as a path to salvation, urging believers to seek divine grace rather than personal empowerment. God, as conceived by Christianity, is an emotionally charged being whose favor must be sought through prayer and submission. Salvation is painted as unattainable without divine intervention. Christianity thrives in secrecy, fostering a culture of shame, concealment, and self-denial.

The body, in Christian teachings, is despised as corrupt, and bodily care is seen as indulgent. Cleanliness and hygiene are often condemned as vain or sinful. Historically, this disdain for the physical led to actions like the closure of public baths after the Christian conquest of Cordova. Cruelty—toward oneself and others—has also been deeply rooted in Christian practice. This includes a hatred of unbelievers and a willingness to persecute those with differing views. Somberness and self-denial are prized, while joy and celebration are discouraged. Christian dietary laws, often restrictive, aim to produce a state of nervous tension that mirrors the inner turmoil celebrated in religious devotion.

As Christianity spread from the underprivileged classes of the ancient world to barbarian tribes, it encountered strong but undeveloped individuals—those more inclined to aggression than introspection. Unlike Buddhism, which aims to heal spiritual exhaustion, Christianity seeks to subdue raw and untamed energy. To appeal to barbaric societies, it adopted elements of their culture: blood sacrifices, disdain for intellectual pursuits, and rituals rooted in violence and fear. Christianity's aim was not refinement but control—weakening the strong to civilize them.

Buddhism speaks to societies that have grown weary from their own refinement, offering a return to peace and balance. It fosters a moderate spirit and a strong body, appealing to those who are spiritually advanced but tired. Europe, with its lingering aggression and lack of spiritual maturity, remains unprepared for Buddhism. Christianity, by contrast, thrives in societies still in their early stages of development. It lays foundations where none exist, but it does so by taming, weakening, and controlling.

Buddhism seeks to restore strength and serenity in the later stages of civilization. Christianity, however, rises at the start, shaping cultures through domination and suppression rather than elevation or enlightenment. One is a call to peace for the weary; the other, a strategy to subdue the wild and untamed. Both religions, in their own ways, leave profound marks on the societies they touch.— [4]

The psychological type represented by the Galilean figure is still recognizable, but it was only in its most distorted and degraded form—altered and burdened by foreign elements—that it could serve the purpose for which it has been used: as the model of a savior for humanity.

The Jews are arguably the most remarkable people in history. When faced with the existential question of whether to continue or perish, they chose, with extraordinary determination, to exist at any cost. This decision came at the price of fundamentally altering all aspects of nature and reality, both internally and externally. They opposed the very conditions that had traditionally allowed civilizations to thrive, rejecting natural laws and creating an idea that defied them. Religion, culture, morality, history, and psychology—one by one, these were reshaped by the Jews into their opposites, their natural meanings overturned.

This phenomenon appeared later on, magnified and imitated to a vast degree, in the form of the Christian Church. Compared to the "people of God," Christianity offers no originality. It is a mere imitation. In this way, the Jews became the most influential people in world history. Their legacy has so deeply distorted human reasoning that a modern Christian can hold anti-Semitic views without realizing that such views are the natural conclusion of Judaism's influence.

In my Genealogy of Morals, I provide the first psychological analysis of the fundamental ideas behind two opposing moral systems: noble morality and ressentiment morality. The latter is born from a denial of the former. The moral framework of Judaism and Christianity falls entirely into this second category. To reject everything associated with the elevation of life—such as strength, beauty, power, and self-approval—required an extraordinary instinct for ressentiment. This instinct, sharpened to the point of genius, invented an "other world," where affirming life itself became the greatest sin.

Psychologically, the Jews display extraordinary vitality. Faced with conditions that seemed insurmountable, they consciously chose to ally themselves with the instincts of decadence—not because they were overtaken by those instincts, but because they saw them as tools for defying the world. Far from being decadent themselves, the Jews mastered the art of appearing so. With unparalleled theatrical skill, they took control of all decadent movements (such as Paul's version of Christianity) and transformed them into forces more powerful than any philosophy or movement that affirmed life directly.

For those who sought power through Judaism and Christianity— primarily the priestly class—decadence became a tool rather than an affliction. These figures had a vested interest in making humanity sick, in corrupting its understanding of "good" and "evil," "truth" and "falsehood." This manipulation not only endangered life but also slandered it. By redefining values in a way that served their aims, they weaponized decadence to achieve influence and control.

The history of Israel serves as a critical example of how natural values can be distorted and denatured. Five key observations highlight this process. Initially, during the period of the monarchy, Israel maintained a natural relationship with its world, grounded in strength and self-assurance. Jahveh, their god, embodied their sense of power, pride, and aspirations. He symbolized their hope for victory, their connection to nature, and their reliance on life's necessities—like rain for their crops. Jahveh was the god of justice because he represented the confidence and authority of a people who held power and wielded it with a clear conscience. This was a typical belief system for any nation that felt secure and dominant.

The religious practices of the time reflected this natural outlook. The people expressed gratitude for their triumphs, for their prosperous herds, for the fruitful seasons. Their god was intertwined with their sense of destiny and their pride in their achievements. Even when adversity struck—internal strife and the looming threat of the Assyrian empire—this perspective lingered as an ideal. They longed for a leader who would be both a valiant warrior and a fair judge, a vision upheld by the prophets like Isaiah, who critiqued and satirized the shortcomings of their times.

However, reality failed to meet these hopes. Jahveh, once the embodiment of their might and promise, no longer seemed capable of fulfilling their needs. Instead of abandoning him, his followers redefined him. This reinterpretation came at a cost: Jahveh's character was denatured to fit a new narrative. No longer a god who reflected Israel's pride and power, he became a god of conditions and obedience—a god wielded by religious leaders to enforce their moral and social agendas.

The clerics used Jahveh's name to create a new framework of understanding: happiness became a reward, and suffering was rebranded as punishment for sin. This moral manipulation introduced the fraudulent concept of a "moral order of the world," which replaced the natural understanding of cause and effect with artificial, moralized causation. Nature itself was undermined by this reinterpretation, leading to an entire system of thought that denied the natural world and its laws.

Jahveh was no longer the god who inspired courage and self-reliance or offered help and wisdom. Instead, he became a god who demanded submission and compliance—a tool for control. Morality, which should have been a reflection of the conditions necessary for a healthy, thriving community, was now twisted into something abstract and life-denying. It became a perversion of human imagination, casting a shadow of suspicion and guilt over existence.

Jewish and Christian morality thus represent a profound corruption. They transformed chance and misfortune into guilt, labeling unhappiness as sin and prosperity as temptation. The result was a profound physiological distortion— a sickness of the soul wrought by the burdens of conscience. This morality doesn't reflect the instincts that nurture life and vitality; instead, it opposes them, poisoning natural joy and freedom with fabricated guilt and fear.

The idea of God was distorted; the concept of morality was twisted—and yet the Jewish priests didn't stop there. They erased the entire history of Israel, discarding it as if it were worthless. These priests achieved a complete falsification of history, a process that much of the Bible clearly shows. With unparalleled arrogance and in defiance of tradition and historical facts, they reinterpreted their people's past in religious terms. In doing so, they turned it into a ridiculous system of salvation, where every offense against Yahweh was punished and every act of devotion to Him was rewarded. This manipulation of history would seem far more disgraceful to us if thousands of years of church- led historical distortions hadn't already dulled our sense of truth in historical matters.

Philosophers supported the church in this deception: the falsehood about a "moral order of the world" runs through the entire history of philosophy, including even the most recent ideas. What does a "moral order of the world" mean? It claims that there is a "will of God" that permanently defines what people should and shouldn't do. According to this view, the value of a nation or an individual is measured by how well they obey this divine will. It also suggests that the fate of a nation or individual is determined by this will, which rewards obedience and punishes disobedience. But reality shows us something completely different: the priest—a parasitic type of person who can only exist by undermining healthy views of life—misuses the name of God. He labels the social order, in which he has the authority to determine all values, as "the kingdom of God." He refers to the methods for creating this order as "the will of God." With cold and calculated cynicism, he judges entire nations, eras, and individuals by how much they submit to or oppose priestly power.

Watch how they operate: under the influence of the Jewish priesthood, the great era of Israel became an age of decline. The Exile, with its long sequence of disasters, was rewritten as punishment for that earlier great age—when priests had not yet taken control. They turned the powerful and completely free heroes of Israel's history into either miserable zealots and hypocrites or entirely "godless" figures, depending on their current agenda. They reduced every significant event to a senseless formula: "obedient or disobedient to God."

They went even further: the "will of God" (which essentially means the tools needed to maintain the priests' power) had to be clarified, and for that, they needed a "revelation." In simple terms, they committed a massive literary fraud by fabricating "holy scriptures." With elaborate ceremonies, days of penance, and loud mourning over the supposed sins of the past, these scriptures were officially presented. They declared that the "will of God" had always existed as an unchanging truth, but humanity had neglected the "holy scriptures."

However, they also claimed that the "will of God" had already been revealed to Moses.

What actually happened? The priest had, once and for all, clearly outlined what he wanted—down to the tiniest detail. He specified the tithes he was entitled to, from the largest offerings to the smallest (not forgetting the tastiest portions of meat, as priests were big fans of steaks). In short, he explained exactly what "the will of God" required. From that point on, life was organized so that the priest became essential at every major life event—birth, marriage, illness, death, and even meals (or "sacrifices"). The priest was always there, interfering with natural life and calling it "sanctification."

Here's the key point: every natural habit, every institution that arose from human instincts—such as the state, justice, marriage, care for the sick and poor, and all the essentials of life—was devalued and even reversed in its purpose by the parasitism of priests. Through their actions, all these things, which once had genuine value, were reduced to nothing or even turned into their opposites, thanks to what they called the "moral order of the world."

The idea requires authority—a force that can assign values is necessary, and the only way this authority can generate such values is by rejecting and condemning nature. The priest achieves this by devaluing and defiling nature; this is the only way he can sustain his existence. What is labeled as disobedience to God—though it truly means disobedience to the priest and "the law"—is now called "sin." The path to "reconciliation with God" is, unsurprisingly, precisely the one that most tightly binds individuals to the power of the priest. He alone holds the keys to salvation, or so he claims. From a psychological perspective, the concept of "sin" is vital to every society built on an ecclesiastical foundation. Sin becomes the most reliable weapon of power, the core tool for the priest's survival. He thrives on sin; without the concept of "sinning," his role would collapse entirely. The fundamental rule is clear: "God forgives those who repent," which, in plain language, means "those who submit to the priest's authority."

Christianity emerged from a foundation so decayed that every natural value, every aspect of life that was real and uncorrupted, faced direct opposition from the ruling class's deepest instincts. It developed as a relentless war against reality itself, a war so intense and unyielding that no subsequent movement has surpassed it in its hostility toward life. The so-called "holy people," who embraced priestly values and redefined all aspects of life through priestly labels, consistently condemned the natural world as "unholy," "worldly," and "sinful." This mindset reached its ultimate expression in Christianity, where even the last remnants of reality—the concept of a "holy people" or the "chosen people" of Jewish tradition—were rejected. Christianity went so far as to deny Jewish identity itself, pushing this rejection of reality to an extreme that bordered on self-destruction.

This phenomenon is of extraordinary importance: the small, rebellious movement associated with Jesus of Nazareth represents a reawakening of the Jewish instinct, though in an altered form. It is, in essence, the priestly instinct taken to such an extreme that it could no longer tolerate the priesthood itself as a reality. It sought an even more fantastical state of existence, a vision of life more disconnected from reality than any ecclesiastical system before it. Christianity, in its essence, denies the church as much as it claims to uphold it. I find it impossible to identify the true target of the rebellion attributed to Jesus, whether accurately or not, if it was not the Jewish church. And by "church," I mean it in the exact sense we use the word today.

This was a revolt against the established order of things: the "good and just," the "prophets of Israel," and the entire hierarchical structure of Jewish society. It was not a rebellion against corruption but against the systems of caste, privilege, and formalized tradition. It rejected the notion of "superior men" and cast aside everything the priests and theologians represented. Yet, the hierarchy under attack by this movement, however briefly, was the very structure that ensured the Jewish people's survival. This social and religious framework was their lifeline, their last vestige of independent political existence. To challenge it was to challenge the most deeply rooted national instinct and the strongest will to survive that humanity has ever witnessed.

Jesus, the saintly anarchist, rallied the marginalized—the outcasts, the "sinners," and the despised—against the established order. He appealed to those who had been excluded from society, encouraging them to rise up against the institutions that defined their lives. If we are to trust the accounts in the Gospels, his words were so radical that they would earn him exile or imprisonment in any modern society. This man, who stirred up the downtrodden and defied the foundations of his community, was undoubtedly a political criminal, at least insofar as it was possible to be one in a society so lacking in political structure. His challenge to the status quo sealed his fate. The inscription on the cross— declaring him "King of the Jews"—is proof enough. He did not die for the sins of others, as is so often claimed, but for his own rebellion against the order of his time. There is no credible reason to believe otherwise, no matter how frequently this narrative is repeated.

Whether Jesus himself was aware of this contradiction—or whether it was the only contradiction he recognized—is an entirely different question. Here, I am led to the profound psychological mystery of the figure we call the Savior. To begin, I must admit that few texts challenge me as much as the Gospels. My difficulties, however, differ entirely from those that spurred the scholarly curiosity of the German intellect to one of its most remarkable achievements. Many years ago, like all other young academics, I immersed myself with the meticulous passion of a philologist in the work of the incomparable David Strauss. At that time, I was twenty years old, and the intellectual exercise was a delight. Now, however, I find myself too serious for such endeavors. What interest do I have in resolving the contradictions of "tradition"? How can one seriously refer to pious legends as "traditions"?

The hagiographies of saints form one of the most dubious literary genres that exist. To scrutinize them with the tools of scientific inquiry, when no corroborative historical documents exist, seems to me to doom the entire endeavor from the start. It is no more than a sophisticated form of idle scholarship. What genuinely matters to me is not the historical accuracy of these accounts but the psychological type that emerges from them—the character of the Savior. This type may be discernible in the Gospels, however distorted or burdened it may be with later additions. It appears in the same way that the figure of Francis of Assisi emerges in his legends—not because of them, but in spite of them.

The focus here is not on whether the accounts in the Gospels truthfully record what Jesus did, said, or how he met his end. The real question is whether his type remains conceivable to us—whether it has been faithfully transmitted across time. All the attempts I have encountered to interpret the "soul" of Jesus through the Gospels strike me as marked by a shocking superficiality. For instance, M. Renan, that performer of psychological tricks, introduced two thoroughly inappropriate notions to explain the nature of Jesus: the concept of the genius and that of the hero. These are deeply flawed interpretations, for there is nothing more fundamentally opposed to the essence of the Gospels than the concept of a hero.

The Gospels present a perspective that is the complete antithesis of heroism or the taste for struggle. They embody a rejection of resistance, transforming even the inability to oppose into a moral virtue. Consider the phrase "resist not evil!"—arguably the most profound sentence in the Gospels and perhaps their central theme. It encapsulates a state of being in which blessedness arises from peace, gentleness, and an incapacity to harbor enmity. This is the core of the "glad tidings": the revelation of the true life, the eternal life, as something already discovered and present—not as a distant promise, but as a reality within. This life is rooted in a love that knows no barriers, no exclusions, no distances. Jesus claims nothing uniquely for himself. In his view, every person is a child of God, and as such, all are equal. To frame Jesus as a hero is to commit a profound misinterpretation.

Equally flawed is the application of the term "genius" to Jesus. Our modern understanding of "spirituality" and intellectual sophistication has no relevance to the context in which Jesus lived. His world operated on entirely different premises. From a physiological standpoint, a completely different term would be more appropriate. We know, for instance, of a condition involving an extreme sensitivity of the tactile nerves, where sufferers recoil from physical contact and avoid any solid grasp.

Taken to its logical extreme, such a disposition could manifest as an instinctive aversion to reality—a retreat into the intangible, the incomprehensible. It might express itself as a distaste for anything fixed or concrete, whether customs, institutions, or temporal structures like time and space. Such a mindset feels at home only in a realm devoid of tangible reality— a purely internal world, an imagined "true" or "eternal" realm.

This perspective finds its perfect expression in the idea: "The Kingdom of God is within you." Here lies the ultimate psychological retreat: a turning away from all external realities, a flight into the inner sanctum of the self, where the external world is not merely rejected but The instinctive rejection of reality, the profound aversion to the world as it is, stems from an acute sensitivity to pain and irritation— a sensitivity so extreme that even the slightest "touch" becomes unbearable. Every sensation cuts too deeply, leaving no space for even the smallest confrontation with discomfort. This kind of deep susceptibility alters the way a person interacts with the world, leading to an instinctive exclusion of all hostility, all boundaries, all aversions. This avoidance arises not out of a moral stance, but from the overwhelming experience of suffering that even the smallest resistance or compulsion to resist causes. Such resistance feels not only intolerable but harmful—something prohibited by the basic instinct for survival. In this state, peace and joy become conceivable only when all forms of resistance are eliminated, even toward the most harmful or dangerous forces. Love, then, becomes the sole possible response, the last conceivable avenue for life to continue.

These two physiological realities—this extreme sensitivity to pain and the absolute rejection of resistance—are the fertile ground upon which the doctrine of salvation has grown. I see this as a remarkable and elevated form of hedonism, one that paradoxically emerged on the most unhealthy of foundations. It is worth comparing this to the salvation doctrine of paganism, particularly Epicureanism, which bears similarities to this phenomenon but with a vital difference: Epicureanism is infused with Greek vigor and energy. Yet Epicurus himself was a quintessential example of decadence. I was the first to recognize him as such. His philosophy, too, revolves around the avoidance of pain, even of the most minor discomforts. Ultimately, such avoidance leads naturally and inevitably to a religion of love, which can be seen as the endpoint of this trajectory.

I have already shared my perspective on this issue. It begins with the assumption that the type of the Savior has come down to us only in a distorted and highly altered form. Such distortion is not only likely but almost certain, given the many factors that could have influenced the preservation of this figure. The environment in which this enigmatic person lived undoubtedly left its mark on him. Furthermore, the early Christian communities, shaped by their own struggles and history, must have added layers of meaning and character to the figure of the Savior. These additions were often tailored to serve their own needs, whether for propaganda or for rallying believers during times of crisis. The milieu of the Gospels is itself peculiar—a strange, unsettling world reminiscent of the scenes from a Russian novel, filled with societal outcasts, nervous disorders, and what might now be called "childish simplicity." Such a setting would have inevitably coarsened and simplified the type of the Savior.

The earliest disciples, in particular, likely struggled to comprehend such an extraordinary figure. To make sense of him, they had to reshape and recast him into forms they could understand. This meant translating a life full of symbols and mysteries into something more concrete and familiar. In their hands, the figure of the Savior took on attributes they could relate to: the prophet, the messiah, the moral teacher, the miracle worker, and even the fiery judge. Each of these roles represented opportunities to misunderstand his essence. Over time, these layers of interpretation became inseparable from the original type.

One cannot overlook the tendency of all veneration, especially within sects, to erase the unique and often unsettling traits of the figure they revere. What is strange, individual, or challenging is smoothed over, replaced with more palatable, conventional qualities. It is deeply regrettable that no Dostoevsky lived during the time of this fascinating figure. Dostoevsky, with his ability to capture the sublime mingled with the morbid and the childlike, might have portrayed this Savior with the depth and complexity he deserved. As it stands, the Savior, as a type of decadence, may indeed have been a profoundly contradictory figure, combining the sublime with the fragile. Such a possibility cannot be ignored. Yet the historical record works against this idea, for such contradictions, if present, would likely have been preserved with greater accuracy and objectivity. Instead, what we find suggests a systematic reshaping of the figure to suit the needs of early Christian propaganda.

This reshaping has created an apparent contradiction between two vastly different images of Jesus. On the one hand, we see the peaceful preacher of the Sermon on the Mount, a figure reminiscent of a new Buddha, bringing a message of inner peace and harmony to a land far removed from India. On the other hand, we have the fiery, combative figure—a bitter adversary of theologians and ecclesiastics—whom Renan, with his characteristic malice, exalted as "the great master of irony." I have no doubt that much of this venom, and just as much of this supposed brilliance, was injected into the concept of Jesus by the heated rhetoric of early Christian propaganda.

It is well known how unscrupulous sectarians can be when shaping the image of their leader to suit their own needs. When the early Christians found themselves in need of a cunning, argumentative, and sharp-witted theologian to challenge rival theologians, they fashioned such a figure out of their Savior. They placed ideas into his mouth with little hesitation, ideas that were essential to their mission but utterly foreign to the Gospels themselves. Concepts like "the second coming," "the last judgment," and a host of promises and expectations common in that era were attributed to Jesus, despite their clear divergence from his original teachings. In doing so, they created a figure that served their purposes but moved further away from the reality of the man who had once lived.

I must emphasize again that I oppose any attempts to portray the Savior as a fanatic. Even the word impér ieux used by Renan is enough to dismantle the entire idea of the type. The message of the "glad tidings" is simple: contradictions no longer exist. The kingdom of heaven belongs to the innocent, to those who approach life with the openness of children. The faith expressed here is not a militant faith. It does not battle against anything, for it has always been present, from the beginning. It represents a sort of spiritual regression to a childlike state. Physiologists would recognize this as a delayed or incomplete maturity in the organism, a result of degeneration rather than development.

This faith does not rage, it does not condemn, and it does not seek to defend itself. It carries no sword, and it has no awareness of the divisions it might one day cause, setting man against man. It does not rely on miracles, rewards, promises, or scriptures to prove its validity. It is entirely self-contained, its own miracle, its own reward, its own promise, its own "kingdom of God." This faith does not express itself through doctrines or formulas; it simply exists and protects itself by avoiding such constructs. Certainly, the cultural and educational influences of the time shaped its language and symbols. In early Christianity, one finds a distinctly Judaeo-Semitic flavor, such as the idea of eating and drinking at the Last Supper, which reflects this context. This idea, like so many other Jewish concepts, was later misinterpreted and altered by the church. But even this must be understood as symbolic language, a mode of parable, rather than literal belief.

Indeed, this anti-realist perspective is grounded in an understanding that the world itself is symbolic. The figure of Jesus would have spoken differently depending on his cultural context. Among Hindus, he might have used the language of the Sankhya philosophy; among the Chinese, he might have spoken in the terms of Lao-tse. The underlying message, however, would remain unchanged, for the symbols themselves are secondary to the truth they aim to convey. In this sense, Jesus could even be described, with some interpretive freedom, as a "free spirit." He cared nothing for established norms, for institutions, or for rigid rules. For him, the "letter kills," and all that is established stifles the true essence of life.

To Jesus, life was an inner experience, an unfolding truth that could not be confined to words, laws, or doctrines. His concepts of "life," "truth," and "light" referred to the innermost realities of existence. Everything else—the natural world, the material reality, and even language—served merely as signs and allegories pointing to these inner truths. It is crucial to avoid being misled by ecclesiastical prejudices when interpreting this symbolism. The wisdom of Jesus was not bound to religion, worship, history, science, politics, psychology, art, or any worldly knowledge. His "wisdom" was, paradoxically, a profound ignorance of these things. He did not engage with culture because he had no need to resist or oppose it— he simply did not acknowledge it.

The same applies to his relationship with the state, social structures, labor, war, or even the concept of the world as understood by ecclesiastical authorities. He did not deny the world, for he was completely unfamiliar with the ecclesiastical notion of "the world." Denial itself was foreign to him; it was not something he was capable of. Likewise, Jesus lacked any inclination to argue or to defend his beliefs through logical proofs. His "proofs" were entirely internal— flashes of insight, feelings of bliss and self- assurance, simple manifestations of what he called "power." His doctrine did not contradict others, because it did not recognize that any other doctrines existed. It could not even conceive of opposition. When confronted with differing views, it responded not with arguments but with a heartfelt lamentation for the "blindness" of others, a genuine sympathy for those without "light."

The psychology of the Gospels contains no trace of guilt, punishment, or reward. The concept of "sin" as something that creates a barrier between God and man is entirely absent. The essence of the "glad tidings" is precisely the abolition of this distance. Eternal bliss is not something promised for the future, nor is it conditional on specific actions. It is understood as the only true reality, with all else serving merely as symbols to help describe it.

This perspective on life gives rise to a completely new way of living—a distinctly evangelical way of being. A Christian is not defined by belief but by action, by a way of living that reflects this inner reality. He does not resist those who oppose him, neither outwardly nor in his heart. He does not distinguish between people based on nationality, religion, or ethnicity; he sees no difference between neighbors and strangers, Jews and Gentiles. His love and forgiveness extend to everyone. He harbors no anger and despises no one. He neither appeals to courts of justice nor abides by their rules; he refuses to swear oaths or divorce his wife, even in the face of infidelity.

Beneath all these actions lies a single guiding principle, a singular instinct from which all else flows. This instinct is the foundation of the evangelical life, shaping every aspect of how the Christian exists in the world.

The life of the Savior was the living embodiment of this way of being, carried out with such purity that even his death was a continuation of it. He required no formulas, no rituals, no intermediaries in his relationship with God—not even prayer. He had moved beyond the entirety of the Jewish framework of repentance and atonement. For him, the only path to feeling "divine," "blessed," "evangelical," or a "child of God" was through a way of life. It was not through "repentance," not through "prayer and forgiveness" that one reached God. The Gospel way itself was the pathway to God; it was God.

The Gospels effectively abolished the Jewish concepts of "sin," "forgiveness of sin," "faith," and "salvation through faith." They denied the entire structure of Jewish religious dogma, offering instead the "glad tidings" as a radical alternative. What the Gospels introduced was not another doctrine but a profound reorientation of life—a rejection of all external rules and beliefs in favor of a direct and lived experience of the divine.

The deep instinct of the Christian, the internal guide that shows how to live in a way that feels like being "in heaven" or "immortal," even amid the ordinary struggles of existence, is the sole psychological reality of what is called "salvation." It does not depend on adopting a new faith but on living a new way of life. This distinction is fundamental to understanding the essence of the Gospel message.

If I have grasped anything about this extraordinary symbolist, it is that he recognized subjective realities as the only true realities. For him, "truths" were internal experiences, deeply felt, while everything else—nature, history, time, and space—was secondary.

These external realities existed only as symbols, materials for parables to illustrate inner truths. The concept of "the Son of God," for instance, does not represent a specific historical figure, a concrete individual tied to a particular moment in time. Instead, it signifies an eternal fact, a psychological symbol that transcends time entirely.

This same symbolic understanding applies to the God of this symbolist, the "kingdom of God," and the "sonship of God." These are not crude, literal notions but profound metaphors for experiences and realities beyond ordinary comprehension. Nothing could be further from the true spirit of the Gospels than the institutionalized, ecclesiastical interpretations of God as a person, of the "kingdom of God" as a future event, or of the "kingdom of heaven" as a distant paradise. The idea of the "Son of God" as a literal second person of the Trinity is equally alien to the original message of the Gospels.

Such interpretations—if I may use a strong metaphor—are like thrusting a fist into the eye of the Gospels. They demonstrate a profound disrespect for the symbolic language of these texts, a kind of historical cynicism that reduces profound spiritual metaphors to clumsy dogma. Yet, for those who look carefully, the meaning of symbols like "Father" and "Son" remains clear—at least to those capable of understanding them. The "Son" symbolizes the experience of entering into a state of universal transformation and beatitude, while the "Father" represents the sensation of eternity and perfection itself. Together, these symbols articulate the spiritual experience of profound unity and fulfillment.

It is almost embarrassing to compare this elegant symbolism with what the church has made of it. The ecclesiastical interpretation, with its rigid and literal stories, often seems closer to mythological tales like those of Amphitryon than to the profound psychological and spiritual truths that the Gospels intended to convey. The reduction of such sublime metaphors into crude literalism is not only a misunderstanding but a distortion that has shaped history in ways that obscured the original depth of these symbols[13] at the very threshold of Christian "faith," we find the introduction of a dogma—a belief in the "immaculate conception." And what has this dogma achieved? By insisting on a so-called purity in conception, it has ironically stripped conception itself of its natural purity. In elevating it to the status of a miraculous event, it has sullied the simple, inherent beauty and sacredness of natural processes. This is not a celebration of life but a rejection of its reality, a denial of the very essence that makes existence profound. The concept, meant to sanctify, instead diminishes. By defining "immaculateness" through exclusion, it casts a shadow over what should be whole, complete, and untouchably pure in its natural state.The "kingdom of heaven" is not a distant promise, not something to be anticipated beyond this world or after death. It is not a place, nor an event to be awaited. Instead, it is a state of the heart, a condition of being. The idea of natural death, as it is commonly understood, is entirely absent from the Gospels. Death is not a transition, not a passage to something greater; it belongs to a different realm altogether—a realm that is merely symbolic, useful only as an allegory. For the bearer of "glad tidings," concepts like the "hour of death" or the crises of physical life hold no meaning. Time, measured in hours and days, is irrelevant to his message. The "kingdom of God" is not something to come in the future, not something to wait for. It does not belong to yesterday, today, or tomorrow, and it is not tied to the hope of a millennium. It is a living experience, something felt within. It is everywhere and yet nowhere at the same time.

The bearer of "glad tidings" lived and died in alignment with the way of life he taught—not to "save mankind" in the sense of erasing their sins, but to reveal a new way of living. His life was his message, and his death was its culmination. He faced his accusers, the judges, and even the executioners with a demeanor that reflected his teachings. He resisted nothing, did not defend his rights, and did not attempt to escape his fate. On the contrary, he accepted the ultimate penalty, even invited it, as an extension of his message. On the cross, he prayed, suffered, and loved— even for those who inflicted harm upon him. His way was one of submission, not defiance; love, not condemnation. To defend oneself, to show anger, or to assign blame—these were actions entirely foreign to his nature. Instead, he embraced even the Evil One, responding with love rather than resistance.

We, the free spirits, are perhaps the first to grasp the profound integrity of this way of life—something misunderstood for nineteen centuries. Only now are we beginning to comprehend the instinct and passion for truth that characterized this figure. He waged a quiet war against the "holy lie," a lie more insidious and dangerous than all others. His integrity stood in opposition not only to falsehoods but also to the structure that emerged in the aftermath of his teachings: the church. Mankind, motivated by selfishness and a desire for advantage, created the church out of a denial of the very principles the Gospels embodied.

For those who look for signs of irony in the great drama of existence, Christianity offers one of the most staggering examples. That humanity would kneel before something that directly opposes the essence of the Gospels—their origin, meaning, and guiding law— is a profound paradox. The concept of the "church" sanctifies precisely what the bearer of "glad tidings" rejected and left behind. This contradiction stands as a monumental example of world-historical irony, unmatched in its magnitude.

Our age prides itself on its historical awareness, yet it continues to delude itself into believing that Christianity began with the crude tale of a miracle worker and savior, with the spiritual and symbolic elements added later. In reality, the reverse is true. The history of Christianity, from the moment of the crucifixion onward, is the story of an ever-deepening misunderstanding of an original symbolism. As Christianity spread to larger, less sophisticated populations, it became necessary to simplify and vulgarize its teachings to suit the limited understanding of these masses. The result was a progressive coarsening of its message.

To meet the demands of a growing and increasingly unrefined audience, Christianity absorbed the rituals and beliefs of various underground cults of the Roman Empire. Over time, it became entangled with the superstitions and irrationalities of countless sickly ideologies. It was Christianity's fate to adapt itself to the needs of the most base and degraded, resulting in a faith that became as distorted and corrupt as the needs it served. From this degeneration emerged the church—a manifestation of barbarism masquerading as spiritual authority. The church became the embodiment of hostility to truth, to nobility of spirit, to intellectual discipline, and to spontaneous human kindness.

Christian values, which were meant to be noble and transformative, were replaced by a system that served only to perpetuate dishonesty and power. It is only now, through the perspective of free spirits, that we have re-established the true dichotomy between the values of the church and the noble values of the Gospels. This recognition restores the greatest of all contrasts in values—a contrast that had been obscured by centuries of misunderstanding and distortion.

I cannot help but sigh here. There are days when I am gripped by a despair deeper than any melancholy—an overwhelming contempt for humanity. Let me be clear about what I despise and whom I despise: it is the modern man, the man of today, the one I am forced to call my contemporary. This man of today suffocates me with the stench of his decay, his moral rot, his empty words, and his hollow convictions.

Toward the past, I feel no such disdain. Like anyone who seeks to understand, I approach history with tolerance—a kind of restrained generosity. With grim patience, I walk through the millennia of human madness, whether it is called "Christianity," "Christian faith," or the "Christian church." I do not hold humanity accountable for its historical delusions; those times were shaped by ignorance and circumstances beyond the understanding of those who lived them. But when I turn to the present—when I confront the modern age—my restraint crumbles. A new level of revulsion overtakes me. This age knows better. It has no excuse. What was once mere sickness has now become something grotesque and indecent. Today, it is indecent to call oneself a Christian. And that is where my disgust begins.

I look around me, and I see that not a shred of what was once called "truth" remains intact. The word itself—truth—has become unbearable. Even the sound of a priest speaking it is intolerable. Any person with even the slightest sense of honesty must know that when a theologian, priest, or pope speaks today, he does not merely err— he lies. And he knows he lies. Gone are the days when such falsehoods could be excused as innocent or born of ignorance. No, the priest knows full well that there is no "God," no "sinner," no "Savior." He knows that "free will" is a fabrication, that the "moral order of the world" is a sham. The deeper reflection and self-mastery required to face these truths leave no room for pretense. No honest man can claim ignorance of these facts anymore.

The ideas of the church are now exposed for what they are: the most vile counterfeits ever conceived. These notions were created to corrupt nature, to undermine natural values, and to poison human vitality. The priest is no longer a figure of mystery or reverence; he is revealed as the ultimate parasite, the venomous spider spinning his web of deception to ensnare and subjugate. We now see the true purpose behind the sinister inventions of priestly doctrine: their concepts—"the other world," "the last judgment," "the immortality of the soul," and even the very notion of the "soul"—were never anything more than tools of domination, instruments of cruelty. Through them, the priest secured his power, holding humanity in a grip of fear and self-loathing.

We know this now. Our collective conscience has awakened to the truth. We understand the grotesque legacy of these lies, the profound degradation they have wrought upon humanity. They reduced people to a state of self-abasement so pitiful that it inspires only disgust. The very sight of the human soul, corrupted by these lies, is enough to provoke revulsion. Yet, despite this awareness, the world continues as before. Nothing changes. The last remnants of decency and self-respect seem to have vanished entirely.

What are we to make of modern statesmen, men who are otherwise bold, pragmatic, and openly anti-Christian in their actions, still calling themselves Christians and taking communion? What could be more hypocritical? A prince, commanding armies, embodying the egoism and pride of his people—yet without a hint of shame, he declares himself a Christian. And whom does Christianity deny? What does it call "the world"? To be a soldier, to be a judge, to be a patriot; to defend oneself; to act with honor; to pursue one's advantage; to feel pride—all these basic human instincts and values are now labeled anti- Christian.

What does this mean for the modern man who still calls himself a Christian? It means he is a walking contradiction, a monstrosity of falsehood. Every action he takes, every instinct he follows, every value he demonstrates in his daily life stands in direct opposition to the creed he professes. And yet, without a trace of shame, he continues to cling to this identity, declaring himself a Christian as though the word still held meaning. This is the height of hypocrisy, the final degradation of honesty, integrity, and authenticity in the modern age.

Let me take a step back and recount the true story of Christianity. The very word "Christianity" itself is a profound misunderstanding. At its core, there was only ever one Christian, and he died on the cross. The "Gospels" died with him. From the moment of his death onward, what came to be called the "Gospels" became the complete opposite of what he had lived and taught. They became "bad tidings," or what might more aptly be termed a Dysangelium. It is a fundamental error—indeed, a nonsensical one—to view "faith," particularly faith in salvation through Christ, as the defining characteristic of the Christian. True Christianity lies solely in the way of life lived by the one who died on the cross. His way of being, his life, and his actions were the essence of what it means to be Christian.

This way of life remains possible, even now, and for certain people, it may even be necessary. Authentic, primitive Christianity—the original way of being embodied by Christ—can still exist in any age. It is not about faith, but about action—or, more accurately, a deliberate avoidance of certain actions. It is not about a belief system but about a fundamentally different state of being.

Psychologists understand that states of consciousness, or the acceptance of something as true, are of negligible importance compared to the instincts that drive human behavior. The entire notion of reducing Christianity to an intellectual acceptance of "truth" is a profound error. It negates the very essence of Christianity. To equate being Christian with mere belief is to misunderstand it completely. In reality, there are no Christians. The person who, for two thousand years, has been called a "Christian" is nothing more than a psychological self-deception. When examined closely, this so-called Christian, despite all his "faith," is governed entirely by his instincts—and what base instincts they are!

Throughout history, faith has served as little more than a disguise, a mask that conceals the true forces at work: instincts. Consider the case of Luther, for instance. His "faith" was merely a front, a justification that veiled the instinctual drives operating behind it. Faith, in this context, is the quintessential Christian form of cunning. People proclaim their faith loudly, but their actions invariably follow the dictates of their instincts. This has been the pattern in every age.

The ideas within the Christian worldview have no contact with reality. Instead, they are driven by an instinctive hatred of reality itself, a rejection of the world as it is. This hostility to reality is the primary force underlying Christianity—the one true motive power of its existence. And what does this imply? That the entire structure of Christianity is built on a foundational error, a misconception that conditions everything about it. Replace any one of its erroneous ideas with a genuine reality, and Christianity collapses entirely. It cannot survive without its errors.

When viewed dispassionately, Christianity stands out as one of the strangest phenomena in human history—a religion not only built upon falsehoods but actively creative and ingenious in inventing falsehoods that harm life and poison the human spirit. It is a spectacle that might well amuse the gods, particularly those who are also philosophers. These gods, like the ones I encountered in the famed dialogues at Naxos, might find themselves momentarily entertained by this peculiar drama. Once their disgust—and ours—subsides, they might even feel a glimmer of gratitude for the absurdity of it all. Perhaps this strange exhibition is the only reason our small, wretched planet deserves even a passing glance from omnipotence—a brief flicker of divine interest.

Let us, then, not underestimate the Christians. The Christian, though false to the point of innocence, is still far above the ape. In fact, applying a well- known theory of descent to Christians is nothing short of polite. In their case, such a theory becomes a courtesy, a small concession to civility in the face of the endless spectacle they provide.

The fate of the Gospels was sealed by death—by the death on the cross. Everything turned on that event, that unexpected and shameful end. The cross, a symbol of degradation reserved for the lowest strata of society, carried an appalling paradox that confronted the disciples with a profound and inescapable question: "Who was he? What was he?" The shocking nature of his death shook them to their core, filling them with dismay, a sense of profound insult, and even a suspicion that such an end might refute the very cause they had believed in.

The haunting question, "Why this way?" loomed over them, demanding an explanation.

In their minds, everything had to be accounted for; everything had to have a reason, not just any reason, but the highest and most divine. The love of a disciple does not tolerate chance. For them, there could be no accidents in the life of their Master. It was this desperate search for meaning that opened the chasm of doubt. And then came the inevitable question, striking like lightning: "Who put him to death? Who was his true enemy?" The answer, clear and immediate, was the dominant powers of Judaism, its ruling class.

From that moment on, the disciples found themselves in opposition to the established order. Jesus was suddenly reimagined as a figure in revolt against authority, against the structures of power that had condemned him. Until then, the militant, defiant side of his character had been absent from their understanding. They had seen him as embodying the opposite: a message of peace and reconciliation. The very essence of his life and teachings— the way he lived and the way he died—had been misunderstood by his closest followers. They failed to grasp the central point of his death: the example he set, his total freedom from and transcendence of ressentiment. His death, far from being a defeat, was meant to demonstrate his teachings in the most profound and public way imaginable.

Yet his disciples could not forgive his death. They did not respond with the serene calmness of heart that his teachings demanded, nor were they willing to follow his example by embracing a similar fate. Instead, they were overtaken by the most unevangelical of emotions: revenge. They could not accept that the cause might end with his death. To them, there had to be recompense, a settling of accounts, a divine judgment. But nothing could be further from the Gospel spirit than the concepts of "recompense," "punishment," and "judgment."

With this shift, the popular Jewish expectation of a messiah surged back to the forefront of their thinking. They refocused their hopes on a future event, an apocalyptic moment when the "kingdom of God" would arrive with vengeance upon Jesus' enemies. They transformed his teachings, which had been a living realization of the kingdom of God, into a promise of something yet to come. This was a profound misunderstanding. The Gospels had proclaimed the kingdom of God as something already present, as a reality embodied in Jesus' life and teachings. To relegate it to a future event was to undo its fulfillment and misrepresent its essence.

At the same time, their grief and rage twisted their understanding of Jesus himself. Suddenly, all the contempt and bitterness they harbored against the Pharisees and theologians became projected onto the character of their Master. In this, they remade him in their own image, turning him into a figure who opposed the Pharisees and theologians by embodying their very characteristics—he was now a Pharisee and theologian in his own right, wielding the same tools of denunciation and judgment that he had once transcended.

Their veneration of Jesus also took a distorted and extravagant form. They could no longer accept his message of equality—that all men are children of God. This teaching, so central to his Gospel, was abandoned in their need for revenge and superiority. They elevated Jesus far above themselves, turning him into something entirely separate and inaccessible. In doing so, they mirrored the actions of the Jews in earlier times, who had distanced themselves from their God by elevating him to an unattainable height as a way of asserting dominance over their enemies.

Thus arose the constructs of the One God and the Only Son of God— born not out of the teachings of Jesus, but out of the disciples' inability to reconcile his death with their own instincts for vengeance, superiority, and power. What had once been a message of profound equality and present fulfillment became distorted into a doctrine of separation, hierarchy, and deferred hope. The faith that emerged from this distortion bore little resemblance to the life or teachings of the man who died on the cross.

From this distortion sprang an absurd and tragic question: "How could God allow such a death?" The bewildered and desperate reasoning of the early Christian community answered this riddle with a terrifying absurdity: God had sacrificed his son for the forgiveness of sins. And in that moment, the spirit of the Gospels was extinguished. The central message of Jesus—the abolition of guilt, the denial of any separation between God and man, the living embodiment of unity with the divine—was replaced with the abhorrent idea of sacrifice for sin. And not just any sacrifice, but the most barbaric form imaginable: the sacrifice of the innocent for the guilty. This was not salvation; it was a regression to the worst kind of paganism, dressed in the language of holiness.

Jesus himself had eradicated the concept of "guilt." He denied the existence of a chasm between God and humanity, and his life was the demonstration of this denial. His "glad tidings" were the announcement of this unity, not as a privilege for the few but as a reality for all. Yet, with this new doctrine of sacrifice, his message was corrupted. Bit by bit, the figure of the Savior was transformed by doctrines entirely foreign to his life and teachings: the doctrine of divine judgment, the second coming, the resurrection, and the idea of death as a necessary atonement. These alterations shifted the meaning of the Gospels away from the here and now, away from the realization of blessedness in this life, and toward the promise of a state of existence after death.

The worst of these distortions came at the hands of St. Paul. With the audacity of a rabbinical logician, Paul cemented the indecent idea of the resurrection with his infamous claim: "If Christ did not rise from the dead, then our faith is in vain." This single declaration reduced the essence of the Gospels to a doctrine of personal immortality—the most contemptible and unfulfillable promise imaginable. Paul did not stop there; he preached this immortality as a reward, entrenching the idea that faith was transactional, something done for the sake of a future payoff.

What, then, truly ended with the death of Jesus on the cross? It was a new, original attempt to establish peace and happiness on earth—a movement akin to Buddhism, but distinct in that it promised nothing and sought to fulfill everything here and now. Buddhism fulfills through its teachings and practices; Christianity, corrupted from its outset, promised everything and fulfilled nothing. And what followed the "glad tidings" of the Gospels? The most disastrous possible news: the doctrines of Paul.

In Paul, we find the complete antithesis of the "bearer of glad tidings." He was not the messenger of peace but the architect of hatred, the embodiment of its relentless logic and vision. Everything in Paul's work was sacrificed to this hatred: above all, the figure of the Savior himself. Paul nailed Jesus to the cross a second time—not with nails, but with his words and doctrines. The life, example, teachings, and even the death of Jesus were repurposed and twisted to serve Paul's own agenda. The essence of the Gospels—their meaning, their law—was obliterated under the weight of Paul's theological contrivances.

What Paul left in place of historical truth was a fabrication. He erased the actual history of Jesus' life and death, inventing a narrative that suited his needs. The yesterday and the day before yesterday of

Christianity were wiped clean, rewritten to align with Paul's vision. The history of Israel itself was recast to serve as a prelude to Paul's version of the Savior. In his narrative, all the prophets were reinterpreted as having foreshadowed his "Christ," and the entire religious history of humanity was manipulated to appear as though it culminated in Paul's theology.

The figure of Jesus, his teachings, his way of life, his death, and even the meaning of that death—nothing escaped this falsification. The concept of the "risen" Jesus became the focal point, and Paul shifted the entire weight of Jesus' life to this fabricated event. The real life and teachings of the Savior no longer mattered. For Paul, what was important was the death on the cross, and more than that, what could be built upon it.

To see Paul as sincere or honest, as someone who genuinely believed in the hallucination he claimed as proof of the resurrection, would be an absurdity for any psychologist. Paul was a man who willed the end and therefore willed the means. He knew what he needed to achieve his goals and was unbothered by the untruths he propagated. The fools to whom he preached were quick to accept these fabrications, swallowing his claims without question. For Paul, what mattered was power, and he used Christianity as a vehicle for priestly dominance.

The concepts, teachings, and symbols he introduced all served one purpose: to subjugate the masses and organize them into obedient mobs. His doctrine of immortality, and with it the promise of judgment, became his most potent tool for establishing priestly control. This invention, this mechanism of power, was so effective that even Islam later adopted it wholesale. Mohammed borrowed Paul's central device—the belief in the immortality of the soul and the judgment to come—as the cornerstone of his own religious structure. In Paul, the priesthood found its most cunning architect, and Christianity became a religion of domination rather than liberation, a faith of control rather than fulfillment.

When the center of gravity in life is shifted away from life itself and placed in a "beyond"—into nothingness—then life is robbed of its very essence, its meaning, and its balance. The grand falsehood of personal immortality undermines all reason and natural instincts, dismantling the very foundation upon which life thrives. Once this lie takes hold, everything in the human instinct that supports life, fosters its flourishing, and secures its future is cast under suspicion. The instincts that once guided humanity to thrive now become threats to the salvation of the soul. To live in such a way that life loses all meaning—this becomes the new "meaning" of life.

Why cultivate a sense of civic responsibility? Why take pride in one's lineage or honor one's forebears? Why work together, trust one another, or concern oneself with the common good? Why strive to contribute to the betterment of society? Under the Christian doctrine, all these are mere distractions, temptations leading one astray from the "straight and narrow path." Life becomes reduced to a single, all-encompassing command: "One thing only is necessary."

The poisonous idea that every man, by virtue of possessing an "immortal soul," is equal to every other man, regardless of his character, accomplishments, or contribution, leads to an absurd inflation of the self. In this distorted vision, the "salvation" of each insignificant individual is elevated to a matter of infinite importance, as though the laws of the universe should bend and nature itself should be suspended for the sake of the petty concerns of small-minded bigots and those teetering on the edge of madness. This grotesque exaltation of selfishness—this transformation of vanity into cosmic significance—is contemptible beyond measure. And yet, it is precisely this appeal to personal vanity, this flattery of the weak and the downtrodden, that Christianity owes its success. By magnifying the self-worth of the "botched," the dissatisfied, the downtrodden, and the refuse of humanity, it gathered to itself the disgruntled masses, those who found life too harsh and unforgiving.

The "salvation of the soul" is, in plain terms, the proclamation that "the world revolves around me." This doctrine of poisonous self-importance, masquerading as equality, became the cornerstone of Christianity. Under its influence, the principle of "equal rights for all" was introduced as a sacred truth, and from the dark recesses of human envy and bad instincts, Christianity launched its most insidious attack. It declared war on every instinct of reverence and respect for distinction between individuals, undermining the essential prerequisites for any upward movement, for any progress in civilization.

From the ressentiment of the masses, Christianity forged its most potent weapon—an unrelenting assault on all that is noble, joyous, and elevated in life. It turned its sights against the very happiness and vitality of the earth, dragging everything down to its level. To grant "immortality" to every Peter and Paul, to proclaim that every soul is of equal worth regardless of its merit, was the greatest and most vicious affront ever inflicted upon noble humanity. It flattened the peaks of human greatness, extinguishing the spark of aspiration and excellence that drives civilization forward.

And let us not overlook the corrosive influence that Christianity has exerted upon politics. Today, no one dares to stand for special rights or the right to rule. The courage to take pride in oneself and one's equals, the honor of noble distinction, and the "pathos of distance" that separates the exceptional from the ordinary—all of these have been eroded by the Christian lie of the equality of souls.

Our politics is gravely ill with this lack of courage. The aristocratic ethos, the belief in the refinement and elevation of a select few, has been shattered by the falsehood of equality. This same lie now fuels the belief in the "rights of the majority," which continues to ignite revolutions. But every revolution, guided by Christian values, inevitably devolves into a grotesque carnival of blood and crime. Let us not be deceived—Christianity is the root cause. Its teachings have inverted the natural order, turning every uprising into a revolt against what is noble, strong, and elevated in life.

Christianity is, at its heart, the revolt of all that creeps upon the ground against all that soars to great heights. It is the gospel of the "lowly," designed to drag down what is lofty and magnificent. Rather than uplifting the weak, it lowers the strong, reducing the sublime to the mediocre and the extraordinary to the common.

In its obsessive glorification of the downtrodden, it has made a virtue of smallness and a sin of greatness, leaving humanity poorer, weaker, and further from its highest potential.

The Gospels stand as a profound testament to the corruption that had already taken root within the earliest Christian community. What Paul later developed into a fully articulated system, with the unrelenting logic of a rabbi, was in fact merely the culmination of a decay that began with the death of the Savior. These texts must be read with the utmost care, for behind every word lies a complexity that challenges even the most discerning reader. I must admit—though I hope it will not be held against me—that it is precisely this complexity that offers unparalleled joy to a psychologist. The Gospels are a masterpiece of psychological refinement, not naive in their corruption but deliberate, an artful triumph in the realm of spiritual and moral manipulation.

In this sense, the Gospels stand alone. They are unlike any other part of the Bible. Here, we are unmistakably among Jews, and this fact is key to understanding their nature. The genius displayed in the Gospels is the genius of creating a profound delusion of personal "holiness," a skill unmatched in any other book or by any other people. This elevation of fraud—both in language and in posture—to the level of an art form is not a random occurrence or the product of individual talent. It is, rather, the result of centuries of Jewish tradition and practice, honed to perfection.

Judaism, with its relentless focus on "holiness," appears in Christianity as the ultimate refinement of this art: the fabrication of holy lies. After long centuries of training and discipline, this practice reached a level of mastery in the Christian tradition. The

Christian, in this sense, is the perfected Jew, not merely inheriting this talent but multiplying it. He is, in a way, threefold the Jew. The instinct to adopt only those concepts, symbols, and attitudes that align with priestly practice—while instinctively rejecting all other forms of thought and value—is not just tradition. It is inheritance. It operates with the force of nature, passed down and deeply ingrained.

The entire world, even the greatest minds of its most enlightened eras, has allowed itself to be deceived by this artifice. The Gospels have been read as books of innocence, which in itself is a testament to the extraordinary skill with which the deception was executed. The naïveté of their readers is astonishing. If these sanctimonious frauds and self-appointed saints could be seen in their true form, even for an instant, the farce would collapse. It is precisely because I cannot read a single word of theirs without picturing their theatrical piety—their rolling eyes, their false humility—that I have had enough of them. Their hypocrisy is intolerable.

For most people, however, books are just literature, and they fail to see beyond the surface. Let us not be deceived by the words "judge not," for these same figures condemn to hell anyone who stands in their way. In exalting God, they glorify themselves. In demanding virtues that suit their own needs, they present themselves as warriors for goodness, truth, and light. "We live, we die, we sacrifice ourselves for the good," they proclaim— though in reality, they simply act as they are compelled to by their base instincts. Forced by their hypocrisy to slink in shadows and conceal their true motives, they convert this necessity into a virtue. Their lives of humility are not a choice but a defense mechanism, rebranded as proof of their piety.

This brand of humble, chaste, and charitable fraud is a morality designed to manipulate. The Gospels are, at their core, texts of moral seduction. These people understood the utility of morality as a tool for control. Morality became their ultimate device for leading humanity by the nose. The conscious conceit of being "chosen" hides behind a veil of modesty, but this modesty is a mask for arrogance. They, the "community," the "good and just," claim a monopoly on truth and virtue, while relegating the rest of humanity—"the world"—to the status of outsiders.

This is the most dangerous form of megalomania the earth has ever seen. These small-minded bigots and liars claimed exclusive rights to concepts such as "God," "truth," "light," "spirit," "love," "wisdom," and "life," as though these ideas were synonymous with themselves. They sought to set themselves apart from the rest of humanity, to elevate their pettiness to the level of universal truth. They turned values on their heads, declaring that the Christian was the ultimate measure of all things—the salt of the earth, the standard of humanity, and even the arbiter of the final judgment.

This disaster was made possible only because it found fertile ground in the pre-existing megalomania of Judaism. The Judaeo-Christians, once they found themselves in conflict with mainstream Judaism, had no choice but to adopt the same tactics of self-preservation that Jewish instincts had long employed— only now, they used them even against the Jews themselves.

Christianity became, in essence, a "reformed" Judaism, a mirror image of its parent tradition, wielding the same tools of exclusion and self-glorification.

Let me offer a clear example of what these petty minds have projected onto the figure of their Master—the unfiltered creed of "beautiful souls":

" And whosoever shall not receive you, nor hear you, when ye depart thence, shake off the dust under your feet for a testimony against them. Verily I say unto you, it shall be more tolerable for Sodom and Gomorrha in the day of judgment, than for that city" (Mark 6:11).

How evangelical indeed! This is the language not of humility or grace but of vengeance and condemnation. It reveals the deep corruption that pervades the very foundations of the Gospels, transforming what could have been a message of peace into one of division, arrogance, and self-righteousness.

"And whosoever shall offend one of these little ones that believe in me, it is better for him that a millstone were hanged about his neck, and he were cast into the sea" (Mark 9 :42).

How very evangelical indeed! A message of love and humility expressed through threats of punishment so severe they border on the grotesque. What a curious way to inspire goodness—by invoking images of drowning with millstones.

"And if thine eye offend thee, pluck it out: it is better for thee to enter into the kingdom of God with one eye, than having two eyes to be cast into hell fir e; W her e the worm dieth not, and the fir e is not quenched" (Mark 9:47).

Ah, but it is not truly the eye that is meant here. This is not about the literal removal of body parts but about severing ties with anything deemed "sinful"— and yet, the language is unmistakably barbaric. How perfectly these words reflect the Christian preoccupation with violence as a means to sanctity, a moral calculus that prefers mutilation to perceived impurity.

"Verily I say unto you, That there be some of them that stand her e, which shall not taste of death, t ill they have seen the kingdom of God come with power " (Mark 9 :1).

Well lied, lion! A bold proclamation, indeed, yet how many centuries have passed since these words were spoken, and where is this "kingdom of God"? How prophetic, how divine—until one recalls that such declarations of imminent glory were never meant to be verifiable. A clever evasion of accountability.

"Whosoever will come after me, let him deny himself, and take up his cross, and follow me" (Mark 8 :34).

Here we see the core of Christian morality, built not on affirmation but on denial—of the self, of life, of joy. For... what? A promise, a vague reward in the beyond. As a psychologist might note, the very logic of these "fors"—the reasons behind the self-denial—undermine the morality they seek to uphold. And that, of course, is what makes it quintessentially Christian.

"Judge not, that ye be not judged. With what measure ye mete, it shall be measured to you again" (Matthew 7 :1).

What an astounding notion of justice—justice as a mirror of one's own actions, as if the universe were a tit-for-tat mechanism. This "just judge," it seems, operates less on principles and more on the whims of reciprocity.

"For if ye love them which love you, what reward have ye? do not even the publicans the same? And if ye salute your brethren only, what do ye mor e than others? do not even the publicans so?" (Matthew 5:46).

Here lies the principle of "Christian love": a love that demands distinction, that insists upon being extraordinary, and most of all, that expects payment in the form of eternal reward. Selfless, indeed!

"But if ye forgive not men their trespasses, neither will your Father forgive your trespasses" (Matthew 6 :15).

Quite compromising for this "Father" figure, who seems less like an embodiment of divine mercy and more like a scorekeeper, eager to withhold forgiveness if his terms are not met. A deity of conditional grace, at best.

"But seek ye first the kingdom of God, and his righteousness; and all these things shall be added unto you" (Matthew 6 :33).

"All these things"—the necessities of life, food, clothing, shelter—will apparently be provided. A promise that, to put it mildly, is far from accurate. Earlier, this God even dabbled as a tailor, fashioning garments for his chosen ones. How practical!

"Rejoice ye in that day, and leap for joy: for , behold, your reward is great in heaven: for in the lik e manner did their father s unto the prophets" (Luke 6 :23).

The audacity of such a statement! The "rabble," with their self-glorifying comparisons, dare to liken themselves to prophets. What impudence, what megalomania, to align their grievances with the legacies of those who truly shaped history.

"Know ye not that ye are the temple of God, and that the spirit of God dwelleth in you? If any man defile the temple of God, him shall God destroy; for the temple of God is holy, which temple ye are" (1 Corinthians 3:16).

What sanctimonious arrogance! To equate oneself with a "holy temple," to assume divine indwelling, and then to invoke destruction for those who fail to uphold this illusion of sanctity— one cannot heap enough contempt upon such pretension.

"Do ye not know that the saints shall judge the world? and if the world shall be judged by you, are ye unworthy to judge the smallest matters?" (1 Corinthians 6 :2).

Not merely the ravings of a lunatic, unfortunately, but the calculated rhetoric of one seeking dominance. And yet, Paul does not stop here.

"Know ye not that we shall judge angels? how much more things that pertain to this life?"

The delusion expands further. Saints judging the world was not grandiose enough—now they will judge angels as well! This is no longer mere arrogance but a flight into the absurd, a theology built on unbridled megalomania and the elevation of mediocrity to cosmic significance. Such impostures reveal the true spirit of early Christianity: not a doctrine of humility but a machinery of control and self-aggrandizement.

"Hath not God made foolish the wisdom of this world? For after that in the wisdom of God the world by wisdom knew not God, it pleased God by the foolishness of preaching to save them that believe. Not many wise men after the flesh, not many mighty, not many noble are called: But God hath chosen the foolish things of the world to confound the wise; and God hath chosen the weak things of the world to confound the things which are mighty; And base things of the world, and things which are despised, hath God chosen, yea, and things which are not, to bring to nought things that are: That no flesh should g lory in his presence." (1 Corinthians 1:20ff)

To truly grasp the psychological depth of this passage—arguably one of the clearest expressions of the moral framework underlying a Chandala morality— one must revisit the first part of my Genealogy of Morals. There, the stark opposition between noble morality and the morality born from ressentiment and impotent vengefulness is laid bare. Paul, above all others, stands as the supreme apostle of vengeance. His vision is one of turning every instinct of the downtrodden into a weapon against the powerful, of exalting weakness as virtue while condemning strength as sin.

What is the natural consequence of such a framework? It is that one would do well to handle the New Testament with gloves. The filth contained within it practically demands such precaution. To linger among the early Christians, even through the medium of their texts, is as unpleasant as mingling with Polish Jews— not because of any particular grievance against them, but simply because neither leaves behind a pleasant aroma.

In all my examination of the New Testament, I have not found a single instance of genuine humanity—nothing free-spirited, kind, open-hearted, or upright. The instincts for vitality and elevation, the first steps toward greatness, are entirely absent. What remains are the lowest instincts—vindictive, envious, cowardly—and even these lack courage. The text reeks of a shutting of the eyes, of a pervasive self-deception, of a cowardice that cloaks itself in virtue. Compared to this, every other book feels clean, invigorating, even joyful.

After reading Paul, I turned with relief and delight to the immortal Petronius. How different his tone—so wanton, so charming, so alive! Petronius possesses that enduring health and cheerfulness that breathes life into his words. Of him, one might echo Boccaccio's description of Cesare Borgia: "è tutto festo"— completely festive, completely sound.

In stark contrast, the early Christians made a critical miscalculation. Their attacks on others served only to highlight the worth of their adversaries. Anyone denounced by an early Christian emerges unscathed, if not elevated, by the association. Indeed, to be the target of such hatred becomes a badge of honor. The New Testament unwittingly inspires admiration for everything it condemns. Even the Pharisees and scribes—regular objects of its venom—gain a certain dignity. To be so hated, one must have had qualities worth despising. Hypocrisy? As if early Christians could level such a charge without irony! Their hatred of privilege required no justification other than its existence. Privilege alone was enough to provoke their wrath.

The early Christian—and, I fear, the last Christian as well—is driven by an instinctive rebellion against privilege in all its forms. His war for "equal rights" is eternal, born from an unrelenting need to elevate his weakness by tearing down the strength of others. For such a man, every standard—be it intellectual, moral, or aesthetic— becomes "worldly" and therefore evil. The Christian moral code transforms nobility, beauty, freedom, and pride into vices, while raising mediocrity, timidity, and submission to divine virtues.

It is impossible to ignore the dishonesty inherent in every word uttered by such a figure. His values are corrosive, his actions destructive, and his instincts toxic. Yet, paradoxically, his hatred serves as a reliable measure of value.

Whatever the Christian priest condemns, we may be certain is worth preserving. In this way, the Christian, especially the priest, becomes an inverted criterion of worth.

And what of the figures within the New Testament? Only one stands out as worthy of honor: Pilate, the Roman viceroy. His noble Roman disdain for the Jewish quagmire in which he found himself is unmatched. One Jew more or less—what difference did it make to him? His scorn for the petty drama before him added a touch of Roman dignity to a text otherwise devoid of it. Pilate enriched the New Testament with its only statement of enduring value—a single question that is both its critique and its undoing: " W hat is truth?"

With this question, Pilate dismissed the sham seriousness of those who surrounded him. He stood apart from their lies and self-delusions, embodying the clarity and strength of a world that saw beyond petty moralistic games. In this moment, the Roman viceroy became the unintentional savior of the text— a beacon of realism in a sea of falsity.

What sets us apart is not that we fail to find God—in history, in nature, or even beyond nature—but that we reject what has been honored as God. We do not see such a figure as "divine" but as pitiable, absurd, and ultimately harmful. We regard this so- called God not merely as an error but as a profound crime against life itself. We do not merely deny the Christian God; we deny that such a God could be God. Were someone to present us with proof of the Christian God's existence, it would make us believe in him even less. In simple terms: deus, qualem Paulus creavit, dei negatio—the God as Paul created him is the negation of God.

A religion like Christianity, which fails to engage with reality on any level and crumbles the moment reality asserts itself, must inevitably set itself against the "wisdom of this world." Christianity cannot coexist with science, clarity, or intellectual integrity. It thrives only by poisoning, defaming, and vilifying all disciplines that demand lucidity and rigor, all qualities that embody the freedom and nobility of the mind. Faith, as Christianity defines it, is not merely separate from reason—it is a direct veto against reason. In practice, faith requires falsehood at any cost.

Paul understood this necessity. He knew that the lie, packaged as "faith," was indispensable. The church later inherited and institutionalized this insight from Paul. The God that Paul invented for himself—a God who "made foolish the wisdom of this world"—is not divine revelation but a reflection of Paul's own will to power. This God is the expression of a Jewish instinct to impose one's will upon others by declaring it divine law (thora). Paul's war was not only theological but also deeply practical: he sought to eradicate the "wisdom of this world," which he identified as his greatest threat. His specific enemies were the philologists and physicians of the Alexandrian school. These practitioners of knowledge represented everything that stood in opposition to Paul's invention.

No one can be a philologist or a physician without, in essence, being an Antichrist. A philologist sees through the veil of the "holy books," exposing their fraudulence. A physician discerns the physiological degeneration of the Christian ideal, diagnosing it as incurable. To the philologist, Christianity is a literary deception; to the physician, it is a symptom of sickness.

Has anyone ever truly understood the famous story at the beginning of the Bible? The narrative of God's mortal fear of knowledge? It has gone unnoticed by most, yet it reveals the fundamental anxiety of the priestly mind. This priest- book par excellence begins with the acknowledgment of the priest's only real danger: knowledge. Ergo, "God" faces the same peril. The story of Eden is not about humanity's fall but about the priest's struggle to maintain control.

The old God, entirely spirit, entirely priestly, entirely "perfect," strolls through his garden in boredom, seeking diversion. Even gods cannot escape the tedium of eternity. In his idleness, he creates man—a creature to entertain him. But man, too, grows bored. God, moved by pity, creates animals to distract man, but they fail to suffice. Man seeks dominion over them, rejecting the role of mere animal himself. So God creates woman, ending boredom—but also beginning a cascade of unintended consequences. Woman, the second mistake of God, introduces chaos. Priests have always known that "woman is a serpent" and that "from woman comes all evil in the world." And what was her ultimate crime? She introduced man to knowledge.

Through woman, man tasted the forbidden fruit of the tree of knowledge. And God, realizing his mistake, was seized by terror. Man, his greatest blunder, had become a rival. Knowledge threatened to make man godlike, spelling the end for both gods and priests. Thus, the moral of the story becomes clear: science, as the pursuit of knowledge, is the ultimate sin, the origin of all other sins. This is the essence of priestly morality: "Thou shalt not know." Everything else follows from this foundational command.

But God's terror did not make him less cunning. How could he defend himself against knowledge? The answer came in stages. First, he expelled man from paradise. Happiness and leisure foster thought, and thought is dangerous. Man must be made to suffer— only suffering can keep him from thinking. So the priest invented distress, death, childbirth's agonies, old age, decrepitude, and above all, sickness. These miseries served as tools of control, preventing man from indulging in dangerous curiosity.

And yet, despite these efforts, knowledge continued to grow. The edifice of human understanding rose higher and higher, casting a shadow over the gods. Desperate, God took another step: he invented war. By dividing peoples and setting them against one another, he ensured that they would be too consumed by conflict to pursue knowledge. War, among other things, is the greatest disruptor of science. And yet, even war could not fully halt humanity's progress. Knowledge flourished in defiance of all obstacles.

Finally, God resolved to end it all. "Man has become scientific— there is no help for it," he concluded. And so, his ultimate solution was the flood: to drown mankind, to erase his greatest mistake. Yet even this failed to extinguish humanity's thirst for knowledge. The legacy of science and reason persists, growing ever stronger, while the gods and their priestly servants continue to weaken under its light.

The opening of the Bible lays bare the entire psychology of the priest. The priest's singular and greatest fear is science—the clear and systematic understanding of cause and effect. This fear is not accidental; it is foundational. Science, the pursuit of knowledge, thrives only under favorable conditions. To seek knowledge, a man must have time, intellectual abundance, and the freedom to explore. But this is precisely what the priest cannot allow. For the priest, the solution has always been simple and consistent: "Man must be made unhappy."

From this logic emerged the concept of "sin." Sin is the priest's weapon, the first invention deployed to stifle the human mind. Guilt, punishment, and the so-called "moral order of the world" were all crafted to stand against science, against liberation, and against humanity's progress toward self-empowerment. These ideas redirected man's gaze inward, away from the external world and its truths. Instead of looking at the world with reason and curiosity, man was taught to close his eyes and suffer. Suffering became his condition—his justification for needing the priest. The physician, who sought to heal suffering and restore strength, was replaced by the "Savior," whose role was to deepen man's dependence on the priestly class.

This invention of guilt and punishment—along with doctrines of "grace," "salvation," and "forgiveness"—constitutes a lie of the highest order. These concepts are utterly without psychological reality; they exist solely to undermine man's sense of causality. They deny the natural consequences of actions and replace them with supernatural fabrications. Cause and effect are transformed into the whims of invisible forces: "God," "spirits," and "souls." These fabrications reduce natural outcomes to "moral" consequences, cloaked in rewards and punishments. In doing so, they destroy the foundation of knowledge itself, perpetrating the greatest crime against humanity—the deliberate obliteration of understanding.

Sin, this act of man desecrating himself, was invented for one purpose: to make science, culture, and human elevation impossible. The priest's power depends entirely on the perpetuation of sin. Through it, the priest rules.

At this point, I cannot refrain from offering a psychology of "belief" and the "believer"—for the benefit of those who still claim to believe. If anyone still fails to recognize how indecent it is to be "believing," or how much belief signifies a decline, a broken will to live, they will soon enough. My words are clear even to the deaf.

Among Christians, there exists a peculiar criterion of truth often referred to as "proof by power." It follows a simple formula: "Faith makes one blessed; therefore, it is true." This argument, if we may call it that, is entirely circular. One might immediately object that the blessedness faith promises is not a demonstration of truth—it is merely a promise, suspended upon the condition of belief. "One shall be blessed because one believes." But even this promise, rooted as it is in a wholly transcendental "beyond," remains undemonstrated and un-demonstrable. How can such a claim serve as a proof?

The so-called "proof by power" reduces to a mere belief that the effects promised by faith will eventually manifest. Translated into a formula: "I believe that faith makes me blessed; therefore, it is true." But this reasoning is absurd as a criterion of truth. Let us assume for the sake of politeness that faith's promise of blessedness can be demonstrated—not merely hoped for or whispered by the suspicious lips of priests. Even then, could the sensation of blessedness— pleasure, in technical terms—ever serve as a proof of truth?

The answer is unequivocal: no. If anything, pleasure often serves as a proof against truth. When sensations of pleasure influence the judgment of what is true, they render such judgments deeply suspect. Pleasure proves nothing beyond itself. Why, then, should one assume that truth must be accompanied by agreeable feelings? Why should truth be easier, more comfortable, or more pleasurable than falsehood? Experience, particularly the experience of disciplined and profound minds, teaches the opposite. Every small victory for truth has come at an enormous cost—sacrificing the comforts of the heart, the bonds of love, and the securities of human trust.

The pursuit of truth demands greatness of soul. It is the hardest of all services, requiring courage, sacrifice, and an unrelenting commitment to intellectual integrity. And what is this integrity? It is the refusal to yield to the seductions of comfort, pleasure, or convenience in matters of understanding. It is the relentless demand that we face the world as it is, not as we wish it to be. This is the true meaning of intellectual honesty, the cornerstone of any genuine elevation of humanity.

It means that a person must be strict with their own heart, reject the appeal of "beautiful feelings," and treat every "yes" and "no" as a matter of conscience. Faith may make people feel blessed, but that does not make it true—it is, instead, a lie. The fact that faith, in certain situations, can create a sense of happiness does not prove that the ideas behind it are real. The happiness caused by being fixated on one belief does not validate that belief. In truth, faith does not move mountains; it creates mountains where none existed before. This becomes clear enough with a simple walk through a lunatic asylum. Of course, this would never be obvious to a priest, whose instincts compel him to deny reality, insisting that illness is not illness and asylums are not asylums.

Christianity depends on sickness in the same way that the Greek spirit thrived on a superabundance of health. The true purpose behind the entire system of salvation offered by the church is to make people ill. Even the church itself, when viewed honestly, seems to aim toward turning the world into one enormous madhouse, a kind of universal Catholic asylum. The ideal type of religious person that the church desires is, in fact, a typical décadent. Whenever a religious crisis overtakes a society, it is marked by epidemics of nervous disorders.

The "inner world" of the religious person is indistinguishable from that of someone who is overstressed and worn out. The so-called "highest" states of mind celebrated by Christianity as supremely valuable are often epileptic in nature. The church has only ever regarded the insane or outright frauds as holy, all under the pretense of honoring God.

At one point, I even described the entire Christian method of penance and salvation as a deliberate way of cultivating madness on ground already prepared for it, ground weakened and unhealthy. Not everyone can be a Christian; one cannot simply "convert" to Christianity. Instead, a person must already be sick enough to be drawn into it.

We, on the other hand, who have the courage to embrace health and even contempt, have every reason to despise a religion that teaches people to misunderstand their own bodies. Christianity clings to the superstitions surrounding the "soul" and makes a "virtue" out of inadequate nourishment. It views health itself as an enemy, a form of temptation, or even as the devil. Christianity convinces itself that a "perfect soul" can live in a broken and decaying body, and to justify this, it creates a twisted concept of "perfection." This so-called perfection is nothing more than a pale, sickly, and irrational state of mind, which it calls "holiness." This holiness is not a sign of strength or vitality but instead a series of symptoms—signs of a body that is impoverished, weakened, and permanently disordered.

As a movement within Europe, Christianity has always been an uprising of all the rejected and discarded elements of society— those who, under the banner of Christianity, now sought power. It was not the decline of an ancient, noble civilization that gave rise to Christianity, as some claim. This idea, which is still widely believed today, is entirely false and deserves to be challenged. Christianity did not emerge from the decay of classical antiquity. On the contrary, when the weak and marginalized classes of the Roman Empire were drawn into Christianity, the noble classes of the time were at their strongest and most refined. Christianity's triumph was the victory of the majority, the rise of democracy with its instincts for resentment and revenge.

Christianity was never tied to any one nation or race; it was a universal call to all those who felt disinherited by life. Its allies were found among the oppressed, the outcasts, and the sick. At its core, Christianity harbors a deep resentment against health and vitality. It despises everything that is strong, proud, and beautiful. Consider again the infamous words of Paul: "And God hath chosen the weak things of the world, the foolish things of the world, the base things of the world, and things which are despised." This sums up Christianity's entire approach: through this mindset, décadence triumphed.

The symbol of God on the cross encapsulates this victory, yet its deeper meaning is often missed. Christianity elevates suffering to the divine. Anything that suffers or hangs on the cross is declared sacred. This extends to humanity itself: because we all suffer, we are all divine. From this logic, Christianity proclaims that only it is divine.

Thus, Christianity achieved its victory by destroying a nobler way of thinking. It remains, to this day, the greatest misfortune to have befallen humanity.

Christianity opposes all forms of intellectual well-being— it can only use a form of reasoning that is flawed and sickly, which it presents as "Christian reasoning." It aligns itself with everything irrational and curses the "intellect" as though it were a sin, condemning the pride of a healthy, functioning mind. Since Christianity inherently thrives on sickness, the Christian concept of "faith" must also be considered a form of sickness. The church, therefore, bans all direct, honest, and scientific paths to understanding as dangerous and forbidden. From the very beginning, doubt itself is treated as a sin.

The complete lack of psychological clarity in priests is immediately apparent just by observing them—it is a direct symptom of their state of décadence. Similar traits can be seen in hysterical women and in children suffering from physical and emotional weakness: a distorted instinct, a delight in lying simply for the sake of lying, and an inability to see or move straightforwardly. Faith, in this sense, represents a willful refusal to acknowledge the truth. The pietist or priest, whether male or female, is fundamentally dishonest because they are ill; their instincts demand that truth must never be allowed to win. For the believer, anything that leads to sickness is considered good, while everything that stems from vitality, strength, and abundance is deemed evil. This instinct to lie is what marks someone destined to become a theologian.

Another sign of the theologian is their complete unsuitability for philology. By philology, I mean the art of reading carefully and thoughtfully—the ability to understand facts without twisting their meaning or abandoning caution, patience, and subtlety in interpretation. Philology, in this sense, is the practice of restraint in understanding. This applies whether one is reading books, interpreting news, analyzing major historical events, or even examining weather statistics—let alone the so-called "salvation of the soul."

The way theologians, whether in Berlin or in Rome, explain a passage of scripture, a personal experience, or even a military victory by calling upon the lofty imagery of the Psalms of David is so absurdly bold that it could drive a philologist mad. And what can one say when pietists and other such simple- minded folks claim that the "finger of God" is responsible for turning their mundane, insignificant lives into miracles of "grace," "providence," and "salvation"? Even the smallest amount of intellectual effort—or common decency—should be enough to expose the childishness and unworthiness of such claims.

Imagine encountering a god who always cured your cold at just the right time or arranged for you to step into a carriage precisely as it started to rain. Such a god would appear so ridiculous that he would have to be abolished, even if he truly existed. A god reduced to the role of a household servant, a mailman, or a walking almanac—at his core, he would be nothing more than a name for the most foolish kind of chance.

The idea of "Divine Providence," which is still believed by a significant portion of educated Germans, is itself one of the strongest arguments against the existence of God. It is so absurd that no stronger argument against God could be imagined. And if nothing else, it is a powerful argument against the Germans themselves.

It is far from true that martyrs prove the truth of a cause; in fact, I would argue that martyrs have nothing to do with truth at all. The way a martyr loudly proclaims what he believes to be true, throwing it in the face of the world, shows such a low level of intellectual honesty and such an inability to engage with the problem of "truth" that there is no need to refute him. Truth is not something one person possesses while another lacks; this kind of thinking is the mark of peasants or peasant-like apostles such as Luther. The more intellectually honest a person is, the more modest and careful they will be about claiming knowledge. To truly know even a few things and to gracefully admit ignorance about everything else—that is the hallmark of someone with intellectual discipline.

The way prophets, sectarians, free-thinkers, Socialists, and church leaders understand "truth" is nothing more than proof that they have failed to begin even the smallest intellectual discipline or self-control required to discover real truth. The deaths of martyrs, we should note, have been unfortunate events in history. They have led people astray. The simple-minded conclusion that many idiots, women, and common folk draw—that there must be value in a cause for which someone dies, or for which, as in early Christianity, people willingly seek death—has done immense harm to the pursuit of facts and the spirit of investigation. Martyrs have not helped truth; they have harmed it. Even today, the mere fact of persecution gives unwarranted respect to the most baseless sects and beliefs.

But why should this be? Does the value of a cause increase simply because someone has died for it? An error made honorable through martyrdom is still an error—it has merely gained a dangerous charm. Do you theologians imagine we will grant you the privilege of being martyred for your lies? The best way to deal with a cause is to respectfully put it aside and let it fade. That is also the best way to deal with theologians. This was the great, world-shaping mistake of every persecutor: they gave undue respect to the causes they opposed, gifting them the seductive appeal of martyrdom. Even now, women kneel before an error because they have been told that someone died on a cross for it. But is the cross an argument?

There is only one figure who has said what has needed to be said about this for thousands of years—Zarathustra. They left bloody marks along their paths and convinced themselves that blood proved the truth of their beliefs. But blood is the worst evidence for truth. It corrupts even the purest teachings, filling hearts with madness and hatred. What does it prove when someone walks through fire for their beliefs? Far more meaningful is when a teaching emerges from within one's own fire.

Do not be deceived: great intellects are always skeptical. Zarathustra himself is a skeptic. The strength and freedom that come from intellectual power— especially an overflowing abundance of it—express themselves as skepticism. People with rigid convictions are not the ones who shape what is truly fundamental in values or lack of values. Those who cling to convictions are like prisoners; they cannot see far enough ahead, nor can they see what lies beneath them. By contrast, someone who wishes to speak meaningfully about value and non-value must be able to view hundreds of convictions below and behind them, understanding their place from a great height.

A mind that strives for greatness and seeks the means to achieve it must necessarily be skeptical. True strength and independence of thought require freedom from all forms of rigid belief. This grand passion, which serves as both the foundation and the driving force of a skeptic's existence, is more enlightened and more commanding than the skeptic himself. It enlists every part of his intellect into its service, makes him unsparing, and gives him the courage to use methods others might call unholy. At times, it may even permit him to adopt convictions, but only as tools. Conviction becomes a means to an end, a device that can accomplish much when wielded wisely. However, a grand passion never submits to conviction—it rules over it as a sovereign.

On the other hand, the need for faith, for something absolute that demands unwavering belief, reveals a weakness. The "man of faith," no matter what he believes in, is fundamentally dependent. Such a person cannot set himself as his own goal, nor can he find purpose within himself. The believer does not belong to himself; he is merely a means to someone else's end, waiting to be used. His instincts lead him to exalt an ethic of self-denial above all else. He embraces it willingly, driven by prudence, experience, and even vanity. Every kind of faith is, at its core, a symptom of self-denial and self-alienation.

When one considers how vital it is for the majority of people to have external rules and restraints to guide them, it becomes clear why belief and conviction are so necessary. For the weak- willed—and especially for women—order, control, or even a higher form of slavery is the only condition under which they can thrive. Convictions provide these individuals with structure and support; they are, in a sense, their backbone. To maintain this rigid framework, such people must avoid seeing many things and remain entirely partial. They become completely absorbed in their chosen cause, judging all values with unshakable certainty. But these very traits place them in opposition to the truthful person, who values openness and inquiry.

The believer is not free to ask whether something is "true" or "not true" based on his own conscience. To do so would be to undermine his entire foundation. His pathological narrowness of vision turns him into a fanatic— examples include Savonarola, Luther, Rousseau, Robespierre, and Saint-Simon. These figures stand as stark contrasts to the strong and liberated spirit. Yet the grandiose postures of such sickly minds, these intellectual epileptics, often captivate the masses.

Fanatics are dramatic, and humanity is more inclined to admire a striking pose than to listen to well-reasoned arguments.

Let us take another step into the psychology of conviction and "faith." Some time ago, I raised the question of whether convictions might actually be more dangerous enemies of truth than lies. Today, I want to state this question more directly: is there any real difference between a lie and a conviction? Most people believe there is—but then, most people believe many things that are questionable. Every conviction has a history. It begins in primitive forms, passes through stages of doubt and error, and only later becomes a firm belief. What if falsehood itself is simply one of these early stages of conviction? Sometimes, all it takes is a change of people: what the father believed to be a lie becomes a conviction for the son.

I call it lying when someone refuses to see what is right in front of them or refuses to acknowledge it for what it truly is. It doesn't matter whether this lie is spoken aloud or kept within—it remains a lie. The most common lie is the one a person tells themselves; deceiving others is comparatively rare. This deliberate blindness, this refusal to see the world as it is, is often the first requirement for belonging to any group or party. To be a partisan is to be a liar. Consider, for example, the German historians who are convinced that Rome represented tyranny, while the Germanic peoples brought liberty to the world. What is the difference between this conviction and a lie?

Is it any surprise that all partisans—like those German historians— instinctively cling to moral platitudes? Morality survives largely because party members of every kind feel they need it constantly. "This is our conviction: we proclaim it to the world; we are willing to live and die for it. Let us respect everyone who holds strong convictions!" I have actually heard this argument from anti-Semites. But the opposite is true! An anti-Semite does not become more respectable simply because he lies out of principle.

Priests, who are more cunning in these matters, recognize the problem with convictions—that is, with lies elevated to principles because they serve a purpose. To avoid this issue, they have borrowed a clever tactic from the Jews: they introduce concepts like "God," "the will of God," and "revelation." Kant, with his categorical imperative, took a similar approach. According to this reasoning, there are questions about truth or falsehood that humans cannot answer. The most important questions, the ultimate problems of value, lie beyond human comprehension. To know the limits of reason—this, they claim, is true philosophy.

Why, then, did God reveal his will to humanity? Surely, God would not do something unnecessary. The argument goes that humans could not figure out for themselves what is good or evil, so God had to teach them his will. From this perspective, the priest does not lie. The questions of "true" or "false" do not apply to the matters the priest discusses. After all, how can one lie about something if it is impossible to know the truth of it? Thus, the priest becomes merely the voice of God.

This kind of priestly reasoning is not unique to Judaism or Christianity. It is a hallmark of the priestly mindset throughout history, whether among ancient pagans or the priests of later décadence. (Pagans, by the way, are those who say "yes" to life and use "God" as a term to affirm all things.) Terms like "law," "the will of God," "holy books," and "inspiration" are nothing more than tools by which priests gain and maintain power. These concepts are the foundation of all priestly institutions and of every priestly or priestly-philosophical form of government.

The "holy lie" is not exclusive to one religion. It appears in the teachings of Confucius, the Code of Manu, the Quran, and the Christian church—and even Plato was not free of it. Whenever you hear the phrase "Truth is here," you can be certain of one thing: the priest is lying.

In the end, the question becomes: what is the purpose of lying? My main objection to Christianity lies in the fact that its so- called "holy" ends are nowhere to be seen. Instead, it leads only to destructive outcomes: poisoning minds, spreading slander, denying life, despising the body, and degrading humanity with the concept of sin. Because its ends are harmful, its methods are equally harmful.

In contrast, I have an entirely different reaction when reading the Code of Manu. This work is incomparably more intellectual and refined; it would be an insult to intelligence to even mention it in the same breath as the Bible. The reason is clear: the Code of Manu is rooted in true philosophy, not the foul mix of rabbinical legalism and superstition that pervades the Bible. It offers even the most discerning psychologist something of substance to explore. Most importantly, it stands fundamentally apart from any kind of Bible. In the Code of Manu, the nobles, philosophers, and warriors maintain their rightful authority over the masses. The text is filled with noble values, a sense of completeness, and an affirmation of life. It reflects a triumphant, self-assured embrace of existence—the entire work seems to glow with sunlight.

In the Code of Manu, the topics that Christianity treats with crude vulgarity—such as procreation, women, and marriage—are addressed with earnestness, respect, and a deep sense of love and trust. How can anyone seriously give children and women a book like the Bible, which contains repulsive teachings such as: "To avoid fornication, let every man have his own wife, and let ever y woman have her own husband; ... it is better to marry than to burn"? Is it possible to call oneself a Christian while accepting a worldview that corrupts the origin of humanity with the doctrine of the immaculata conceptio, reducing it to something base and shameful?

I know of no text that speaks with more delicacy and respect about women than the Code of Manu. These ancient sages and elders have a gallantry toward women that is nearly impossible to match. Consider this passage: "The mouth of a woman, the breasts of a maiden, the prayer of a child, and the smoke of sacrifice are always pure." Or this one: "There is nothing purer than the light of the sun, the shadow cast by a cow, air , water , fir e, and the breath of a maiden." And finally, this striking statement— perhaps another holy lie, but a charming one nonetheless: "All the openings of the body above the navel are pure, and all below are impure. Only in the maiden is the You can clearly see the unholiness of Christianity's methods by comparing its goals with those of the Code of Manu. When you place these two entirely opposite sets of goals side by side and examine them closely, the contrast becomes undeniable. Any serious critique of Christianity must expose its means and ends as contemptible. A book of laws like the Code of Manu originates from the same source as any truly good legal code—it represents the accumulated wisdom, insight, and ethical experimentation of many centuries. It brings long processes of trial and error to a conclusion; it codifies rather than creates.

Such codification relies on an essential principle: the methods used to establish the authority of a hard-won truth must differ completely from those used to prove or explain it. A lawbook does not include arguments for its laws, nor does it recount their utility or origins. To do so would undermine the imperative tone, the commanding "thou shall" on which obedience depends. This is where the issue lies. At a certain point in a people's development, the wisest among them—those with the most hindsight and foresight—declare that the period of experimentation in determining how life should be lived has ended. Their task then becomes to gather as much as possible from the lessons learned through these hard and often painful experiences. The priority shifts to ensuring stability and avoiding further experimentation, preventing values from remaining in constant flux, endlessly questioned and redefined.

Two strategies support this goal. First, revelation: the claim that the laws are not of human origin but were given by divine power. This suggests the laws were not discovered through trial and error but were instead perfect, eternal, and miraculous from the start. Second, tradition: the belief that the laws have stood unchanged since the dawn of time and that questioning them dishonors one's ancestors. By grounding the authority of law in the idea that it was both given by God and upheld by the forefathers, a powerful double layer of legitimacy is created.

The higher purpose of these strategies is to slowly shift people's focus away from thinking consciously about right and wrong and instead instill instincts that operate automatically. Such automatism is essential for achieving mastery and perfection in the art of living. Writing a lawbook like the Code of Manu is an effort to provide a society with the tools to achieve future greatness and aspire to mastery in life. For this to happen, adherence to the law must become unconscious—this is the purpose of every so- called holy lie.

The caste system, the highest and most central law of the Code of Manu, does not represent arbitrary invention. It reflects a natural law of the highest order, one that no modern ideas or human whims can alter. In every healthy society, three fundamental types of people naturally emerge, each distinct yet interdependent. These groups differ in their physical and intellectual characteristics, their roles in society, and their sense of fulfillment. Nature, not Manu, determines who belongs to these castes: those with superior intellect, those with physical strength and temperament, and the majority who display mediocrity. The first two groups are the chosen few, while the last represents the larger mass.

The highest caste—the smallest and most exceptional group—embodies perfection and possesses privileges unavailable to the rest. This caste represents happiness, beauty, and all that is truly good in life. Only the most intellectually gifted have the right to beauty and nobility; only they can transform goodness into a strength rather than a weakness. Pulchrum est paucorum hominum—beauty belongs to the few. For these superior individuals, vulgarity, pessimism, or indignation at the imperfections of the world are unworthy traits. Indignation and pessimism are the attitudes of the Chandala. For the most intellectual among us, the world appears perfect. They understand that even what is beneath them, what is distant, what is flawed— even the Chandala—is part of that perfection.

The most intelligent and strongest individuals find joy where others would only see hardship. They thrive in challenges, embrace self-discipline, and transform asceticism into a natural instinct. For them, difficult tasks are privileges, and they find pleasure in carrying burdens that would crush anyone else. Even the pursuit of knowledge becomes a form of asceticism for them. These individuals are the most honorable of all, but they are also the most cheerful and charming. They rule not because they desire power but because they embody it; it is impossible for them to occupy a subordinate position.

The second caste consists of those who uphold the law and maintain order—noble warriors, protectors, and judges, with the king as their highest expression. This caste serves as the practical arm of the intellectual elite, taking on the more arduous tasks of governance and carrying out their directives. They are the followers and loyal enforcers of the highest caste's vision.

Nothing in this system is arbitrary. To suggest otherwise is to dishonor nature. The caste system reflects life's fundamental principles, ensuring societal stability and allowing for the development of higher types. Inequality of rights is not a flaw—it is a necessity for the existence of rights at all. A right is always a privilege, aligned with one's place in the natural order. Even mediocrity has its privileges.

Life becomes more demanding as one ascends to higher ranks. The air grows colder, and the weight of responsibility increases. A high civilization is like a pyramid—it can only stand on a broad base of mediocrity. This foundation is crucial, as most professions— craftsmanship, commerce, agriculture, science, and much of art— require mediocre abilities and aspirations. Exceptional individuals would find such roles unsuitable. Mediocrity is a form of happiness for the majority, as they are naturally inclined toward specialization and mastery of a single task. To despise mediocrity is unworthy of a deep thinker; it is the necessary condition for the emergence of the exceptional.

When exceptional individuals treat those of average ability with greater care and consideration than they do their equals, it is not merely out of kindness but a recognition of duty.

Who do I despise most among today's crowds? The rabble of Socialists, those preachers to the Chandala who corrupt the instincts of the working man. They make him resentful, envious, and dissatisfied with his simple, contented life. They teach him revenge and poison his natural sense of joy. The true injustice is not in unequal rights but in the lie of "equal" rights. What do I call bad? I have already answered: anything born of weakness, envy, or revenge. The anarchist and the Christian share the same origin.

In the end, the purpose behind a lie makes all the difference. Does it serve to preserve or to destroy? Christianity and anarchism are alike in their ultimate goal: both aim for destruction. History provides overwhelming evidence of this. Compare Christianity with the Code of Manu, which sought to turn the conditions for life's flourishing into an enduring social order. Christianity, in contrast, defined its mission as destroying such an order—precisely because life thrived under it. The Code of Manu represents the careful application of wisdom gathered over centuries, a means of harvesting the fullest possible benefits from life's long and difficult experiments. Christianity, on the other hand, destroyed that harvest in a single night.

Consider the imperium Romanum, the Roman Empire—a monumental achievement of organization under the most challenging conditions. It was unparalleled in history, a masterpiece of order and strength, standing as a model against which everything before and after seems crude and clumsy. Yet the so-called "holy" anarchists of Christianity turned the destruction of this empire into a sacred duty. They sought to dismantle "the world"—their term for the Roman

Empire—until nothing remained. Even crude conquerors like the Germans and their ilk were able to take control of the ruins.

The Christian and the anarchist are both décadents. Neither is capable of contributing anything constructive; instead, they act only to dissolve, poison, and weaken. Their hatred is directed at everything strong, enduring, and life- affirming. Christianity was the vampire that drained the lifeblood of the Roman Empire. Overnight, it wiped out the vast achievements of the Romans, who had cultivated the soil for a great culture that could endure and develop over centuries. This simple fact is still not fully understood.

The Roman Empire, as we know it from history and from the increasing understanding of its provinces, was only the beginning of something even greater. It was a work of grand-scale artistry, destined to prove its worth over millennia. To this day, nothing comparable has been built—or even imagined— on such a scale, with such an eternal vision. This Roman organization was so robust that it could survive even poor leadership. The personalities of individual emperors mattered little—this is the hallmark of truly great architecture. But not even this structure could withstand the most corrupting force of all: Christianity.

These stealthy Christians, creeping through society under the cover of night and secrecy, drained people of their interest in real, tangible things and their instincts for reality. This cowardly, soft, and deceptive group gradually alienated every noble and virtuous soul that had once aligned its purpose with Rome. Concepts like hypocrisy, secrecy, and dark ideas about the sacrifice of the innocent and mystical union through blood-drinking became dominant. At the heart of it all was the slow-burning revenge of the Chandala—the lowest, most resentful instincts turned into power. Rome succumbed to the very type of religion that Epicurus had fought against.

To understand what Epicurus battled, one need only read Lucretius. Epicurus did not oppose paganism; he fought against what we now recognize as Christianity—the corruption of human souls through ideas of guilt, punishment, and immortality. He stood against the cults of the underground, the hidden Christianity that was already taking root. Denying the concept of immortality was, for Epicurus, a genuine act of salvation. His victory was clear: in Rome, every respectable mind was Epicurean—until Paul arrived.

Paul embodied the Chandala hatred of Rome and the world, wielding it with a genius for destruction. As the quintessential Jew, Paul recognized how the small Christian sect could ignite a "world fire." With the symbol of "God on the cross," he unified the subversive elements and anarchist movements across the empire, forging them into an immense force. "Salvation is of the Jews"—this became the Christian formula.

Christianity was the culmination of all underground cults, including those of Osiris, the Great Mother, and Mithras. Paul's genius lay in recognizing this and exploiting it. With ruthless disregard for truth, he attributed to the "Saviour" ideas that would resonate with adherents of every Chandala religion. He reshaped Christ into something even a priest of Mithras could accept. This was Paul's "revelation" at Damascus: he realized that belief in immortality was essential to devalue life on earth, that the concept of "hell" could conquer Rome, and that the notion of an otherworldly "beyond" would spell the death of this world.

Nihilist and Christian—they rhyme in German, and they do much more than rhyme.

The entire labor of the ancient world was wasted. I can hardly find words to describe the outrage this inspires in me. When we consider that all this effort was only the foundation for a project meant to last thousands of years, the entire purpose of antiquity seems to vanish! Why did we have the Greeks? Why did we have the Romans? All the essential tools for a scholarly culture were already in place. The methods of science were developed, humanity had mastered the unmatched art of reading with purpose—a vital skill for maintaining a cultural tradition and uniting the sciences. The natural sciences had already aligned with mathematics and mechanics, progressing steadily. The sense of fact, that most valuable sense of all, had established its schools, and its traditions had lasted for centuries.

Do we fully grasp this? Every critical element necessary to begin great work was ready—and the most essential part, methods, was already there. These methods are the hardest to develop and the most fiercely resisted by laziness and habit. What we have painstakingly reclaimed today, through relentless discipline and effort—despite lingering bad instincts and remnants of Christian tendencies within us—was already present two thousand years ago. Keen observation, a steady hand, patience, attention to detail, and a commitment to truth—all these existed long before. Beyond that, there was a refined sense of tact and taste, not as mere mental exercises or the awkward pretensions of "German" culture, but as something deeply embodied, instinctive, and real. All of it—lost! Overnight, it was reduced to a memory.

The Greeks! The Romans! Their instinctive nobility, their refined taste, their disciplined inquiry, their genius for organization, their dedication to securing humanity's future, and their resounding affirmation of life—all embodied in the Roman Empire, a reality that transcended art, becoming truth and life itself. All of it swept away in a single night—not by a natural disaster, nor by the crushing feet of barbaric invaders like the Teutons. No, it was undone by cunning, sneaky, bloodless parasites. It wasn't conquered; it was drained dry. Hidden resentment and petty envy took control. Everything wretched, sickly, and filled with malice—the entire ghetto of the soul—rose to power.

If you read any Christian agitator, like St. Augustine, you can clearly sense the kind of vile characters that rose to prominence. Yet, it would be a mistake to think these leaders of Christianity lacked intelligence. On the contrary, they were incredibly clever— so clever that their cunning seemed almost saintly. What they lacked, however, were respectable, honest, and clean instincts. Between us, they were not even men in the truest sense. If Islam holds Christianity in contempt, it has every right to do so. At least Islam assumes it is dealing with men.

Christianity destroyed the entire harvest of ancient civilization for us. Later, it also wiped out the entire cultural legacy of the Muslim world. The magnificent Moorish culture in Spain, which was closer to our senses and taste than ancient Greece and Rome, was crushed. I won't say by whom. Why? Because its origins lay in noble and manly instincts. It affirmed life, even the rare, refined luxury of Moorish life. Yet the Crusaders waged war against something that deserved their reverence, something so advanced that even the culture of the nineteenth century pales in comparison. What did they seek? Booty. The Orient was wealthy. Let us be clear: the Crusades were no more than organized piracy. The German nobility, with its Viking roots, fit naturally into this role. The Church knew precisely how to manipulate them.

The German noble was always the Church's loyal guard, always in service to its worst instincts—and well-paid for his loyalty. It was through the strength of German swords, the sacrifice of

German blood, and the courage of German warriors that the Church succeeded in waging its relentless war against everything noble on Earth. This raises painful questions. The German nobility stands outside the history of higher culture. The reasons are obvious. Christianity and alcohol—the two great forces of corruption.

In essence, there is no meaningful choice between Islam and Christianity, just as there is none between an Arab and a Jew. The decision has already been made; no one can pretend otherwise. Either a person is a Chandala, or they are not. "War to the knife with Rome! Peace and friendship with Islam!" This was the sentiment and action of Frederick II, that great free spirit, that genius among German emperors. What does it say that a German must first be a genius, a free spirit, before they can even feel decently? I cannot fathom how a German could ever truly feel Christian.

The entire labor of the Renaissance, the last great harvest of civilization in Europe, was destroyed—and the Germans were responsible for it. Do we truly understand, or will we ever understand, what the Renaissance was? It was the reversal of Christian values, an attempt, using every available instinct, resource, and genius, to bring forth the triumph of nobler, higher values. This was the greatest war in history, the most crucial question ever posed—it is my question too. The Renaissance was a direct and fundamental attack on Christianity, aimed at its very core. It sought to replace its values with those that affirmed life, embedding these ideals into the instincts and desires of those at the center of power.

I imagine what could have been—a vision so enchanting, so luminous with beauty and art, that it seems otherworldly. It was a spectacle of significance and paradox, rich enough to make the gods of Olympus erupt in eternal laughter: imagine Cæsar Borgia as pope! Do you understand now? That would have been the triumph I long for even today. It would have swept Christianity away forever.

But what happened? A German monk named Luther came to Rome. With all the bitterness of a failed priest, he rebelled against the Renaissance. Instead of appreciating the miracle unfolding before him—the conquest of Christianity in its very heart—his hatred grew. Religious men think only of themselves. Luther saw only the corruption of the papacy, failing to see that the old sin, the original corruption that was Christianity itself, was no longer sitting on the papal throne. In its place was life, vitality, a triumphant yes to all that is bold, beautiful, and exalted.

Luther attacked this miracle and restored the church. He crushed the Renaissance, rendering it meaningless—a grand, wasted effort. Oh, what the Germans have cost us! Their work has always been futility. The Reformation, Leibniz, Kant, so-called German philosophy, the wars of "liberation," the empire—all of it substitutes for what was once possible, for what is now irretrievable. These Germans, I confess, are my enemies. I despise their unclean thinking, their cowardice before an honest yes or no. For a thousand years, everything they have touched has been tangled and corrupted. They are responsible for Europe's half-measures and compromises, for its sickness—and for Protestantism, the filthiest and most incurable form of Christianity.

If humanity can never rid itself of Christianity, it will be the Germans' fault.

And now I come to my final judgment. I condemn Christianity. I accuse the Christian church of the most profound corruption imaginable. It seeks to bring about the worst kind of decay. It has corrupted everything it has touched, turning every value into worthlessness, every truth into a lie, every act of integrity into spiritual depravity. And let no one speak to me of the "humanitarian blessings" of Christianity! The church's very existence depends on suffering. It creates suffering to sustain itself, to ensure its survival.

Consider the "worm of sin." This misery was a gift from the church to humanity. Or the idea of "equality of souls before God," which served as a tool for the resentment of the base-minded. This explosive idea has led to revolutions, to the modern drive to overthrow entire social structures. Christian dynamite!

Christianity's so-called "humanitarianism" is nothing but a mockery. It has turned humanity into a contradiction, a self-destructive force, driven by lies at any cost. It has cultivated contempt for all that is good, honest, and natural. Its ideals— anemic and "holy"—have drained life of its vitality, love, and hope. The notion of an afterlife denies reality itself. The cross has become the symbol of the most insidious conspiracy ever devised—against health, beauty, intelligence, kindness, and life itself.

This is my eternal accusation against Christianity. I will write it on every wall, in letters so large that even the blind can see. I call Christianity the greatest curse, the deepest corruption, the most insidious revenge. It spares no means— however poisonous, hidden, or small—in its war against life. I call it the one immortal stain on the human race.

And yet humanity marks time from the dies nefastus, the day this calamity began—the first day of Christianity. Why not from its end? Why not start today, with the reversal of all values?

The End

Thank You for Reading

Dear Reader,

We hope this timeless classic has sparked your imagination and enriched your literary journey. Now that you've turned the final page, we want to share a vision for the future of reading—one where every classic you've ever wanted to explore is at your fingertips, in a format that best suits your life.

We'd like to invite you to gain immediate, unlimited digital & audiobook access to hundreds of the most treasured literary classics ever written—along with the option to secure deluxe paperback, hardcover & box set editions at printing cost. Together, we can spark a new global literary renaissance alongside our small, independent publishing house called "The Library of Alexandria."

Thousands of years ago, the Library of Alexandria stood as a beacon of knowledge—until it was lost to history. We aim to reignite that spirit of preservation and discovery right now, in the modern age— only this time, it's accessible to all, in every language and every format.

Picture a world where every timeless classic, novel, poem, or philosophical treatise is not only available to read but also updated for today's readers—modernized, translated into any language or dialect, and ready to enjoy in any format you choose, whether that is in an eBook, audiobook, paperback, or deluxe hardcover & box set version a printing cost.

By joining our movement to rebuild the modern Library of Alexandria, you become part of an unprecedented mission to offer:

- **Unlimited Audiobook & eBook Access to the Greatest Classics of All Time**

  Instantly explore thousands of legendary works, from Plato and Shakespeare to Jane Austen and Leo Tolstoy. All are instantly ready to read or listen to, giving you a complete literary universe at your fingertips.

- **Paperback & Deluxe Editions at Printing Costs:**

  Purchase any title in a paperback, deluxe hardbound, or deluxe boxset edition at printing costs, shipped right to your doorstep. Curate your personal library of Alexandria with editions worthy of display—crafted to last, designed to captivate, and delivered straight to your door.

- **Modern translations for Contemporary Readers in all languages and dialects**

  Discover a vast selection of classics reimagined in clear, current language—no more struggling with outdated phrases or obscure references. Next to the original versions, we aim to offer translations in as many languages and dialects as possible.

  As we continue our translation efforts and add new languages, readers everywhere can connect with these works as if they were written today. By bridging linguistic divides, you're contributing to ensuring that these timeless stories become more meaningful, accessible, and inspiring for people across the globe.

- **Your Personal Library of Alexandria:**

  Over the months and years, you'll curate a unique physical archive of classics—each volume a testament to your taste, curiosity, and love of knowledge. It's not just about owning books—it's about curating a cultural legacy you'll cherish and pass down for generations to come.

- **Join a Global Literary Renaissance:**

  Your support fuels an ongoing mission: allowing us to reinvest in offering deluxe print editions (including special boxsets) at their true cost, broaden the range of available formats and translations, and extend the reach of these works to new audiences worldwide. By joining today, you're not just preserving a legacy of masterpieces; you set in motion a powerful wave of literary accessibility.

We are more than a publisher—we're a movement, and we can't do it alone. Your support lets us scale our mission, preserving and reimagining history's greatest works for tomorrow's readers.

Become a Torchbearer of knowledge.

Thank you for picking up this book and allowing us into your literary journey. As you turn the pages, know that you're part of something larger: a global effort to keep these stories alive, share their wisdom across borders and generations, and spark a true cultural revival for the modern era.

If this resonates with you—please consider taking the next step by visiting:

www.libraryofalexandria.com

With gratitude and a shared love of knowledge,

The Modern Library of Alexandria Team

Visit:

www.libraryofalexandria.com

Or scan the code below: